THE FIRST MILLION
IS ALWAYS THE HARDEST . . .

The banker spoke to Genie calmly. "You're a beautiful young woman. You also need to borrow money. I have money to lend. So I have an arrangement to propose. One hat will facilitate our having a good banking relationship."

Genie's stomach clenched. There was no mistaking his meaning. But she forced a diplomatic expression. "What re the terms of the arrangement which will make my banker happy?" she asked.

'I suggest we see each other one or two nights a week, depending upon my schedule, for as long as you owe the bank money."

A shiver ran through Genie's body. She had lost her capacity for outrage, but hope and humiliation mingled in her blush. She leaned over and kissed him lightly on the lips.

You," he said, "are an unusual woman."

═══════════

MAJESTIC DREAMS

WILLIAM SAXON

PINNACLE BOOKS NEW YORK

MAJESTIC DREAMS

Copyright © 1983 by William M. Mayleas

A Pinnacle Books edition, published by special arrangement with Macmillan Publishing Company.

Macmillan edition published in 1983
Pinnacle edition / February 1985

ISBN: 0-523-42270-9

Can. ISBN: 0-523-43265-8

Printed in the United States of America

PINNACLE BOOKS, INC.
1430 Broadway
New York, New York 10018

9 8 7 6 5 4 3 2 1

I would like to dedicate this book to my wife, Davidyne, and my daughter, Alexandra. Two ladies who have put up with me for a long time.

Acknowledgments

While quite a number of people assisted me in the writing of this book, I would first like to thank Ms. Arlene Friedman, Senior Executive Editor of Macmillan Publishing Company, who took over the project at a most critical time. Thank you for your advice, your good taste, your sense of style, and your technical skills as an editor.

Also her assistant, Andrea Raab, who provided her own editorial input plus her special charm to soothe the nerves of a nervous author. Then there was the superb work done by the copy editors, Felice Sabbagh and Ginger Heinbockel, with their green pencils and hundreds of pink slips. And Gai Boocher, who was able to decipher my handwriting and type a large part of the original manuscript. Finally, Julian Bach, who took on an unpublished writer and found the appropriate publisher for the work.

Thank you. Each and every one of you. Individually and collectively.

MAJESTIC
DREAMS

PART ONE

1983

1

It would not be accurate to say that New York was experiencing its typical January weather. It had been too consistently cold to be typical. Usually there were short breaks in the below freezing temperatures, when the thermometer might climb out of the teens and twenties into the thirties or forties. And the knowing New Yorker would remark, ''Ah, yes. The January thaw. Happens every year.'' But this January there were no thaws. Still, if you were superstitious, you didn't complain. The worst of the winter snowstorms that had seemed headed for the city had veered off at the last minute to bury houses and roads from Hartford to Boston and as far north as Maine under a heavy blanket of snow before moving off the coast to spend their fury in the Atlantic.

Several air traffic controllers, exhausted from the long hours they had put in since the abortive controllers' strike, sat in the Common IFR Room at Mitchell Field in Long Island talking and arguing. A low pressure area had formed off the coast of Florida and had started moving up the East Coast with ever-increasing speed, drawing gale force winds in its wake. Worse, a classic high pressure front just east of the Rockies was forcing frigid air eastward. As the cold air moved, it picked up moisture from the Great Lakes and transformed itself into a blizzard. The gale from the south and the blizzard from the west were now on a crash course. The computer projected the path of the collision along a line over New York City and Long Island. Unless something happened to change the projected path of one front or the other, New York City was about to be inundated with snow.

The day had started with a bright blue sky, a cold wind, and unusually clear air. But the storm systems were moving so fast that, even though it was only 3:00 P.M., there was no sky; only a dark, ominous ceiling which was dropping rapidly, cutting off the tops of the tall buildings and heralding the vast approaching army of snowflakes. As projected, the storm was intensifying; and everyone was concerned. Jack Reardon, a heavyset man with iron grey hair, thick shoulders, and an even thicker waist, sat motionless. He felt isolated, alone, with the storms rolling in on him—a breath of white destruction clutching at his airports. His airports, because he was in charge of the shift. How long could he keep the fields open? One hour? Maybe two? But what then? Where would he send the planes? Upstate New York and New England would be a howling, white hell. Airports as far south as Atlanta could be imprisoned, like New York, under a glistening shroud of snow.

He turned to Joe Collins, a sallow-faced man with thinning black hair and a thick black mustache, who was studying the weather map. Joe was next in command. "Joe, do you think we should shut her down?"

Joe didn't like the question. "You know how many planes are heading this way right now?"

"I know."

"If the sun comes out, the news media will have a field day."

"I don't think it will come out."

"We'll look like damn fools if it does."

"It won't."

There were moments of silence. "I'm not going to make the decision," Joe said in a flat voice. "You're the boss. You do it."

Reardon shook his head in resignation. What did old Truman say? "The buck stops here." And it did. "Shut the fucking thing down, Joe."

They punched the buttons that linked them to every air traffic control center in the country. Within seconds the word flashed to San Francisco, Los Angeles, Dallas, Houston, Chicago. Soon the control towers in all the major airports were full of cursing men frantically sorting out which planes would depart for where and which would be held.

* * *

A silver DC-9 with the name ConVert-Co painted in large red letters on the nose and tail of the plane was starting down the takeoff runway at Chicago's O'Hare airport. The pilot and copilot were concentrating on doing what they were very highly paid to do—get the plane off the ground. The radio connecting the plane to the control tower squawked. "Control Tower to ConVert-Co. Come in, please."

A rich, deep woman's voice spoke, and a slender manicured hand rested on the copilot's shoulder. "Don't answer for five seconds, Harry." She counted. "One. Two. Three. Four. Five." The plane was gathering speed with every second. "Now! Answer!"

"ConVert-Co to Control Tower. Come in."

"Control Tower to ConVert-Co. Abort your takeoff. All flights to New York are cancelled. Blizzard condition."

The woman spoke again. "Don't answer for three seconds." She looked at the dial indicating their ground speed. One hundred seventy-five miles per hour. It was too late to stop them.

The pilot and copilot realized exactly what she had done. "ConVert-Co to Control Tower. Too late to abort." The plane lifted off the ground.

"Get into flight pattern C. We'll bring you in as quickly as we can."

"I'll do the talking, Harry." The woman's voice was soft and low as she spoke into the microphone. "This is Eugenia Szabo. Gentlemen, we thank you for flight pattern C. However, we're cleared for La Guardia, and La Guardia's where we're going."

The voice in the tower sputtered. "La Guardia's closed. You can't land there."

"We can and we will."

"The FAA will hear about this."

"Quite so. That's your job." Her voice had the firmness peculiar to those accustomed to having their orders obeyed without question. "My job is to get to New York. And, gentlemen, we were off the ground before you gave the order. Out of your control, gentlemen. Ciao." She broke the air to ground connection.

Luke Jonas stared at the woman as she straightened up in the engineer's seat behind the copilot. Her heart-shaped face was composed. Her neck made a beautiful line to her shoulders. She raised her eyebrows and with them her rather heavy eyelids. For a moment her grey eyes looked amused, like a slightly wicked Madonna. "Damn fools," she murmured.

But Luke was beginning to sweat. His physical reflexes were much quicker than his mind, and he only now realized how much he resented the danger she had placed them in. The FAA and a blizzard in New York.

Genie Szabo could read his mind, and she knew his anger was about to show. "Don't worry, Luke. I'll take the FAA heat. You were only following orders. And we were not in air space controlled by the tower when they told us to turn back."

Luke muttered half to himself, "The hell we weren't."

She continued. "Are we on our filed flight plan?"

"Not quite." He disliked having to answer her.

"Get us on the plan and keep us on it."

Luke Jonas smothered his rage. Did she think she could control the blizzard in New York? That the whole universe would submit to her will? All he allowed himself to say was, "We're on dead center now."

"Good. Stay there. How long before we're due in La Guardia?"

"Two hours, eighteen minutes."

"All right. I'm going back to take a nap. Wake me when we're fifteen minutes from landing. I just hope the bastards won't keep us circling for hours."

"They won't." Harry was as angry as Luke. Also concerned for his safety. "Not with this weather. We'll probably be the only plane crazy enough to be coming in. Unless they divert us to another airport."

Genie puzzled over this bit of information. Divert them? Not land at La Guardia? Oh, no! "Are we over water?" she asked finally.

"Yes. Our route takes us over Lake Michigan and then . . ."

"Dump enough fuel so we have only thirty minutes extra flying time."

The two men turned and stared at her. She stared back, maintaining her calm, composed, friendly bearing. "Yes, Luke.

Dump the fuel! That way they'll have to let us land. Those clowns are scared out of their pants. They always make things sound worse than they are. You know as well as I most crashes are caused by pilot error, and neither of you is paid to make errors. Are you?''

Luke shrugged. He was afraid of the woman, mortally afraid, and for the life of him, he couldn't explain why.

"Do it!'' Genie left the cabin.

Luke and Harry exchanged looks. They were both veterans of World War II, the Korean War, and years of working for commercial airlines. They had been lured away from the security of their jobs by six figure salaries and lots of free time. But there were moments, and this was one of them, when they wished they hadn't been so greedy. Luke laughed nervously and said, ''All right, kiddo. Let's do what the boss lady wants. She's right. It is the only way they'll let us land.'' By now their flight plan had taken them well out over Lake Michigan. If they were going to dump the fuel, it was the time.

Harry Harper did a rapid calculation. ''Let go tanks four through six. That'll give us a little more breathing space. We should have about an hour extra flying time.''

"The boss lady wants thirty minutes.''

"Listen, Luke. I don't like that broad. But I've got to admit I admire her. If she were a man, I'd say she had brass balls. I don't. I'm scared. And I've a wife and three kids in school who'd be scared too if they knew what we were doing. A little bigger safety net won't hurt.'' Luke agreed, and the dumping operation was rapidly completed. Then they settled down to let the autopilot fly the jet to New York.

Although her brother, Max Szabo, used the plane as often as she did, the rear cabin had been decorated to please Genie. The interior was divided into two sections. All the seats had been removed, and the front section was now a conference room doubling as a dining room and bar. The sleeping quarters, for use by either Max or Genie, took up most of the rear cabin and there was a sensual elegance about the room. The fur throw on the round oversized bed, the soft antelope-patterned rug, the carved wooden statuettes of a primitive man and woman embracing, the perfume and cosmetics on a granite-topped hand-painted lacquered vanity, the special curtains running down both sides of the cabin all seemed to cry out, "female." The only exceptions were the functional luggage racks, large built-in closets, and a huge brown leather chair which Max frequently used to sleep in rather than bother to undress and climb into the bed.

Genie sat in what had come to be known as Max's chair staring into space. She hadn't slept much in the past three weeks. There had been too much to do, too many people to talk to, and, afterwards, too much to think about. But for the moment, she had lost all trace of weariness. Her body was held erect in the chair by the straight line of her shoulders and her concentration, which had the steely look of a woman who drives herself without mercy toward whatever she wants. Then, abruptly, she let herself go, slumped down in the chair, kicked off her shoes, stretched out her legs like a worn-out Raggedy Ann doll. Her legs were long and beautiful, perhaps a little too slender for the rest of her wide-hipped, full-buttocked, narrow-waisted, and large-breasted body. She had deep-set eyes which were two long rectangular cuts edged by the parallel lines of heavy lashes. There was strength in her full soft mouth that was pink under a colorless lip gloss; not flirtatious, yet challengingly feminine. Her chin was narrow but square, ending in a surprising dimple. Her pale skin, temporarily drained of color, now seemed luminous, framed as it was by a luxuriant mass of curly blue-black hair worn close to her head in tight ringlets. Genie had the kind of beauty painters, not fashion photographers, meant when they spoke of beauty.

Her abrupt collapse betrayed the exhaustion of her body, and for a moment, she felt an emotion she'd held back for many years. The only words to describe it were "this is not the way I expected my life to be." She thought, you're tired, and she watched her mood with detachment, knowing it would pass. If emotional satisfaction was the response to the great things the world has to offer, if she loved her family, if she loved her work, if all those things were true, there was still one feeling she was missing. To find a man who could equal her capacity for love. She had known such a man once, but. . . . She pressed her face into her hands, a gesture she had seen her mother make many times. After a while she raised her head. It was pointless to think of him. Today's life would be all she would ever have of the total life she once wanted. It was as it was.

She reached into the refrigerator, took out a split of Mumm's '59, a small tin of beluga caviar, and a box of Carr's water biscuits. She washed the caviar down with several glasses of champagne which she sipped out of a glass of pure rock crystal. The sunlight shining through the window struck the glass turning it iridescent and creating a series of prisms which broke up the white light into all the colors of the spectrum. Genie marvelled at the beauty man and nature had produced, then turned away, the proposal she had prepared for her brother running through her mind. It was crucial for her to be in New York in the morning. She had to talk to their bankers as soon as possible to arrange the financing which would enable ConVert-Co to purchase a large apartment house on the North Side of Chicago. This morning, at the closing, she had advanced $250,000 on an option to buy the building. But they had only thirty days to make good on the option. Otherwise they would forfeit the two-fifty and lose the building as well. Pausing in her concentration, Genie noticed that she felt herself revived as always by the hard exhilarating pleasure of work.

She decided to take a quick nap. It was only a matter of slipping off her panty hose, pulling her dress over her head, tossing it aside, and unhooking a wisp of a brassiere. Then she pulled back the deep blue silk satin sheets and slipped into bed, drawing the sheet and a light cashmere blanket around her. She closed her eyes but sleep didn't come quickly. She was still too keyed up from the closing and thoughts of the meetings to come. She remembered how, when she was a child, she'd decided the most important thing anyone could own was their own home. People like her parents. Average people. It gave them security and dignity. How, when she was twenty-four, she had told her brother the two of them would build a real estate empire founded on the idea that all Americans had the right to own the roof over their heads. Even if the roof was an apartment ceiling, one should own it. It had never occurred to her that women do not run real estate empires, and it had never occurred to her brother. The passion for her dream had helped her make peace with herself, to come to terms with her inner loneliness. Even Max didn't realize how much the dream meant to her. How much. . . . Then she was asleep.

2

Sitting behind his desk on the thirty-first floor of 299 Park Avenue in New York City, Max Szabo was talking on the telephone to a private detective in Boston. Max was a tall, powerfully built man who had been an athlete when he was young. He was now thirty-eight years old and he weighed the same as he had at twenty-one. His thick blond hair, brilliant blue eyes, and ruddy skin were a throwback to a Magyar heritage, as was his quick violent temper. His hair was combed straight back from a low, broad forehead. His jaw was heavy and square, his nose straight; when he smiled, his whole face lit up in a bawdy masculine humor. Max exuded male virility and strength, combined with an open and friendly manner, a ready laugh, and a quick wit. All this made him attractive to both men and women. But the fact was the one person with whom he did not feel at constant war was his sister, Genie. Now he was giving the detective a very hard time for what he considered good and sufficient reasons.

"What the fuck do you mean, you have no line on the Elliot kid?" He listened for a moment. "That won't fly. I don't give a damn if you think she's social or what school she went to. She dropped out because she wanted to drop out. She didn't lose her scholarship, and her family didn't lose their dough. Just remember that. She dropped out to work in some crummy joint in South Boston, as a topless dancer . . ." He was interrupted by a ping and a flashing light. His secretary wanted him. "I'm putting you on hold for a minute. Hang on."

He punched the button on the tilted panel next to his desk, connecting the intercom. "What is it, Rose?"

"Miss Moore is here."

Max looked at his watch. She was on time for once. "Send her in, and hold all calls except anything from Miss Szabo."

11

He switched back to the detective while keeping his eye on the door to his office. It opened, and a tall, slim woman with dark curly hair walked in. She leaned against the door for a moment before moving toward the couch in an exaggerated mockery of a burlesque queen's hip swinging glide. Her movements were a comic contrast to the classic style of her Harris tweed suit and the Burberry raincoat she carried over her arm. He gestured toward his private bathroom and continued his conversation with hardly a break. "Listen to me, Barry. A girl just came in. She's in her twenties. Graduated from Smith or Wellesley. One of those sister schools. And she's smashed. Nobody forced her to shoot up cocaine. Or Quaaludes. Or whatever she's taking. It's all her idea. And she's here because she wants to be here. Hell! She insists on being here. And you know what? She's going to do whatever I tell her to do. Fuck me, suck me, whatever I want. And you tell me Elliott's kid is straight because she's social and went to Sarah Lawrence. You're nuts." He listened to the reply. "You tag her. I want proof. I want pictures. She's doing a number with someone. And now that you mention Sarah Lawrence, it's probably a girl. Also I'll bet she's into the heavy stuff. It's the rich kid rag. You don't understand. Deep down those rich kids think they're untouchable. They're not bound by the rules of us ordinary stiffs. Well, we'll see how long Elliott holds out when he sees those shots." He laughed. "We'll suggest selling them in every porno bookstore in Boston. Poster size. And we'll save the best ones for Elliott's wife. Also for his friends, neighbors, relatives, and the boys at the bank where he does whatever he does. Just tail the kid with your handy Rollei, and let's see what you get."

There was another question.

"Too long. Two weeks. No more. Every week that cocksucker's held us up cost us over fifty grand. That's right. Fifty thousand dollars. Now get your ass moving!" He slammed the phone down.

Stacey Moore had been listening behind the bathroom door. As soon as she heard the phone slam, she appeared, naked as usual. Stacey knew exactly what was expected of her this afternoon. It had been the same for the last two years.

When Stacey Moore met Max Szabo four years ago, she was only a few years out of Radcliffe. He'd had the wrong college, but the right social class. She was trying to make a go of a catering business that concentrated on corporate accounts. Though her parents could have helped her, being more than merely rich—members of her immediate family either sat on or controlled the board of directors of six of *Fortune*'s five hundred leading American corporations—Stacey had chosen to go it on her own. Nobody had helped her great grandfather found the huge Moore fortune. Nobody needed to help her. She had pitched Max for the ConVert-Co account, and they ended up that evening in his apartment. Sex with Max was a new experience for Stacey. She had found the young men in her own set too familiar, too boring; and even the most ambitious corporate man found the idea of sex with her somewhat profane. It was troublesome enough that she had beauty, brains, and breeding. When you added the huge family fortune to the holy trio, it seemed like screwing the chairman of the board. When they did, the sex was tame, reverent, so respectful it almost seemed an offense against nature.

Not so Max. Not only didn't he know who she was, if he had known, he wouldn't have given a damn. His fucking was direct, even brutal. Not only was he bigger and stronger than any man she had ever known, but his penis was longer, thicker, and, it seemed, harder. When he entered her, it was like a club or a horn entering her. It was a goring that did not hurt but made her want to retaliate with the same fury. Stacey was caught by the bestiality of the man. He incited her to unleash her most violent desires. From the depths of her body, from a place she had not known even existed, came a fever that could not be satisfied, that could not have enough of Max and Max's club inside her.

Although it no longer mattered as much, her business profited as well. When Max set out to convert a rental apartment house to condominiums, the sale often started with a huge party for the tenants. It was part of the sales plan. Stacey was irritated when Max added several new girls to her staff; girls who could neither cook nor serve nor clean up after the party. But they could and did fuck. "All part of the business, honey. What's good for the business is good for the country," was his answer. Stacey wasn't a Moore for nothing. It was a cynicism she well understood. But her first real experience of how far Max's commitment to the business went occurred about a year and a half after they had met. They had put together a huge party, huge even by ConVert-Co standards, to convert an entire building complex in Dallas. Max had included the usual female assistants. But this time the assistants weren't enough. A lawyer, the leader of the tenants' group opposing the conversion—and there always was a group opposed to any conversion—wasn't having any of the liquor, the food, or the girls. He seemed to have a fix on Stacey. She told Max, and he nodded and smiled. "Interesting, honey."

As the party wound down, the lawyer asked her if she was free the next day. He had tickets to the Cowboys football game. They could have a real Texas steak after the game. Max was standing nearby and heard the proposal. "Of course she's free. You are free, aren't you, Stacey?"

Later that evening in bed, she said, "Max, you know there's more on his mind than football and steak."

"So?"

"Max, he expects me to go to bed with him."

"So?"

"What do you mean, 'so'? Don't you care?"

"Of course I care, honey. I feel lousy. But if you have to fuck him to make the deal, fuck him!"

She was hurt by his words, but before she could object, Max returned to the business of satisfying her. He took her again and again with a fierceness that made her whole body vibrate. Drugged by her physical need of him and frightened of his reaction if she objected, Stacey did as Max dictated. She had to get very drunk to do it, and she had no memory of what happened or even if she enjoyed it. It didn't seem to make any difference. After two nights with Stacey, the lawyer agreed to support the conversion. Several months later Stacey discovered Max had a tape recording of Stacey and the man talking while in bed. It was an obscene tape which could have damaged the man's career at Texas Enterprises where he was employed as house counsel. To say nothing about what it would have done to his marriage. The experience told her what Max thought of her. But it didn't help. Stacey was turning into a woman she no longer recognized.

From that time on, Stacey was one of the girls. The only difference was Max still saw her. Less and less fequently, though, as time passed. And the more he stayed away, the more intense her needs grew. Needs only he could satisfy. The less he called her, the more she called him. That he was an animal was meaningless. She was an animal, too. That he came to disgust her was nothing compared to the disgust she felt for herself. To make up for the times he couldn't or wouldn't see her, she dulled herself with increasing amounts of alcohol, other men and finally drugs. But in spite of everything, he continued to use her, and she continued to want to be used.

Today was typical. She had drunk two double straight gins at lunch along with her usual pill. Her head was light, and she had some difficulty keeping her steps steady.

"Stoned again!"

"That's right. Who cares?"

"If you don't, no one does."

She reached the couch, fell backward and spread her legs. "What will be your pleasure today? This? Or this? Or this?"

The performance disgusted Max as she knew it would. It was a gutter game she had come to play. How much could she befoul herself? It gave her a certain pleasure to see his revulsion.

Max didn't bother to take off his shirt and tie. He slid his pants over his socks and stepped out of his shorts. The sight of his club had its usual effect. She could feel her body begin to throb. Whatever he wanted, whatever he did was all right just so long as he could make her feel this way.

"Suck it. Suck it good."

"Please, Max. Fuck me first. I need you inside me."

"I said, suck it!" He jabbed his prick into her mouth.

She began to caress him. It took only a few minutes before she could tell he was ready to come. She moved her lips up and down the length of his penis while her tongue rubbed against the tip. Max came in huge spurts that filled her mouth faster than she could swallow. Some semen dribbled down one side of her mouth.

When she could speak, she pleaded, "Now, Max. Please come inside me." She knew he could have two or three orgasms before he lost his erection. She gathered her courage and glanced at his face. He was looking out the window.

"Goddamn it. Look at that snow. And Genie's flying in from Chicago."

"Max!" Stacey reached for him. "Max! Please!" The ab-

ject need in her voice startled even her. Then as though through
the wrong end of a pair of opera glasses, she saw Max getting
dressed.

This was not the first time she had been used and betrayed,
but for some reason, today was different. He hadn't even bothered to fuck her. He was a sadistic shit, and she was a damn
fool, a masochist. She recognized again that she had chosen
this, this depravity; she was hooked on booze and drugs and a
man who wouldn't waste five seconds to throw her a rope if she
was being dragged to her death in quicksand.

What was he doing? Making a phone call? A phone call
about his sister. His sister! Oh, Christ! What chance did she
have, had she ever had? Her competition was his own flesh and
blood. His sister.

"What's the matter, Max? Worried about Genie? Don't
worry, sweetie. That bitch'll survive."

"What did you say?"

"I said your precious sister, the woman you love, will survive."

"What did you call her?"

"Several things. Bitch. The woman you love. Take your
choice."

Before she was aware he had moved, Max was in front of
her. It was the first time she had ever touched a nerve. It
couldn't be because she had called Genie a bitch. No! The
woman you love—that had done it. She smiled up at him. His
rage seemed to blur the outlines of his body. Yes. That was
why today was even worse than usual. It was Genie.

"You've got a case on your own sister." She was laughing
so hysterically tears streamed down her cheeks. No wonder he
had picked her. She looked like Genie. She was a substitute.
"In anthropology that's called primary incest. Animals on a
lower scale of evolution than human beings practice it. How
about it, Max? Ever screwed Genie? Ever dreamed of screwing
Genie? Are you a lower form of animal life? Like say an ape.
Ever fantasized Genie while we were fucking?" She watched
him struggle with himself. She got to her feet and put an arm
around his neck, fondling him through his pants. She whispered
in his ear, "It's all right, Max. It's me, Genie, making love to
you. Live out your fantasy. Fuck me. Fuck your sister."

Those were the last words she clearly remembered. Max hit

her. She had a dim recollection of being lifted and flying through the air. When things sorted themselves out, she found herself on the floor of Max's private secretary's office, still naked, her clothes scattered about her. The first thing she saw was Rose, one hand in front of her face hiding her shocked expression and her other hand running nervously through her neartly combed grey hair. Finally she was able to focus on Max. He was in the doorway to his office.

"Rose, get her dressed and have her thrown out. If she ever comes back, call the police." He retreated into his office and slammed the door. Stacey got to her knees. Her jaw and head hurt, but she didn't want Rose's help. Slowly, carefully, she dressed, while Rose remained at her desk, eyes wide open and mouth agape, still patting her hair. Stacey realized the violence within her was the reaction to her sudden release. The rage shaking her body was the final recognition of her hatred of Max. A hatred so consuming, so virulent, it filled her being absolutely, obliterating all her former self-contempt. She was free to think with calculated purpose. She was glad he hadn't given her a chance to warn him. Oh, yes! She had come for the usual reason. But there was something else she had intended to tell him. To protect him. Now he wouldn't know. And she was delighted. He'd have no time to get his ass out of the sling.

For the first time in years she would use her family. They would complete what others had started. She was grateful for what they were. For who they were. For who they knew. Max had forgotten who she was, and he'd find out his mistake soon enough. She was a Mcore, and the Moores could be killers, too.

After Max slammed the door to his office, he stumbled into the bathroom, barely making it to the toilet before throwing up. He kept vomiting until there was nothing left but phlegm and stomach bile. Finally he was able to stop, blow his nose, and clear his head. That cunt! That fucking cunt! Comparing herself to Genie. And then accusing him of wanting to make love to her. His own sister! What a crock of shit! Of course he cared for Genie. She was his sister. It was natural to care about one's sister. He began to get angry all over again. Just let Stacey come near him once more, begging him to forgive her. When he was finished forgiving her, it would take a Swiss watchmaker to put the pieces together—providing, of course, there weren't any pieces missing.

He looked out the window again. The damned snow! Still very angry and a little frightened, he called the weather bureau. "Snow starting early this evening. Continuing all night. Ending by tomorrow morning. Accumulations of one foot or more. High winds will cause drifting and make driving hazardous . . ." There was more which only irritated Max. Make driving hazardous? How about flying? He dialed La Guardia.

"You're closing the field? What about incoming planes?"

"They'll be diverted to other airports."

"Sure. Where? This storm's up and down the East Coast."

"I know. Now if you'll excuse me, I have other calls to answer."

"No! I won't excuse you. I . . ." The line went dead as the connection was broken. "Goddamn bitch!" He yelled into the dead line. Max swivelled his chair to stare again out the window. It was snowing much harder.

He dialed his secretary. "Has anyone heard from Miss Szabo?"

Rose, still in a state of semishock, stammered, "No, Mr. Sz-Szabo. Not a w-word. I'd have informed you if there w-were."

"Get me the control tower at O'Hare."

"Yes, sir."

He waited for the phone to ring. In seconds he lost patience. "What the hell's happening?"

"I'm sorry, I can't get the tower number."

"Put me on." He waited.

"May I help you?"

"Who is this?"

"Information, sir."

"Good. What's the number of the control tower at O'Hare?"

"We don't have that number, sir."

"Give me your supervisor."

The supervisor was on the line almost at once. "What's the problem, sir?"

"I want to speak to the control tower at O'Hare Airport, and information won't give me the number."

"Not won't, sir. Can't. She doesn't have it."

"Who does?"

"The FAA in Skokie."

"What's the number of the FAA in Skokie?"

She gave him the number. When the phone was answered, he asked, "What's the number of the control tower at O'Hare?"

A man's voice replied. "Who is this?"

"Max Szabo. Why?"

"I'm sorry, but we're not allowed to give out that number without special authorization."

"I've got a very good reason. My sister's plane was supposed to leave O'Hare for La Guardia, and I'm concerned about the weather."

"Why don't you call the airline?"

"It's a private plane. Our plane. ConVert-Co."

He heard an obscenity at the other end of the line. "You own that plane?"

"Our company does. Why?"

"That's your sister on the plane?"

Max's control of his temper began to slip again. "Why all the damn questions? I just want to find out where she is."

"I'll tell you where she is. Your sister took off against instructions from the control tower. She refused to get into a flight pattern as ordered and return to the field. She, the pilot, and the copilot are in lots of trouble if and when they land. And they're heading directly into a hell of a blizzard."

"She's on her way to La Guardia?"

"I'd like to wring her neck."

Max's voice got very quiet. "Between us, it's lucky you can't touch her. However, I understand your problem. I'll wring it for you." He hung up the phone and thought about Genie. She'd refused to obey some order. Nothing new in that. She usually did exactly as she wished. Some kid sister! He looked again at the snow. Damn it! She'd better be right. They could square it with the FAA, but the bastards were right about one thing. She was coming into La Guardia in one hell of a blizzard.

He called the garage where the company kept its cars. "Charlie, which of our cars handles best in deep snow?"

"The Merce, Mr. Szabo."

"Which Merce, Charlie?"

"I'm sorry, sir. The 300 Cabriolet. It has twelve cylinders up front and a lot of weight in the rear. I'll put some sandbags in the trunk for better traction and chains on the rear wheels."

"O.K. Miss Szabo is on her way to La Guardia. The airport is officially closed, but she'll find a way to land. Meet her as usual at Butler."

"Yes, sir. When is she due?"

"I'm not sure. Just get out there and wait for her." He hung up. There was nothing more he could do. He would wait for her phone call. If he had been a man who prayed, he would have prayed now.

The buzzer rang in the rear cabin. Genie was awake at once. "I'm up. Thanks for the buzz, Harry."

"I think you'd better come up front. We're in communication with the control tower at La Guardia, and they're not friendly."

"I'll be right there." In spite of the urgency, she washed her face, applied her eye makeup, ran a comb through her hair, and only then slipped on her panty hose and brassiere. She found a pair of high boots in a closet. Where was her dress? Had she hung it up or tossed it somewhere? She was too exasperated to look for it. So she grabbed her mink coat and slipped it on, belting it tightly to cover her from the curve of her chin to the tops of her boots.

A tense argument was going on in the cockpit between La Guardia and Luke.

"I told you, ConVert-Co. We are closed! The nearest open field is Chicago."

"Sorry. That's two hours flying time. More, considering the headwinds. We have about one hour of fuel remaining."

"Bullshit. That plane holds a hell of a lot more than that."

"I only know what my gauges tell me."

"Damn it! I'll be back to you."

Genie asked, "Where are we?"

"About a hundred miles northwest of La Guardia. If they let us land, we'll be down in less than ten minutes."

"Why one hour of fuel? I told you to dump everything and leave only one half hour to spare."

Luke looked at Harry.

Harry mumbled, "I misjudged the tailwinds. We made a quick trip. Saved fuel."

He was lying, but this was neither the time nor the place to make an issue of it.

The control tower was back. "We can't bring you in here. The runways aren't plowed. They're a mass of snowdrifts and ice. Try Kennedy."

"Give me the mike. This is Eugenia Szabo speaking. We will not try Kennedy, Philadelphia, or Boston, or anywhere else. We are going to land at La Guardia." She paused to allow her words to sink in. "Unless you wish to be responsible for a plane crash, you will monitor us and keep your radar tight and steady." She asked Luke, "Have we picked up their radar?"

"Yes, Miss Szabo."

"La Guardia. We've got your radar. We're coming in on it."

She heard the stubbornness in the voice from the tower. "I told you the runways are unusable."

"They're just as unusable everywhere else. We are coming in."

The controller gave up. It was his responsibility to get the plane down. "All right. Are you familiar with the airport?"

"You must be one of the new boys. This is ConVert-Co. We're based at La Guardia. Of course we know the runways."

"O.K. We'll take you straight in. Runway two. Set her down with minimum air speed, give yourself as much runway room as possible, and hit the reverse thrust at once—hard! There's so much ice and snow your brakes won't do you much good. We'll try to monitor your approach."

Genie looked at Luke. He was clutching the controls. The bones on the back of his long thin hands seemed about to poke through his skin. "Relax, Luke. It's a piece of cake."

"Some cake! Sit in the engineer's seat, and buckle your seat belt. This is going to be rough."

Genie snapped her seat belt and pulled it tight. Then she crossed her legs and waited. She became fully aware she hadn't bothered to find her dress. Her fur coat was too warm. She began to perspire. Her panty hose rubbed against her crotch, and her whole body tingled with sudden desire. She uncrossed her legs, shifted in her seat to relieve the friction, and wondered at her sexual reaction to the danger.

It was time to get the plane down. Within seconds the DC-9 dropped into the clouds. There was a sudden jolt as they passed from the clear air. Genie glanced out the window. There was nothing to see but dirty cotton clouds.

Luke asked Harry, "Flaps?"

The copilot studied the radar. "Thirty seconds and counting." The seconds passed slowly. Then, "Flaps." Two pairs of hands moved as one. The plane shuddered and made a high-pitched, grinding screech that lasted until the flaps were locked in place. They were less than a thousand feet up, and their airspeed had dropped to 150 miles per hour. "Five minutes to touchdown, I hope." They still couldn't see a thing. Cross winds picked them up and began tossing the plane around. Both men fought the controls to keep the DC-9 level and on the glide path. Still no sight of ground. Harry spoke to the control tower. "ConVert-Co to tower. Can you read me?"

"I read you."

"We're about five hundred feet and dropping. Still on glide path. How low does this stuff reach?"

"Ceiling varies from one hundred feet to zero. But you're coming in fine. Wait! You're too high. Drop down!" The voice had an edge of hysteria which infected the listeners. "Drop down. You're too high! Too high!"

They were fighting a sudden updraft. Then, grudgingly, the updraft released them, and the plane began to drop.

"That's better." The voice was back under control. "Drop your landing gear." A shudder ran through the plane, and a grinding sound, similar to the screeching caused by the flaps moving into place, was heard. The landing gear gave the wind something additional to grab onto. Controlling the plane became even more difficult. "You're still too high. Drop another fifty feet. Now!"

The plane settled down still further causing a sinking sensation in Genie's stomach. The tower continued, "You should be out of it at any moment."

Three pairs of eyes tried to pierce the grey cotton. The plane was vibrating and bouncing about. Genie felt the sweat of fear mingled with her body's heat pouring through the open pores of her skin.

"Wait a second. We're coming out. Jesus Christ, it's really snowing. I can't see a thing!"

"What'd you think it was doing? Raining pennies from heaven?"

A particularly vicious gust of wind flung the plane sideways. Genie's head cracked against the side of the cockpit. It momentarily stunned her. Now Harry and Luke were working together to bring the plane back on course. They strained to pierce the solid white wall. Genie squinted. She thought she saw something close and dead ahead. Luke reacted immediately. There was the field. But they were too low. A loud crash deafened them. The plane seemed to pause, hang for a moment, then bounce up as Luke instinctively slammed on the power.

"What the fuck was that?" Harry yelled.

"We hit the goddamn water and bounced. Just pray we still have our landing gear."

"Oh, shit!"

"Yeah. Shit! ConVert-Co to tower. We see you. We just bounced off the water. I don't know what's under the plane, but we're coming in."

"Take her down early, and I mean early! I think I see your landing gear."

Luke set the plane down and down. There was the water that had almost swallowed them. For a panicky moment the field disappeared in a thick gust of snow. The gust passed, and they saw the landing pier stretching out into the bay to greet them. They were over the pier. Luke set the plane down as though the strip was glass. The landing gear seemed to hold. "Reverse thrust. Full throttle." Genie was thrown forward against her seat belt. It cut into her stomach forcing the breath from her lungs. The plane was slowing but not rapidly enough. Luke called out, "Brakes. Gradual. Now full!" They skidded and bumped down the runway, now on the ground, now in the air. They began to slew sideways. Both men caught the motion. They overcorrected and slid in the other direction. This time there was no stopping them. They did a 180-degree turn and came to a stop facing the end of the pier—the direction from which they had come. By guess and by God, they had landed.

Genie wrapped her arms around her body. She felt clammy, dizzy, and her head hurt. She vaguely remembered banging it. The pilots sat in their seats shaking their hands to get rid of the cramps which had set in.

Luke spoke first. "I wouldn't care to try that again."

Harry said nothing.

They were directed toward the west end of the airport, the area called Butler-La Guardia, where the privately owned planes were kept. Luke guided them to the proper parking place. Finally they saw a member of the ground crew of Butler waiting for them; his bright orange parka and fluorescent sticks gleamed in their headlights. He motioned them forward, a little to the left, and forward again. Then he dropped his sticks. Luke braked to a stop and cut the twin jets.

"Open the doors, Harry. I'll call the office and tell them we've arrived." Harry swung the door open and was hit by a blast of icy air and heavy gusts of snow. After dropping the aluminum stairs, he jumped out of the way. Genie asked, "You and Luke can't get home from here, can you?"

"No. My wife isn't going to drive here from Fair Lawn. Not in this weather. And Luke's wife, Mary, is in Westchester."

"I'll arrange for a car to pick us up. You can both stay in the company apartment in the city. Call your wives and tell them you're here."

Harry's voice took on an edge of sarcasm. "Thanks. We intend to."

"I'll call from the passenger waiting room. Luke and you join me as soon as the bird is in her nest." She was almost at the terminal when a huge black man appeared out of nowhere. "Charlie! What are you doing here?"

"Waiting for you. Mr. Szabo sent me to pick you up."

Genie smiled with appreciation. "A true keeper of the faith, my brother. Which car did you bring?"

"The Merce. The 300 Cabriolet."

"I'm going to call Mr. Szabo. You find Harry and Luke and tell them they have a lift into the city. I'll meet you all inside." She made her way through hip-high drifts to a dimly lit door and went directly to a pay phone.

"Genie! Where the fuck are you?" Max sounded angry and worried.

"Max, dear, watch your language. But I do like to see you're a dedicated worker. Still slogging away in the office at five-thirty."

"You're at Butler. "She heard his sigh of relief. "Is Charlie there?"

"The first face I saw after landing. That's how I knew I wasn't in heaven."

"A good thing. They're against the profit motive. You all right?"

"Only my first grey hairs. Thanks for sending Charlie. Your display of confidence in my immortality is heartwarming."

"You're welcome. Just a typical day in the life of the Szabos. What time will you be in tomorrow?"

"Nine-thirty. Max, we made the deal." The words brought a sparkle to her voice. "Now the lawyers go to work."

"I'll see you at nine-thirty."

"With bells and boots on."

His fears over, Max felt a surge of pride in Genie's courage. "Well done, kidlet. Well done."

Genie's apartment was the penthouse of a tall building on Sutton Place. If one only counted the number of rooms, the apartment would not be considered unusually large: a living room, dining room, library/office, kitchen, a master bedroom, and a maid's room. But the room count was deceptive. Each room was oversized. The actual apartment was over three thousand square feet, not including the huge terrace.

When she finally arrived home, Genie was much too tense to sleep; on a whim, she decided to relax in the heated, outdoor Jacuzzi. One advantage of her penthouse privacy was that she could lie naked in the spa. The infrared heating lamps mounted against the wall cast a pale, red glow over the steam rising from the spa and kept the area from becoming too cold.

In spite of the soothing action of the bubbling water, Genie found it difficult to shake the tension of the flight. Lovemaking would have done that, but she didn't know a man about whom she cared enough to call. The depression she had felt on the plane returned, and she realized how long it had been since she really cared for a man. She accepted how great her loss was, her loss as a woman, a wife, a mother. She was thirty-six, and the clock was ticking. It was already difficult for her to have a first child. In another few years her biological clock would make having a baby dangerous.

The Jacuzzi was large enough for her to stretch full out. As the combination of hot air and water caressed her, she willed herself to relax. Her brandy glass was on the edge of the spa. She sipped the Napoleon brandy and felt the heat pass through her body, adding to the soothing action of the water. Finally the combination of the spa and the brandy achieved its purpose.

She lay quietly, spent, luxuriating in the blessed peace. Now it took an effort for her to stay awake.

Stepping out of the steaming pool, Genie put on her terry cloth bathrobe, turned off the air jets and entered her bedroom. She dropped her robe on the carpet and slid into bed, asleep even as her head touched the pillow.

3

The radio alarm went off promptly at 7:00 A.M. Despite the exhausting trip and the lack of sleep, Genie felt fit and alert. She padded across the thick white rug to her bathroom, used the toilet, and finished by splashing cold water on her face. Then it was back to the bedroom and into a pair of panties, an exercise brassiere, and leotards. One wall of her bedroom consisted of a combination of windows and French doors opening out onto the terrace. The second wall was a series of closets with twin built-in chests of drawers, all of which was hidden by four huge sliding doors covered with mirrors. Her bed, night tables strewn with books and magazines, several chairs, and a small table were against the third wall. But the fourth wall was unusual. It had two doors, one leading to the bathroom and the other to the hall, and also concealed a fifteen-foot space which appeared when a button was pressed and the wall slid sideways to reveal a compact gym.

Genie gave the same energy and meticulous attention to keeping herself in shape as she gave to everything she did. The daily exercise routine was more than vanity, though she certainly meant to look as attractive as possible for as long as nature, with some help, permitted. Beyond good looks, she knew that, given the stress of her business life, a healthy body was essential for success. On the few occasions when Genie failed to achieve her immediate goal, it was never for lack of energy.

The gym consisted of a special table with cutouts to hold a set of stainless steel hand weights which she used to firm her arm and pectoral muscles so her breasts wouldn't sag. There was a narrow, lightly padded bench upon which she could either lie flat or sit while using the weights and a tilted ramp held in place by bolts fastened into the wall. The ramp made the leg-ups and sit-ups which tightened her stomach muscles and buttocks more difficult. A stationary bicycle completed the gym.

Genie started her routine. First the five-pound hand weights. The weeks in Chicago had left her a little out of shape; and by the time she was ready for the bicycle, she was panting and sweating heavily. She set the tension on the bicycle at three and stood up on the pedals to start. Once the speedometer reached twenty miles per hour, she sat down on the bicycle seat. This completed an electrical connection and a motor could be heard. A small platform with a TV set bolted to it was lowered from the ceiling. While she bicycled, Genie watched the morning news on "The Today Show." She noticed at once that the interviews were taped, and there were no theatrical or movie reviews. What news there was concerned the snowstorm. It had turned out to be worse than the weather bureau predicted. A high pressure ridge out in the Atlantic Ocean had stalled the storm over the northeast coast. The city had received over twenty inches of snow with wind-blown drifts up to six feet high. All the highways into and out of the city were closed. Snow flurries were expected to end later in the morning, and clearing was predicted. The temperature was fifteen degrees Fahrenheit or minus nine degrees Celsius. The windchill factor made the temperature feel like zero degrees Fahrenheit or minus eighteen degrees Celsius. The report confirmed her decision yesterday to fly in, storm or not. Given today's weather conditions, there was no telling how long she would have been stuck in Chicago if she had obeyed the control tower instead of her own instincts.

When she climbed off the bicycle, the television set shut itself off and the platform retracted to the ceiling. She pushed the button that brought the wall panel back into place, hiding the gym. Then she pushed another button next to the window which opened the heavy lined drapes. To her delighted surprise, the room was flooded with brilliant sunlight. Whoever had prepared the TV weather forecast had read the computer printout rather than looked out a window. It was Genie's opinion that weather forecasters never looked out windows. Too unsettling. Suppose what one saw was different from what the computer printout claimed? Trust one's eyes or the computer printout? Better not to have to make that kind of decision.

She thought about the day ahead. In good weather, the walk

from 54th Street and Sutton Place to 49th and Park Avenue was pleasant. Today it would be a bitch. She'd be slogging through drifts every inch of the way. There was no use even thinking about a car or cab until the streets were plowed. So how was she going to get to work?

Genie never questioned whether or not Max would be there. They had arranged to meet. Max would be there.

While applying her makeup, she thought again about the various ways to get to the office and had an idea that tickled her. She would ski to work. She was a good enough skier to handle the slopes, crevasses, and ravines of 54th Street. Skiing down Park Avenue would be a lark! She could use her backpack to carry a dress, lingerie, and shoes to change into at the office.

She rang the kitchen. Nina, her housekeeper, answered.

"Nina, my usual breakfast, please."

"Yes, madam."

"I'll be there in ten minutes."

"Yes, madam. Madam will be home for lunch?"

"No, Nina. I'll call you about dinner."

She sensed Nina's silent protest at the idea of madam going out in such weather. Nina had never accepted the fact that Genie worked. Rich people didn't work. It had occurred to Genie in the past to tell Nina the reason she was rich was because she worked. But there was no point in explaining such things to Nina who liked nothing better than her time off when Genie was out of town.

She dressed. Special long johns to hold the warm air close to her skin. Stretch knickers in black with a thin red stripe down each side. Her knee-length stockings were a matching shade of red with a thin black stripe down the sides. A black cashmere turtleneck sweater completed her outfit. She looked in the mirror and liked what she saw.

Seated at a small butcher block table in the kitchen, Genie surveyed Nina's breakfast and smiled. A little more than she'd asked for, but what the hell. She was starving. All she'd had yesterday was champagne and caviar. While she ate, she nodded and smiled as Nina explained that it was madness for madam to go out in such weather.

Breakfast completed, she prepared to leave. After buckling her boots, she selected a short grey fox jacket and a matching Astrakhan hat. As a last thought, she added a pair of black suede after-ski boots to her pack. The pack hitched in place, she gathered her skis, poles, and gloves.

Fortunately, the elevators were automatic. She didn't relish walking down forty-two flights of stairs carrying her skis and poles. She would if she had to, but she was relieved when an elevator arrived.

Once on the cleared sidewalk in front of the building, she stood for a moment enjoying the fresh clean air and the deep soft silence. Then she stepped into her cross-country bindings, snapped them shut, and took a deep breath. Working her way to Park Avenue through drifted snow, a high wind, bitter cold, and up and down slopes of the city streets would be another morning workout.

It was. When she arrived at Park Avenue and 49th she was perspiring from the exertion. The sweat felt good. It was healthy sweat, not like last night's nervous sweat. She unsnapped her bindings, shouldered her skis and poles, and struggled through the drifts to the building. A small space had been shoveled clean in front of the revolving door. After some maneuvering, she managed to fit her skis, her poles, and herself into one section of the door.

Inside, she stamped her boots to get most of the snow off them and went to the rear bank of elevators. One was waiting. She probably was the first person to use it that morning. Unless Max had beaten her to the office.

At 9:30 sharp, as she and Max had planned last night, Genie entered the office of ConVert-Co. The heavy wooden door was unlocked. Max was ahead of her. She stood her skis against the corner of the entrance hall and allowed them to drip onto the slate floor, sparing the decorator's "divine Orientals." That reminded her to take off her boots and put on her dry after-ski boots. Then she went in search of Max. He wasn't in his office though his suit coat hung over his desk chair. She heard the toilet flush in his bathroom, and it occurred to her that Max had slept in the office. In a moment he appeared, clean shaven in a fresh shirt.

"Beat ya," he chortled.

"Rat! Foul play. You slept here."

"You betcha. Anything to win, kidlet. Now don't tell me about the flight. I've heard enough horror stories this month."

"Just say we made it. Any coffee around?"

Max smiled. "I made some."

The coffee was strong. Max had chosen Genie's favorite blend, which was ground for her every week at Zabar's. She sipped it, savoring the flavor. Finally Max broke the silence. "You mentioned in passing last night you put together the Chicago deal. Unless it's a secret, fill me in." Genie gave him the terms of the deal, and Max whistled. "We have to put up fifteen million in cash on top of two mortgages? Fifteen million! What does he think he owns—an oil well?"

"I beat the price down from twenty."

"What about the mortgages?"

"In round numbers, they total about thirty-five million."

"A million here, a million there, and pretty soon you're talking money. What're the interest rates?"

"The first is a goodie. Eight-and-a-half percent on twenty-five million. Standard self-liquidation over thirty years."

"Now tell me the bad news."

"The second is for ten million, sixteen percent interest. No amortization. A balloon payment in five years." Genie studied Max over her coffee cup. "I know what you're thinking. Our seller is very bright or he has very good tax advice. He's borrowed ten million dollars tax free, and uses taxable income to pay the interest on the loan. Then he sells us the building before the ten million dollar mortgage comes due. It's beautiful."

"Yeah! Except we don't have five years to pay off that mortgage, do we?"

"Right again. We have three and a half years. Max, dear brother, I know the problems, but top buildings are scarce. This is top. That should make it easier to convert."

"It's a good location, but top it isn't. Top is Lake Shore Drive. The Gold Coast."

"It's as close to top as we can get. The Gold Coast is gone."

"If it's close enough, we'll call it Gold Coast North. What's in a name?" He sounded grim. "How many apartments, and how many rooms?"

"Two hundred forty-three apartments. About eleven hundred rooms. Perfect for professional couples."

Max started to do some mental arithmetic then switched to a calculator. "That's about twenty-three thousand a room average, and over a hundred thousand per apartment. How many professional couples can afford that—except psychiatrists?"

He shook his head and frowned. "When you see Herb at the bank, see if you can get them to agree that an income of two-and-a-half times the maintenance qualifies the buyer for a bank loan. If we're lucky and the people living there are in reasonably good financial shape, maybe most of them can get in with only ten percent down. We're going to need all the help we can get selling this deal."

"How much help, Max? If it's too tough and I made a mistake, we can always drop the option."

"And the next building we want will only cost more. Decent merchandise is getting scarcer than virgins. And more expensive. Plus interest rates are rising. Again!"

Genie had been concerned for some time with rising interest rates. She knew, as did Max, that ConVert-Co was on a funny treadmill. The money they made on a building conversion was being swallowed up by the repayment of the bank loans that made the purchase of the building possible, plus the huge interest they had to pay on the loans until they were repaid. All they needed were several sticky buildings where the tenants refused to buy the apartments, and their bankers could get difficult about demanding repayment of the loans.

She pulled out of her own thoughts to hear Max saying, "We can't even take a reasonable time to convince the tenants to buy the apartments any longer. We don't dare keep inventory. If we own something for more than six months, we have to raise the price of the apartments because the interest rates on our loans rise."

"Why don't we sit back and ride out the interest rates? Sell off what we have and wait? The recession's so bad, the Feds will have to loosen up or the country will be back in 1932. We're not the only ones in a squeeze."

Max thought about that. "Maybe. Personally I think they're religious fanatics. High interest rates are their hobby horse to break inflation, and the country be hanged. Anyway, you're the dreamer and schemer. I'm only the reamer. You call the shots."

"I don't like your division of labor. You've got your own stake in the dream. And I'd get into the selling if you'd let me."

"That's not your end of the business. You've got enough to do as is."

"Why so grim, Max? We're not in that bad shape."

"No. But if I can't move that Boston albatross pretty soon, we could be."

"The sale that tough?"

"It shouldn't be. There's some opposition, and you know Boston. I think we've finally got the handle though. Won't know for a week or two. Oh, yeah. That reminds me. We'll need another caterer. I tossed Stacey out on her ass yesterday."

Max's face had no expression, but his eyes told Genie more than she wanted to know. "What do you mean, you tossed her out?"

"She's become a real pain."

Genie hesitated before asking the next question. "How rough on her were you?"

"We did not part as good friends. But we did agree to part."

"Oh, Max! Damn it! When will you learn to control your temper?" She sipped the last of her coffee. Her mind was full of thoughts. Thoughts of Max, of their business problems, of Stacey Moore and her family's banking connections. Max paid no attention to such things, but Genie could only hope there wouldn't be any nasty feedback. Feedback that could hurt ConVert-Co. "Your romances aside, I'll put some time in over the next few weeks to do an internal audit. It'll tell us where we really stand. But I still have to see Herb. Providing you want to go ahead with Chicago?"

"I think so. The idea of making that guy a present of our two hundred and fifty thousand annoys me. But find out where we stand before taking on anything new."

"Agreed. I'm going to my office to shower and change. Hopefully some of our more loyal, overpaid, wage slaves have arrived? At least someone to run the switchboard."

"If there's no one there, we can take turns on the board ourselves."

She laughed. "Someone ought to be here by now. Try the phone."

Max dialed, and the operator answered. If nothing else, the telephones at ConVert-Co were being taken care of.

Genie had just finished changing when her phone rang. "Yes?"

"Miss Szabo, there's a call for you from a man who says he's an old friend. His name is Paul Husseman. Shall I put him through?"

"Ask him to hold. Tell him I'm on another line, but I won't be long." Her words were rapid, almost staccato. She leaned back in her chair trying to catch her breath, to remember and not remember at the same time. Paul Husseman? How long had it been? Twelve years, five months, three days and—she looked at her watch—almost thirteen hours. She could feel herself begin to shake. Could she actually speak to him? After ten deep breaths, she felt capable of controlling her voice. "Paul! What a surprise after so many years." In spite of her efforts, her voice sounded terrible. High. Forced. Almost shrill.

"Genie, I'll make this short. I apologize for bothering you, but it's important I see you at your earliest convenience."

He sounded as she remembered. His voice was deep. Slightly theatrical. Clipped consonants. Perhaps a little deeper than when they had been young and in love. She gathered her courage. "How important is important?"

"Important enough or I wouldn't have telephoned you."

She thought, get it over with as quickly as possible. "Hold on for a moment." She walked to the window. By some miracle a single lane on each side of Park Avenue had been plowed. The lane snaked its way between stalled cars that had yet to be removed. "Where are you, Paul?"

"In our apartment in the Majestic."

Now she had to struggle harder to maintain an even tone. "Would lunch be soon enough?"

"Lunch would be fine. Twenty-One? Twelve-thirty?"

"Are they open?"

"I called in advance. They'll be open."

"You were so sure I'd see you?"

"Of course not. But as I said, it is very important."

That was like Paul. For a moment she was tempted to change her mind. How could anything Paul said to her be important anymore? He caught her thought as though she'd broadcast it. "Don't, Genie. This *is* important. If I can stand our meeting, so can you."

Genie gave in. "All right. I'll be there."

She hung up the phone and stared at the white ceiling. What could be so important? So urgent? She closed her eyes. And then, as though a dam had broken, buried memories of her youth flooded back, invading her mind, filling it to the brim with so many brilliantly etched scenes, so many forgotten but familiar faces. Her mind was spinning in a thousand directions. It wasn't only Paul. It was Andre Husseman. And Rebecca. Ralph Gluck and her own father and mother. It was the Majestic itself. Some mind-numbing anesthesia had suddenly worn off, and she could no longer defend herself against the pain of memories. She could only sit in her chair, cradling her head in her arms, letting her memories take possession of her, thinking how it had all started with Paul when they were children. Seemingly, they'd met by accident. Or was it an accident? Looking back over the long perspective of years, she wondered if it was pure chance? The odds against her ever knowing Paul had been so high. Why had Andre Husseman—and his wife—permitted it to happen? Why? She had no answers, and she accepted she would never have any. But it had happened. She and Paul had met. Had fallen in love. And so much of her life followed from that meeting and their falling in love.

PART TWO

1957–1968

4

One warm morning in late May, Andre Husseman was relaxing in his favorite chair, waiting for his wife. The chair was in what the original building plans had called a sun porch. Unlike the rest of the Husseman apartment, which was furnished predominately in French and Italian antiques, the note here was informality, with sisal matting on the floor, comfortable wicker chairs, and footrests with cushions covered in natural sailcloth.

While he waited, Andre looked absentmindedly out the windows thinking about his past and present. He thought about his father, Paul Husseman, after whom he had named his son. His father, born of hardworking Alsatian-Jewish immigrants, had a gambler's eye for the main chance and a shrewd instinct for business. He also had an unwavering determination to die a very rich man, and had almost achieved his goal. But when the nation's economy came apart after the stock market crash in 1929, his luck turned. It had taken all his father's energies and persistence to keep the family's real estate holdings together. It was a time when buildings were half-empty and the half that was rented was occupied by people who were usually three months behind in paying their rent. The days, months, and years of running from bank to bank to forestall foreclosures on his properties plus his losses in the stock market took their toll. But his father's tenacity, when other men threw in the towel, had ultimately paid off. The strain cost him his life—he lived just long enough to see the market and real estate begin the long climb back and died of a massive heart attack on 42nd Street in front of the Bowery Savings Bank, exactly fifteen minutes after receiving congratulations from the president of the bank along with the deed to a factory building on 38th Street and Eighth Avenue. It remained for Andre to become the multimillionaire his father had longed to be.

Andre Husseman inherited much of his father's instinct for the main chance. He was known to have a keen eye for business situations, and some of his associates considered him as opportunistic as his father. Often these traits came as a surprise to men who didn't know him. Andre had the tall slender look and the easy grace of an overbred idler. His blond hair had turned white at an early age and added to his distinguished appearance. His face was well modelled, fine, and sensitive, and might have suggested weakness were it not for an unusually square chin. It more truly represented Andre Husseman's true nature. He was not a weak man.

Andre looked at the traffic winding through Central Park. Glancing south, he could see the skyscrapers of the city silhouetted against the sky. New York was his city. The foundation of his wealth. He'd made astute use of the government laws that had made building so profitable right after the war, and his construction company built residential buildings mostly in the upper West Bronx and Queens. Now there was a new game in New York City. It was called Title One construction. His architects had plagued him to become involved. Finally he had, but only after making certain the law worked exactly as they claimed. It meant additional millions of dollars' profit with very little risk. That was the kind of business he understood, and looked for.

It was the profits produced from these business ventures that made his apartment in the Majestic, the trips to Europe, the many servants, and other luxuries possible. The Majestic was one of the premier buildings on the West Side of Manhattan, and the Hussemans occupied the largest apartment in the building. Andre smiled as he remembered the head-to-head confrontation his father had had with the builder when he insisted the builder live up to the terms of the lease he had signed. Their apartment was to be on the top two floors of the south tower, and that was exactly what he insisted upon regardless of the extensive subdivisions the builder planned for the rest of the apartments, subdivisions that had been forced upon the builder first by the stock market crash in 1929 and by the real estate collapse that followed.

A sound interrupted Andre's thinking of things past. Sara Husseman, a tall, solidly built woman with a handsome face dominated by bright green eyes and auburn hair, had finally arrived. Usually very much in command of herself, this morning her green eyes seemed larger and greener against her pale face. A tiny frown wrinkled her usually smooth brow. He knew she had been dealing with some problem or other with the servants, but he doubted this was the cause of her concern. Sara Husseman was accustomed to servants. Her treatment of the staff—a cook and butler couple, the chauffeur, Rebecca's governess, and the general housekeeper and her two twice-a-week assistants for the heavy work—though exacting and firm was nonetheless tempered by a quiet sympathy and considerable kindness.

"What is it, Sara?" Andre asked, rising from his chair and taking his wife's hands. "Tell me, what's troubling you?" He led her to the wicker couch and sat in a chair facing her.

For a moment Sara Husseman felt awkward with her husband. She feared she might not live up to his image of her, and that, as always, was of primary importance to her. Then she recovered her composure, reminding herself that Andre was generous of heart, generous with his time and money, generous in his understanding of other people's problems. He was trying to be understanding now. She was proud of him, and her concern that she might tarnish her own image in his eyes was not worthy of her husband.

"What is it?" he persisted.

Sara leaned back on the couch, consciously adopting a relaxed attitude, and said, "It's the Szabo child, Andre. Genie Szabo."

"What about her?"

Sara cleared her throat and said firmly, "Rebecca insists on inviting Genie to her birthday party. I'm against it."

"Why?"

"She doesn't go to school with Rebecca. And she won't know any of the other children."

"If she was a visiting relative, would you mind?"

"No." With his quick perception, Andre had put his finger on the heart of the matter. "It's what you suspect. She's the super's daughter."

"I see." Andre was silent. The Husseman family was very rich. Originally he had believed it important that his children understand not everyone had the privileges of money and the lifestyle and attitudes having money makes. He felt they might learn something valuable from knowing the Szabo children. With this in mind, he'd spoken directly to their father, Zoltan Szabo. He'd explained he had noticed the Szabo children kept very much to themselves, and he wondered if it would be an imposition on Zoltan to permit Max and Genie to get to know his children? Zoltan agreed. And in the course of time, the two sets of children, coming from vastly different backgrounds, became friends. Now the idea appeared to have repercussions. "Genie's being the super's daughter matters?"

Sara blushed. "In a way, yes, and in another way, of course not." She had, originally, also been in favor of their children becoming friends with Max and Genie. And that was exactly why she was at odds with herself. "Let me explain," she said. "I know we agreed that Max and Genie's playing with Paul and Rebecca was a good idea. But then they're alone. This is a children's party, and that's a very subtle thing." She hesitated before stating her case as fairly as she was able. "Children are not adults. They have not yet learned to restrain themselves. They can be unbelievably cruel. The right group has to be invited or they will not mix. And the right number. The games and food are more important than for the most formal dinner party we have ever given. It would be easier to handle a dozen adults, each on a different weight-loss or salt-free diet. For children, the food has to be sweet but not too sweet. Easy to eat, but not so soft there might be a temptation to throw it around. The games must be the right games. If they're wrong, the children won't play. They'll sit and sulk. But if they're too active, the children will run wild. Above all," she said in a resigned voice, "the children must know each other. A child who knows no one, a child such as Genie, will be left sitting in a corner."

"Rebecca will include her in the play."

"No. She may try, but in the end, she'll be running between Genie and the rest of her friends. Because they won't accept Genie. Especially when they discover she's not a relative or a friend from camp, but the super's child. And they will discover it even though Rebecca hasn't invited anyone else from the building."

"I still believe Genie should be invited."

Sara was perplexed. She had not liked what she had said, and she certainly did not like the picture it gave of herself. But she was realistic, and she was convinced Genie's presence would be a mistake. There was another unspoken reason why she felt the time had come to place more distance between her children and the Szabos. Paul. Paul was thirteen and approaching puberty. Her mother's instinct had picked up something between Paul and Genie.

"It's a matter of balancing choices," Andre said. "Although I must say I'm impressed with your practical analysis of children's parties. Who would have thought there was so much involved? But there are two additional points to be considered. First, Rebecca will be hurt if we go against her wishes. It is her party. Second," and the outer edges of his mouth turned up in the beginnings of a faint smile, "don't you think it's wiser that Rebecca, and even Genie, discover, at this age, the limitations of our society? There are things Rebecca Husseman can and cannot do. And the same can be said for Genie Szabo."

Sara reconsidered her opposition to Genie's presence. Yes, painful as it might be, it would be a lesson to the children if they exposed Genie to Rebecca's friends. Though Rebecca and Genie were both ten years old, both attractive, lively, and intelligent, they were destined for different lives, and it would be better for them to realize it sooner rather than later. "You're right, my dear. We'll invite Genie." Her mind turned to practical matters. "I was considering inviting her by telephone, if I had to. But now I'll send her an invitation as I will all the other children."

"Very wise, Sara. A good decision." And the two Hussemans smiled at each other with complete understanding.

Genie had been kept after class by Miss Brown, her teacher. Miss Brown had snow white hair and a nose as red as her apple dumpling cheeks. "Genie," her teacher said, leaning forward so Genie could smell the mint she chewed, "you turned in an A plus assignment. Child, you have a gift for numbers. It's supposed to be ungirlish, but forget that. It will prove a great asset when you grow up."

Genie, who had been holding herself rigid wondering what she'd done wrong, relaxed and flushed with delight. "Thank you, Miss Brown. Thank you very much.'' The terrible dragon of the fourth grade had said she'd done well. She licked her lips. ''Uh—Miss Brown? My brother's been waiting for me since three o'clock. Could I please leave now?''

''Oh, yes. Max. Go, child. It's all right.''

Genie ran for the door, then down the hall with its dim lights and dirty walls. She saw Max waiting and watching the boys play in the school yard. There were always two games going, sometimes three. One played by the Irish kids. Another by the Negroes. Once in a while the Puerto Ricans got enough kids together to grab a portion of the playground. A few more Puerto Ricans and there would be three groups in a concrete yard that was barely large enough for two. Genie and Max were Hungarian. Their father was afraid one day a gang, it made no difference which gang, would decide to get the Hungarian kids. So he insisted they come home right after school.

As she ran to Max, a ball bounced off the playground wall towards him. He caught it and threw it back with an easy graceful motion. There were some calls he should come and play, but Genie saw Max shake his head. Their father's word was law. Then she was at his side, slipping her small hand in his.

Max looked down at his little sister. ''Kidlet, the old dragon keep you after class? What's eating her?''

Genie heard the anger in Max's voice. ''She liked my homework and wanted to tell me. That's all.''

They left the playground and walked east on 70th Street. The area was run down, almost a slum. The sidewalks were cracked, the factories had broken windows and were mostly vacant, the tenements were dark and dingy. Close to the buildings everything smelled of urine. Genie thought how odd it was that just two blocks north was 72nd Street with its stores, expensive apartment houses, and rich people. Here, only poor people. As they neared Amsterdam Avenue, an old drunk tottered towards them, stumbled, almost fell, caught himself, and leaned against a lamp post. In the bright light of the late spring afternoon, Genie could see his watery, frightened eyes. She wanted to help him, but Max hurried her on. She looked back and saw the poor man had fallen over the fender of a car and was vomiting into the street.

At the corner of 70th and Amsterdam, Max waited for the

light to change. The wind coming off the river made his dark blond hair fly and his ruddy complexion redder. All the Szabos except Max were dark-haired and pale-skinned. Genie was a typical Szabo. Long-legged, coltish, with a strong, heart-shaped face. Even at ten, she was beautifully ugly as little girls who are destined to grow up to be incredibly lovely women are apt to be. She wasn't aware why, but somehow she knew she would always get her way with men—with her father and brother and even with the boys in her class.

The light changed to green, and Max, seeing the street was clear, held Genie's hand tightly as they crossed. They headed north. At 72nd Street, they played a game to see whether they could cross both Broadway and Amsterdam Avenue on the same green light. Some days it was too crowded, and they couldn't push their way through. Today they could. When they reached the east side of Amsterdam, Max stopped to let Genie catch her breath. The first part of the adventure home was over.

Walking east, Max and Genie could see the windows of the Eclair Pastry Shop across the street. Occasionally their father would bring home a small box from the Eclair and there would be a celebration. They stopped to stare at the roast beef, turkey, and other foods in the window of Fine and Schapiro, a restaurant with funny waiters that served special food Jewish people loved—soup with knaidlach, gefilte fish. Sometimes the Szabos ate there. They loved the food as much as the Jewish people.

As always, they paused for a moment on the southeast corner of Columbus Avenue and 72nd Street. The most wonderful part of the walk home was about to begin. It would have been quicker to walk south to 71st Street and east to the Majestic. But then they'd miss standing on the corner of Central Park West watching the tenants of the Majestic arrive. The Szabo children had no understanding that among the people who lived in the Majestic, all were not equal. Some were wealthy, some comfortable, and a few struggled to pay their monthly rent. All seemed equally grand, equally mysterious, equally worthy of envy.

A taxi drew up, and the outside doorman, Moe, rushed to open the cab door and help a lady in some kind of fur piece out of the cab. Genie knew Moe worked for their father. At least she thought he did, because their father gave Moe orders. As the lady hurried toward the main entrance, the inside doorman, Michael, opened the door for her and for Moe, who was now carrying some packages wrapped in silver paper. The children smiled at each other. It was time to go home or their mother would worry. As they passed the canopy, Moe said hello. He knew they would not use the main entrance. Even though the ground floor apartment in which they lived had an entrance from the lobby, they were barred from using the lobby without special permission. And the only reason for special permission would be if children of the tenants invited them to play in their apartment. As Anna Szabo had explained several years ago, this was not likely to happen. The tenants were aristocrats, and the Szabos were, if not actually peasants, only one generation removed. In Hungary mixing between classes wasn't possible. She saw no reason to suppose it would be different in the United States. They were to be polite but distant, and make no overtures of friendship toward anyone living in the building. The tenants' children would probably ignore them; if they didn't, they would make fun of them behind their backs.

Their mother's warning words were never out of Max and Genie's minds. They'd become awkward when in the presence of the tenants' children. This was unfortunate, because the young and attractive Szabos originally had been often approached by other children looking for playmates, who came from families that made no such class distinctions as Anna. Still, the two Szabos obeyed their mother and shied away saying, "Thank you, but I'm busy." Their refusal to mingle set up barriers that at first puzzled the other children, but as time passed, led to a general attitude of who-needs-them-anyway. Thus Anna's words of warning became a self-fulfilling prophecy, and Max and Genie were left alone, forced to depend solely on each other for friendship, fun, and warmth.

There was one exception to Anna's rule: the Husseman children. After Andre had spoken to Zoltan, Anna and Zoltan had one of their few serious disagreements over what action they should take.

"I don't care what Mr. Husseman wishes. It is wrong."

"Why is it wrong?"

"It is wrong for our children to play with the Husseman children, and you know why. They do not belong together."

"But Mr. Husseman has said it is all right. He's asked for our permission." Zoltan was a patient man, and he hoped, once Anna understood that a tenant actually wanted Max and Genie to play with his children, she would agree.

"I refuse to give my permission. No! You must tell Mr. Husseman I said no."

"I cannot do that, Anna."

"You must!"

Zoltan had never before seen his wife take such an unyielding stance. Her refusal forced him to remind her of the realities of their life. "Anna, listen to me. Mr. Husseman is a tenant. He has asked us for a favor. If we refuse him this favor, he might complain to Mr. Carson at Brown, Harris, and Mr. Carson will tell us to leave. I will lose my job, and we will have to move from this beautiful apartment."

Faced with the possibility of Zoltan losing his job and their being forced to move from a home she had come to love, Anna reluctantly surrendered. "Yes, it is true. People like us cannot offend people like the Hussemans. We must do as he wishes." She shook her head, sadly, and said, more to herself than Zoltan, "It is still wrong. He will hurt Genie."

Over the years Zoltan had learned to ignore certain remarks made by his wife. Something had happened in Hungary long before they'd married, and he had no wish to dwell on what was past. It was enough for him that they now lived in the United States, and she'd agreed to do what they had to do.

Today, as Max and Genie walked down Central Park West, the bus from the Riverdale Country Day School for Boys drew up, and Paul jumped out. He saw them and waved as he always did. Max thought the wave was for him, but Genie knew it was special for her. They walked around the corner and west on 71st Street past the entrance on that side. The doorman, Pat, said hello. He also knew the special rules regarding the children. At the wrought iron gate leading to the service entrance, they went down the worn wooden steps leading to the courtyard. Then they climbed the rusty iron stairs that led to the rear entrance of their apartment. Max rang the bell. It took only a few moments for their mother to open the door.

Anna returned to the kitchen and handed Genie an already opened envelope. The envelope was large, almost square, and made of heavy expensive paper.

"What's in it, Genie?" Max asked.

Genie pulled a white card with a pink border out of the envelope. The printing was in deep red. She read it aloud. "You are cordially invited to attend the tenth birthday party for Rebecca Sara Husseman." There was the time, date, and address, and some small printing at the bottom right hand corner that said RSVP. She wondered what that meant. A second look in the envelope produced a smaller card, a note, and an addressed stamped smaller envelope. The card read, "I will—will not—be able to attend the party for Rebecca." The note said, "Please omit presents." The address on the envelope that went with the smaller card was: Miss Rebecca Sara Husseman, The Majestic, 115 Central Park West, New York 23, New York. Genie was puzzled. "Where is the invitation for Max?"

"This is a girl's party. No boys are invited."

"Not even Paul?"

"Not even Paul."

Genie's disappointment lasted only a second. The party sounded like it would be a lot of fun.

Anna regarded her daughter with a mixture of pride and fear. She was so proud of Genie's independent spirit, but she was afraid for her, too. She was certain that spirit would get her into trouble. There was no room for Genie's spirit in their world. Theirs was the world of the servant. Anna hated doing what she knew she had to do. "I don't think it's right for you to go to Rebecca's party, Genie. These are rich people. You're the super's daughter. I don't think it's right."

"Why not, Momma? Why not? You said it was all right for us to play with Paul and Rebecca." Genie was trying hard not to cry.

"That's different. But we'll talk to your father tonight, we'll see what he thinks."

That made Genie feel better. She knew she was her father's favorite. He would say yes.

* * *

After finishing their milk and cookies, Genie asked Max if he'd like to play their game.

Max knew how upset Genie was, and he wanted to please her. "I will, if you will."

"I will, if you will."

"I will, if you will."

The "I wills" went back and forth, faster and faster in a confused jumble. Finally Anna stopped them. "Play in the living room, and let me prepare supper." Two chairs were pushed out, and two pairs of legs raced into the living room.

The living room was a good-sized room. It was painted white and furnished with a big overstuffed couch, several easy chairs, and the usual assortment of tables and lamps. There was a worn rug on the waxed hardwood floor. The windows looked out on 71st Street. Though the sofa and easy chairs were spotless and the wooden tables had been polished to a high gloss, everything had the look of secondhand furniture. Love and care had replaced money. The entire room was dominated by two huge multicolored maps, one of Budapest and the other of Western Europe just before the start of the Second World War. The map of Budapest had a large circle at the corner of two streets very near the Danube. The words "our home" were meticulously lettered in bright red paint next to the circle. The map of Europe had a line, drawn with the same care and the same bright red paint, that started in Budapest, and, after numerous stops, led to Lisbon, Portugal. From Lisbon it headed west and extended as far into the Atlantic Ocean as the map allowed. The children knew the circle on the map of Budapest was the spot where their parents had lived, and the line on the second map was the route they had taken to escape the Nazis on their way to the United States.

Max and Genie settled themselves on the threadbare Oriental rug in the middle of the room. Max spoke first, not waiting for agreement before starting. "What if we were rich enough to buy new furniture?"

Genie laughed. "What if we had a new soft rug like Paul and Rebecca?"

It was Max's turn. "What if we owned the baseball field in the park?"

"What if we paid rent like the other tenants?"

"They'd have to let us use the regular entrances to the building. What if we were rich like the other tenants?"

Genie thought about that.

During the short moment of silence they heard the telephone ring in the kitchen. Then Genie clapped her hands. "I've got the best 'what if' . . ." Max waited. "What if we owned the Majestic?"

Max's mouth fell open. "Oh! What if we did?"

At that moment their mother appeared. "That was Mrs. Husseman on the phone. She invited both of you upstairs to play with Paul and Rebecca. It would only be for an hour. Do you want to go?"

Genie jumped up. "Oh, yes! Let's go!"

Max agreed mostly because he knew how much Genie wanted to go.

Anna took charge. "Then it's settled. Off you go." She led them to the front door which opened onto the lobby.

Pat greeted them. He had been called and knew the Szabo children could use the lobby. "I'll take care of them, Mrs. Szabo."

Anna returned to the apartment, and the children followed the large man in his splendid black uniform along the wide hall. He took them to the elevator operator at the C/D elevator bank, which served the largest apartments in the building.

On their way to the elevator, Genie studied the elaborate inlaid metal and wood, the marble floors, the leather chairs and sofas, and the many mirrors with figures of men and women etched in them. "Max," she whispered. She could hardly control her voice. "Oh, Max! What if we really owned the Majestic?"

That evening at supper Zoltan Szabo listened patiently. He was a tall, imposing man with thick black hair just beginning to show a touch of grey, a broad body, and large hands with very clean nails and blunt, square fingers. The hands both looked, and were, competent. A thick black mustache gave his face an almost fierce appearance. Only his eyes belied the image of strength. They were very dark, deep set, and he rarely looked directly at people when speaking to them. They were always shifting around as if to assure himself he was really here, really in the United States, really eating the good food Anna put on the table, really in this apartment his job provided for his family.

Though Zoltan agreed with his wife's attitude toward the party, by the end of the supper the hurt look on Genie's face almost caused him to change his mind. Anna sensed his impulse to surrender and sent the children to their rooms to do their homework. "We'll tell you what we decided before you go to sleep." After the children left, Anna and Zoltan remained at the dining room table. Anna spoke first. "I don't think she should go. We decided a long time ago, the children must not mix with the tenants."

"But she wants to go so badly."

"And I don't like her attachment to Paul Husseman."

Zoltan was startled. "What attachment? She's only ten, and he's what? Twelve? Thirteen? They're children."

"They won't be children forever. And if it comes to something else, it will come to nothing. Genie will be hurt." She repeated her deep felt feeling. "They're not from the same class."

Zoltan remained silent while Anna reconsidered the possibilities. If she allowed Genie to go to the party, Anna was certain she'd be ignored by Rebecca's friends, and Rebecca would choose her friends over Genie. Genie would be hurt. But perhaps that wasn't so terrible. She was young. She'd recover, and she'd learn a lesson. She'd begin to understand something of what life had in store for her. Anna Szabo had no way of knowing her thoughts coincided exactly with those of Sara Husseman. So Anna came to a decision. "I think we should let her go. I'll make her a new dress for the party."

"I thought you said you didn't want her to go?"

"I've changed my mind."

"Why?"

Anna considered telling her husband her real reasons, but she decided against it. If he thought Genie would be hurt, he'd want to protect her. She invented a reason. "The look on her face, Zoltan. She'd be so disappointed if we didn't let her go."

Zoltan knew his wife. She wasn't telling him the truth. But he asked himself, did he really want to know the truth? Wasn't it enough that Anna had changed her mind? Genie would be so pleased. That was what mattered.

Leaving Zoltan to sip his coffee and brandy, Anna went to tell Genie. Once alone, Zoltan forgot about the party. There was something else on his mind. He had heard a rumor that a wealthy group of tenants had an idea the tenants should buy the building. Turn it into a cooperative. He had no idea what a cooperative was, but anything concerning the building that he didn't understand could be a threat to him and his family. He knew a lawyer with offices on 72nd Street. Tomorrow he would ask the lawyer what a cooperative was. Then he would decide how concerned he should be, a little or a lot. It didn't occur to him not to worry.

5

Genie's dress was ready a week before the party. Anna had made a classic Hungarian dress—a wide white skirt, a small vest laced with a black ribbon, and a white blouse with puffed sleeves, worn with white stockings and black shoes. The vest, which was red, had beautifully embroidered piping around the edges. Genie's hair was washed, cut, and held in place by a high hat made out of white linen. When she looked at Genie in the dress, Anna realized how successful she had been. Her daughter looked exactly like the child of a landowner she had once seen in the old country before the war. Her dress was not the dress an American child would wear to a party. It wasn't supposed to be.

Studying herself in the mirror, Genie wasn't pleased. She didn't want to offend her mother, but she was certain she had never seen any child dressed this way. She ran her hands down the wide skirt in a vain attempt to make it seem less wide. She looked at her white stockings and wondered what the other girls would think. She looked so different, almost funny. For the first time in her life, she felt embarrassed. But all she said was, "Momma, it's beautiful."

Anna managed a smile. "You look lovely. Like a real aristocrat."

"What's an aristocrat, Momma?"

That called for a careful answer. "Well, it's someone who is better born. From a family that owns property."

"Are Paul and Rebecca aristocrats? Were they better born than I was." She'd been taught in school that all Americans were born equal. Momma didn't think so. Did money make them better? She asked the question again. "Momma, are Paul and Rebecca better than we are? Are their friends better?"

Anna hugged Genie. "Nobody's better than you, dear."

53

Genie chewed on her lip. She had a sudden insight. "You didn't want me to go to the party because you think the other kids are better than I am."

"I don't want you to get hurt."

"How can I be hurt? There won't be any fights." She didn't respond to her mother's hug in her usual affectionate way.

Anna felt shamed by her own child, as if she were the child and Genie the parent. It was her fault, and she would put a stop to it. "We've talked enough about our betters. You are going to the party, and you will have a wonderful time." The ending of the conversation didn't satisfy Genie, and Anna knew it. However, there really was nothing she could say that would satisfy her daughter. She certainly could not tell her the truth.

After Genie had gone to her bedroom to hang up her party dress, Anna returned to the kitchen. The dress and the talk about aristocrats made her question her actions. Was this the right thing for her to have done? Should she have made Genie an American dress and allowed events to take their course? Slowly, sadly, she shook her head. Everything she knew, everything that had happened to her, told her she was right. If her parents had been as concerned about her as she was about Genie, she might have been spared so much. Spared Anton and Count Balacz. Spared the years of fear and shame that still haunted her.

For as long as anyone could remember, the Dozsa family had farmed a small corner of rich land in the "Little Alföld" between the Danube and the Rabá rivers. And as far back as history was taught in the small school Szuszuanna attended, the ancestors of Count Vladislav Balacz had owned the land the Dozsas farmed and the house in which they lived. The first Count Balacz received his title from the King of Hungary, Louis the Great, in 1362, and his descendants ruled the lands bordering the city of Pâpa with absolute power. They survived the Ottoman invasion—a Count Lothar Balacz led a body of soldiers in the battle of Vienna in 1683, which finally halted the invasion of Europe and routed the Turks. After the battle of Vienna, the Magyars ranged through Central Europe, on occasion reaching as far west as the Rhine. The ferocity with which they raped, looted, tortured, and destroyed was unusual, even for those chaotic times. They became so infamous that the British, finding the word "Magyar" difficult to pronounce, short-ened it, and a new word with which to frighten both children and adults came into wide usage. "Magyar" became "ogre." Finally the Magyars made their peace with the Habsburgs in 1699 and returned home to Hungary. When the Dual Monarchy was established in Vienna under the Emperor Francis Joseph and the emperor guaranteed the civil rights of all non-Magyars, Count Gyula Balacz drank a toast to his emperor with rich, golden Tokay wine and ignored the edict. No one except the Balacz family had any rights on his land. Even the end of the First World War and the establishment of Admiral Miklos Horthy as provisional head of state brought little change to the land owned and controlled by Count Vladislav Balacz.

Like all his ancestors, Count Balacz considered the peasants who farmed his land, tended his horses, cattle and sheep, and worked in the large, rambling two-story half-castle, half-villa ancestral home his subjects. And his subjects obeyed him as their lord. Of what use was it to complain to the local magistrate when the local magistrate was appointed by and served at the pleasure of the count? No one considered leaving the count's land and traveling to the city of Pâpa to complain about injustices. A peasant belonged to the land, and buried deep in the heart of every peasant was the knowledge that a part of him belonged to the count.

When Szuszuanna Dozsa was ten years old, Count Balacz's estate manager approached her father, Nandor Dozsa. "Your daughter has been honored by our lord."

Nandor removed the leather harness from his shoulders; the harness was attached to a heavy iron plow. He'd been working the land, making deep furrows in the soil before planting wheat. He wiped the sweat from his eyes. "In what way, sir?"

"She has been chosen to serve in the great hall." He pointed to the top of the gentle rise where the count's home could be seen. "She will be taught to sew, dust, clean, cook, and serve the count and his family. She will also be taught by the same tutors who teach the young Count Anton."

Nandor agreed. "That is a great honor. When do you wish my wife to deliver her to the hall?"

"On Sunday, after church. Wash her well. Dress her in her finest clothes. Do not bring along anything else. The countess will see to it that she is provided for."

"Will Szuszuanna be allowed to visit us?"

"Every Sunday after church she will spend the afternoon with you. But she must be returned to the hall by sundown. In time for dinner."

So Szuszuanna began a new life. She bathed twice a week, changed her garments after every bath and worked in the house of the count. Szuszuanna was a tall, strong child with black hair and black eyes which stood out in startling contrast to her white skin. Most of her time was spent with Count Anton, either at study or at play. Often, when she was hard at work in the kitchen or running between the formal rooms downstairs and the sleeping quarters on the second floor, she was interrupted by the cry, "Szuszuanna, Count Anton wants you. Stop whatever you're doing. He's in the maze. You must find him." Or, "He's by the moat. Go to him." Or. . . . Although Szuszuanna was unaware of it, most of the servants were jealous of her and whispered behind her back of other duties for which she was being trained.

Count Anton Balacz was a stocky boy with red-blond hair, blue eyes, and a ruddy complexion. Although short, he was heavy-boned and well muscled for his age and gave promise of growing up to be a powerful man. He had only one physical oddity—an oddity characteristic of all his ancestors since they'd left the plains of Western Siberia in the sixth century. His legs were badly bowed from having spent too many hours on a horse when he was very young. No one thought anything of it. All the male Balaczes had bowed legs. Why should Count Anton be any different? His nature, as well, was that of a Balacz. He could be happy, graceful, even charming, one moment, and in an instant change to become angry, violent, sadistic. When he was happy, it seemed to Szuszuanna that all the sun which shone on the land shone for her. And when he was angry and hurt her, it was as though the heavy storm clouds that so often rolled in from the far-off Alps were gathered over her head. Actually, Anton had no conception of being either charming or sadistic. At all times he was himself: Hungarian, a count, and a product of fourteen hundred years of pure Magyar blood.

It never occurred to Szuszuanna to complain when Anton hit or pinched her, making her white skin black and blue. That she should be allowed to spend so much time in his presence was, in itself, a wondrous thing and made up for all the bad days.

Above all, there were the good days to remember and cherish. It seemed to Szuszuanna that there were so many good days, it was easy to forget the bad ones.

As the years passed, Szuszuanna came to like Count Anton Balacz more and more, admire him and, eventually, to love him. By the time she was sixteen, she'd reached her full height. Like most women of peasant stock, her breasts and hips were large and round. Thanks to the wholesome food she'd been fed, there was a glow of healthy energy in everything she did. She dreamed beautiful dreams of living with her count, even fantasized she'd been born of noble parents and had been stolen away by Gypsies who had left her with Nandor Dozsa. Soon her true parents would be discovered, and she would take her rightful place beside Count Anton. She asked herself, why should it not be so? Did not Anton like her better than anyone else? He told her he did, and he'd taken to holding her hand and kissing her when they were alone. His kisses made her head spin, her knees buckle, and her body ache for him. He had not been content with kisses. His hands had become familiar with her breasts, her thighs, even the place between her legs. Szuszuanna understood and welcomed what she knew would follow. Like most children raised on the land, the sexual act held no mysteries for her. When one has seen a stallion mount a mare, or a bull, a cow, what mysteries are left? Except those of loving and caring: human mysteries.

For a while, Anton's hands had remained outside her clothes. Then everything changed. The day had been hot, and even the setting of the sun did little to dissipate the heat being given off by the warm earth. After dinner, Anton and Szuszuanna met, as arranged, under a partially ruined arch which had once supported a bridge over the moat. There, in the still darkness, Anton unlaced her blouse and kissed her bare breasts. When he said, "I love you," Szuszuanna thought she might faint. He lifted her skirt and caressed the places he'd previously only touched. Szuszuanna was helpless to stop him. Her surrender was complete. His words, "I love you," were far more compelling than the physical act. When he mounted her, there was a moment of shock, followed by some pain, followed by nothing. After he'd satisfied himself, Anton withdrew, helped her to her feet, allowed her to lace her blouse, brush herself off, and return to the house. In a hypersexual state, Szuszuanna was convinced Anton planned to marry her. Even though she knew her parents were peasants, she'd been raised in the great hall, and she would be a good wife to the Count Anton Balacz.

Several days later, Szuszuanna stole into Count Balacz's library. She was looking for a book which would guide her as to how great ladies, Countess Balacz, for example, conducted themselves at balls or when paying a visit to a neighboring estate. She heard footsteps and voices and had just enough time to jump for an open door which led to a stone terrace. It was the count and Anton. Szuszuanna knew she had no business listening to other people's conversation—above all not the conversation between Count Vladislav Balacz and his son—but at that moment, nothing could have stopped her.

"Well, Anton, how is it coming along with Szuszuanna?"

Anton appeared to be in one of his bad moods. "All right, I guess."

"Too slow for you?"

"Yes. Thank you for providing me with Maria."

Szuszuanna's hand flew to her mouth. Maria? Who was Maria? What did he mean?

Count Vladislav laughed. "Oh to be young and on fire again!"

"Why must I have Szuszuanna. I like Maria much better."

Szuszuanna bit her hand. Anton! A hammer was pounding at her brain.

"Maria is a fine, well-paid prostitute. She's been paid to teach you about sex. But she's almost thirty. Besides, Szuszuanna loves you. You will explain to her what it is you desire from her, and she will learn to please you. A woman in love is a much more satisfying mistress than a whore."

"Maybe."

"You listen to your father, Anton. I've watched that girl. If I hadn't picked her out for you years ago, I'd take her myself."

"Take her. I give her to you." Anton continued. "When I had her last week, she lay on the ground and didn't move. As far as I could tell, she might as well have been dead. Even when I told her I loved her—as if such a thing could be possible: a Count Balacz in love with a peasant—she did not move. . . ."

Those were the last words Szuszuanna heard. She ran from the terrace all the way home. By the time she arrived, her father had returned from the fields. He and her mother listened to her story, and she saw a darkness settle over her parents' faces.

Nandor asked, "What should we do, Katarin?"

"I don't know. Why did you believe Count Anton loved you? You're a peasant. He's a great lord's son. How could you think such a thing was possible?"

"It is a mistake I will never make again."

Katarin said a silent prayer. "Please, dear God. She's a child. Don't let her be pregnant."

"Does anyone know you're here?"

"No, father."

"I have an idea. But we must act fast before you're missed. And, Katarin, it is important you remember that we have not seen Szuszuanna. We do not know where she is. Or the count will be angry with us, and we will be forced to leave our home and land."

"What should we do, Nandor?"

"I have a cousin in Budapest. Szuszuanna, you must walk all the way to Pâpa. Momma will give you food, and I have money for the railroad ticket from Pâpa to Budapest. You must leave as soon as it is dark."

Szuszuanna cried all the way to Pâpa and most of the way to Budapest. Eventually she stopped crying, found her father's cousin and began a new life. Whether it was because, for once, God was listening to a mother's prayer, or because Anton had chosen the wrong time of the month to mount Szuszuanna, when the day came for her menstrual blood to flow, it did. As a result, Szuszuanna suffered no serious physical consequences from Anton's act. In addition, the education she'd received from the Balacz tutor enabled her to obtain a job, first as a housekeeper and later as a governess. She remained a governess until she met and married Zoltan.

As far as Anna was concerned, her daughter was making the same mistake she had made. The Hussemans were no different than the Balaczes, and Paul and Rebecca were other versions of Anton. The Szabos were peasants. The Hussemans aristocrats. It was her duty to protect Genie. Genie was strong as she was strong. She had survived and found a man from her own class to love and marry. So would Genie.

The invitation said the party would run from 2:30 to 5:30.

Anna insisted she wait until 3:00. She didn't want Genie to be the first to arrive. Genie didn't understand, but she obeyed her mother as always. When the grandfather clock in the hall chimed three, Genie prepared to leave. At the last moment she insisted on leaving off the high, starched white hat. It looked too silly.

While waiting for the elevator, three other children arrived with their mothers. They stared curiously at her dress and wondered where her mother was. It seemed all solved when the elevator arrived and the operator greeted Genie by name. Mothers and children assumed she lived in the building. The elevator rose to the thirty-first floor where a Husseman maid waited by the open apartment door. She greeted Genie with a familiarity that prompted one of the mothers to look at Genie more carefully. Not only was the child oddly dressed, but the overly familiar tone of the help was puzzling.

Rebecca and Mrs. Husseman were waiting in the hall to greet Rebecca's friends. Sara Husseman extended her hand and said, "Come in, Genie. Rebecca and I are delighted you could come." Genie had no idea what to say so she shook Mrs. Husseman's hand and rushed to hug Rebecca. Then she heard Mrs. Husseman give the same welcome to the other children and receive the same answer each time. "Thank you for inviting me." That was what she should have said. She'd know better next time. As the guests continued to arrive, there was nothing for her to do except move on into the living room.

The servants had rolled up all the rugs and pushed the furniture in the living room and playroom against the walls. Within a half hour there were over thirty-five children in the two rooms with a few stragglers still to come. Genie didn't know a soul except Rebecca who had been running between her friends and had no time for Genie. The party wasn't anything like what Genie had imagined. Everything wasn't all right or fun, or friendly; she discovered that in this crowd of chattering, teasing, talking little girls, she was utterly alone. She wandered around the rooms always on the outskirts of conversations, ignored. Then one of the girls who had ridden up in the elevator with her happened to be standing alone next to her.

"Do you live in the building?" she asked.

Genie nodded.

"What floor?"

"The ground floor."

The girl seemed confused. "What's your name?"

"Genie Szabo. What's yours?"

"Laura Barron."

"Do you go to school with Rebecca?"

"No. We belong to the same temple. Temple Emanu-el on Fifth Avenue. Which temple do you belong to?"

Genie wondered if a church was the same as a temple. "St. Elizabeth of Hungary Church."

There was a silence as Laura tried to adjust to the new situation. Genie wasn't Jewish. She lived on the ground floor. She wore a funny dress. "What does your father do? Mine's a lawyer."

Genie swallowed. She could lie and say her father was a lawyer. Or a doctor. The temptation was strong, but that would mean she was ashamed of her father. She couldn't do that. "My father is the superintendent of this building."

Laura was startled. Her building had a superintendent. But the only time he and his son had been in their apartment was when something went wrong. They were always dirty, and smelled bad. She certainly never expected to meet either of them at a party. Slowly her features underwent a series of changes, going from curiosity to superiority to scorn. "Well, it's nice to meet a superintendent's daughter. I never have before. Now I have to go and play. Bye."

Genie felt a shame she had never felt before. Was this what her mother meant when she talked about being better born? She became even more aware of not belonging at the party. The girls had started choosing up teams for some game in the living room, and no one asked Genie to join. Maybe she could sneak out the back door and go home. Instead she went into the playroom. Sara Husseman found her sitting on the floor in the corner, her hands folded in her lap. Sara realized her plan had worked only too well, and the blatant lack of kindness of the children dismayed her. Even worse, she'd caused the misery she was now seeing. She reached down and took Genie by the hand. "Come with me. They're going to play a game. 'Paint the Doll.' You should be on one of the teams."

Genie let herself be urged along. Once in the living room, Mrs. Husseman announced in a loud voice, "Genie Szabo is going to be on team three." She led her to one of five groups of girls, the one with Rebecca in the center. She was going to force Rebecca to pay attention to her friend whom she had insisted on inviting. "Rebecca, Genie's going to be on your team. I'm sure she'll do splendidly."

Rebecca had already heard from Laura Barron about the strange girl in the funny dress whose father was the super. Most of the other girls had also heard about Genie. They had never met anyone like her, and they didn't want to meet her now. But Rebecca felt a twinge of discomfort at her own and everyone else's meanness, and since her mother's voice carried authority, she said, "Yes, Momma."

Genie moved closer to Rebecca. She asked, "How do you play Paint the Doll?"

Before Rebecca could answer, a large fat girl, dressed in an expensive white dress with lace inserts, interrupted loudly. "She's never played Paint the Doll? Who needs her? Let Addie's team have her." Betsy Rubin was thoroughly spoiled. She had not been disciplined either by her parents or her school.

Genie was not now so easily intimidated. Not with right on her side. "Mrs. Husseman wants me to be on Rebecca's team." It was her trump card, and she waited for Rebecca to second her. But Rebecca, feeling trapped between Genie and Betsy, said nothing. She was sorry she had invited Genie in the first place. Genie's dress was stupid. She didn't know anybody. She didn't even know how to play a simple game any five-year-old knew. She didn't fit. After a long pause, she found her voice. "I'll teach her, Betsy. She'll do fine."

Betsy persisted. "I don't want to play with her. We'll lose with her. She's the super's kid. She looks queer and funny."

"I am not queer and funny." Genie's temper began to rise.

"Yes, you are. Isn't she, Rebecca?"

Rebecca swallowed hard. "She's all right." The words lacked conviction.

"No, she isn't. She's a mess!"

The room filled with girls shifting about nervously and smothering giggles. They were glad they weren't the butt of Betsy's rage. Genie didn't know that most of the girls hated Betsy Rubin as much as she did. Behind her back they referred to her as the Blimp. Fat, loud, stupid, she also had a nasty temper. Many a child went home from school in tears, black and blue as a result of Betsy's pinching. But fat, loud, and stupid as she was, she was one of them.

Mrs. Husseman had listened to Betsy and Genie clash. She saw and was ashamed at her daughter's timidity. She felt again a self-disgust at the plan to embarrass Genie. The child was hurt, and worse, she didn't like what the events told her about her own daughter. They would have a long talk after the party. But first things first. What was important was to make Betsy play with Genie. She took charge. "That's quite enough, Betsy. I told you Genie's on the team. Rebecca, explain to Genie what she's to do, and we'll have no more nonsense."

The adult world had spoken, and even Betsy surrendered. Rebecca explained, "Each team has a large doll. The idea is to cut out the paper clothes and use the special paint to paint the doll to make it lifelike. The team that does the best job, according to Momma, Mrs. Barron, and Mrs. Stein, wins the game. What would you like to do?"

Genie thought she would really like to go home, but she answered, "I've helped my mother make clothes. I'll cut out a set of clothes."

Rebecca handed Genie the scissors and a sheet of heavy paper with the costume printed on it. Betsy took over painting the doll's face. Rebecca worked on the toenails. Other children did the fingernails and cut out different costumes.

Slowly, carefully, Genie started cutting along the lines. Suddenly an elbow was jammed into her back almost causing her to miss a cut. She turned around to see Betsy with a nasty grin on her round face.

"You're in my way, dope," Betsy hissed.

"I am not!" Small spots of color appeared on Genie's cheeks.

"Shut up, stupid," muttered Betsy turning back to her own painting. The girls quieted down again as each concentrated on her own work. Then Genie felt a hand push against her back.

There was grinning Betsy. Genie spoke very softly. "You quit it this minute! You've more than enough room, and you're trying to make me make mistakes."

"What a dummy you are."

Betsy's words and actions bothered Genie, but she didn't want to make a scene. She had to concentrate on cutting the best dress ever. Concentrate. Now and then she felt something light on her back. When she looked over her shoulder, Betsy seemed absorbed in painting the face of the doll. Genie didn't trust her. She had to hold herself together, fusing her fear and loathing into concentration on her work. At least Betsy had stopped pushing her.

Rebecca was sitting next to Betsy and saw what Betsy was doing. She was painting the back of Genie's red vest black. Rebecca was too ashamed of Genie and too frightened of Betsy to say anything.

Genie finished ahead of the other girls. Just as Betsy was about to touch her vest with another dab of paint, Genie stepped back to admire her work. The brush, which had been resting lightly on her back, now pressed firmly into it. The black paint was spread over a wide area. Genie spun around and caught Betsy in the act of yanking her wet paint brush away. The back of Genie's vest was now exposed to the mothers who were sitting on the couches watching their children. Genie heard them gasp.

She reached behind and felt the back of her vest. When she looked at her hand, it was black with paint. Genie exploded. She grabbed the paint brush out of Betsy's hand and smeared Betsy's face and dress with paint. Then she took the entire bottle of paint and poured it over Betsy's hair. She ran the brush up and down Betsy until it was dry, smearing her thoroughly.

Betsy was stunned. No girl had ever dared to attack her physically. "I'll kill you," she screamed, grabbing Genie by the hair and shaking her. Genie kicked Betsy in the shins as hard as she could. Betsy let go of Genie's hair and doubled over screaming, "Owwwww. You hurt me."

Genie yelled back. "You started it, you big fat nitwit."

Betsy launched herself at Genie who stepped aside and struck out her foot to trip Betsy. Off balance, Betsy fell against a low, lacquered Chinese table. The table splintered under Betsy's weight. She lay amidst the wreckage sobbing, "I want my Momma! I wamt my Momma!"

Not surprisingly, there was silence. Then Genie screamed, "You people! You're awful. You're not better. You're worse."

Before Mrs. Husseman could reach Genie, she ran from the room. When she reached the foyer, the elevator doors were opening, and she collided with Paul and Andre Husseman who were returning from a day at their country club. Andre grabbed

Genie and was startled to find his hand covered with sticky black paint.

Beside herself with fear, Genie managed to squirm out of his grasp and ran for the door to the fire stairs. Paul started after her, but was stopped by his father, as Mrs. Husseman appeared at the apartment door.

"What on earth's happened, Sara? What's going on?"

"Everything went wrong, my dear. Everything!"

Andre realized they must not include Paul in their talk about Genie and the party. "Paul, go after her. No. Not the stairs. You'll never catch her. Take the elevator and meet her on the ground floor, and send that vest back with Albert. We'll have it cleaned. Then take her out for an ice cream soda or whatever she wants." He turned to the elevator operator. "Albert, take my son down. No stops. And bring back the vest. I'll take care of you later."

"Yes, sir."

As soon as the elevator door closed, Sara told Andre the disastrous events of the party. What Andre had not counted on were raw childish emotions. Simply to ignore, to exclude, to barely tolerate Genie was not enough. They had to kick, pull hair, and paint each other. He had been wrong, and it gave him a warning. Though it had not been discussed, Andre, like Sara, had noticed the budding affection between Paul and Genie. What had happened would only strengthen Paul's attachment. But now was hardly the time to interfere. First, Rebecca's party had to be patched up, if possible.

Genie tripped and fell several times running down the stairs. She bruised both her knees and tore her white stockings. Finally she couldn't run any further. She sat on the cold grey steel of the third floor landing gasping for breath, her body shaking with silent tears. Her mother was right. She and her whole family were outsiders in the Majestic. Before today she had imagined she could be friends with Rebecca. Faced with today's reality, she knew she was unacceptable. She was the super's daughter. That said it all.

Paul, having waited for her on the ground floor, finally started up the stairs. He found her still sobbing. After lifting her to her feet, he helped her take off her vest, and then hung it on the bannister. "Don't cry, Genie. We'll send the vest up to mother with the elevator man, and she'll have it cleaned."

Genie wiped her cheeks with the back of her hand. She forced herself to stop crying. "Thank you for helping me." She wasn't going to show Paul how badly she had been hurt. "And thank your mother for offering to have my vest cleaned."

She sounded so cold, so remote. Paul understood she was shutting him out, and he felt a greater loss than he had ever known. "Don't be angry with me. I had nothing to do with whatever happened."

Genie's eyes were overflowing with tears again, and she murmured, "They don't like me. They just don't like me."

"They're dumb fool girls. Rebecca likes you."

"No, she doesn't."

"She invited you to the party, didn't she?"

"She shouldn't have. She didn't want me there. Nobody wanted me there. I looked so silly." For a fleeting moment, she wondered why her mother had made such a funny dress!

Paul could feel her misery so clearly it was as if he had been there himself, had suffered everything Genie had suffered. He managed to say, "I'm so sorry whatever happened, happened. Truly, I am. Please don't cry. I like you." He added, "You know you're my best friend. My very best friend in fact."

"Am I really?"

"Yes! Really!" He wanted more than anything else to make her feel better, so he tried to change the subject. "Aren't you hungry after all that crying?"

"A little." She did feel better. If Paul cared, what did it matter about Rebecca and her stupid dumb friends?

He took her hand in his and smiled. "Let's go to the Eclair and have ice cream and cake. We'll have our own party and forget those silly girls."

Paul was right. He was always right. He seemed to Genie to be the only person left in the world besides her family. Everything would be terrible without him.

6

There had been a change in the Majestic. Using Rebecca's birthday party as an excuse, Paul asked his father to see if anything could be done about altering the rules so that Max and Genie could use the regular building entrances and the public halls. Andre had always thought the restriction an unfortunate bit of snobbery, and agreed to approach Brown, Harris, Stevens, Inc., the managing agents, with the requested minor change. At Brown, Harris, an ex-Californian named Jack O'Neil had recently been given the management of the building. O'Neil had no idea there was a restriction on the children's use of the entrances, and he agreed to talk to Irving Sacher, the building owner, about removing it.

It turned out Sacher had no idea the restriction existed. In fact, no one could remember how it came into existence. Sacher had only one question. "Are the children well behaved?"

"As far as I know, they're very well behaved."

"Then forget it. Let the kids use whatever entrance they want."

This decision made, the news went from O'Neil to Husseman via telephone and to Zoltan via a typewritten notice as part of the weekly exchange between the building and the managing agent. When the tenants learned, via the gossip route, of the change, three women complained to their husbands about how the standards of the building were being lowered. Their husbands listened, agreed, and did nothing. The only person with a strong objection was Anna Szabo. Anna knew the restriction had never existed. It was invented by Zoltan, at her insistence, to keep the children in their place. And Genie's experience at Rebecca's party strengthened her conviction that the restrictions had been right in the first place.

"It's a mistake. It will give them wrong ideas about their station in life."

"Do you want me to forbid them to use the entrances?"

"Yes. I want you to forbid them."

"How can I?"

"You are their father. They must obey you."

"They will not understand. They will think it is un-American."

"I don't care what they think. It is right that they use the service entrance. The school teaches them terrible things. It would be better if they stopped attending the school."

"You know they must go to school. It is a law." For one of the few times in his marriage Zoltan found it necessary to enter into areas of Anna's beliefs he preferred to avoid. "What terrible things are they being taught?"

"That your being a super does not matter. That they are. . . ." If Anna had allowed herself to say aloud what she actually felt, she would have finished by adding, "as good as the tenants. They are not." She did say, "That they have a right to play with the children of the tenants. They do not, and it will come to trouble."

"And you believe that is wrong? Terrible?" Anna nodded. "Is it possible, Anna, that things are different in the United States than they were in Hungary? Maybe we are the ones who have been wrong. Maybe they are as good as Paul and Rebecca Husseman. And their playing with the other children will not cause trouble."

The look of deep sorrow Zoltan had seen many times touched Anna's face and then was gone. It was replaced by a stubborn refusal to believe anything other than what past experiences had shown her to be true. "No. I am right. The school, this country, is wrong. Someday they will all realize it."

As it always had, Anna's memory of old injuries prevented Zoltan from probing further, and his instinct to compromise prevailed. "I don't know. You may be right. However, I still cannot forbid them from using the main entrances. You know Mr. Husseman has talked to Mr. O'Neil, the new man at Brown, Harris, and Mr. O'Neil went to Mr. Sacher. If we continue to insist Max and Genie use the service entrance, they will not understand."

Caught between what she knew was right and what Mr.

Sacher, the owner of the Majestic, had ordered, once again Anna surrendered. "Do what you must do." She was frightened. Where would this American stupidity end? First the Hussemans. Then the school. Now this. Even her husband was changing. What else could happen to them?

Another and more important change was about to take place in the Majestic. Zoltan Szabo sat at an old wooden desk in his small office off the north corridor of the building. It was Friday before the Labor Day weekend, and he had two problems with which to contend; one was practical and the other somewhat theoretical. The practical problem was water leaks. August had been a very wet month, and the complaints about the crumbling plaster in the window reveals had mounted. In addition, a portion of the ceiling below the solarium had fallen into the dining room of the Gilman apartment during a formal dinner party. Mrs. Gilman took to her bed with a migraine, and Dr. Gilman called his lawyer. Threats were made regarding legal action for physical and psychological damages.

The theoretical problem on Zoltan's mind was Jack O'Neil. Why was O'Neil coming to see him on a Friday afternoon before a long weekend? Usually on Fridays O'Neil took a late lunch, had his three martinis, and disappeared for the rest of the day. Today O'Neil was on his way to see him. Undoubtedly it had something to do with the building about to become a cooperative.

The plan had been in the works for almost a year. Its original sponsors, Andre Husseman and Ralph Gluck, had gradually won over most of the tenants. Then, after a long negotiation during which the deal was off and on several times, a contract had finally been signed with the owner to purchase the building. Privately Zoltan thought the tenants were crazy. To pay thirty-two dollars a share or twelve thousand dollars cash for a five-and-a-half-room apartment like 9C West? In addition to the mortgage? It was much too high.

After the contract had been signed, Andre Husseman, his wife, and their children left on their annual eight-week vacation in Europe. They were due back in several days. Zoltan thought about Genie. Max had had a fine summer, but Genie moped about the house. She missed Paul. The continued closeness between Genie and Paul bothered Anna and himself. However, there seemed to be nothing they could do about it.

His thoughts returned to the building. There were still some tenants who had not agreed to buy their apartments. A few, such as Mrs. Robbins in 12F, didn't have the money and were terrified of going to a bank to try to borrow it. Zoltan knew Mrs. Robbins lived on a small trust and Social Security. He had told all the maintenance men they were to make whatever repairs that might be necessary in her apartment, and they were to refuse any tips offered. She would offer out of pride, but he knew she couldn't afford the few dollars.

Jack O'Neil packed his briefcase and prepared to leave his office. At thirty-four, he was the youngest vice-president at Brown, Harris and proud of his success. He looked in the mirror again. Originally from California, his hair had been bleached almost white from days spent on a tennis court under the hot San Diego sun. Now it was ten years later, and his hair, while as thick as ever, had darkened and his waistline had begun to bulge. He'd have to start watching it.

He considered the commissions he'd earn co-oping the Mighty Majestic. They would be huge. He planned to sock away any money he could spare in a special account. If there was enough, he would lease and furnish a small apartment in one of the new buildings on the East Side. He'd tell his wife it was for late evening work that made it too late for him to take the train to Greenwich. If the work load of the last few months continued, that would even be true some of the time. Diane wouldn't like it. These days she didn't like anything, including him. No wonder he found himself women who were available, eager for a quickie at lunch or from five to seven in the evening. Yes, an apartment in New York was at least a partial solution. He thought about the leisurely evenings with a wealthy divorcee he'd recently met. The thought was enough to stir the beginnings of an erection. He shook his head. Enough! Back to business. He had an unpleasant job ahead of him.

He'd taken soundings of a number of tenants who would be shareholders after the contract closed, and the vote seemed overwhelming. How was he to explain it to Zoltan? The Szabos were going to be told to vacate their apartment. The space would be sold as an apartment or converted into additional doctors' offices.

Actually it was a rotten idea. A building like the Majestic needed a superintendent on the premises as much as possible. And the only other possible space that might serve as an apartment was in the basement with a few windows that looked out on the courtyard and some small ventilator shafts that poked out just above the sidewalk. There were the additional problems of the smell, fumes, and noise from the oil burners and the vibration from the subway on Central Park West.

When the idea was first proposed a month ago, he'd pointed out all the negatives and was told to keep his mouth shut. They could always change managing agents. If the Szabos didn't like it, they could leave. The building would get another super along with another managing agent. For a building like the Majestic, both were a dime a dozen. Faced with that threat, O'Neil refrained from mentioning the basement apartment would not be legal. The answer would have been, "Building inspectors are always paid off."

The leader of the group, Ivor Andersen, was hell-bent on holding down the costs of everything. Last week he had put it on the line. "Get it straight, Jack. I don't like Szabo and I don't like his kids, but that has nothing to do with it. It's a matter of money. The Szabo apartment is worth at least six thousand dollars, maybe seventy-five hundred. And the super's job is a prize. With tips and what he steals in kickbacks, I'll bet Szabo clears over twenty thousand a year plus the free apartment. I don't give a damn what you think. When I'm president of the building, I'll run it my way. So get used to it now."

Andersen was an arrogant son of a bitch and a fool to boot. The wrong man for the job. There were good men in the Majestic, but none O'Neil approached were interested in being president. So Andersen would be elected by default. The best he could do was warn Szabo to start looking around. He was a fine superintendent and would find something quickly enough. It was unfortunate Brown, Harris couldn't transfer him to another of their buildings. Andersen would get so sore he'd carry out his threat to change managing agents. They'd lose the Majestic which, if not the most prestigious building they managed, was the biggest in terms of management fees and commissions. Also, plans were in the works to use the example of the Majes-

tic to help them convert all the rent-controlled buildings on
Central Park West from the Century on 61st Street to the
Beresford on 81st Street. The commissions would be staggering. He had friends at Douglas Elliman to whom he could
mention Szabo. And Brett, Wyckoff was another possibility.
But it was going to be a disagreeable talk, and putting it off
wasn't going to make it any easier. He might as well get going.

Mrs. Robbins was leaving Zoltan's office after a harrowing
conversation. She was frantic about the prospect of buying her
apartment. Her eyes were red rimmed from weeping and lack of
sleep. She could only speak in broken sentences. Zoltan gathered she had one daughter living in Dallas who was no help.
The daughter had five children of her own, hadn't seen her
mother in years, and was going through divorce proceedings.
She had no room in her house for her mother and no money to
spare. Mrs. Robbins was alone. Her panic was contagious.
Zoltan thanked God for his wife and children, for their being so
close he would never be old and alone.

Jack O'Neil passed Mrs. Robbins on his way to Zoltan's office. He started to give her his usual professional smile and
stopped. As she shuffled past him, she wiped her eyes with an
already sodden handkerchief. Jack couldn't remember whether
or not she had signed the agreement to purchase her apartment.
The sight of Mrs. Robbins increased his anxiety about the
meeting with Zoltan. He thought again who might be rounded
up to oppose Andersen. He was the wrong man for the job and
would end up harming the building, all the shareholders, and
Brown, Harris. It was then that Jack O'Neil made what for him
was an unusual decision. He decided to go out on a limb.

Zoltan looked up. His face seemed composed, but the conversation with Mrs. Robbins had given him an alarming premonition. His eyes leaped to O'Neil's face trying to guess what
was coming.

"Good afternoon, Mr. O'Neil. Sit down, please." He motioned to the old wooden chair next to his desk.

"Zoltan, I forgot to tell my secretary something. It'll only
take a minute." He reached for the phone. "Jessie, I'm going
to stop off at the office on my way to the train. Would you put a
list on my desk of all the tenants at the Majestic, their apartments, whether or not they've signed the agreement and note if

we've actually received their checks. . . . Yes, Jes, I do realize you may have to catch a later train to Fire Island in order to do this little thing for me. But there are some of us who have to work over the weekend . . . Just do it! Bye, Jes.''

He replaced the phone and ran a finger under his collar. It felt too tight. "Since I'm stopping at the office, I might as well take all the approved bills with me. It'll save a messenger on Tuesday.''

Zoltan handed him a thick envelope which disappeared into Jack's briefcase. He had already picked up O'Neil's discomfort. And the extra work over the weekend? He started to fish for a reason. "Is Brown, Harris concerned over Dr. Gilman's lawsuit?''

Jack forced a laugh. "No. Dr. Gilman was one of the first to sign the co-op agreement. He would hardly sue himself. The roof is one of those things that will be taken care of after the closing. Zoltan . . .''

The moment Zoltan heard the tone of O'Neil's voice, he knew his fears were justified. He braced himself for whatever was coming. "Yes . . .''

"You know that after the Majestic goes co-op, the shareholders will elect a board of directors to run the building, and the board will elect a president?''

"Yes, I know." He also knew that Brown, Harris would continue to manage the building. He had prepared himself for the change. And he didn't believe for a moment that Jack O'Neil had come on Friday afternoon to brief him on technicalities. Something far more serious was troubling him.

O'Neil continued. "You'll still do the things you do now. In fact, I wouldn't be surprised if you find you have additional men to do some of the things Mr. Sacher wouldn't agree to. Like fixing the solarium roof.''

Zoltan still didn't understand. Why was Mr. O'Neil talking like this? Trying to put a good face on things? The problem must be very serious. He was almost at the point of asking him directly, when O'Neil began to speak rapidly. "Zoltan, it's Ivor Andersen. He's going to be elected president of the Majestic, because no one more appropriate wants to run against him. And I can't stop the damn fool.''

Zoltan considered what he had just heard. If he was to fix the solarium and have more men working for him, then Andersen didn't intend to fire him. He'd been a good superintendent. A very good superintendent. He didn't think there was a better one in the city. The Mighty Majestic needed constant babying to keep it running. They must know that. He leaned forward wanting to ask, stop him from what? But his courage deserted him when he saw the concern in Jack O'Neil's face.

"No. I can't stop him. He simply won't listen."

Zoltan couldn't contain himself. "What can't you stop?"

O'Neil blurted out the words, "Andersen wants to sell your apartment. He thinks the building can get six thousand dollars, maybe a little more, for it."

Zoltan rocked back. He felt as if he'd been struck across the head by a great fist.

"It's a lousy idea, but I can't stop him."

Zoltan tried to moisten his lips. His mouth was dry. "Where will we live? My family? My wife and children? Where?"

"There's a space in the basement. We use it for furniture storage. It would take some fixing up. A bathroom and kitchen . . ." The look on Zoltan's face stopped him.

Zoltan opened his mouth. Nothing came out. Finally he managed to speak. The words were disjointed. "Three windows on the court! My children! No light! Bad air! The fumes from the burner aren't healthy! The subway noise!"

"I agree. It isn't a fit place to live." O'Neil realized he must have known all along what a terrible shock he was going to give Zoltan or he wouldn't have put off telling him until he had almost run out of time. That apartment was Zoltan's home. The roof over his family's head. The proof of what he had accomplished in his life, and now he was going to lose it. "Zoltan?" Zoltan looked at him. "Listen! Nothing's settled yet. I just wanted to warn you. That's why I'm going back to my office. I want to review the tenant list again. Maybe I missed someone—someone appropriate to run against Andersen." Then he took another risk. "This must be confidential. If it should come out, I could be in serious trouble." He studied Zoltan, expectantly.

Zoltan heard the words from a great distance, but he couldn't respond. His mind was full of the fact that his family was about to lose their home.

"Damn it, Zoltan. Listen!" Jack O'Neil was on the edge of his chair. He was sick of the whole subject and sicker at the thought that he was going to risk his own job to try to help this man who couldn't even seem to listen. "If this actually happens, I'll put you in touch with several real estate firms as good as Brown, Harris. You're an excellent superintendent. You'll get another job easily."

"Another job?" Zoltan had never considered another job. This was the job at which he had intended to spend the rest of his working life. And even if he found another job, might not the same thing happen again? He was a super. That's all. He could never own his own apartment. He could always be forced to move. The Ivor Andersens of the world would see to that. O'Neil meant well. He must thank the man. "I appreciate what you've told me, Mr. O'Neil. I'll have to talk this over with my family." Suddenly he felt an overwhelming need to be alone. He had to think. How to get rid of O'Neil? "But right now there's work to be done. The Hussemans cabled from Paris. They'll be home on Monday, and I have to air out the apartment before their servants come in to clean up."

O'Neil had a sudden vision of Zoltan standing next to an open window on the thirty-first floor. "You will be careful about those windows?"

"Of course I'll be careful. I won't break anything."

O'Neil felt relieved. No! Zoltan Szabo was not the kind of man to commit suicide and desert his family. "Now listen," he said again. "Nothing's set yet. Another man, a better man, may run against Andersen. And finally, if everything is lost, you can still get another job. I'll come up with something."

"I know. It will turn out all right. And thank you for telling me. Thank you very much."

Zoltan sat alone in a rarely used section of the park. He couldn't bring himself to look at the Majestic, and didn't see the long black limousine cruising slowly down Central Park West. He didn't see it park in front of a fire plug alongside the Dakota.

But as they walked home under the shade of the trees on the park side of the street, Max and Genie did see it. They had rented a boat and had been rowing on the pond in Central Park.

"Hey, look at that car, Genie. That's a real boat."

"It looks more like a hearse to me."

"A hearse?" The light changed. They crossed the street and stood at the north corner of 72nd Street. Even as they did so, the black limousine started to move away from the curb. Both the car and the children waited at 72nd Street for the light to change. When it did, the children hurried across, but the car waited at the corner. It seemed to be waiting for someone.

A grey limousine, very much like the black one, was parked at the south end of the bus stop, and a huge brute of a man, his muscles bulging even in his well-tailored grey chauffeur's uniform, was leaning against the door smoking a cigarette.

"That's Mr. Costello's car," Genie whispered. "I heard he's a gangster." As she spoke, Moe ushered a stocky man in a dark suit with iron grey hair out of the building. As soon as he saw the man, the chauffeur dropped his cigarette and slid behind the wheel of the car.

Max said, "His wife gives me great tips whenever I do any errands for her. I guess she can afford them."

Costello noticed the children. He motioned to Max to approach him. Neither of them saw the black limousine slide across the street just ahead of the light change. "Max, my wife wants you to go to the little picture frame store on Columbus Avenue. You know the one. They'll give you a painting for her. Can you get there before they close?"

Even though they were late for supper, Max knew it would be all right with Momma. He was doing what a tenant had asked him to do, and getting paid for it. "Yes, sir. Genie, tell Momma I'll be home in fifteen or twenty minutes."

"Okay." Genie was the only one facing the street and the only one to see the black car which was almost abreast of the Majestic canopy. She nudged Max. "Look at that car. It still looks like a hearse to me."

Frank Costello and Max turned automatically to see what Genie was talking about. Costello reacted instantly. He'd seen the face of death too many times in too many disguises not to recognize an old enemy. He yelled, *"Nome di Dio! Assassini! Luigi! Aiutto!"* Then with a quick swipe of his arm he tried to knock Max out of death's way. Genie fell to the sidewalk.

Max grabbed the arm that had struck him trying to keep his balance and pulled Costello with him. As he did so, several men in the hearse started shooting. It was ironic that Costello's attempt to push the boy out of the way saved his own life. The men in the car were professionals. They were paid to kill, not wound. But the difference between a bullet striking squarely between one's eyes and a bullet that grazes one's head is about four inches. And the difference between a bullet that hits in the middle of one's stomach and one that enters the flesh at the side of a grown man's waist is less than a foot.

Costello was dragged to his knees on top of Max. Most of the hail of bullets passed over his head. Three struck him, but none in a vital place. The last bullet knocked him away from Max and back into the outer lobby of the Majestic.

Then it was over. Costello's chauffeur had also seen, heard, and understood. Several seconds too late he had his grey limousine between the hearse and the sidewalk. The opportunity was lost, and the killers knew it. The black car picked up speed and disappeared around the corner at 71st Street.

Moe had dropped to the sidewalk where he lay holding his head and shaking. The inside doorman was huddled against the wall in shock, useless. Costello was lying in a rapidly spreading pool of blood. Only Max seemed able to act with purpose. He realized immediately that the bleeding had to be controlled. Remembering the first aid techniques he had learned in school, he ripped off his threadbare T-shirt and was about to tear it into strips for bandages when he was grabbed under the arms and lifted into the air.

"Stay away from the boss, kid!"

"Listen, you idiot," Max shouted in frustration, kicking his feet in the air. "Mr. Costello's bleeding to death."

"If you don't let my brother put a tourniquet on his wounds, he may die," Genie cried.

"Let me go. He knows me! Ask him."

There was no expression on Costello's face, but a look flickered between the two men, a look born of years of intimacy. And Louie understood.

"Go ahead, kid. Do whatever you have to."

Max went back to ripping his T-shirt to the proper lengths. Fortunately the shirt was so worn and thin that it tore easily.

"Shouldn't we call a hospital?" Genie asked.

The chauffeur seemed to collect his wits. "Yeah. We need a hospital. And some friends to keep him company. I gotta make some calls. Where's the nearest phone?"

"Take him to our apartment, Genie. Run!"

Genie hurried into the building followed by the chauffeur. Max unbuttoned Costello's suit and shirt exposing a chest wound. Then he unbuckled the man's belt and removed his pants. His shorts were blue silk with the initials FC on the right leg. The blood was beginning to obscure the monogram. Max tied a bandage around Costello's scalp wound and a tourniquet around his upper leg. Each strip of cloth was wound as tightly as possible and tied with a square knot. He wished he had a stick to make the tourniquet tighter, but at least the blood had stopped spurting from his leg. After that he rolled the last of the cloth into a ball and held it against the chest wound. Just as he finished, the chauffeur, Genie, and Anna returned.

People from the Majestic and passersby had crowded into the lobby. An ambulance could be heard, and seconds later, it pulled up in front of the building. Shortly after the ambulance came a police car, then more police cars followed. The first officer to enter saw Costello and gave a long low whistle.

The hospital attendants replaced Max's makeshift bandages, lifted Costello onto a stretcher, and carried him to the ambulance.

Only after the ambulance had left, its siren screaming, did a detective question Max and Genie.

"Did either of you kids see the shooting?"

Max answered. "We both did."

"Did you see who did it?"

"No. The shots were fired from a black limousine."

"A hearse," Genie added.

"What do you mean? Was it a limousine or a hearse?"

"It was a limousine. It just looked like a hearse."

"Where did it go? Did you get the license plate?"

"It went around 71st Street. I didn't get the license plate. Everything happened too fast, Did you, Genie?"

"No, but I think it was a Jersey plate."

The detective sighed. "They always are. You kids live here?"

Anna spoke up. "They're my children. My husband's the superintendent of the building. We all live here."

"What're your names?"

"Genie Szabo."

"I'm Max Szabo." He spelled their names for the detective.

"You got a phone number?"

Anna answered. "Can't you leave my children alone? They don't know a thing."

"I know that, ma'am." He was very worried and didn't want to show it. Any attempt to knock off a *capo di capi* of the Mafia was bound to start something, and that something could be a first class shooting war between the families. He wondered which source of income was in dispute—drugs, whores, gambling, loan sharking? Big money makers! But all he said was, "It's just a routine I have to follow. What's your number?"

"Tr 3-9886."

"Thank you." He might have more questions for them after he did some work running down the black hearse.

At that moment, Zoltan entered the lobby. The crowd, the police, the reporters, who had finally arrived and were taking pictures, the blood on the floor, everything confused him. He went directly to Anna. "What in heaven's name is going on?"

"Someone shot Mr. Costello. It's terrible. Such awful things go on all over. Even in the Majestic."

"Yes, even in the Majestic," Zoltan agreed.

But at least that night at supper he didn't have to talk about the terrible thing that might happen to his family. Everyone was too busy talking about Mr. Costello.

The next afternoon a package arrived for Max Szabo, from Sulka, a store on Park Avenue that specialized in very expensive men's haberdashery. It was hand delivered to Moe at the main entrance of the Majestic by a small compact man wearing a dark brown suit. The man would go unnoticed in a crowd unless one was looking hard for a very special person. There was something too neutral about him.

When the inner doorman gave the package to the hallman who delivered to Anna, she was thoroughly annoyed. What was Max doing buying things in a store like Sulka? And what did he use for money? The clothes sold there were far too expensive. She opened the package and found, to her further irritation, three handsome boy's shirts. One white, one blue, and one tan. Then she noticed a small envelope in the pocket of the tan shirt. She opened it and found a card inside. The card read, "Max, thank you for the use of your shirt. I owe you more than three. Should you ever need more, call me." It was signed Frank Costello.

Anna's irritation was replaced by awe. She could hardly wait for Max to get home so he could see his present. These were shirts he would use only on very special occasions. Max arrived home late in the afternoon and was just as pleased and impressed as his mother. So was Genie. When Zoltan came in for supper, the children had to show him the shirts. There was a great deal of talk about the shooting and the part Max had played.

"What a nice thing for him to do," was Genie's opinion. "Even though Max did save his life."

"I wouldn't go that far." Max was preening, sitting at the table wearing the blue version of the shirt.

"I would," Genie insisted. She had clipped an article from the *Daily News* which referred to a teenager who had first bandaged Frank Costello's wounds. A doctor commented that the early bandaging made it possible to remove the bullets at once without the use of blood plasma. No one had any idea who the teenager was. The police hadn't explained, and the Szabos decided to keep it that way. There was some concern that the men in the hearse might come back to take care of anyone who helped Mr. Costello.

While she listened somewhat distractedly to the children, Anna became aware Zoltan was keeping something from them. And continuing to watch him at dinner added to her conviction. He hardly ate anything, and he wasn't joining in the conversation the way he usually did.

As far as Genie was concerned, the arrival of the shirts vied for importance with the imminent return of Paul Husseman. Max, though glad to see him, was more interested in the reopening of school. He was entering his first class at the Joan of Arc School on West 93rd Street. The school had a much larger playground, and Max would finally be able to play baseball with boys his own age and even older. Zoltan had agreed he could stay after school and participate in the school athletic programs. With Max at Joan of Arc, Genie would have to walk by herself to and from their old school, P.S. 199, on West 70th Street.

The talk returned to yesterday's excitement. The word from Moe, the source of most of their information, was that Mr. Costello was out of danger, progressing nicely, and would be out of the hospital in due time. Moe added there had been a quick meeting of certain tenants who expected to be elected to the board of directors to discuss whether or not a man as notorious as Frank Costello should be allowed to buy his apartment. They had no choice. The same offer had to be made to all the tenants. The decision was accepted with some relief as no one at the meeting wanted to be the one to tell Frank Costello he wasn't welcome at the building in which he had lived for so many years. He might have taken the rebuff less gracefully than one would have liked.

The talk about the board of directors and buying apartments seemed to agitate Zoltan. Usually a careful and well-coordinated man, he knocked over his wine glass, spilling the red wine over the clean white tablecloth. Zoltan insisted on fussing with paper towels to mop up the mess. Then he subsided into a deeper silence, and the meal dragged to an end. The children sensed something very threatening in the air.

Genie put her hand on his arm. "Daddy? What is it? Why don't you talk to us?"

Zoltan looked around the table and wondered how he was going to tell Genie he had failed her—failed his entire family. He gazed at her pale face, and was moved as only she could move him. She would forgive him. He looked at the questioning face of Max. Max loved him. He hoped Max would forgive him as well. Then he turned to Anna. Her grey eyes were so full of love for him he found at last the strength he needed. He touched her cheek, and began to explain.

"Mr. O'Neil came to see me yesterday. He told me the changes in the buildings were about to begin. There will be a board of directors and a president. It appears Mr. Andersen will be president. They will be in charge of the building."

The children riveted their eyes on their father's strained face. Though they understood he was about to tell them something terrible, they reached out for him with love trying to make him understand. Whatever had happened, it wasn't his fault.

"What is going to happen . . ." Zoltan started to say. "What will happen," he repeated, "is that Mr. Andersen plans to sell this apartment. Our apartment. To another family. For six thousand dollars, maybe more." Telling his family the truth took every ounce of courage he had, and he was unable to look any of them in the face. His eyes ranged from wall to wall, from floor to ceiling; and once he turned to look through the door into the living room.

Anna sat still, while Genie and Max exchanged bewildered glances.

"But this is our home," Max said. "He can't sell it."

"Yes, he can. He can sell our home."

"We won't move."

"Max, we have no choice."

"Then we'll buy the apartment." Genie couldn't conceive of giving up their home.

Zoltan couldn't bring himself to answer her.

Anna had no questions. Even as the world began to spin out of control, she was able to lay her hand on Zoltan's to comfort him. How could this happen? How could they lose their home? Their home! The roof over their heads!

Zoltan tried to explain the situation again. "We'll have to move. I don't know where." He made no mention of the suggestion they live in the basement. "And, Genie, we can't buy the apartment. We don't have the money. Even if we did, we still couldn't buy it. I'm the superintendent of this building, not a tenant. They won't sell to me."

Anna finally spoke. "If we can't stay, and you don't know where we can move, what will we do? Where will we live?"

"I don't know. We'll have to talk about it."

Max had his own solution. "Dad, you should quit. There's no one who can take care of this building the way you can. You can get another job."

"That's what Mr. O'Neil said. He even said he would help me. But I don't want another job." His voice sounded desperate. "The same thing could happen again."

"Daddy?" Genie asked, as her fright increased. "Daddy, Paul and Mr. Husseman are coming home in two days. I could speak to Paul, and maybe . . ."

Zoltan interrupted, and looked directly at Genie. What she had suggested would be the final acknowledgement of his failure as a man. To use his daughter's friendship with a boy to influence the boy's father? "No, Genie," Zoltan said. "You will not speak to Paul or any other of the Hussemans. This is our problem. Not theirs."

After Max and Genie were in bed and had been kissed good night, Anna and Zoltan sat in the living room discussing what was happening. An hour later they were no closer to a solution than when they began. Zoltan dropped his head in his hands. He looked at his wife through spread fingers. "I've done my best, Szuszuanna." It was a measure of the grief he felt at what he considered to be his failure as an American man, as an American husband, and as an American father that, without realizing it, he referred to his wife by her full name, Szuszuanna.

"I know, dear. I know." Anna cared for him deeply. He was so fine and good. And now such terrible things were happening to them.

"I'll tell Mr. O'Neil on Tuesday that I'll have to look for another job. He said he would help."

Zoltan wondered how much help Jack O'Neil would really provide against what was coming. O'Neil had his own job to worry about.

Anna agreed he should speak to Mr. O'Neil as soon as possible. Then they went to bed, thankful to God for his allowing them to be together. They lay in each other's arms, holding close that blessing which had carried them through so much: their love and trust. So it had always been, and so it always would be. No matter what else happened in their world, that love and trust remained the rock upon which their life was built.

Genie lay in the dark with her hands clasped behind her head. She realized once again that they were the super's children, and that fact made them less than other people. What was worse, she now knew her beloved father had no solutions. He did not earn enough money to provide for the security, even survival, of his family. Money! Lots of money! That was what made the difference in the United States. Her mother was both right and wrong. She remembered their conversation about aristocrats. Maybe people were born aristocrats in Hungary. She didn't know. But she did know that in the United States, money made aristocrats. In the United States, it was possible to make money and *become* aristocrats. That was part of what she had learned in school. That was what this country offered. Neither her mother nor her father understood. When she grew up, she would know how to make money. No Ivor Andersen was going to make her move out of her apartment. In spite of the terrible trouble her family was in, Genie almost smiled as she thought of the future.

7

Gertrude Robbins had been waiting all day for Ivor Andersen to arrive. He had telephoned that morning, telling her he would like to see her at five. Much to her own surprise, she agreed. And now she found herself actually looking forward to his coming. She even wished to celebrate it. It was as though by some magic all her fears about the future had evaporated the way alcohol evaporates in an uncorked wine bottle.

She sat in her chair in the kitchen by a window overlooking 72nd Street, staring out the window but seeing nothing. She hadn't eaten or drunk anything all day, because she was neither hungry nor thirsty. In a strange, exalted state, she was absorbed in taking deep soundings of her being, discovering passions and memories and longings which she had avoided for years.

Gertrude Robbins had lived as a coward, always afraid of the perilous demands living might make. Now she was remembering her life as though in a confused waking dream, remembering how as a young woman she had been so afraid. She had taken no risks, having been unaware then that the most dangerous thing in life is to be afraid.

Now it was four o'clock, and Ivor Andersen was due to arrive in an hour. Gertrude Robbins decided to take off the bedraggled bathrobe she usually wore and dress as though for an occasion. Yes, it was an occasion. She would wear her vine print dress, her best shoes, and her stockings without runs; what she wore on those rare days when she left the apartment to sit in the park.

Promptly at five o'clock the doorbell rang; Gertrude hurried to answer it as though it was someone she longed to see. She opened the door and smiled her most winning smile.

Ivor Andersen stood in the hall. He was a medium-sized

man, overweight, in his mid-forties, wearing a dark, double-breasted business suit. His face was ruddy and round; a creased, moonish face. His eyes, narrow and cold, examined her with contempt. He despised her as he despised anyone weaker than himself. As a lawyer who specialized in litigation, he gained his satisfactions in life from forcing people to their knees. He was good at his work. It gave him the only pleasure he knew, but, though he won their cases, he knew clients often disliked him. They thought him sadistic, and they were right.

But in dealing with this aging woman, the bully, the sadist could have his field day. Gertrude was meat and drink to Andersen. He would thoroughly enjoy terrifying her.

"Would you come in, Mr. Andersen?" she said.

"Yes, Mrs. Robbins. I can't stay long, and I want to have a word with you about this apartment."

"I know, Mr. Andersen. I've prepared some coffee. Would you like a cup?"

"No, Mrs. Robbins." Then he found himself forced to add, "Thank you." What's the old bag up to, he wondered? Putting on airs? He followed her into the living room; once there, he was reassured by the mess he saw. Dust over everything. The furniture worn and threadbare. It looked like a room no one had lived in in years. Which was the truth. Gertrude spent most of her days in the kitchen or in bed.

She sat in a chair and indicated that Andersen should seat himself on the couch. He did, and the weight of his body on the cushions caused clouds of dust to rise and swirl in the late summer sunlight. The dust made Andersen sneeze, and Gertrude laughed.

Her lack of embarrassment outraged him. "Let's get to the point, Mrs. Robbins. Your name is not on the list of tenants who have agreed to buy their apartments."

"Really, Mr. Andersen. I hear quite well. I wish you wouldn't raise your voice."

Something in her tone startled him. It carried within it the note of power. Obeying an instinctive reaction to power, he lowered his voice to a reasonable level. "Should you decide not to buy this apartment, you will have to move."

Gertrude kept her eyes on him. "Mr. Andersen, do try to be more cheerful about the world."

"I'm just stating the facts."

She held a little handkerchief to her mouth. "But I have so much to consider. Do I want to stay here, or not? Once you buy an apartment, you're really settled. And I've lived in this building since it was first built. Why, I remember when you moved in." She ran a finger lightly along her bottom lip. "Wasn't your name Thomas I. Andersen? I seem to remember that."

Andersen didn't like being reminded he had changed his name, dropping the Thomas as too ordinary and using his middle name as his first. Most people seemed to have forgotten, but not this old crone. He pulled himself together. "We still need an answer!"

"I know you do, you poor man. Still . . ." She paused to give her words full weight. "My cousin, a captain of industry, feels I should travel—live in Europe for a while. In Paris particularly. I do speak French fluently." She sighed. "I simply don't seem able to decide." She gave Andersen the privilege of a half smile.

He almost smiled back. This was not the cringing, weeping creature he had expected. And what was that number about a captain of industry? He hadn't heard anyone use that old-fashioned a term in years. She probably had wads of dough buried in safe deposit boxes all over town. The world was full of eccentrics. He'd better be careful. "Now, Mrs. Robbins, of course you must do what's best for you. We understand that, but would you be kind enough to make up your mind? Otherwise, with the greatest of reluctance, we will have to ask you to move."

Gertrude wasn't finished with him yet. "Mr. Andersen," she said in a soft voice which somehow sent a shiver down his spine, "you sound like the big, bad wolf at the door. Remember Little Red Riding Hood? 'Oh, Grandma, what big eyes you have.' " She watched him. "Of course, today, if Little Red Riding Hood discovered it wasn't her grandmother, it was really a wolf, she'd take an automatic pistol out of her jacket pocket and shoot the wolf dead. It's not so easy to frighten little girls anymore."

Ivor Andersen's hair rose a little on his head. He might be in some personal danger, and he wanted to get out of the apartment as rapidly as possible. "Mrs. Robbins, you do as you please, and if you'll excuse me, I really must be on my way." Without another word he hurried to the front door and left.

In spite of herself, Gertrude couldn't help laughing. She had had a far clearer understanding of the visit than he had given her credit for. Andersen had come to terrorize her and she had beaten him at his own game. Today had given her the only victory she had ever won. In fact, it was the only battle she had ever fought. But the victory had come too late. However, she still had enough courage for one final triumph. She would write first to that nice Jack O'Neil at Brown, Harris, mail the letter downstairs in the building post box, and then she would see. A great calm had come over her. She realized the fear she had finally faced and to which she had always surrendered was that most dangerous of all fears—the fear of living.

Zoltan and Anna were suddenly awake. Someone was ringing their front doorbell. Ringing! Ringing! Both Szabos heard it plainly. "What's wrong?" asked Anna.

"I don't know. The oil burner. A blown fuse. Anything. I'll see."

"At this hour?" Anna glanced at the bedside clock. It was 1:30.

"At any hour. It's my job." Zoltan shook off his light fitful sleep and slipped his feet into the slippers beside the bed. Then he put on his bathrobe and hurried towards the door of the apartment where the bell was still ringing.

Anna followed her husband, her hands trembling slightly as she reached for her flannel robe. She found Max and Genie standing side by side in the living room, wide-awake and waiting. This added to her distress.

"Momma, what is it?" Max was ready to do battle with any and all enemies.

"Has Mr. Andersen come to get us?" asked Genie, clutching Max's hand.

"It's nothing. Nothing. Go back to bed," Anna answered, putting her arms around her children.

"No!" Max resisted. "I want to know what's happening."

By this time, Zoltan had opened the door. There were Mr. and Mrs. Tilson from apartment 12G. He was in a tuxedo, she in something black, floor-length and glittering. Evidently the Tilsons were returning from a formal party.

"Mr. Szabo, I hate to bother you at this hour . . ."

"It's all right. What is it?"

"I think there's something wrong on our floor. When we got off the elevator, we could hardly breathe. The landing is filled with gas."

"Gas! Anna, put the children to bed. I'm going upstairs." Zoltan ran to his office to get a key to 12F. The key to Gertrude Robbins's apartment.

When Zoltan and the Tilsons arrived at the twelfth floor of the F/G line, Zoltan opened the door of 12F. A burst of gas poured out of the apartment. Zoltan turned quickly to the elevator man. "Hold your breath, and get the windows open as quickly as possible."

Zoltan ran through the gas-filled rooms toward the kitchen, knowing exactly what to expect. Hoping he wasn't too late; knowing he was.

Yes. There she was seated by the open oven door while the gas continued to pour out. He shut off the gas, opened the kitchen window, and stared at the small limp form. She had slipped back in her chair, her mouth falling open, seemingly asleep. He knelt to hear her heart and felt for her pulse. The body was still warm. But he was stopped short by her face, so harassed and frightened in life. It had an exalted look. All the worry and care with which her face had been marked had vanished.

That night Genie and Max slept very little. The police were in and out of the Szabo living room questioning Zoltan. They couldn't hear much of what was being said, but they knew Mrs. Robbins was dead and the body had been taken to the morgue.

The following day a reporter came to interview Zoltan, but there was only a short report the next day in the *Daily News*. The reporter had made no connection between Gertrude Robbins's death and the co-oping of the building in which she lived, and those who might have enabled him to make the connection chose not to. Without being told in detail, the children picked up fragments listening to their parents. Mrs. Robbins had probably committed suicide rather than be evicted from her apartment. The knowledge threw Genie and Max into a state bordering panic.

A day later Max made a decision. By now he accepted, though he couldn't understand it, that his father wouldn't fight.

It was up to him to fight for the family. Just thinking about what he must do made him afraid. But he knew he must do it. While Genie had been forbidden to speak to Paul Husseman, he hadn't been forbidden anything. And he wasn't about to ask permission. Max thought the unthinkable. He wouldn't speak to Paul Husseman. Max would speak to Andre Husseman, himself.

On the Tuesday after Labor Day, Max waited outside the Majestic for Andre Husseman to appear. It was 8:15 A.M. He was sweating with fear, having carefully gone over the possible consequences of his actions. And the consequences might be disastrous. Andre Husseman was one of the men who had initiated the move for the Majestic to go co-op. He might even be in favor of the Szabos losing their apartment. Max reasoned that if that was true, it didn't matter what he did. He couldn't make matters any worse.

Promptly at 8:20 the Husseman limousine appeared. The bronze front door opened, and Moe held it as Mr. Husseman walked to his car. Max made the greatest effort of his young life. Before the man disappeared into the car, he called out, "Mr. Husseman?"

Andre Husseman turned and saw him. "Max? Good morning. Shouldn't you be on your way to school, young man?"

"Yes, sir. But I have to talk to you."

"Now?" Andre realized Max must be troubled. He said, "If you have something you want to discuss with me, get in the car, son. I'll drive you to school. We can talk on the way."

Max jumped into the car, and Andre followed at a more leisurely pace. "Where is your school, Max?"

"The Joan of Arc on 93rd Street between Columbus and Amsterdam."

Andre gave the instruction to his chauffeur, and the car pulled away from the curb. "Now what's bothering you, Max?"

Suspicious, cautious, and wary of the world in general, Max admired Mr. Husseman. He had no way of knowing that Andre Husseman and he had a great deal in common in the way they perceived the world. It was this unrealized similarity transmitting itself to Max that gave him the final confidence to speak out.

He blurted out, in a voice not always steady, the problem facing the Szabo family. How the new board of directors and the president, Ivor Andersen, were planning to sell the Szabo apartment as a co-op and throw them out.

Andre was impressed with Max's precise explanation of the situation. Of even greater interest were his lucid reasons why a building such as the Majestic needed a super on the premises as much as possible. As witness what had happened to Mrs. Robbins. Suppose Zoltan Szabo had not been around, and no one knew what to do. The danger of a gas explosion had been very real.

By the time Max finished, they were in front of the school.

"That's an interesting piece of information, Max. Let me think about it."

Max was shuffling his feet on the floor of the car, nervously. "Mr. Husseman, my father will be very angry if he finds out I spoke to you."

"Then we won't say anything about it, will we?"

"Thank you, sir." Max smiled for the first time in days. What he had done was an act of desperation. It was also an act of defiance of his father's wishes. While he was willing to accept the punishment for his behavior, he was relieved his father would never know his oldest son had disobeyed him. The disgrace his father would feel far outweighed the fear of any punishment he might receive.

"Now off to school before you're late." Andre Husseman assumed the boy's relief came from the fact of escaping Zoltan's anger. As the limousine wound its slow way downtown through the park, Andre told his driver, "Willie! I want no gossip about our taking the Szabo boy to school."

8

When Jack O'Neil arrived in his office Tuesday morning, he reviewed his mail. There was one letter in the pile that startled him. It was from Gertrude Robbins. He'd heard from his secretary that she'd committed suicide over the weekend, and he remembered the last time he'd seen her in the Majestic. The news of her suicide gave him a bad turn; as he opened the letter, he wondered what a letter from a dead woman was doing on his desk. Jack was only mildly superstitious. He avoided walking under ladders and knocked upwards on wood. That was about it, but for the first time in his life, it seemed to him he was hearing a voice from the grave.

The letter, while written in a clear precise hand, contained words which were blurred as though the ink had been wetted. As he read on, the blurred words explained themselves.

Dear Mr. O'Neil,

I am writing this letter with tears streaming down my face. Tears of pride. For once in my life I have acted with courage. When I was younger and more ashamed, I thought to have courage meant one must not be afraid. Now I know better. I understand fear in a human being is a natural thing. And to have courage does not mean one is not afraid. It means one sees the danger, is afraid, and at the same time does what one must do.

So I have taken that step and defied my fear. This morning Ivor Andersen telephoned asking to visit late this afternoon. I agreed to see him knowing full well what he wished. When he arrived, we spoke for a short time. In our conversation I lied to him. But I lied bravely, though I swear to you I have never lied before in my life. I led him down the garden path, so to speak, allowing him to think I might buy my apartment. I did that because I realized he had come for no other purpose than to frighten me. He wanted to tell me that they would evict me if I did not agree to buy immediately. He would have so enjoyed seeing me beg for mercy. If you doubt my words, remember, Mr. O'Neil, I have lived in the Majestic since the building first opened. And ever since he moved in some five years ago, I have watched Ivor Andersen going in and out of the building. He is the worst sort of tenant. He has no manners, he curses the doormen, he jumps in front of people waiting for cabs. The handymen tell me he is planning to be the president of the Majestic. Forgive the bluntness of an old woman, but he gives off the odor of garbage. And what he touches becomes garbage.

So now I will tell you the truth. I have not a penny with which to buy my apartment. That fact leaves me with only one thing left to do. And because I am brave, I do it gladly.

Sincerely,
Gertrude Robbins

By the time he finished the letter, Jack O'Neil was having a hard time not adding his tears to the already smudged ink. The conflict between his awareness of the risk he would have to take and the responsibility laid on him by Mrs. Robbins's letter must be resolved. Over the Labor Day weekend, Jack O'Neil had had second thoughts about contacting Andre Husseman or Ralph Gluck. Though either would make an excellent president, they were both extremely wealthy and exceedingly busy. He had finally come to the conclusion that no matter how he felt about the Szabos, he had no business sticking his nose into the politics of the Majestic. He could live with Ivor Andersen. And if that vicious, vindictive bastard ever found out that Jack opposed his election, Jack would lose his job. So he'd put aside the list of signed tenant applications and tried to forget the whole thing.

But the letter shook him. He read it again, trying to arrange his thoughts. And out of his conflict came a deeper self-knowledge. He had come near committing a sin. The sin of cowardice. If he cared one whit for his self-respect, he would have to do something about the Szabos and Andersen. Even if it cost him his job.

He picked up the phone and asked Jessie to call Andre Husseman.

"You just saved the company a dime, Mr. O'Neil. He's on the other line asking to speak to you."

On any other day this curious coincidence might have struck Jack as something out of the ordinary. But today was an odd day. "Put him on."

"Good morning, Jack. I trust you had a pleasant Labor Day?"

"Very pleasant, thank you."

"I wonder. If you happen to be free, could you have lunch with me?"

Jack laughed. "You must be clairvoyant, sir. I was about to call you for exactly the same purpose."

"Good! We start then at least with a partial meeting of the minds. By any chance were you planning to call Mr. Gluck as well? He and I are having lunch. We'll be a threesome."

For an instant Jack was too surprised to answer. All he could manage was, "I didn't know he was in town."

"He's in town."

Jack had the distinct impression that, without stating the problem, Husseman and he were joining forces to meet it. "Would you and Mr. Gluck like to have lunch at the Harvard Club? It might be convenient for both of you."

"Nothing is convenient for Gluck but his office. We'll lunch there."

"Fine. What time?"

"Twelve-thirty. See you then." He hung up.

Although Jack O'Neil knew the address of Ralph Gluck's office, he'd never had a reason to go there. The office exceeded anything he'd imagined. It was in the penthouse of a building Gluck owned on 53rd Street and Park Avenue and had the flavor of both office and studio, being at the same time handsome, utilitarian, and yet, somehow, artistic. It seemed to consist of two rooms, an outer office with a semicircular window where Gluck's secretary sat, and the huge inner office where Gluck worked. O'Neil guessed it had once been most of the entire apartment.

The office on three walls consisted of floor to ceiling curved glass held in place by thin strips of anodized bronze and opened onto a generous terrace overlooking Park Avenue. Building plans, city maps, and blueprints were all neatly arranged on a series of Lucite pegboards attached to bronze poles which also extended from floor to ceiling. They could be swivelled to allow or obstruct the rays of the sun from entering the office. Along the one solid wall were custom-designed bronze bookcases on which books on real estate, law, finance, taxes, history, and art, even some fiction, stood. Gluck's desk sat on a raised platform and was unlike any desk O'Neil had ever seen—it was a huge glass drawing board that could be lit from below. There were building plans and business papers neatly stacked in several piles.

Andre Husseman had arrived before O'Neil and was seated, somewhat uncomfortably, in a very low modern chair. He was forced to look up at Gluck. The two men were having a heated discussion.

They stopped when O'Neil entered, and Gluck left his desk to shake hands with O'Neil. "I'm starving, young man. What held you up?" His surprisingly clear, attractive baritone voice was curt but polite.

"Traffic . . ." Jack started to explain.

"Standard excuse. Let's argue over lunch." Gluck walked toward the bookcases at the far end of the room. O'Neil thought again how unusually Gluck was built. He couldn't have been more than five feet eight inches tall, and yet he must have weighed 230 pounds or more. His hands and his torso were those of a giant. It was as if his body had grown faster than his legs. At the moment the Creator was completing him, Gluck had slid from his fingers and, with his typical impatience, went off on his own. The result was that his legs were almost those of a dwarf when compared to the rest of his frame. If they had been in proportion, he would have towered over O'Neil, who was a solid six feet one.

"I've taken the liberty of ordering for all of us. I know the menu."

"All drugstore menus are the same," O'Neil said, grinning.

"Drugstore!" Gluck laughed. "I haven't had lunch in a drugstore since I made my first million, and that was a long time ago. Pavillon's my drugstore. They send up lunch every day."

He took one of the books off a shelf. Behind the book was a silver button. He pressed it, and the bronze bookshelves swung back. Except for the fact that sunlight flooded the office, it might have been a scene from a James Bond movie. However, the open bookshelves revealed nothing more sinister than an elegant wood-panelled dining room which was furnished, unlike the office, with beautiful antiques. The early eighteenth-century Venetian dining table could have seated twelve but was now set for three with crystal and silver. Two black-coated waiters, who must have entered via another door, stood at attention next to a food cart. The conversation which had been interrupted, first by O'Neil's arrival and then by lunch, continued.

"Are you sure of that clause in the bylaws?"

"I'm positive, Ralph. I had it inserted myself. Article Seven, Section A, Paragraph One. It specifically states that all tenants must occupy the apartments they buy. They cannot own apartments they don't live in. The idea was to prevent speculation in the apartments that aren't bought."

"You object to speculation? The free enterprise system that built your country isn't good enough for you?"

"Not at all. What I object to is speculation in the building in which I live. It cheapens the building."

"You're oversensitive. And I signed that damn piece of foolishness?"

"You certainly did. Didn't you read the bylaws?"

Ralph Gluck pressed his finger lightly on a particular spot on the wall. A small panel opened, and a shelf, on which a brown telephone stood, extended itself toward Gluck. Gluck picked up the phone and said, "Ellen, get me Jerry, the boy genius." He glanced at Andre. "Jerry's my damn fool lawyer. He went over the bylaws because I was too busy." There was a short period of silence. Then Gluck exploded into the phone. "Listen, you overpaid astigmatic Blackstone dropout. With your fine eye for detail, it's a miracle your name is spelled correctly on your letterhead. Or were your bifocals fogged when you happened not to read the bylaws of 115 Central Park West? Yes. I refer specifically to Article Seven, Section A, Paragraph One . . . Oh, you did see it. And you let me sign an agreement that prevents me from buying any other apartments in the building except for the one I fuck in?. . . Jerry, the tragedy is, it's not your tragedy alone. It's now mine. I thought you were a real estate lawyer. I suggest your true calling is chasing ambulances

. . . Oh, shut up and go to pieces like a man! Remember, I'm in the real estate business. I buy and sell real estate. Would I, if I was in my right mind, sign an agreement that prevents me from buying up the available apartments in 115 when I can resell them at a nice profit? I hope you have many old friends who will stand behind you, because suddenly I realize you have taken advantage of my immensely generous nature. And I have a growing conviction you are shortly going to need a new job.'' He slammed the receiver down. ''You know, Andre, at least ten percent of those apartments would have been vacant within three years. That deal was found money, and I'm an ordinary man with ordinary greed. Article Seven, Section A, Paragraph One hurts my digestion.'' He looked again at Andre. ''I detect a dangerous romanticism in your nature. You're the kind who would overinsure a stinking tenement, hire Benny the Torch, and then telephone the fire department because some kid has a dog stuck on the third floor.'' He shook his head disgustedly. ''Let's eat. It'll settle my stomach.''

The food and wine were excellent and the conversation mindboggling. Professional though Jack was, he had trouble following the rapidity with which they tossed around tax concepts and numbers. Also he was growing more and more uncomfortable. The millions that Gluck and Husseman bandied about made him tongue-tied. How was he going to be able to bring up the problem of a potentially homeless superintendent and his family to these men with such huge wealth?

It was Husseman who finally rescued him. ''Jack, you were going to call me this morning about lunch, and you agreed to Ralph joining us. You had something on your mind you wanted to discuss?''

''I did.''

''Was it about the Szabo family and Ivor Andersen?''

''Yes.'' Jack was thankful Husseman understood. ''Andersen wants to throw them out. He plans to sell the apartment or make it into doctors' offices.''

''That asshole with a bookkeeper's brain,'' Gluck exploded. ''Doesn't he know that a building like the Majestic must have a top superintendent available on the premises? What happens when a lady gets her hair net caught in a light switch? Or the elevators break down?'' He turned to Husseman with a gleefully wicked smile. ''Andre, you had better get in shape. I can just see you walking up those thirty-one floors to your apartment. If you hadn't inserted that damn clause, I'd have bought an apartment for the Szabos and given it to them. That would have ended the whole problem."

"You know you couldn't do it."

"Do you really think anyone could have stopped me? Besides, there's little I'd like better than being known as the most hated man in the Majestic."

While this byplay was going on, Jack O'Neil was studying Ralph Gluck's face. He was struck by such a terrifying impression of extraordinary strength and even violence, he was glad not to have Gluck as an enemy.

Andre nodded to O'Neil. "It was the Szabo problem that brought up Article Seven, Section A, Paragraph One. Ralph actually was going to make them a gift of their apartment."

"And now I'm perfectly willing to let the building go to hell. Andre tells me Andersen wants to be president. Let him! The idiot! We agree to pay over three million dollars cash for the building, and he's going to fuck it up for six thousand dollars. After the super's apartment, he'll get rid of the elevator men. They cost money. The building will become the first thirty-two-story slum on Central Park West. By then I'll have sold my apartment." He glanced at Husseman. "Are you sure that nitwit will be president? Who told you?"

"He's the only one running. One of the women told my wife yesterday," Andre lied.

"He plans to be," O'Neil added. "He's already visited Brown, Harris with his ideas."

"And I suppose you called us together to discuss this disaster?"

For a second Jack O'Neil squirmed uncomfortably. The look on Gluck's face was pure deviltry. "As a matter of fact, I did. The Szabos aside, he's not the right man for the job. I had hoped one of you would agree to run against him."

Ralph smiled. "I do admire your guts, O'Neil. You protest. You speak up. You stand up for the things you believe, and the devil take the hindmost. Am I right?"

"Not exactly, but in this case, I felt . . ."

"And of course Brown, Harris knows nothing about this meeting?"

"No, and it would be embarrassing if they found out."

"You bet your sweet ass it would. I know your boss. If Andersen found out, your company would lose the building. You sure know where to put your loyalties. I wouldn't risk having you on my payroll. However, that's not my problem. I'll let you nurse your guilty secret, but as far as running against Andersen, not I. In fact I think I'll give him some advice to make sure he wins."

Husseman started to laugh. "Cut it out, Ralph. You're not that vindictive."

"The hell I'm not. Dear neighbor, I never forgive or forget. You've given me additional proof of human perfidy and the foolishness in having faith in the greed of rich acquaintances. From here on, Andersen is my man."

O'Neil realized that through no fault of his, the lunch had gone all wrong. Though he'd had far less wine than either man, he felt slightly drunk.

Looking at the grin on Gluck's face, he realized Gluck knew exactly how much damage he was doing. He fumbled in his coat pocket and pulled out the letter he had received from Gertrude Robbins. He handed it to Gluck without comment.

When he finished reading it, Gluck looked down at the remains of the meal on his plate. Then he signalled for the waiter to refill his wine glass and passed the letter to Husseman. Gluck sipped at his wine while Andre read the letter. It seemed to O'Neil that something had gone out of Gluck's eyes. His face was covered by a mask.

Husseman frowned. "Didn't she know he couldn't evict her? The apartment could be sold, but the owners would have to wait for possession until she moved or buy her off."

O'Neil shook his head. "She was a frightened, or should I say brave, old woman."

"Do you still like your Ivor Andersen, Ralph?"

"It's my feeling that most people are damn fools who deserve what they get." He paused and rubbed his chin. "Still, it strikes me that, given even my inhumanity to my fellow man, Andersen has the instincts of a crooked dogcatcher. He just lost my vote."

That sounded better to O'Neil. He heard Andre ask, "Then you would consider running for president?"

"No. But I'd back you."

"I don't want the job."

"Neither do I."

"If neither of us run, Andersen will be elected president"

"Having defended myself against a variety of lawsuits in my day, I doubt . . ."

"No one remembers or cares."

"Anyway, I have no patience to speak in an appealing, persuasive tone to anyone. Especially to a bunch of idiotic shareholders."

"Come on. You're highly respected. You understand real estate. And you can read a balance sheet."

"So can you. Furthermore, there's the matter of personality and political appeal. You've got that. Look at that white hair. The ladies go for things like that. Have you ever thought of running for public office?" He laughed. "Senator Husseman. This election could be the start of another career. I wouldn't turn down the opportunity if I were you."

"Then don't. You run and you be the senator."

"I couldn't be elected. Most people dislike me. Including your wife."

"It's those damn cigars you smoke in the elevators. The children can't breathe."

Cluck roared. "Well, you know what they say." He imitated W. C. Fields's voice. "A man who hates dogs and children can't be all bad."

"Not funny."

"Isn't it?" Still laughing, he said, "Okay. Stuck is stuck. One of us has to run. So let's get an unbiased opinion." He took a silver coin out of his pocket and spun it on an empty plate. "Pick it up, Andre. Make sure it's legit."

"What do you mean, legit?"

"It has a head and a tail."

Andre fingered the coin. It was an 1881 silver dollar worn almost smooth from decades of handling. He stood it on its edge and watched it fall. Heads. Seemingly absentminded, he did the same thing a number of times. Always heads. On several occasions he tilted the coin ever so slightly before he spun it. Tails. He handed the coin back to Gluck.

"I'll spin the coin. You call it while it spins. If you call it right, you win. Wrong, you lose. The loser runs for president."

Andre realized Ralph had recognized he knew the coin was slightly weighted to come up heads. All he had to do was watch

Gluck's fingers as he spun the coin and he could be pretty certain which side would come up. Ralph was going to make him choose which of them would run for president. What an interesting, complicated man. "All right. Jack, do you understand what we're doing?"

"Yes."

"Spin the coin, Ralph."

"Certainly, Andre." He put the coin in the center of a clean dish and gave it a firm spin. There was no tilt. Andre considered his call. He knew he had a better chance than Ralph to win the election. Too many people disliked Ralph. And it was important that the building not be allowed to run downhill. The first step in preventing that was to keep Zoltan Szabo as the building superintendent. The choice wasn't really a choice.

"Tails," he said, knowing it would be heads.

He heard Ralph laugh.

The coin spun. Finally it started to slow down and wobble. Then it clattered to a stop.

"I'll vote for you, Andre. You were born to be president of the Majestic."

9

The meeting hall of the Spanish and Portuguese Synagogue had been rented for the first shareholder meeting of 115 Central Park West, Inc. The meeting was set for September 15. The days before the election dragged by for the Szabo family. The knowledge that they would be forced to move shortly after the building went co-op preyed on their minds. It seemed to Zoltan and Anna that their entire lives had ended in failure. Sometimes they actually wished they had never left Hungary. Hungary offered no false promises of security as the United States did, before it broke them.

Genie struggled daily with her feelings of helplessness. Though it was still late summer and the weather was warm, a chill seeped into her body. Sometimes she wondered if Paul was avoiding her. They'd hardly seen each other since his return from Europe. During the week before the election, he disappeared completely. In this one thing, Genie was correct. Andre Husseman wanted to distance his family from the Szabos so that there would be no cry of favoritism when he took his stand against selling their apartment. He invented many tasks to keep Paul busy.

A need, raw and inexorable, was growing within Genie. That evening, when her father first told the family of Ivor Andersen's plans, she'd made a vow, a personal, private vow which she would not share even with her brother. When she grew up, she would work with every ounce of strength, with every fiber of her being so that neither she nor her family would ever have to worry about having a safe home. She would be rich. She would be powerful. She would act, not be acted upon. This need would return, again and again. It would never leave her as long as she lived.

And even as Genie tossed and turned at night, struggling with her newly discovered realities, so Max, by a different road, arrived at the same wretched conclusion. He had done what he had done. He had defied his father, acted on his own, and spoken to Andre Husseman. Now, as far as he could see, Husseman had done nothing. In choosing to defy his father, Max knew he had passed judgment on his father as a man. A brave man would have stood up to Andersen. Would have forced him to back down. But his father wasn't brave. Not by Max's standards. The guilt caused by his newly discovered contempt for his father's lack of courage resulted in his trying to prove his own courage by getting into fights almost every day in school. And, curiously, beating up the boys in school taught Max another hard lesson. Bravery and strength were not enough.

Though he could also beat up every boy close to his own age in the Majestic, though he yearned to prove himself superior, he knew he wasn't. By universally accepted standards, he wasn't superior. He was inferior. And it was out of this feeling of inferiority that Max's character began to take final shape. When his time came, he would not allow anyone to stand in his way. He would rise above his father and take his whole family with him. He would be forever single-minded in his pursuit of money—vast sums of money—and the power that vast sums of money control. For only money and power could protect his family, as even his strength and courage could not.

Representatives from Brown, Harris, Stevens, Inc., headed by Jack O'Neil, were at the meeting hall on September 15 well before 7:30. The first act of the shareholders would be to elect a board of directors who would then elect a president and other officers.

Zoltan Szabo had been requested to attend the meeting. He was to sit at the entrance and check every shareholder as he or she entered. Jack watched the door, waiting for the arrival of Husseman and Gluck. He had heard nothing from either of them since their meeting, and he knew how arbitrary the rich and mighty could be. They just might have shelved the idea of running for the presidency as too much trouble.

People started arriving at about 7:30. Andersen and six other men arrived promptly at 7:45. They comprised the known slate hoping to be elected as the board of directors. O'Neil noted they seated themselves in the front row. He kept looking at the door. Where the hell were Husseman and Gluck?

It was almost time for the meeting to start. Silently cursing the rich bastards, he climbed the three steps leading to the stage and stood in front of the blue velvet curtain. Before calling the meeting to order, he gave one last look at the door. There were Andre Husseman and his wife entering followed by Ralph Gluck and five other men and their wives.

Jack waited for them to get settled and called the meeting to order. "As you know, I have been acting president of 115 Central Park West, Inc. for the last," he looked at his watch, "three hours, thirty-five minutes, and almost fifty seconds. It is clear to me I have been in the seat of power far too long." The joke was rewarded with far more laughter than it rated. It seemed everyone was nervous. "My assistant, Mark Levine, was elected secretary of the corporation at the same time. As secretary of 115 Central Park West, Inc., Mr. Levine, can you certify there are enough shareholders present to constitute a quorum?"

"Mr. President, I can. Out of 102,000 shares issued and outstanding, there are 98,626 shares represented by people present tonight."

"Thank you, Mr. Secretary. I now declare this meeting open for business. The first order of business is to nominate and then elect a board of directors. Do I hear any nominations?"

Ivor Andersen stood up. "O'Neil, I move the nomination of the following six men." He read off six names. Each man stood up as his name was called and was duly seconded by another of the group. When he finished, one of the six raised his hand.

"The chair recognizes Edward Walker."

"I would like to nominate Ivor Andersen to complete the seven board members."

"Do I hear a second for the nomination of Mr. Andersen?"

"I so second."

"Are there any other nominations?"

For a moment no one moved, and then a hand was raised.

"Mr. Gluck?"

"I would like to place in nomination Andre Husseman."

"Do I hear a second?"

A man sitting next to Gluck rose. "I second the nomination."

Husseman rose. "I would like to place in nomination Philip Davis."

"Are there any seconds?"

Another man rose. "I second the nomination."

And so it went until there were seven additional candidates including Ralph Gluck.

It was obvious the unexpected opposition had caused some surprise among Andersen's group. He raised his hand.

"The chair recognizes Mr. Andersen."

"O'Neil, I have the proxies for over sixty-five thousand shares in favor of we seven to serve as the board of directors." He tossed the package on the table. "Count them. They constitute a majority of the votes. We can go through the motions of an election, but I think that settles the issue."

Andre Husseman raised his hand and after being recognized said in a pleasant, even voice, "I would like to remind the chair that any proxy can be cancelled by the person who gave the proxy providing that person is actually present at this meeting. I believe Mr. Levine stated that there were over 98,000 shares represented out of a possible 102,000. It seems evident that most of those who signed proxies are present and can now vote in person."

"That's correct, Mr. Husseman," Mark Levine agreed.

"And those proxies held by Mr. Andersen representing shareholders who are not here will be added to Mr. Andersen's vote count."

"Correct, sir."

Andersen knelt in front of his group, whispering. He turned towards the stage. "Agreed. We'll have a formal election."

Andre wasn't finished. "I have a further suggestion, Mr. O'Neil. Since we now have two slates of directors running, let each group select a spokesman who will state the group's idea on how the building should be managed. After all questions from the floor are answered, a vote can be taken."

Again Andersen's group went into a caucus. Finally he agreed.

"Have you decided who will speak for your slate, Mr. Andersen?"

"I will."

"And you, Mr. Husseman?"

"It seems I will."

"Does either of you have a preference for who will speak first?"

Andre spoke first. "I'd like to lead off. That is if Mr. Andersen has no objection."

"Well, I do object."

"You'd rather speak first?"

"I would!"

"Then I waive. By all means, do so, sir."

Andersen realized he'd been mousetrapped. The one who spoke last would have the last say. But it was too late to retract. He scrambled onto the stage, reached for the microphone, and started to speak. His mottled red face was redder than usual, and his plump body jiggled as he moved. His speech consisted of his plans to put the building on a sound financial footing. Among the changes he would put into effect were automatic elevators and elimination of delivery of mail to the apartment doors. The inside doormen could be let go, and the entrances on 71st Street and 72nd Street locked eliminating additional men. He would make an apartment out of the solarium and sell the super's apartment to cut everyone's maintenance a little. The total projected savings would be substantial. He concluded with one statement, "Ladies and gentlemen, if you elect us, you'll have people on the board who work for a living"—he accented the next phrase—"made their own money and know how to save a buck. Not waste it." He jumped off the stage with a satisfied smile.

O'Neil returned to the microphone. Everyone was buzzing about the direct insult to Andre Husseman. "Mr. Husseman, it's your turn."

Andre's first words were, "My apologies to Mr. Andersen for having inherited some money. I hope the remaining shareholders won't hold it against me. In point of fact, it's given me a bit of an advantage. I had to learn early in life not only how to make money but, equally important, how properly to spend it. Along these lines, let's look at what Mr. Andersen proposed and what it would mean to our building. I agree we need new elevators, and automatic elevators are a fine idea for emergencies, but . . ." Then he cited the crime statistics in automatic elevators. One by one he demolished Andersen's proposals as detrimental to the success of the building as a cooperative in the long run. When he finished, he went into the reasons for his agreeing to run. In a quiet and sad tone, he described the suicide note Mrs. Robbins had left. "I am certain Mr. Andersen had no intention of driving Mrs. Robbins to her death. In fact, like all his other suggestions, he was trying to save some money for all of you. However," and he paused letting the utter silence fill the room, "that is not the way I believe you feel the Majestic should save money." Andre continued. "I have managed buildings almost since the day I was born. Among the many valuable lessons that experience has taught me is that where a luxury apartment house of the size of the Majestic is concerned, one of its most valuable assets is a competent superintendent. We have such a man in Zoltan Szabo. Mr. Andersen has told you of his plan to turn Mr. Szabo's apartment into another co-operative. However, he did not give you the complete details of his plan. He has also suggested that the Szabos live in the basement in an area next to the oil burners and subways. The space is illegal for that kind of occupancy, so it will be necessary to satisfy every building inspector not to mention the police, fire, and sanitation departments. The annual cost of satisfying them will exceed the income we might receive. Plus, we will lose the services of Mr. Szabo, who will find another job in a building where his family will be able to live decently. The pity is Mr. Andersen, though a fine lawyer, has no knowledge of either real estate, in general, or the New York Building and Occupancy Code or apartment real estate management in particular."

No longer able to control himself, Andersen shot to his feet. "I don't believe for a moment that addlepated old broad ever wrote that letter. I know your type, Husseman. I see them in court every day and you planted it. So I'd like to know just what you're getting out of this."

Once again the shareholders were stunned by the personal attack. Andre didn't bother to look at the man. He handed the microphone back to O'Neil and returned to his seat.

O'Neil waited for him to sit down before he spoke. "Ballots are by the ballot box." He pointed to a corner in the rear. "Please form a line and Mr. Levine will have a ballot ready for you when you reach the table. All you have to do is place a check beside the name of Andersen or Husseman. The vote will be for one complete slate of directors or the other." He'd been correct in preparing two sets of ballots. If Husseman had failed to show up or not run for office, the ballots would have had only Andersen's name. He had given Mark instructions earlier to follow the course of the meeting, and to choose the correct ballots when the time to vote came.

Andersen realized for the first time that O'Neil had known Husseman was going to run. While the others lined up, he moved to the edge of the stage and whispered, "You cocksucker! I'll fire you and your fucking firm for this."

"You very well may. If you're elected." When the voting was completed, he said, "I would appreciate it if both Mr. Andersen and Mr. Husseman counted the ballots along with Mr. Levine."

The votes were added up, then totalled again. Both men returned to their seats, and Levine brought the results to O'Neil. He read them out loud. "Mr. Ivor Andersen, 18,387 votes plus 2,475 proxies for a total of 20,862 votes. Mr. Andre Husseman, 80,269 votes. I hereby declare the Husseman slate the winners."

The meeting ran on for several more hours. Finally it was over. O'Neil patted Zoltan on the back. "We did it. We really did it."

Zoltan began to feel dizzy. "Yes. I can't tell you how much I owe you."

"You owe me nothing. You make my job easier. Go home, man! Tell your family!"

Zoltan gratefully agreed. It was all he could do to keep from running out of the hall.

When Zoltan opened the door to the apartment, Anna, Genie, and Max were playing cards, a game called Go Fish.

They heard Zoltan's key in the lock and all three had turned in unison towards the door. They watched him enter, and their eyes opened wide, questioning him, expecting the blow to fall.

Zoltan was exhausted, so exhausted that his face did not convey the relief he felt. He had to use words. "Anna! Genie! Max! It's settled. We don't have to move."

Anna had lived so long with the fear her mind could not accept her husband's words.

"Is it true?" Max asked. "True?" Max studied Zoltan's face, a face he had loved all his life. A face he no longer trusted.

"It's true. Absolutely true. Andre Husseman, not Andersen, was elected president, and we can keep our apartment." Genie ran to her father, her whole body heaving as she released the fright she had held back for so long. She was sure Paul had done something to save them. It didn't matter that there was no way he could have even known. He must have known and done something.

At last the despair that had engulfed Zoltan for weeks seemed to ease. He smiled at Anna over Genie's head. "It's true, dear. It's really true."

Anna went to Zoltan's side, and looking up at him, she smiled a tremulous smile and kissed him on the cheek. "I've been so frightened."

Zoltan's weary eyes brightened. "I know, dear. I know."

Anna reached for Genie and took her in her arms. Zoltan stroked her hair and murmured softly, "It's all right, Genie. We're safe. It's all right."

The conviction in his father's voice finally reached Max, and he slumped forward, his face in his hands. He didn't even want to mention the part he might have played in saving them. He had learned too much about the world in the past few weeks and was simply glad his courage might have been of some use. But he wasn't sure how much. The rich and mighty lived by different rules than those governing ordinary people. And he was not yet rich and mighty.

After Genie and Max had finally gone to bed, Zoltan and Anna sat holding hands. Both of them were very tired now and much more knowing about the world they had made. The world that had allowed them to keep their home. This time.

10

Zoltan and Anna never recovered from the final loss of their innocence. Originally they had cherished a dream, not of riches, but of a kind of secure life. Now they came to accept the truth. Their family would never have the kind of security they so deeply desired. That belonged only to the wealthy. And they would never be wealthy. Even in the United States, they were almost as vulnerable as they had been in their native Hungary. They were still peasants, American peasants, and they would always be peasants. Yes, they had a few more choices, more freedom of a sort. The police couldn't come in the middle of the night and take them away. Zoltan had to remind Anna of this fact.

"Other things can come. Other things have already come."

"Of course. We must be careful. We will try to save money." He sighed. "But we can go to a movie. Or a restaurant. Or most places that people go."

"If we have the money. And, Zoltan, we will never have much money."

"Are you not happy? How much money do we need?"

"I'm happy. We don't need much money to be happy. But I'm afraid too. Suppose you had no job, and we had no money? Even to buy food."

"We will always have enough money for that."

"I hope so."

But if the elder Szabos came to live with their constricted view of the New World, neither Genie nor Max was able to understand or accept what had happened. Shortly after the shareholder meeting, they found a trellis-covered walk in Central Park behind the band shell and overlooking the 72nd Street transverse. The walk had many benches where they could sit and talk about the terrible things that had happened and came to be known to them as the time of the troubles.

Over the years, it became their habit to stroll to this covered walk, to sit and have long, serious talks about almost anything. Sometimes school, sometimes each other, usually full of their young dreams, meaningless opinions, but always returning to the eternal and hypnotic appeal of the Majestic and the people who lived there.

Most of their information as to who was doing what to whom came from what could be described as a highly intelligent domestic espionage system. With studied innocence, the Szabo children had plugged into the network of people who serviced the building. Doormen, elevator men, handymen, maids, governesses, laundresses, delivery boys, anyone and everyone, even their parents, all provided grist for their spy mill.

"Mrs. Soames dropped a diamond earring down the toilet," said Genie.

"She's too fat to fall in herself. That idiot," was Max's answer.

"And Elias Kahn is going on an African safari. Isn't that nuts?"

"Africa! Yuk! Spiders! Cannibals! Tigers! I'd rather go to Paris. Tiffany Frumkis bought her entire trousseau in Paris."

"Donald Hawkins gets private tennis lessons at the West Side Tennis Club in Forest Hills."

"Debbie Miller just got a horse for her birthday. I'd love owning a horse."

"What does she need with a horse? She's got a Jag."

"Silly. You can't ride a Jag."

Innately shrewd and perceptive, they had years to learn the vast differences between the life of the apartment owners of the Majestic and the life of the less fortunate. It seemed to them that the people in the Majestic lived in luxury, totally isolated from the threats the Szabos and similar families might have to face at any moment. And they long ago accepted their parents' statements that each friendly face concealed contempt, each sociable greeting hid condescension. That they were less than equal. The psychological bruises they sustained day after day left their indelible mark. And unlike more fortunate children, they dared not turn to their parents for help. Their parents were helpless to protect them. So there was no one to run to, no one to talk to, no place where they felt themselves safe.

Along with the knowledge that they could not talk to their parents went a reluctance to talk, even to each other, about the importance of making money. If Zoltan was not what Zoltan was, he might have made money. He was highly competent. Then why didn't he find work that would have earned him more money? Kept his home and family safe?

So making money—lots of money—became an all but sacred idea which they dared not mention lest it suggest a failure of love, a loss of faith in their parents. But money and how to make it was what Max and Genie thought about obsessively. And living as they did, in enemy country, with a need to keep even their parents at a distance, inevitably, helplessly, they grew more dependent on each other for safety and reassurance. Only Paul Husseman was accepted into their circle of trust. And then only fully by Genie.

One evening in the spring of 1962, when Genie was fifteen and Max seventeen, during one of their endless talk sessions, Genie turned from Max and looked across the park at the twin towers of the Majestic. She could see the windows of the Husseman apartment. She thought of the parties that went on there, parties to which, with the one exception, she had never been invited. She thought about Paul. With enough money, she might marry Paul Husseman. Marry Paul! The idea made her shiver, and thinking of what it would be like sent unexpected and strange but delicious sensations through her body. In her fantasy, the Hussemans couldn't object to Paul marrying a Genie Szabo worth millions.

Max, ever sensitive to her moods, gently prodded her. "What are you dreaming about?"

Genie was reluctant to become involved in a conversation about Paul. She wondered what else she could tell Max. The wild-tempered boy who teased her, pulled her hair, quarreled with her, had always been her staunchest ally. But the boy she had never ceased to worship would not be her ally when it came to Paul. Max was almost a grown man now, and if possible, a grown man with stronger opinions than he had had as a child. The promise of great size and strength, which had been apparent as a boy, had been fulfilled by his middle teens. He was a natural leader. A born athlete. He was chased by all the girls in his class. There was a strength in his face that seemed to call out, "Look at me! I'm a man! A male!" She decided he was too handsome for his own good and was glad she was his sister and could love him with safety.

"Come on, kidlet. What's eating you? Cat got your tongue?"

Still searching for something to tell him, she said without thinking, "I was dreaming about college. I might study finance. I'm very good with numbers."

"Who ever heard of a woman financier?" Max teased. "Don't waste your time. Take up teaching. Women are good teachers. You can teach math."

His sarcasm irritated Genie more than it ever had before, and it was unusual for her to be irritated at all at him. She was a straight A student at Hunter High, and she expected to be accepted at Hunter College. Fantasies about her glittering future would soon have to stand the test of reality, and Max was not going to shake her confidence in that future. At that moment she wanted to hit him. "Max, I'm your sister. You've grown up with me, and you don't understand me at all."

Max realized he had said something wrong. "Sorry, kidlet. What am I missing?"

"You're missing me." She cleared her throat and then said, simply and bluntly, "I want to make money. Teachers don't make money. Not the kind of money I want to make."

Her words brought Max up short. "Why? Do you think money's that important?"

"Isn't it? Look, I remember the time of the troubles just as clearly as you do. It would never have happened if we had money. That's why I want money. Barrels of it."

So it was finally out. In an effort to justify the implied criticism of her father, she added, "In school we're studying history. And the fact is for thousands of years only a very few people had money. Kings. Nobles. The Church. A few merchants. The rest were peasants. Serfs. Slaves. The way Momma always says. You were born a landholder, an aristocrat, or you weren't. And there wasn't a thing you could do about it. You were stuck." She knew exactly how she was going to continue. "In the United States it's different. We may be the super's kids, but we don't have to be superintendents. We can be anything in the world!'' Carried away by her vision of the future, she gripped Max's arm. ''Anything!''

''You think so, too?''

Genie squeezed his hand. ''I know so. Just wait.''

Genie's thoughts and the intensity with which she expressed them surprised him. He'd always known she was smart, but he hadn't expected her to understand their situation that clearly. She was different from the girls at school. Like him, she realized the importance of making money. Most girls only knew how to spend it. Money was power. The power their father never had. The power Max longed for so desperately. ''Then you don't think money is the root of all evil?'' he asked.

''Stop teasing me. No. Money is freedom. Money is security.''

Genie's fantasies were concrete and practical. She wanted security. She wanted her own home. She wanted a large bank account. Or maybe stocks and bonds. She'd heard Paul talk about his father's portfolio. She wanted so much money she would never have to stop and think if she had enough money in the bank to pay for something she wanted. The way Paul didn't think; and yes, she wanted Paul. But she wouldn't tell Max that.

''Now it's your turn,'' she said. ''What are you thinking?''

''I was thinking money is power. You can tell people where to head in. The way old man Gluck did. You can get things done.''

Genie laughed remembering Ralph Gluck. ''He certainly did get things done.''

''I was also thinking that girls usually think about having a man take care of them. About boyfriends, sex, marriage, babies. That's all the girls I know think about. How come you don't?''

''I think about those things too.'' Genie blushed slightly. ''But I also think about making money.'' She laughed. ''After all, I'd be a better catch if I were rich.''

Yes, you sure are something, Max thought. With or without money, you're a real catch, sister mine. There's not a guy around who wouldn't be proud to be seen with you. Christ! You are special! These thoughts caused a sudden and unexpected feeling of jealousy in Max. Not even that damn Paul Husseman is good enough for my sister. He knew as he had never known before how much he truly cared for her. No other woman could measure up to Genie.

He got up and stretched. "Kidlet, I think we ought to go home. Even if we don't own it."

"Yes. Let's go home. Someday we may own it. Or a reasonable facsimile." Genie's face was very still. They linked hands, Max and Genie, the way they had for so many years, and with Max leading the way, they made their way home to their parents' apartment in the Majestic.

11

The apartment was empty; grabbing her bath towel and robe, Genie hurried to the shower. She stood under the warm water soaping herself with the special Elizabeth Arden soap Paul had given her. As the water streamed down her body washing away the suds, Genie touched her skin, first her arms and then her stomach. Her skin felt so smooth. Almost without thinking, her hands cupped her breasts. They were full. Sensitive. Her period was due in a day or two.

Her hands brushed her nipples and a ripple of excitement ran through her body. Though it wasn't as exciting as when Paul touched them. She'd be seeing him soon, and the thought made her shiver.

During the summer, for the first time in their lives, they had been able to see each other regularly. Paul had argued that he was nineteen, going into his sophomore year at Harvard, and that it was ludicrous to treat him like a child. He'd been going to Europe with his family for ten years. Now he wanted to stay in New York and spend the summer working in an Off Broadway theater. Finally Mr. Husseman agreed. Genie suspected Mrs. Husseman didn't agree with his agreeing.

Neither did Anna. She still considered it wrong for the daughter of a superintendent to be seeing so much of the prince in the tower. She nagged Genie so consistently that one evening, while drying the dishes, Genie took her first open stand against her mother.

"Momma, I've been thinking how much you dislike my seeing Paul. So I've decided to see someone I think you'll like. Johnny Stadler. We're going out Saturday night."

"The boy who repairs cars in the garage?" Anna was

pleased. "He's such a nice young man. And he works so hard at the garage. It's a good steady job."

"You like him better than Paul?"

"Oh, yes! He's right for you."

"Because I'm the super's daughter, and he's a garage mechanic?"

"Yes. You're from the same sort of people."

Genie had baited the trap neatly. "Okay, Momma. I have to go to a gynecologist."

"A gynecologist?" Anna almost dropped the dish she was drying. "Why, for heaven's sake?"

"To be fitted for a diaphragm. If I see Johnny, he'll insist on our having sex. You don't think for a minute Johnny Stadler would take out a girl twice without sex? And I don't want to get pregnant. So shouldn't we set a date with a gynecologist?"

"We'll do no such thing!" Anna's voice was rising. The idea of teenage sex was not totally new to her, but to associate it with her daughter was too much. It bothered her so much she managed to ignore Genie's knowledge of contraception. "I'm glad your father didn't hear what you said."

At which point the discussion ended, because Zoltan stuck his head in the kitchen and asked, "What's going on?" No one answered him, and when he left, the subject was dropped except for Anna's last words. "If what you say is true, I'd rather you didn't see Johnny on Saturday."

Genie stepped out of the shower and dried herself with a fluffy white towel. As she dried her pubic hair, she felt the tension of unsatisfied desire. Her nerves were unusually awake, alive, sensitive.

It was going to be a warm night. She applied deodorant under her arms and then a puff of powder. She put on her robe for the short trip down the hall to her own room. Even though she was alone in the apartment, in Genie's world one did not walk around naked. Once in her room, she dropped the robe on her bed and put on a clean pair of panties. Next came a light bra, a short skirt, and a blouse that buttoned up the front. Her mother had not allowed her to make a real miniskirt, which was the rage. Her daughter would dress like a lady no matter what her high school friends wore.

Dressed and ready, she settled down in the living room to

read a book of poetry by Edna St. Vincent Millay. She had barely started when the telephone rang. It had to be Paul.

"Hello?"

"Genie!"

She heard the relief in his voice, delighted that she, not her mother or father, had picked up the phone. Somehow, when either of them answered, he became embarrassed. "Hi, Paul. Where are you?"

"I'm leaving the theater now. I'll be home in about thirty minutes."

"Oh?" She tried to keep the disappointment out of her voice.

"I know. I stayed longer than I meant to. Anyway, I'll make up for it. Wait."

"Of course." If Paul was going to succeed in the theater, he had to spend a lot of time at rehearsals. That was the way one learned. He had invested some money in an Off Broadway production and was being allowed to help out. The opening was in three weeks, and she was almost as excited as he was. She'd be so proud of him. "Call me when you get home."

"I've an idea. Suppose I pick up some food, and we eat in? The servants are off. We'll have the whole apartment to ourselves."

A small red flag rose before Genie's eyes, but she ran right through the warning. "Wonderful!"

"And I'll get a bottle of wine."

"I've never drunk a bottle of wine."

"You won't drink the whole bottle, silly. Just a glass or two."

"I'll leave some for you. Don't worry. Just hurry."

"Bye."

She hung up and tried to go back to reading the poetry, but she couldn't concentrate. She thought about being alone with Paul in his apartment, and remembered last fall just before Paul left for Harvard. It was the first time he had really kissed her. He'd taken her home after a movie, but instead of going straight to the door, he'd ducked into an alcove next to the service entrance, put his arms around her, and held her close. She remembered being confused by the feel of his body pressing against her. She looked up at him, and he kissed her on the mouth. Tenderly at first and then with more feeling. Without thinking, she closed her eyes, let her lips part, and his tongue entered and explored her mouth and the tip of her own tongue. The light contact sent a warmth running from her tongue through her whole body. Her legs seemed weak, and a sort of drugged languor settled over her. As his mouth took possession of her, she had to cling to him to keep her balance. Suddenly he let her go, pushing her away as though that was the only way he could stop himself. When he finally took her to the door, he said good night in a voice that was hardly audible.

After undressing that night, Genie discovered her panties were wet. It wasn't menstrual blood. It was something else. This was what her school friends were always talking about. This was why they talked so much about sex. If kissing was so exciting, real lovemaking must be fantastic.

Over the year she learned how wonderful it was. She and Paul saw each other during vacations and on an occasional weekend when Paul would take the shuttle to New York from Boston. From kissing they went on to caressing. First her breasts outside her clothes. Then one late spring day, her naked breasts under a thin blouse. Each step heightened their sexual intimacy until Paul became as familiar with almost every part of her body as Genie was herself. In time he encouraged her to caress him, and gradually, haltingly, her fingers began to explore first his face, then his chest, then his legs, and then more. One evening she felt his sex beneath his pants, and the sense of the power of his male hardness awed her.

Since Paul didn't own a car, there was no place for them to be entirely alone, and all those early stages of lovemaking were done furtively. On the service staircase of the Majestic. In the dark balcony of an almost empty movie house. Shivering in a cool evening in a secluded area of Riverside Park. And always with almost all their clothes on. Though Paul's hands were as familiar with Genie's breasts as with her face, he had never actually seen her bare breasts. And though she could trace the outline of his sex most vividly in her mind's eye, she had never seen the actual object.

One day she sneaked a book out of the school library which dealt with the human body, both male and female. Late at night, alone in her room, she studied the sexual details of the female body, including pregnancy and the menstrual cycle. She discovered she had something called a clitoris as well as a vagina. When she touched her clitoris, she could feel her whole body respond. She started to rub it back and forth and felt such a strong sexual urge, she grew frightened and stopped. She put the book away, but she didn't sleep well that night. She lay in bed, tossing and turning, touching herself and yanking her hand away. Feeling very guilty, she returned the book to the library the next day. From that evening on, only by exercising the strongest self-control was she able to keep her hands off herself. Masturbation was wrong. She didn't know why it was wrong, but it was wrong.

Now she was going to see Paul in his apartment, and for the first time, they would be alone. What would they do? Part of her ached for his body, and part of her hoped he wouldn't ask for more than she felt right about giving.

When the phone finally rang, she rushed to answer it. "Paul?"

"You were expecting Cary Grant?"

"Stop it, silly."

"Give me fifteen minutes to shower and come on up."

Her breath came faster as she pictured Paul in the shower, his naked body looking like a more human version of a sculpture by Giacometti she had seen in an art book. She was barely able to keep her voice steady and say, "Okay. See you in fifteen."

In addition to the duplex the Hussemans had first rented and then bought, they had persuaded the corporation to sell them a small open area on the roof over their apartment. One had to climb a flight of stairs to reach it, but once there, it was worth the short climb. The space was only about twenty feet square. The floor, actually part of the roof of the building, was a beautiful dark red quarry tile. The Hussemans had built a high redwood stockade-type fence on one side to give them privacy. The second side was the room that housed the machinery that operated the elevator at the top of the elevator shaft and the staircase itself, while the final two sides faced Central Park West and 71st Street. They were protected by five-foot-high parapets. The family used the space to barbecue as well as a place to sit and look at the stars on clear nights that were warm enough to be comfortable. There was a redwood table, benches, chairs, and several chaise lounges with mats.

Paul greeted her dressed in a white tennis shirt, a pair of white shorts, and sandals. Genie felt her skirt and blouse were

too formal, but she had no sport clothes. They went up to the
roof. It was an ideal night to barbecue. Paul had bought a steak,
corn, and the fixings for a tomato and endive salad. To Genie's
surprise, he had also bought not one but two bottles of wine.

"Who's going to drink all that wine?"

"You'll have some. I'll drink a little more, and we'll cork
whatever's left and drink it tomorrow. The wine will keep over-
night." Everything was ready except the charcoal fire. He uncorked the bottle of wine; after taking a sip, he smiled and
poured her half a glass. Genie read the label on the bottle.
Château something Rothschild.

"Isn't this an expensive wine, Paul?"

"I guess so. I asked Sam at Sherry's to select something
good. He'll put it on Dad's bill. Sometimes I think Dad supports Sherry's single-handedly."

Genie watched Paul set the coals on the grill, pour lighter
fluid over them, and start the fire. When she sipped the wine,
she was surprised. She had expected something sweet. It did
leave a pleasant taste on her tongue.

Paul noticed her expression. "Don't you like the wine? It's
really very good."

"It's not sweet."

"I know. If it were, it wouldn't go with the steak. Dessert
wines are sweet."

"Oh!" Genie absorbed that information. She tried another
sip. If one wasn't expecting something sweet, the wine tasted
nice. "I do like it." To prove she meant what she said, she
drained the glass. "Another, please?"

Paul smiled. "Honey, you're supposed to sip the wine. A
little at a time. Too much before eating will get you drunk."

Genie was dubious about getting drunk on anything that
tasted as mild as wine. But she agreed. "Give me a little more,
and I'll sip it."

Paul partially refilled her glass and returned to the fire. Genie
went to the parapet. She could see the beginnings of a sunset.
The sky was tinged with red and gold as the sun sank towards
the horizon in New Jersey. It would be a moonless night with
brilliant stars, and very warm. She turned to see Paul watching
her. He had an odd expression on his face, a half smile. "A
penny for your thoughts," she said.

"Not for sale. At least not now. Make me an offer later."

Genie suddenly felt shy. "I will," she said in a low voice. To hide her embarrassment, she turned back to the night. Once the sun actually slipped behind the hills, the color disappeared from the sky. Paul turned on the orange lights which were not supposed to attract bugs.

In spite of her sipping, the wine vanished too quickly. Genie held out her empty glass for a refill.

Paul laughed. "So soon? You have the makings of a lovely lush."

"I did sip the wine, but I guess I sipped too often."

"We'll save you from the clutches of lushdom by food. The fire's ready. I'll start the steak and corn." He had wrapped the corn in aluminum foil. She could smell the steak sizzling on the fire and saw little bursts of flames as the fat dripped off the steak and fell into the white-hot coals. Paul gave her a third glass. As Genie set the table with mats, napkins, dark grey plates, and stainless steel knives and forks, Paul prepared the salad in a large wooden bowl. By the time the food was ready, they had finished the entire first bottle of wine. Genie realized Paul must have been doing his share of sipping while preparing dinner. He opened the second bottle.

The meal was delicious. The steak was *bleu* the way Paul said a steak should be. And the corn was so sweet. Special white corn. Paul had taught her that salad was always eaten after the main course. "To clear your palate for dessert."

In the middle of the meal she felt his bare foot on hers. She slipped off her moccasins so both their bare feet could touch. They said almost nothing, delighting in each other's nearness, in the perfection of the moment. By the time they finished the meal and cleared the table, the sky was dark.

"If I turn off the lights, we can see the stars more clearly," Paul said, looking up at the sky.

"Oh, yes!" Genie looked at the sky.

The stars seemed to leap down at them. She walked to the parapet to look at Central Park and at the stars. Then she heard Paul's steps moving closer to her. She felt his body pressed against her. His arms reached around her waist and pulled her even tighter around him. So tight she could feel him pushing against her buttocks. She stood still, too expectant to move. His hands slipped up and cupped her breasts the way she hoped he would. Paul unbuttoned the top buttons of her blouse and slipped his hands under it. It only took a moment for them to find their way to her bare breasts. His palms caressed her nipples, and his body pushed still harder against the thin material of her skirt. Genie felt an overwhelming need for her body to feel the warmth of the summer night air. She unbuttoned the rest of her blouse and slipped it off.

"Unhook my bra, Paul." He didn't move. "Unhook it, please."

He removed his hands from her breasts very slowly as though he could hardly bear to release them. Her bra joined her blouse on a chair. She stood before him, her dark hair almost invisible against the black sky, her body casting a pale glow against the stars. "Put your hands on my breasts, please."

He held her again. This time her breasts were totally free. Her nipples were hard and extended, responding to his touch. He kissed her shoulder at the exact spot where it curved into her neck. He kissed her again. She turned in his arms. "Take off your shirt. I want to feel your skin against mine."

Paul hesitated. This was Genie. You mustn't, he thought. He hadn't planned this. Not exactly, anyway. But his need for her overcame his hesitation, and he yanked his shirt over his head. Genie reached for him and pulled his chest against her breasts, her nipples against his bare skin. "Genie." He broke away from her. "I think we'd better stop."

But the wine and the nearness of him had done its seductive work. Her nerves of pleasure were laid bare. She reached for him again. "I love you."

"I love you, too."

"Then hold me. Hold me close."

Their bodies melted together. Genie could feel him pressing between her legs. She was overwhelmed by a desire that obliterated all other thoughts. Suspended on the brink of a voluptuous abyss, she knew only that she wanted him. Wanted all of him. She thought, two people who love each other have a right to have each other.

Paul was beside himself. He had been trying hard to restrain his desire for her. But he could not drag himself away from her half-naked body. Her naked skin seemed to fuse them together. He was as much in love with her as she was with him. What then was right? What was wrong? He had thought he could control the limit of their lovemaking, but his body was making demands that were affecting his judgement. Only slightly more sober than Genie, his resistance weakened. He slipped his hands down to cup her behind, lifted her skirt, and felt the bare skin under her panties. Her strong muscles tensed under his fingers. He had made love to her often in his thoughts, but actually to do it?

Genie quivered under his touch. She wanted his hands on her body, touching every part of her. She half turned, freeing herself for a moment, and slid off her panties. Then she returned to him, offering her mouth to him, pressing her body against his, feeling she was falling into the golden sweetness of his flesh.

Paul was unable to control his hands. He let them circle her, his fingers probing to reach further within her. But he couldn't reach the soft, special place he wanted to touch. He loosened his grip, allowing a slight space between their bodies, and slipped his hand between them, raising her skirt so he could caress her belly and then slide down to her pubic hair. Genie seemed unable to resist, unable to respond, caught in a stare of erotic suspense. It was only when his fingers parted the lips of her vagina and touched her clitoris that she came alive. She gasped at the shock and reached for him. His shorts and underwear were still in the way. Her hand fumbled for the zipper, but he pushed it away. Paul made one final effort at control. "Genie, my darling, is this what you want? Do you want us to make love?"

"My love. Oh, my love. All I want is you. To make love to you."

He had done his best. Much more than most nineteen-year-olds would have done. Now he could do no more. His hands trembled as he unzipped his shorts and threw them on a chair. His underwear followed. Genie removed her skirt. They were two young lovers giving no thought to anything but the demands love makes on all of us.

Paul took her in his arms. His penis pressed up against her naked body. Genie could feel her breasts reaching for his touch. Her hips arched forward to accept him. They staggered to the lounge. She fell back. Her legs parted, waiting. Paul began to caress her. Then he pulled back leaving her trembling at the unexpected rejection.

"Please, love," she whispered.

But her total and absolute innocence had awakened in him a

reverence. In the light of her purity, his own past seemed somewhat sordid. Paul had been raised in the European manner. Thanks to his father, from the time he had reached puberty, he had had sexual experiences with several highly knowledgeable women. They had taught him some of the ways of pleasing a woman. However, it is one thing to have a sexual encounter with a semiprofessional, knowing woman and quite another to make love to a sixteen-year-old virgin whom you love. He was terrified of causing Genie pain, the pain he had been told that comes the first time a woman makes love. And this fear robbed him of all knowledge and experience.

"Paul? What is it? What's wrong? Don't you want me?"

"Want you? Darling, I need you! I just don't want to hurt you."

"Hurt me? How could you hurt me?"

"You're a virgin." He began to stammer. "I've been told the first time it can hurt."

Genie realized Paul must have had some experience with other women. At another time she might mind. But not now. Men have their own needs and she had never been available to Paul. His concern for her was his concern for someone he loved. He was hesitating before the fulfillment of everything that had grown between them. He was hesitating because he loved her. She realized that she, who had little knowledge of the arts of love, would have to take the responsibility for what they did. She took hold of his penis and put it against her vagina trying to open wider to receive him. "It won't hurt me, darling. It won't hurt."

Paul slipped his hands between her legs, feeling how wet she was. Gently, ever so gently, he began to move against her clitoris. Her body arched upward towards him.

"Come into me, darling. Please," she murmured, her eyes closed, wanting to be possessed, fully possessed.

Paul let his penis slide between the lips of her vagina. He pushed forward whispering words of love. Once he was completely inside her, he lay still waiting for her reaction. Nothing happened. She had stiffened for an instant and then relaxed. He could feel the walls of her vagina closing around him. Wherever he touched her, she burned. Waves of pleasure swept over her. She waited for the pain, but there was no pain. Only a wonderful sweetness. She lay absolutely still not wanting to miss the sensation. Her arms circled his waist holding him inside her. "Oh, darling! My darling! It's so beautiful."

At last he began to move. Long, smooth strokes to which she responded. Engulfed by their passion, their fresh young bodies were carried along in mounting ecstasy. Genie thought Paul was dissolving into her, becoming a part of her. She ran her fingers down the small of his back. His fulfillment was only a moment away, when suddenly he pulled out. The next instant his penis was spurting milk, white jets of thick fluid on her belly.

Genie was suddenly frightened. "What is it? Did I do something wrong?"

"You! No, my love. It's me who's crazy. I'm not wearing a condom. Suppose I got you pregnant?"

For an instant Genie thought to tell him her period was due in a day or two. She couldn't get pregnant, but some instinct held her back. It would make his sacrifice seem foolish. And her heart glowed with the knowledge of how much he loved her. Her fingers traced the outline of his cheekbone and jaw. "You're so wonderful. You take such good care of me."

"Oh, sure. Great care!" He mocked himself. "I might have gotten you pregnant. And you didn't have an orgasm, did you?"

"I don't know. It doesn't matter." Her head was swimming with colors. All she knew was she wanted him inside her again. She placed his sex between her legs. "Please!"

Being young and in love, he was still hard. He lowered the weight of his body onto her. Now at last his experience came into play. With every thrust he rubbed against her clitoris.

Genie lay waiting, drugged with passion. Paul knew exactly what to do. Without interrupting his movements, his mouth opened over her parted lips, and his tongue touched the tip of her tongue. Each time his penis touched her clitoris his tongue touched her tongue.

A strange thin feeling, almost a pulse beat, began to stir somewhere in her body. She was only conscious of Paul moving in and out of her, his hands caressing her nipples, his tongue licking her tongue. He seemed to move deeper into the core of her. The thin pulse grew, and with it came strange new feelings, feelings she was powerless to control. Unconsciously, she moved in time to the pulse, lifting her legs and wrapping them around his body to receive him as deeply as possible. The pulse grew and grew. It was all that mattered. She gripped his body, glorying in his flesh. Then, like a dam bursting, the orgasm came. Her legs dropped to the ground. Without realizing what she was doing, she hurled herself against him. Up and down. With each wave, she tried to impale herself further on his sex. Always deeper. Always harder. Finally, when the orgasm began to subside, she lay back on the lounge, still treasuring the dying tremors.

Slowly, ever so slowly, Genie came back into her body. Paul was still inside her. She opened her eyes, looked at him, smiled, and kissed him. She sensed his delight, even wonder, at the strength of her orgasm. He supposed it was being in love that made everything so extraordinary.

Only when he felt the last tremors subside did he pull out. He was about to burst. "It's my turn now." Genie nodded. She put one hand on his balls, and with the other, she fondled the head of his sex, enclosing it, pulling it gently. Love made her wise beyond her experience, and she used her hand as a vagina to stroke him the way she imagined her vagina would. She could feel the contractions as he fought to hold back. To prolong the sweet torture as long as possible. Then he couldn't hold it any longer. His body jerked uncontrollably, and his semen squirted through her hands. When it was over, they rolled together, holding each other, lying side by side for a long while, silent, half asleep.

Paul was the first to speak. He was in control of himself, and he felt a need to explain, to apologize. "Genie, my love, I didn't mean for this to happen. I love you so much, but I didn't plan to make love to you." As much to convince himself as to convince her, he added, "If I had planned to make love to you, I would have been prepared. I would have had some rubbers ready."

"I wanted you as much as you wanted me. Next time use a rubber. I want you to come inside me the way you should."

Thus Genie established that this was not going to be the only time they made love. She planned a summer of lovemaking and many a winter weekend after that. She loved Paul. Paul loved her. It was the way it was supposed to be.

12

Max had taken his Scholastic Aptitude Tests the previous
March and then applied to Cornell and, as a joke, Harvard.
None of this meant he had any desire to go to college. He saw it
as a waste of time. This attitude caused some verbal hassles
with Genie. Zoltan only occasionally had something to say, and
Anna was silent. Actually, Zoltan half agreed with Max's desire to go to work, but the other half of him still sided with the
American dream. On one of the few occasions when he offered
an opinion, he said, "A college education is a wonderful thing.
In Hungary people like us would never have the chance to go to
college."

"Up Hungary! This is the United States. And I don't have to
go to college to prove we're better off than we would have been
in Hungary."

Genie disagreed. "Unless you want to be a cowboy, a college degree will give you a much better chance at getting a good
job."

"I don't believe it. Not the kind of job I want."

"You want to be a cowboy? Or raise carrier pigeons?"

"What I want to do will involve brains, which I have, hard
work, which I'm willing to do, energy and charm, which I also
have." He grinned broadly at his description of himself.

"What are you thinking of?"

"I don't know, but I know it's out there waiting for me."
That wasn't true. He knew what was out there waiting for him.
He'd decided a year ago, after watching how Brown, Harris,
Stevens operated, that he wanted to be a real estate salesman.
Unknown to his family, he had answered a newspaper adver-
tisement that offered openings for young men looking for a start
in the real estate business. The name of the firm was Robert
Alpert & Company. Although he was younger than any of the

127

others interviewed, he had made such a good impression Alpert suggested that after he graduated from high school, he come to see him again.

"Pipe dreams. Nothing's waiting if you don't go to college." Genie was adamant.

"A job pays money." Max rubbed his thumb and middle finger together. "College, as we all know, costs money. It doesn't pay you. You pay it."

"You applied for an athletic scholarship. You might get one. You're the best pitcher in the New York City school system. You told me so yourself. Rah! Rah! Rah!"

"Yeah, I might. Give a one! Give a two! Give a three!" He laughed at his own expense. "But even a full scholarship costs money. There're things it won't pay for. Like cheerleaders." Suddenly he dropped the banter. "Genie, the fact is, now that high school's over, I don't give a you-know-what for competition, unless I'm competing for the almighty buck."

Max agreed to hold his decision until he saw how the colleges responded. And they did respond. Much to the Szabo family shock, the joke of applying to Harvard almost turned out to be on them. The Harvard admissions committee considered his application seriously. The rejection was not the usual thank-you-for-applying-but-no-thanks. It suggested Max reapply for a scholarship after completing a satisfactory year at Andover or any similar prep school. A scholarship to the prep school could be arranged. Then they would be delighted to reconsider his application.

The family had barely recovered from the shock at the idea that Max might attend the same college as Paul Husseman when Max heard from Cornell. He'd been awarded a full scholarship—room, board, and tuition. All that remained was that he pass his final regents' exams.

Again the family huddled over the dining room table and talked about Max's choices.

Genie was excited and very pleased. "You know, Max, you got what amounted to two acceptances."

"Oh, sure. With some ifs, ands, and buts."

"Don't be so cynical."

"Okay. Where do you think I should go?"

"Are you asking me or telling me?"

"Dear kidlet, I'm sure you want me to go to Harvard. Where your buddy, Paul, goes."

"Fat chance. You put in an extra year at a prep school?"

"I don't think it's right for you to go to Harvard."

"I'm not good enough, Dad? Or are we not rich enough?"

"It's wrong." Then Zoltan hesitated. "Of course, if you want to . . ."

In spite of Max's efforts to keep his feelings to himself, Zoltan knew he had lost much, if not all, of his son's respect. He had not lived up to Max's idea of how a brave man should behave. Perhaps the flight from Hungary and the first few years in the United States had exhausted his reserves of courage. And without courage, he felt he had forfeited the right to decide what his son should do.

Max turned again to Genie. "I guess, if Harvard is too sacred and you want me to go to college, your choice must be Cornell?"

"Must be."

Max turned abruptly to Anna. "Momma, what do you think? You haven't said a word throughout this caucus."

Anna was certain of only one thing. Max should not attend the same school as Paul Husseman. If Paul Husseman went to Harvard, Harvard was a special place, a school for aristocrats. Whoever had written that letter from Harvard was a fool. In fact, she had serious doubts about either of her children attending college. What could they learn in college that would help them earn a living? Privately she agreed with Max that he should get a job. If he was lucky he could get something in one of the buildings on Central Park West. Mr. O'Neil might help him. Then in time he would have enough experience to become a building superintendent. He could start the way Zoltan had, managing several small buildings. Max was a hard worker. Maybe he could take Zoltan's place when it came time for Zoltan to retire. If Max went to college, Genie might expect to go, too. That would be absolute foolishness. You don't learn how to cook or clean house in college. She would need to know those things to catch a good husband.

"Anna, what are you thinking?" Zoltan repeated.

"What do I think?" Anna's voice was tired and resigned. Since she couldn't bring herself to say what she really believed, she avoided taking any position. "I don't know anything about college. I think Max should decide for himself. He should do what he wants to do."

Zoltan agreed at once.

Max had only been waiting for someone to ask him for his opinion. Now that his mother had, he said what he thought. "All right. You know I'd rather get a job than go to college. But you all seem to want me to go to college. Genie, you've twisted me around your little finger. For my own good, of course. Cornell shall have the pleasure of my company and my live fastball."

That summer, the evenings were never long enough for Paul and Genie. They saw each other consistently, and like people possessed, they made love constantly. It was a time of sexual discovery for both of them. None of Paul's previous experiences had prepared him for the intensity and single-minded devotion to pleasing him that Genie displayed. Or, in fact, his own continuous efforts to give her pleasure.

It all might have ended as an ordinary experience of puppy love. Nothing unusual. A rich young man and the super's beautiful daughter have a passing but pointless affair. But far from the trivial, far from the commonplace, their words, their actions, their commitment became increasingly full of special meaning and beauty. The time together seemed to be the most memorable in their lives. It was the summer in which all the happiness of life collected, and it seemed to belong only to them.

When together in public their manner was polite, almost cool. Any suspicious eye might have actually found them too courteous and overly polite. It was necessary that Genie be home at a reasonable time every evening, which she managed to establish as midnight. The movies usually let out at that time; or if earlier, they might stop for ice cream. To support her position that they went to a lot of movies, she read all the reviews carefully. She could give an accurate account of the films she had not seen. And since it was necessary that the Husseman servants guess nothing, they were all given generous time off. Whatever the servants thought, they kept their opinions to themselves, being glad for the extra time off to spend as they wished. It was also fortunate that due to vacation schedules during the summer, there were many different elevator operators.

The replacements were usually college boys in need of summer work who knew just enough not to know anything.

However, one morning Paul realized his parents and sister would return in two weeks. Usually they came home over the Labor Day weekend, but this year they were cutting their vacation short. He suggested to Genie it was time for a small dinner party that included Max. Not only was it the polite thing to do, it could be expanded, when described to his parents, as if they had been more of a threesome during the summer. Genie agreed, but the idea of Paul and Max together made her very nervous.

Genie and Max had not seen that much of each other over the summer. And when they did meet, her conversation had been very guarded. Fortunately, Max had been busy. He'd spent long days shopping for things needed for college, and equally long nights seeing how many different girls he could sleep with. But on those evenings when they did meet at home for supper or before going to bed, Genie sensed a watchfulness that often left her at a loss for words. Occasionally the devil would nudge Max in the ribs and he'd tease Genie with a question like, "Seen any good pix with Paul lately?"

It was that kind of teasing that would cause Genie to perspire and break into a bubbly laugh. "Oh, sure. On and off. We go to the movies a lot. We're movie nuts. Paul learns from the movies."

"What have you seen recently that's worth my springing for two bags of popcorn?"

"Oh—hmmm. We saw a revival of *Casablanca* last Tuesday."

Max knew she was lying. He'd tried to see *Casablanca* on Tuesday because Genie had told their mother she was going and found the movie house had substituted a sneak preview. "Yeah. That's a good one. Saw it myself." There was something in his grin that warned Genie he knew she was lying. She waited for him to continue questioning her. He didn't, and that left her more worried than ever. Finally she realized he had something on his mind that was at least as pressing as finding out about her and Paul. She was right.

* * *

Shortly after receiving his offical acceptance from Cornell along with printed brochures describing the school and the courses available to him, and telling him he was to register on Tuesday, September 25, he received a typewritten letter with the Cornell logo on it and and title Cornell Athletic Association under it. The letter requested that he report two weeks earlier, on September 11. A plane ticket was enclosed along with instructions on how to get from the airport to the special dormitory reserved for freshmen athletes. All his expenses for the two weeks would be taken care of once he was there.

The request puzzled Max. Why should he have to report early? Baseball was a spring and summer game. The logical person to talk to was his high school coach. They met in front of the yacht basin on 79th Street and the Hudson River. Zack Zacharias read the letter and frowned.

"Was there a physical form for you to fill out when you applied for the scholarship?"

"Not when I applied. But after I received it, there sure was! The only thing they missed was the size of my you-know-what."

"Humph. I assume you filled in the correct numbers?"

"Yeah."

"How tall are you?"

"A little over six feet three inches."

"Weight?"

"About one-ninety-five. But I'm getting heavier."

"I know." Zack looked and sounded sour. "And I assume there were a few questions on how fast you can run? Odd distances, like forty yards? Or sixty yards?"

"Yes."

"What did you say?"

"What could I say? I never went out for track so I wrote, 'Faster than most.'" Max's curiosity got the best of him. "What the hell are you driving at?"

"We'll see. I have a few friends who played ball at Cornell. They'll remember me from the old days. I'll call you tomorrow."

Early the next morning Max got a call from the coach. They agreed to meet at the same place that afternoon. Max was a half hour early for this meeting and waited for the coach to arrive.

Finally he spotted the old man limping along. When he arrived, he didn't say a word. He handed Max a folded piece of paper.

"What is it? Why do they want me so early?"

"Read it!"

Max looked at the paper. There was one word written on it. He exploded. "Football! You know I never played football in my life. I like my knees in one piece bending up and down in one direction." This was true, but it wasn't the real reason why Max never played football. He knew himself far better than his family, Genie included, gave him credit for. It would take one clip, one late hit, one elbow in his face or knee in his groin, one deliberate illegal action, and he didn't know how violently he would react.

"I'll give it to you straight, Max. You're too big, too strong, and your wise-ass crack about being faster than most has got the football coach's balls in an uproar. You're prime beef on the hoof for any football coach. They'll have you lifting weights, and you'll weigh about two-twenty-five maybe two-thirty by next year."

"All that muscle will get in the way of my pitching motion."

"I know. Max, do you have any idea how many people go to Saturday afternoon football games? I'll tell you. Anywhere from 50,000 to 70,000 depending on the size of the stadium. And then there's the possibility of television money. Football supports the entire college sports program. There wouldn't be any baseball scholarships if it wasn't for football."

"Suppose I don't show? I already have my scholarship."

"You don't show, and the alumni association will be all over you. Besides, when you do register, you'll be visited by a few members of the varsity. You'll end up going out for the team, like it or not."

"With football in the fall and baseball in the spring, when do I get to study? I've picked out a course in business administration and one in architecture. They have Saturday classes."

The coach laughed. "Forget it. Unless you're really dedicated. Like a Whizzer White."

"Who was he?"

"A football player who was also a Rhodes scholar. He even played pro ball for a few years. I think he's a lawyer now. Anyway, you're not the type, Max. You'll be taking Phys Ed 101 and Weight Lifting 36."

"So I'll end up knowing less than I know now with a degree of some sort, and four years older."

"That's about it. At least you can read and write."

The conversation left Max more uncertain than ever as to what he should do. The decision weighed heavily on him, so while he could tease Genie occasionally, he didn't have the psychological strength to look too hard at what she and Paul were doing. Probably some kissing and feeling each other up. If it was more than that, he preferred not to know.

On Monday evening Paul called Max and invited Genie and him to dinner the following Wednesday. Something in Paul's voice irritated Max. Maybe it was the knowledge that Paul's father paid his tuition, and Paul was going to college without any of the extra requirements an athletic scholarship placed on him. Whatever it was, listening to Max, Genie became even more concerned.

"Paul, I want to thank you for inviting Genie's lowbrow brother." She didn't hear Paul's answer, but she did hear Max continue to carry on. "I hope my manners won't embarrass anyone."

When he hung up, Genie glared at him. "What was that all about? There's nothing wrong with your manners."

"Glad you know it, kidlet. Nice of you to approve."

"Will you stop talking like that, please?"

"Talking like what?"

"You were pretty rotten to Paul."

"I beg your pardon." He fell to his knees pleading for her forgiveness.

"Oh, get up." With Max kneeling and grinning at her, she wished Paul had never thought of having him to dinner, that Max had not accepted the invitation, and given that both things had happened, she wished more than anything else it was Thursday morning and the darn dinner was over and done with. She was terrified at what Max might guess, and what he would do if he found out how she and Paul actually had spent the summer.

On Wednesday evening, Genie and Max walked down the hall to the C/D line to take the elevator to the thirty-first floor. The elevator door opened, Max stepped aside, and, with an exaggeratedly gallant gesture, waved Genie in first. Then he slouched in at a snail's pace. Genie thought, this is going to be a disaster.

Paul was standing in the door waiting for them. He was dressed more formally than when he and Genie were alone. Long pants and a buttondown shirt replaced the tennis shorts and shirt. After welcoming them, Paul led them to the open area where he and Genie originally made love. This was the first time Max had known such a place existed. Taking her cue from him, Genie pretended to be as surprised as he was.

Paul had planned this evening carefully. First there was the liquor to be taken care of. A six-pack of Lowenbrau was in the ice chest. He had ordered several bottles of wine. Genie would have a glass or two, and he would have the rest. The main course was roast beef which was turning on a motor-driven spit over the charcoal grill. The potatoes were baking on the same charcoal and the salad was already prepared. He had bought a sacher torte in the Eclair which was in the refrigerator downstairs.

In spite of all the preparations, the start of the evening was rough going. Paul had to be careful about implying any intimacy with Genie beyond close friendship. Seeing her sitting on the redwood lounge called to his mind a picture of her, naked, her arms outstretched, asking him to make love to her. He felt his penis swell and congratulated himself at having the foresight to wear a jockstrap. It was damned uncomfortable, but there was no bulge in his pants to embarrass him. Genie aside, what could he talk to Max about? He wasn't interested in sports, and Max wasn't interested in politics, theater, or books. There were long silences when neither Paul nor Genie could think of a thing to say, and Paul filled the gaps by pouring himself more wine.

Then, seemingly out of left field, Max started talking about how much he liked the movies. "I thought *Casablanca* was a darn good movie. You liked it, didn't you, Genie?"

"Did I? I don't remember." She gave Paul a warning look.

"I got the impression you liked it."

"Oh, movies bore me. Let's talk about something else."

"I thought you and Paul were crazy for movies. You see them all the time. You said you were movie nuts."

Paul realized the danger. "We see them, but there's no sense in talking about them. That's what the critics get paid for."

"Film critics bore me." Max was set on pushing the point. "I'd rather know what my friends and relatives think."

"Well, I don't think anything."

"You seem sore at me, kidlet."

"Sore at you? Why should I be sore at you? Let's talk about your live fastball. Or better, I know one thing we're interested in. Let's talk about that. Your future. Making money."

Max agreed. He had made them uncomfortable which was all he had intended to do.

Over dinner, following Genie's lead, Paul started talking about making money. Though far from drunk, he was beginning to feel the effects of the wine and his tongue grew loose. He decided to entertain Max and Genie with the family history. How his father had made so much money. "No, he didn't inherit it. He started with some, but it was really his brains that did it. When my grandfather died, my father wasn't much older than I am. He was twenty-five."

Max was immediately interested. "What did your father do to make money? You said he was only twenty-five."

Paul smiled and leaned back in his chair. "He built 608's."

"What's that supposed to mean? What are 608's?"

"Haven't you noticed the number of six-story red brick apartment houses in Queens, the Bronx, and Long Island?"

"Sure. I've seen the buildings. I even know families living in them."

"They were built so tens of thousands of middle-income families could have a decent place to live. They were built under a government law called 608. The builder paid six percent interest on his mortgage and was allowed to earn eight percent on the cost of the building. That's why they're called 608's."

"I don't understand." Genie's interest was rising.

"It's easy. The FHA guaranteed the bank loans to the builders who built the apartment houses."

"What's the FHA?" Max asked.

"The Federal Housing Administration," Paul answered, a slightly superior tone in his voice.

"An eight percent return isn't bad." Max had picked up Paul's tone when he'd asked about the FHA, and he wanted

Paul to see he wasn't such a dummy. Since seeing Robert Alpert, he'd been studying real estate investments.

"It sure isn't. If a building costs, let's say, a million dollars to build, you're allowed to earn eighty thousand a year."

"One could get rich on eighty thousand dollars per building."

"There's more to it."

"What more?"

Paul hesitated. He was getting into an area that was strictly family business. But he was in love with Genie, and they planned to marry after he finished school. That made the Szabos almost family. He poured himself another glass of wine. The bottle was empty. "I'll get another bottle from Dad's cellar, bring up dessert, and give you the scoop."

Genie tried to stop him. "Do you think you should? Too much . . ." She'd almost said, "Too much wine makes you tipsy," indicating she was familiar with Paul's drinking habits. Max caught the slip.

Once Paul was out of hearing, he couldn't resist asking, "Does he take a bottle to the movies, kidlet? He has the makings of a true wino."

"Oh, no! He's just feeling happy. Festive. I know him."

"And how well do you know him, sister dear?" He let her see his mistrust, his harsh, jealous suspicions.

Genie panicked. "Paul's a good friend. As he's always been."

"How good is this good friend?"

Before she could answer, Paul returned with a bottle of wine in one hand and the rest of the meal balanced on a tray. "Here I am with the nectar of the gods. Does anyone want a glass besides me?"

Genie was so frightened she let caution slip. "I'll have a glass, Paul."

"Coming up, darling."

That settled it for Max. It provoked a rage in him, deeper, more savage than the situation warranted. He knew very well many girls were not virgins. He'd received far more than his share of favors from so-called decent girls. And Genie's life was her own. Part of him knew it was none of his business. But that his sister, his kidlet, spread her legs like some kind of broad for this nowhere rich kid came very close to making him physically sick. He had to wipe from his mind the image of her naked body being kissed and caressed by golden boy. He had to erase the image of golden boy's prick sliding in and out of his sister. He had to! Or sooner or later he would do something neither Genie nor he wanted. Like beat the shit out of the S.O.B.

Paul filled Genie's glass and settled himself on the lounge. "Now where were we? I remember. We were talking about 608 construction and mortgages."

Genie waited for Max's reaction. She'd heard Paul's slip and was terrified at what Max would do. When all Max said was, "Go on, Paul. I'm very interested," she was both relieved and frightened. It wasn't like Max to let the matter pass.

"Did I explain how the FHA guaranteed the building loans so the banks were eager to lend money at low interest rates?"

"Yes."

Paul's laughter began to go out of control. The wine had taken effect. "There are greater compensations." Now there was a note of arrogance in his voice. Genie cringed at the tone. "It's so simple, I'll never know why everyone didn't do it."

"Everyone? It takes a lot of money to build an apartment house." Max was paying total attention.

"Not if you build 608's it doesn't."

"It doesn't?"

"Nope. You mortgage out."

"What does that mean? Mortgage out?"

"It means you borrow more money from the bank than the building cost to build. In fact, Dad walked away with money on most of his construction."

Max was incredulous. "That's legal?"

"More or less. There's a fine line."

"Give me an example of how it worked."

"Easy." Paul poured himself another glass of wine. "Let's say we find a piece of land on which we're going to build a six-story building in Astoria, Queens. The FHA was empowered to guarantee ninety percent of the total construction costs plus ninety percent of the cost of the loan."

"If the FHA guaranteed only ninety percent of the construction costs, we'd have to lay out ten percent. Ten percent of a million dollar building is a hundred thousand dollars. That's not exactly popcorn."

"You don't remember all I said. The trick was to borrow

more money than the land actually cost. Or more than it cost to construct the building.''

''I'm starting to see daylight.''

''I'll bet you are. Let's say Dad bought the land for fifty thousand dollars and had it appraised for a hundred and fifty. The FHA guaranteed ninety percent of the appraised price. You figure out how much that comes to, Genie.''

''One hundred thirty-five thousand dollars.''

''Go to the head of the class.'' Paul reached over and patted Genie's head. She could see Max tense and then relax. ''Now subtract the fifty thousand Dad actually paid for the land.''

''There's an eighty-five thousand dollar profit. Wow!'' Max was duly awed. ''Before you put a shovel in the ground!''

''Exactly. And then there's the cost of construction. Dad could always beat the price per square foot allowed by the FHA. They set a price on a radiator. A generous price. By buying in bulk, Dad could always get the radiators cheaper. They specified one size oil burner and hot water tank. He put in a slightly smaller unit. Nothing major. Just a little here and there. It all adds up, and the building works just as well.''

''What did an average building cost your father to build?''

''Maybe a million dollars, more or less.''

''Say one million. Would it be reasonable to estimate he made a profit of five percent on the construction costs? By borrowing more than the building cost?''

''Ten percent would be closer.''

Max whistled. ''That could add up to a lot of money. Plus what he took home from those beautiful land appraisals.''

''And don't forget we still own the buildings. We still net that eight percent return on the building. And without investing a dime. It adds up.''

Max nodded. ''Doesn't it! There's only one thing I don't understand. I understand cutting corners on construction and coming in way under the loan. But I don't get the land deal. The FHA didn't do the appraising, did they?''

''Of course not. The banks that actually made the loans sent out their own appraisers.''

''If the land cost fifty thousand, what bank appraiser would value it at a hundred and fifty?''

Paul had much too much to drink, and he'd gone too far to stop now. ''Let's say some appraisers found a little money in their Christmas stocking. Money above the bonuses the banks paid them."

Max felt an odd shock. The shock one feels on seeing something totally familiar in a new setting. "Are you saying your father bribed the appraisers?"

"Bribed? No! Never! Say, er, influenced. That's a nicer word."

"Okay. Influenced." Silently, Max repeated *bribed*. Now he had one last question. "If anybody could do it, why didn't they?"

"Because they didn't understand the game. Take your father. He knows more about construction than my father ever did or ever will. He could build a building without a general contractor. That alone would take ten percent off the construction costs."

He swallowed another glass of wine. Sipping was a thing of the past. The wine disappeared in one gulp. Paul leaned his head back and closed his eyes. "All this talk has made me tired." He closed his eyes and was asleep almost at once.

Max looked at him with thinly disguised contempt. "What do we do now? He's out."

"We can't leave him sleeping here. He'll catch cold."

"That's right, kidlet. And he's too big for me to carry downstairs without waking him up. Let him rest a few minutes. Maybe he'll wake up." He looked at Genie. "What's with you and Paul? He called you darling. That's not exactly the same as Eugenia."

"It's a term of affection. Nothing more. We're fond of each other. That's all."

"I don't believe you. I think you two have been doing a number all summer. Fucking like crazy."

"I don't like you when you talk like this."

"I don't like the rich kid screwing my sister."

"We're not screwing."

"You're playing Monopoly?"

His words were harsh, but Genie knew the depths of his feeling. Seemingly outgoing and friendly, she knew Max had no intimate friends ouside of the family, and she was the strongest of his human bonds. His anger masked his real concern. So she confessed. After all her fear of the possible fireworks, it sounded almost cut and dried. "Max, we love each other. And yes, we do what people do when they're in love. We're going to be married when we're older and out of school."

"Fat chance. He'll never marry you. His family won't let him. You're the super's kid. You don't fit."

"You sound like Momma."

"I suppose I do."

"You don't understand. You've never been in love."

"I understand enough about fucking to know I have to be careful about Momma and Dad. You'd better be careful, too. If they ever found out, they'd never get over it."

It was strange. Max's distress was streaked with domestic realism. "Of course I'll be careful. I don't want to hurt them anymore than you do."

"Oh, damn it. You're wrong about Paul."

"I'm not, Max. I'm not!"

For a few seconds there was a silence while Max struggled with all sorts of conflicting emotions. Then the fire of his anger and jealousy seemed to burn itself out against the backfire of his deep love and concern for his sister. He found himself able to turn to practical matters. "For God's sake, at least don't get pregnant. That would really do them in." Max's head and body were bent over as though he had just taken a great deal of punishment. Without raising his eyes, he said, "When it blows, when this great love affair goes pfft, I'm not interested in any I-told-you-sos. Whatever happens, don't do anything stupid. We're a family, and we stick together. Understand?"

"I understand, and I love you, big brother." She went to him, hugging him to her. "But you're wrong. I will be Genie Szabo Husseman."

"We'll see." He looked at Paul who was still asleep. "If you'll help me, I think we can get Sleeping Beauty downstairs to bed without doing him too much damage."

"I suppose we'd better."

As they lifted him from the lounge, Paul stirred and seemed to understand what they were doing. "Where's his bedroom, Genie? You do know, don't you?" In spite of his best intentions, Max couldn't keep the anger out of his voice. Max dumped Paul's body on his bed. Paul moaned slightly in protest and then fell fast asleep.

"That does it. The Husseman servants can clean upstairs tomorrow. Let's go.'' Once in their apartment, they said hello and good night very quickly to their parents.

Anna expressed her usual concern. ''Was everything all right? Nothing happened, did it?''

Max answered for both of them. ''Nothing, Momma. Paul was very tired so we made an early evening of it. That's all. We're going to see him tomorrow.'' He turned to Genie. ''Come into my room for a moment. I have an idea I want to try out on you.''

Genie knew exactly what he had in mind.

''Do you realize how much money Husseman made at no risk?''

''Of course.''

''Do you realize anyone could have done it?''

''I know what you're thinking, but it won't work.''

''If he just had the guts, it would. You heard Paul. He said Dad knows more about building than Mr. Husseman. He could build an apartment house at less cost than anyone.''

''Ten percent less.''

''The only reason we're the super's kids is because Dad doesn't understand how money is made.''

Genie shook her head. ''It's not that simple. He doesn't want to understand.'' Privately she thought that part of what Paul's father had done was downright dishonest. She couldn't imagine her father being dishonest. Beyond the matter of principle, he'd be too afraid. That was the clincher. Their father would always be afraid to take the risks Andre Husseman took.

''Agreed. He hasn't got the balls. But I'm prepared to give him another chance. I'd like to talk to Dad tomorrow at supper. We can spend the day with Paul getting the numbers straight. Take notes so we can present a complete picture.''

''No go, Max. Paul had too much wine. He talked out of turn. He won't again.''

''Your lover boy opened his big fat mouth. Now it's too late for him to close it.''

''Stop calling him my lover boy! Momma and Dad might hear.''

''Paul is going to give us the complete dope. He will, Genie. Believe me, he will!''

''Dad won't do it no matter how much we tell him.''

"Let's give him one more chance to be a man. He's even smart enough to play it straighter than Husseman."

Genie's own desperate desire for money and the idea that their father could make all that money and still be honest was enough to persuade her to try. "I'll talk to Paul first. If he agrees, we both talk. But if he says no, it sticks. Agreed?"

"Agreed!" But even as he agreed, Max thought, that bastard had better come through or, Genie or no Genie, there just may be one battered and bloody Paul Husseman to greet the rich, crooked Andre Husseman on his return. And the reason? The louse seduced my virgin sister.

13

Genie didn't have to call Paul the next day. He called her first, deeply embarrassed and full of apologies for getting drunk and falling asleep. She asked him to meet her for lunch. Paul agreed. He heard the anxiety in her voice and was alerted by the fact that she didn't want to meet him in the apartment. When he arrived at the Ruxton, she was waiting for him.

"What is it, darling?"

Genie managed to smile. "That's it. Darling. Max heard you call me darling last night and guessed everything. In the end, I told him the truth."

Paul reached for her hand. "Oh, Christ! I'm so sorry. I was a drunken damn fool. I didn't mean to make a muck."

Genie stroked his cheek. "It's all right, dear. I made Max understand. We love each other. When people love each other, whatever they do together is right." She pulled her hands back and folded them in her lap. "Max understands."

"That's pretty generous of Max to understand my seduction of his sister."

"We seduced each other." Genie hesitated. "Actually, he's trying to understand. It does bother him." She paused again. "There is one thing you can do that would convince him you mean no harm. It would be a real favor."

"Anything! Just tell me, and I'll do it."

"This is not my idea. It's Max's. All that's important to me is that my parents never know about us."

"What can I do for my future brother-in-law to convince him my intentions are honorable?"

"Max is very interested in real estate. He'll probably go into the business after college. And right now he wants to know more about 608's."

"What more can I tell him? I seem to remember opening my big fat mouth in several areas last night."

"I think he wants more details. Contractors. Numbers. I'll have to be there because I'm the family numbers person."

"Of course I'll tell him whatever I know." Now that there was something concrete he could do to make amends, his self-disgust was slowly dissipating. "Come up to the apartment about two-thirty this afternoon. We'll go over everything."

"Oh, Paul! You are a darling!"

"Sometimes. But I know a better way to prove it."

"You have to see Max first."

"I know. And after that it'll be too late."

"There's tonight."

"No. The servants arrive at five. Cleaning starts the first thing tomorrow. The family's due back Sunday."

"Love will find a way." Genie tried to laugh. They both needed the physical fact of lovemaking to prove nothing had changed between them. But when and where? She settled for, "Anyway, I'm hungry. I didn't eat breakfast this morning."

"I'll bet you didn't." Paul signalled for a waitress.

Late that afternoon after leaving Paul's apartment, Max and Genie went to their place in the park. Max was aware that Paul's information about 608's had caught Genie's imagination. She was as interested as he was.

"It's such a lead-pipe cinch."

Genie sat huddled on the bench, her arms about her body as though she was cold. After a short silence, she disagreed. "It's useless, Max."

"Why? It's a great opportunity."

"I agree, but it's useless."

"Maybe. But we have to give it a try, kidlet. He listens to you." Max put his arm around her shoulder. "Chances like this don't knock on the door every day. Not our door, anyway. And it's our way out, Genie. Aren't you sick of being a second-class citizen?" He was pleading for her support.

Genie said nothing. She would do her best, but nothing Max said would change her opinion.

That night at supper, Max and Genie were unusually quiet. Zoltan talked about how well the installation of new automatic elevators was going. Now they were beginning the rewiring of the entire building. He had supervised the specifications and submitted them to the electrical contractor. As they were finishing their meal, Max said, "Dad, after the dishes are done, Genie and I want to talk to you about an idea we have."

"What kind of an idea, Max?"

"We'll tell you after everything's cleaned up. Then we'll have no interruptions."

Later, in the living room, Zoltan prompted him. "All right, Max. What's your idea?"

"I want to get some notes from my room." Genie and he had spent the end of the afternoon putting Paul's information into shape so Max could explain everything and leave Zoltan the numbers upon which the idea was based. Their father was not a man to make a quick decision on anything, let alone anything as important as what they were going to propose. If he didn't reject it outright, if he studied the possibilities, he just might do it.

Max began. He told how at dinner the previous night, Paul had explained the way Andre Husseman made so much money building 608's. He made no reference to the second meeting that afternoon and finished by saying, "Dad, by using FHA guaranteed loans, one can build apartment houses with no money. In fact, you can walk away with hundreds of thousands of tax-free dollars. The mortgages are borrowed money, debt. What's more, you own the apartment houses and receive income from them."

Zoltan listened with amazement. "You're suggesting I become a builder?"

"Yes! Max moved to the edge of his seat. "Dad, you can be as successful as the Hussemans."

Zoltan turned to Genie. "And you agree this is a good idea?"

"I think it's a wonderful idea. Even Paul says you know more about construction than his father does."

"Where would the money come from to buy the land?"

Genie knew her father wouldn't want to bribe appraisers. "You and Momma have savings. And you can borrow ninety percent from a bank. I'm certain Mr. Husseman would introduce you to the proper bankers."

"But we'd have to move. I couldn't be the superintendent here and be a builder at the same time."

"That's exactly the idea. So we'd move. We almost had to once. This time we'd choose to."

"What do you think, Anna?"

Anna had been listening, unable to believe what she heard. This is what came from things they had been taught in school. Stupid things. And mixing with people above you. You get crazy ideas. Zoltan a builder? Give up his job and their home? She fumbled for an answer. "I don't know. It seems so dangerous. Suppose the building falls down or something?"

Max laughed. "Oh, Momma!"

Zoltan understood. It was Anna's way of expressing how the idea frightened her. "Let me look at the figures, Max." He went over the numbers carefully. "I see. Everything hinges on getting a high appraisal on the land. Suppose the appraiser doesn't think the land is worth so much?"

The best Max could manage was a nervous laugh. "Dad, you've been dealing with inspectors for years. Appraisers are like building inspectors. They're all on the take."

Zoltan shook his head. "Not all, Max. I'm sorry to admit. But not all."

"Okay. Not all, but most. We could use the same bank Mr. Husseman uses. The same appraiser who appraised his land would appraise ours. If he took from Husseman, he'd take from us."

"He probably would."

"About the appraisers, Dad," Genie added. "You notice we save ten percent by your being your own general contractor. Maybe, if we're a little smarter and pay closer attention than Mr. Husseman ever did, we can save even more. Then we wouldn't have to bribe anyone. What do you think, Dad?"

"Nothing is ever as simple as it looks on paper." He saw the anxious looks on his children's faces. Why did they want him to do this so badly? Hadn't they lived good lives with him as a super? Why change things now? In any case, the question was too complicated for him to reach a quick decision. "Genie, Max, let me study the proposal. I'll give you my answer Sunday. Is that fair enough?"

It was the best Max had hoped for. "Of course, Dad. It's too big a decision to make in one night. Sunday's fine."

The subject was changed, and the evening dragged on, slowly, almost sadly. At last it was bedtime. Zoltan watched his children go to their rooms. It was a strange idea. He must think long and hard about it. His eyes turned to the two maps over the couch, to the place where Anna and he had lived in Budapest; then his eyes followed the long, thin line on the 1938 map of Europe—the line that marked how they had come to the United States. He shook his head.

Zoltan slept little that night. He thought of Anna and their small apartment in Budapest. Thinking about Budapest made him remember the last time he had called her by her full name. Szuszuanna. Six years ago, when it had seemed they were going to lose everything. He looked at his wife lying next to him. In spite of everything, she was fast asleep. She trusted him, and would agree with whatever his final decision was. The two maps in the living room kept returning to his mind, and he drifted into another time.

Zoltan and Szuszuanna Szabo were listening to a radio. It was 1938. The announcer was translating a speech made by the prime minister of Great Britain, Neville Chamberlain. Mr. Chamberlain was waving a piece of paper, the Munich Pact, the agreement with the German chancellor, Adolph Hitler, that assured Europe of "peace in our time." Zoltan had recently returned from a long trip on the Danube and Rhine rivers. He worked on a river barge as an engineer, a self-taught engineer. It was his job to keep the creaky, obstinate old engines running and make certain the hull of the barge didn't take in too much water which would spoil the cargo. He had come in close contact with the Nazis on this trip. Out of curiosity, he had purchased a copy of *Mein Kampf* and read it. The book terrified him. It made the Munich Pact a joke. And there was another thing about the book. The Jewish problem. Szuszuanna's grandmother on her father's side had been Jewish. The book stated that anyone with twenty-five percent Jewish blood was Jewish and would be *ausgerotten und ausgeteilt*, ripped out and destroyed. That made Szuszuanna Jewish and subject to the fate Hitler promised all Jews.

He had seen the tanks and planes of the Wehrmacht and Luftwaffe with his own eyes. Why was Hitler building a war machine? A man doesn't build a bicycle to walk. Zoltan switched off the radio.

"There will be a war. Hungary will become a Nazi state."
He looked at his wife. "We have to leave now."

"I know." She was on the verge of tears. "Where can we go?"

"Europe is not safe. France cannot resist Germany. Mussolini will join Hitler. Russia is a communist state. That leaves England. Sweden. Possibly Norway. And the United States. I think the United States would be best. I can find work there."

"The United States? It's so far away—on the other side of the ocean."

"It is far. And it won't be easy. But I don't think we have a choice. We must go."

It took several months to arrange for a visa to admit them to the United States. The trip had been difficult and dangerous, but they made it, arriving in the United States in March of 1939. They stood on the deck of the small boat and saw the Statue of Liberty in New York harbor. That very day, Czechoslovakia was partitioned.

They had only a little money left and spoke a rudimentary English, learned partially in school years ago, but mostly on the long ocean voyage. They settled in a room and kitchen on West 106th Street. The toilet and bath were in the hall. It was a tenement, but it was the Szabo's first home in the United States. Then the struggle for survival began. They improved their English while working at whatever jobs they could find. Anna took in laundry and did housecleaning. Zoltan got a part-time job in an automobile repair shop. They survived the first year by grinding, back-breaking effort. Many a night they lay in each other's arms too tired to do more than hold each other.

On one bitter cold Sunday in January 1941, the oil burner in the building stopped working. There was no heat and no hot water; without hot water, the pipes would freeze and burst. The super was drunk. Even if he had been sober, Zoltan doubted he could do anything.

Using the knowledge that had kept the old rusty river barges operating, Zoltan looked at the burner and saw what was wrong. He went to the repair shop where he worked and took some wire and connectors to replace the corroded parts. Then he fired the burner. It worked. Within minutes the pipes began to clang and clatter as the heat rose, and the building was saved.

On the following Monday, Zoltan received a visit from the

building owner. "Mrs. Harris, in 1D, who is the world's biggest complainer, tells me you saved my building. The oil burner went out Sunday, and you repaired it. Zoltan nodded. "I like a man who can fix things. I own three adjoining buildings a few blocks from here. Tenements like this. I'm offering you a full-time job as super of all three. A free three-room basement apartment with a private toilet goes with the job. Want it?"

"Yes, thank you."

The war had started in Europe shortly after their arrival. With the bombing of Pearl Harbor, the United States entered it. Zoltan registered for the draft, appeared when he was called, filled out all the forms and was sent home. The draft board decided he was not needed. Zoltan had mixed feelings about being rejected, but Anna had none. He had done what the law required, and if Selective Service decided to reject him, that was a great relief to her.

The war created a number of shortages. Among them were competent apartment superintendents. Zoltan heard that Brett, Wyckoff, a large real estate firm, was looking for a super for a huge building on Riverside Drive. He called for an interview, went dressed in his only suit, white shirt, and tie, and was hired on the spot. The only question was when could he start? Zoltan insisted three weeks notice was the minimum he could give his first real employer. The man at Brett, Wyckoff finally agreed.

The building at 135 Riverside Drive was different from the three tenements he'd taken care of. It was twelve stories high, red brick with a large iron pipe railing separating the building from the sidewalk, impressive marble halls, and two elevators. However, many things were the same. Their apartment was still in the basement, and everything in the building from the elevators to the oil burner to the roof needed constant repair. Zoltan had to keep the elevators running, sufficient heat and hot water available, and the tar roof patched and watertight. Supplies were scarce. Neither was it easy carrying Anna twenty-seven blocks to Roosevelt Hospital that snowy night in 1945 when Max was born.

At last the war ended. Zoltan's ability to keep a building operating under difficult conditions came to the attention of Brown, Harris, Stevens, Inc. The superintendent's job had become available at the Majestic, one of the most important buildings on the West Side. The building employed sixty workers, but it had its own problems. A superintendent had to have electrical and mechanical skills, an understanding of paint and plaster, glazing, waterproofing, and be able to manage the huge staff plus cater to the tenants' needs. Zoltan fit the requirements perfectly. He got the job, one of the best of its kind in the city.

"Oh, Zoltan! Our apartment is so beautiful! Six rooms. And on the first floor. Not in the basement." At the age of thirty-seven, Zoltan felt he had a fine job for life. One that put a secure roof over his family's head. That year, 1947, a second child was born, a girl they named Eugenia.

Zoltan rose the next morning thinking of his children. They were right. Becoming a builder would be a truly wonderful thing. He had done a brave thing once in leaving Hungary. But now he was fifty-three, and he had been frightened for so many years. Could he be brave again? He decided to allow himself the luxury of studying the numbers and thinking about the possibilities during the time remaining until Sunday evening.

Max had been on an emotional roller coaster for the last few days. One moment absolutely certain Zoltan would agree, and the next moment convinced he wouldn't. Genie hadn't helped. She was resigned, certain their father wouldn't do it. If their mother had been a different sort of woman, he might have, but she was as she was. Max had several arguments with Genie—one of them shattering.

"He might do it. Don't you think he just might?"

"I think he'd like to, but you saw Momma's face. She'll add to his being afraid. He wants to, but he won't. If nothing else, he'll worry he's too old."

"He's not too old. He's just right. With all the experience . . ." Max grew more heated. "He will. He has to, or . . ."

"Or what? He's our father. You can't beat him up, Max. Whatever he decides is the way it will be." Genie retreated to her room and shut the door.

Max was shocked at the idea he'd consider beating up his father, and even more shocked that that was exactly what had passed through his mind. He knocked gently on Genie's door. "Genie, I only meant . . ."

She opened the door slowly. "I know what you meant." She

patted his cheek. "Look, I want this as much as you do. But you have to grow up. You can't get mad at our father for being what he is."

Sunday was Zoltan's day off. Anna and he spent it in the park, visiting the zoo, taking a rowboat ride on the lake, and walking around the reservoir. Anna waited all day for Zoltan to bring up Max and Genie's proposal. She silently prayed he would not be led astray. On the walk back to the apartment, Zoltan pointed to a small, deserted gazebo standing on a spit of land that extended into the lake.

"Let's sit there. We still have time before supper."

Anna knew the time had come. They held hands looking out at the water. "Have you thought about what Max and Genie suggested?"

"Yes." Anna's voice was neutral.

"Well? What do you think of their idea? Would you like to be the wife of a builder?"

Anna felt her worst fears were about to be realized. Zoltan was going to leave his secure job, give up the home she loved for reasons she did not understand. She studied the dirt and rock under her feet. Then asked, "Why do you want to be a builder? Have you not been happy all these years? I have."

"Most of the time, but . . ."

For the first time in their married life, Anna interrupted her husband. "But now you want to leave your job, leave everything we've worked so hard for to chase a dream?"

"Not a dream, Anna. It is real. I have studied all the information, and I know everything a builder needs to know. I've done most of the things with my own hands." He focused on the one part of the idea that bothered him, and he assumed it bothered Anna as well. "Also, we won't have to bribe anyone."

"But you would have to leave your job?"

"Yes?"

Anna shook her head. How could she explain to her husband that people such as they do not become builders? This belief had become so much a part of her life it almost assumed a religious status. She knew she couldn't give good reasons, but God would punish them. The building would fail, and they would be left with no money, no job, no home. She thought of the recent months. First Max decided to go to college. Now Zoltan wants to be a builder. Next Genie will want to go to college. The world must be mad to permit such things. She faced Zoltan. "Then you are saying you want to be a builder?"

"Yes, I do, but I also want to please you."

Anna realized she must take a position. It went against her nature, but if she did not, the entire family would be lost. So she said what she had to say. "I do not like the idea. It does not please me!"

The blunt way Anna stated her view took Zoltan by surprise. He knew the idea frightened her, but he now realized he had underestimated her fears. "Why, Anna? Why do you not want me to be a builder?"

"Because it is wrong. People should be content to live the lives they were born to live."

"Some people change. Grow."

"I do not want to change, and I do not want you to change."

Zoltan did not know what to do. If he proceeded, his children would be pleased and his wife miserable. If he didn't, he would most likely lose the respect of his children, but his wife would be pleased. It was in the nature of the man to place his own desires last. He would like to be a builder, but to live the rest of his life as a superintendent was not the worst thing in the world. He would be reasonably happy. Above all, he wanted to be fair. What was fair? Max was going to college and then to work. Genie would graduate from high school next year. She would also leave home either to go to college, or to work, or to marry. It would all end the way it started. Anna and he alone. His ultimate loyalty belonged to Anna. Their life together was the one that would endure. But he felt he owed it to his children to make one final effort.

Anna was waiting. She realized if Zoltan had to do this madness, she would follow him. It was a wife's duty to follow her husband, and she had been raised to be a good wife.

So it turned out that Zoltan's basic nature conspired to betray him. Had he put his wishes ahead of everyone, Anna would have had no choice but to agree. Instead he asked again for her approval. "Anna, Max and Genie will be so disappointed if I do not become a builder. If you think about it, you'll see it's a very good idea."

At this, Anna buried her head in her hands; her body racked

with dry sobbing. When she finally looked up, her face was distorted. She said aloud what she had been saying to herself for so many years. "They are young. They will survive. It is good for children to be disappointed. It prepares them for what will happen later in life." Her voice grew stronger. "No! No matter how Max and Genie feel, I do not wish you to leave your job and home."

Zoltan surrendered. The dream would remain a dream. "All right. It is decided." He took her hand again. "We must go home and tell the children. It is not good to keep their hopes up any longer than necessary."

They left the park at 72nd Street and arrived at the apartment to find Max and Genie waiting.

They looked at their father. He didn't have to speak. Genie knew. His whole face said no. She glanced towards Max, wanting to comfort him. He was still staring at Zoltan waiting for his words. He'd refused to see what she saw.

At last Zoltan began. "I've spent a lot of time studying your proposal. It is very well thought out, but . . ."

Max interrupted. He realized what the answer would be. "But you won't do it. Why, Dad?" He needed an explanation very badly.

"Because I can't. Because I'm too old." He could have said that he wanted to and used Anna's hatred of the idea as an excuse, but Zoltan accepted the decision as his. It was his responsibility so he used Anna's arguments as his own. "Because it's wrong for people like your mother and me to try to do things we weren't born to do. And because I don't want to risk losing what we have."

In spite of his love for his father, Max couldn't help saying, "And because you're too frightened."

"You could say that. But you could also say your mother and I have come a long way from our birthplace. I think it's far enough."

"It's not far enough. There's no limit to how far you can reach in the United States. It's not like Hungary."

"Yes it is, in a way. There are always those who go further. Even in Hungary. Not nearly as many as in the United States, but some." He was desperate, pleading with his son for some understanding and continued respect. "I can't do it, Max. I just can't."

"If I were older, I'd do it without you."

"And maybe that would be the right decision for you."

Max made a supreme effort to control himself. This was his father. His family. He stood up and walked over to the couch to face Zoltan. Genie tensed, watching him. He might say or do anything. Zoltan looked up at his tall, strong, blond, Magyar son and waited.

It took Max several minutes to understand and accept his father's reality. No matter what the reason, Zoltan Szabo was going to remain a superintendent, Anna Szabo was going to remain the wife of a superintendent, and Genie and he would always be the children of a superintendent. Although he could not change the past, he would not accept the meaning the past held for his parents. He would not accept the limitations his father had set on his and Anna's life. Once he was secure in that, it was a short step to another decision. If he went to college, it would be as the son of a superintendent, and he would graduate, after four years, still the son of a superintendent. What was worse, as Zack had made clear, he would be no more equipped to make real money than he was this minute. And he'd be four years older. All the doubts and questions he'd been asking himself during the summer resolved themselves. If he was going to make the kind of money Genie and he had talked about so often, if he was going to rise above being the son of a superintendent and carry the rest of his family with him, the sooner he got started the better.

Max sat next to his father, put his arm around the older man's shoulders and hugged him. "It's all right, Dad. It really is. You did what you could do. Now it's up to us."

Genie had watched her brother and knew every twist and turn in his mind. She was so close to tears—she wasn't certain whether the tears were for her father or her brother—she didn't trust herself to speak. When Max turned from Zoltan to face her, she knew what he was going to say.

"I'm sorry, kidlet, but like Dad, I've made a decision. I've had it up to here with being a second-class citizen. No college. No Cornell. I'm going to work."

Genie made no effort to change Max's mind. Even though his words distressed her, a large part of her agreed with them. During the summer, Paul had told her about some of the scholastic limitations an athletic scholarship put on all except the most dedicated students, and Max wasn't that dedicated. And it was also true if the family was going to rise further in the world, if the family was going to seize the rich promise America offered, it would be up to them, up to Max and her. Zoltan and Anna had come as far as they could.

PART THREE

1968–1970

14

Genie opened her eyes and blinked at the daylight filtering through the cotton curtains of her bedroom window. She'd graduated from Hunter College a week ago, magna cum laude. The super's kid took honors. She remembered the look of pride on her father's face, of pleasure on Max's, and her mother's strained disapproving expression. It seemed to Genie she'd spent her life running a race against her mother's disapproval, a race she couldn't win.

Max and she had agreed she would take one week off before putting into operation a plan they'd been discussing for years. She'd spent as much of the week as possible with Paul. They'd made love in every convenient place and some that weren't so convenient. Just thinking about the week of lovemaking was enough to send shivers of delight running up her thighs and through her belly. She knew all she would have to do was touch herself the way Paul did, and she'd have an orgasm. But despite the years of giving herself to Paul, freely and openly, there remained something about masturbation that bothered her. What was beautiful and right with Paul was somehow wrong without him.

Now the week was over, and they had to get on with their lives. Paul was starting a new production, John Millington Synge's *Deirdre of the Sorrows*, and she had an appointment to meet Max at his office for lunch. Max had explained that for once their timing was perfect. He knew of a job opening that had just come on the market. Not just a job, but exactly the job she was looking for. One working for a large real estate firm that managed a number of buildings in Manhattan. The head of the management department needed an assistant. When Genie questioned her qualifications for such an important job, Max laughed and said, "Of course you're qualified. Didn't they

159

teach you everything you need in that college? Besides,'' he gave her a comic wink, ''I've kind of got the inside track on this one.'' He wouldn't tell her what he meant by that, and he wouldn't tell her either the name of the firm for which she'd be working or the name of her boss. He was saving that information for today's lunch. Since Max was playing some sort of game with her, she had no choice but to go along with it.

After showering she looked over her summer clothes. Years ago Genie had learned how to make her own clothes. She preferred dresses cut along classic lines, the kind worn by girls living in the Majestic. They were dresses sold in stores like Bonwit Teller and Henri Bendel; dresses she couldn't afford to buy, even on sale. Fortunately these dresses were also the easiest to make, and Genie had put together a fashionable wardrobe.

Max's office was on the fifth floor of a small six-story building on Fifth Avenue between 48th and 49th streets. Genie stood in front of the building staring up at the large windows on the fifth floor. The name Robert Alpert & Company Real Estate was printed across the windows. She felt a mild disappointment. Never having been to Max's office before and judging from the money he was making, she expected something much grander. The office itself was another suprise. Facing the small elevator was a reception area with the cheapest dark asphalt tile on the floor, a few hard-backed chairs, and a girl sitting at a grey metal desk. She was very busy handling the switchboard while simultaneously doing the bookkeeping. The office occupied the entire floor. There was a low wooden partition that separated the men working at three large, battered desks and a secretary from the rest of the office.

The rest of the office consisted of file cabinets against the two side walls and a twin row of desks between them. The only other windows were in the rear. A conference room took up some of the rear wall blocking whatever light might have come through the rear windows. Except for the conference room, there was no privacy at all. About twenty men of all sizes, shapes, and ages, their shirt sleeves rolled up, were hunched over in chairs at their desks attached, as though by flesh, to phones in their ears. Their job was to lease or sell real estate, and they were doing exactly that. Genie thought they sounded like barkers in a circus.

She waited in front of the receptionist for her presence to be acknowledged. Then she saw Max, his hair falling over his eyes, his shirt collar open, and his tie dangling around his waist hurrying towards her. He had on a light gray pair of pants that matched his grey shirt and tie. Watching him approach had its usual effect. Genie's heart lifted. Next to Paul, he was the most attractive man in the world. He put his hands on her shoulders and all but hugged her. Then he stepped back and looked her up and down, appraising her. He smiled. "Kidlet, you look great!"

"Thank you. And so do you."

"Hungry?"

"Starved. Low blood sugar count."

"Me, too. We'll take in the leg show at Rockefeller Plaza."

They sat at an outdoor table next to the fountain with a huge gold-painted statue of a nude woman looming above them. Genie sipped her wine while Max watched her over the rim of his martini. She waited for him to tell her who she was going to see after lunch. But when he finished his martini, he was off on another subject. He wanted to keep playing his game a little longer.

"I just closed a nice deal with Chic Frocks."

Genie was irritated enough with his game playing to correct him. "It's not chic like in baby chick. It's chic like in sheik. You know. Those guys in the white sheets who ride camels in the desert."

"Stop it. Even if I didn't go to college, I grew up where you grew up, and this guy called his company Chic Frocks. Like in baby chick, as you put it. At least I had the brains to close the deal before giving him the benefit of my superior culture. And you know what he said?"

"What?" Genie was trying not to laugh.

"He said, 'Kid, what's your commission on this deal?' I figured my share came to about eighteen hundred dollars, so I said two thousand. And he said, 'That's great, kid. I take double that out of this joint every week. If I call it Chick Frocks, it's Chick Frocks. Got it?' I got it and got the hell out of there clutching the commission check in my hot clammy hand."

"Oops! Sorry!"

"Forget it. Anyway, it's only one deal, and you know, while leasing and sales are the icing on the cake, managing buildings is the cake itself. That takes real know-how and a numbers mind. You know numbers, and you've had a head start watching Dad since we were kids."

"Will you please tell me what kind of an interview you've arranged for this afternoon?"

"I thought you'd never ask." Max kept a straight face.

"If you don't tell me . . ." She held her wineglass over his head as thought about to pour it over him. That the glass was empty made no difference.

Max held his hands up, palms out. "Don't shoot! Your feet solidly planted on the ground?"

"Go on."

"You're sure you're ready for this?" She didn't answer him. "You are going to work for Jack O'Neil, senior vice-president of Brown, Harris, Stevens, Inc. He needs a new assistant."

The words popped out of Genie's mouth. "But he's Dad's boss!"

"Right! He is Dad's boss."

"Would Dad be working for me?"

"Right again. That's why I didn't tell you sooner. I didn't want you to get the shakes. Or say no."

"Whew! That does take some getting used to."

"Want another drink?"

"No. Max? Exactly how did you set this up?"

There was that damned grin again. "We just happened to share the same virgin last winter. One night she got her dates screwed up, sorry about the bad pun, and we met. Anyway, as the girl faded into the morning mist, it was the start of a beautiful friendship." He smiled. "That reminds me. Did Paul and you ever get to see *Casablanca*?"

"Shut up!"

"Anyway, I spent the rest of the winter getting him laid."

"Isn't he married?"

"My dear sister, as we both know, you are not Miss Goody-Two-Shoes. Married men fuck."

"Would you swear it?"

"Yeah! More so when they have alcoholic wives. Anyway

he does have an opening for an assistant, and he's agreed to meet you.''

"What else does he have an opening for?''

"Nothing. Unless you agree. Just make sure you learn the business.''

"I wonder what Dad will say?''

The laughter disappeared as Max's face clouded over in sudden anger. "I don't give a damn what he says or thinks. He had his chance a long time ago and blew it. Genie, we've talked about this for a long time. Mr. Outside leasing and selling space, and Miss Inside managing the buildings and running the operation. This is your opportunity to become a first-class Miss Inside. If you want to blow it, just keep worrying about Dad.'' Max's expression softened. "Remember, kidlet, it's you and me against them.'' He waved his arm gesturing around the large, open-air restaurant. "And there's one hell of a lot of them.''

"Szabo and Szabo against the world?''

"That's about it.'' Max stretched in his chair. "Let's order lunch, and do not think of me as the family pimp.''

Max left Genie at the door of the Brown, Harris, Stevens, Inc. building on East 47th Street. "He's on the third floor. Expecting you. The job's a shoo-in. Call me when you've finished, and we'll celebrate.''

"I'm meeting Paul tonight at his theater. He's started rehearsals on a new play. Come along. I know you think the theater is a zoo, but you always liked the zoo.''

"Not since I've become a female animal trainer. But call me afterward. I want to hear how you bearded the lion.''

Genie watched her brother walk toward Fifth Avenue. He had a kind of animal grace with just a touch of predatory ruthlessness beneath it. Every woman he walked by glanced at him with interest. Genie felt her determination reinforced by his strength. If Max had such confidence in her, she had to do him proud. Do the family proud. She had to get the job.

The reception room on the third floor of the Brown, Harris office was done in shades of brown. The floors were carpeted in dark brown, the walls were painted beige, and the girl behind the reception desk had managed a deep summer tan even though it was still June. There was a look of surprise on her face.

"Miss Szabo? You're Miss Szabo?"

"Yes. Do you know the name?"

"Well, yes." The receptionist flushed. "Zoltan Szabo is the superintendent of the Majestic. When I saw the name on my appointment calendar, I assumed it was Mr. Szabo. It's such an unusual name."

"I'm his daughter."

"Oh. I see. I'll tell Mr. O'Neil you're here."

Jack O'Neil sat behind the desk in his comfortable office. Along with the same brown carpet as the reception area, a brown leather couch, and easy chairs, one whole wall was filled by a row of brown file cabinets. These files contained the lifeblood of his job—a ten-year record of every transaction in every building he currently managed or had managed in the past. Covering the wall opposite the file cabinets was a collection of photographs of apartment houses; once again all either were or had been managed at one time by him. The address and name—if the building had a name—were below each photograph. The picture of the Mighty Majestic was in the center of the wall. It was twice the size of the other pictures and seemed to be the keystone to the entire collection.

O'Neil was forty-five years old. He sat with his head high and his back straight, with the practiced posture of a onetime athlete. That, along with his slightly too heavy features, his well-manicured hands, his dark blond hair greying at the temples, and his well-concealed paunch, gave him the look of the kind of man one usually sees on television advertising expensive cars. He rose and extended his hand. "It's a pleasure to meet you, Miss Szabo."

"My pleasure, Mr. O'Neil." Genie sat in a straight-backed chair facing the desk.

O'Neil waited for her to settle herself before beginning. "Although, given your background, I'm certain you already know much of what I have to say, I think the best way for us to begin is for me to explain exactly what goes into managing an apartment house in New York City."

Genie smiled at his assumption of her knowledge. "Of course. If you assume total ignorance, there's no chance of leaving me with an incorrect or incomplete understanding of what you expect from your assistant."

"Right! But the fact is you do have an advantage over most of the other applicants for this job."

Other applicants? This wasn't quite the shoo-in Max had painted.

"To begin, we're responsible for collecting the rents in buildings where the tenants lease their apartments and the maintenance in co-ops such as the Majestic. But if collecting monthly checks were all there was to managing a building, there wouldn't be a job for me, and you wouldn't be sitting here. Our major responsibility is to see to it that the buildings are properly maintained, and at the same time not spend so much money that there's nothing left for the owner or, in the case of a co-op, that the maintenance gets too high. The most important person in this process is the building superintendent. You would have to work very closely with our supers." He paused, waiting for Genie to give him the obvious response—how she grew up with a super for a father and was certain she could work very well with supers.

When Genie didn't refer to her father the way he expected, O'Neil understood her reason and liked her self-assurance. "We try very hard to get the best available men for all our buildings, because although a super is paid by the building where he works, he really represents Brown, Harris at that building. An excellent super, such as your father, can make our job much easier. O'Neil laughed. "You know, superintendents are a little like psychiatrists. Very few are excellent. Some are good, but, despite our best efforts, most are average or indifferent. It's when they're average or indifferent . . ."

Genie understood he would never use the word poor when talking about a super hired by Brown, Harris.

Listening to Jack O'Neil extol her father's abilities—abilities of which Genie was very well aware—Genie wondered whether being her father's daughter was such a great advantage. It should be, but it was possible he might be concerned with having another Szabo dealing with the Majestic. Then there was the business of Max and him sharing women. That was also a two-edged sword. He might think the Szabos were occupying too much space in his life.

O'Neil continued. "Along with collecting the monthly

checks and making certain the building is properly maintained without robbing Fort Knox, we also have to deal with the people who live in the buildings, and like all human beings, be they renters or owners, each person is different and has to be treated as an individual.''

' O'Neil studied Genie. There was something disconcerting about this beautiful young woman who sat so still and listened to him tell her things she must have heard all her life. He realized she was highly intelligent. The way she presented herself was evidence in itself. She was a faithful replica of the manner, tone, and dress of the young women living at the Majestic. It spoke well for her powers of observation and her ability to absorb what she had seen. Then he had another thought. There was one question he hadn't considered. What would the shareholders of the Majestic think about his hiring her? Was she one Szabo too many?

As they continued to talk, Genie tried to estimate her man. She realized his first sight of her surprised and pleased him. Jack O'Neil liked to look at and be around attractive women. That gave her a slight advantage. The longer they talked, the more she wanted the job; the more she realized it was the right job for her, for Max's and her future plans. She also came to the conclusion her first concern was correct. Being her father's daughter was not an advantage. She was one Szabo too many. Therefore, it was important she convince this man she was both knowledgeable and professional.

"You know my major in college was math. And I've taken courses in business administration at night. So, I believe, in addition to what I already know, there's very little I won't be able to pick up in short order.'' The time had arrived for her to face up to what had to be O'Neil's major concern. "I probably won't be of much use dealing with the Majestic since, as you say, my father does his job so well.'' She half smiled. "But, when I have to deal with superintendents not quite as capable— average or indifferent to use your words—I certainly would bring a lot of knowledge I acquired at home to bear on the problems.'' She made her point more precise. "That is, in all the other buildings you manage.''

O'Neil was surprised Genie understood his problem in hiring her and had even suggested a solution. She was correct. There was no reason for her to deal with the Majestic at all. Members of the board of directors might bump into her when they came to the office for their monthly meeting or to work on a special problem concerning the building. He wondered how she would handle that. "Suppose a member of the board of the Majestic arrives with a problem one day when I'm out of the office?"

"Andre Husseman once told Max and me that children, drunks, shareholders, and even members of the board of directors have much in common and should be treated in somewhat the same way: With some understanding, with every consideration, but above all, with firmness." She didn't blink as O'Neil roared with laughter. The impact of the Husseman name was unmistakable.

O'Neil vaguely remembered Husseman asking him, years ago, to do away with some sort of restriction regarding the Szabos. If she was good enough for the Hussemans, she certainly should be able to handle anyone else. "Do you know any of the other people in the building?"

"Not as well as the Hussemans, but I know most of them."

"Umhumph." He decided to try another line of questions. "Why do you want to be in the real estate business?"

Her answer was immediate. "It's the business I was born into."

"I suppose it is at that." Jack O'Neil had rarely met a job applicant who seemed as qualified as Eugenia Szabo. What's more, he liked her enthusiasm, understanding, and acceptance of his problems. "What's your idea of a starting salary?"

"Twelve-five. That's what I've been offered by another firm." She gave the number so flatly, O'Neil accepted it.

"Twelve-five is high for a beginner here."

"Oh?" The job was hers. She wanted to fling her arms around him in sheer relief. Now that she knew she was going to be offered the job, Genie looked forward to the negotiations. "What a shame. I'd rather work here. I'd feel so at home." She leaned forward. "What do you think would be a fair starting salary?"

O'Neil considered eleven-five, and they would compromise on twelve. Oh, shit, he thought! Give her the twelve and get done with it. "Uhm. Twelve is as high as we could go."

"Twelve thousand?"

"Yes. And three weeks vacation." He found himself trying to convince her.

"Three weeks vacation. That does add something. Yes. I think for Brown, Harris it's fine."

"Then it's settled? Can you start Monday?"

"For Brown, Harris I could start Sunday."

They both laughed, and O'Neil said, "That won't be necessary. I'll introduce you to our office manager. She'll have the usual forms for you to fill out. W-2's and the like."

Genie watched him go. Only when he left the room did she permit herself to clap her hands together, lean back in her chair, and kick her feet into the air in sheer glee. She thought, wait until I tell Max. And Paul. And Dad. And Mom. The thought of telling her parents brought her feet back on the ground and some of the pleasure left Genie's face.

15

Theater Four was in an old building on Fourth Street that many years ago had been a popular bar and restaurant. Before Paul leased it, it had also been used as a church, a porno film studio, and was empty a good part of the time between such tenants. Now it was enjoying a new life as a theater, but not a Broadway-style theater. Paul's repertory company had no extra money to refurbish the exterior of the building. They needed every penny to put on their plays.

The stage was a platform surrounded on three sides by six rows of benches. The only concession to comfort was that the benches had wooden backs. Should a wooden bench prove too uncomfortable for the tender rear end of anyone in the audience, pillows were available for rent. At the start, Paul had found it surprising how few pillows were rented, but in time he had come to regard Off Broadway audiences as very hard-assed people. Genie sat in the last row of the empty theater and watched Paul directing the actors. As usual, he wore faded blue jeans and a T-shirt that outlined his lean body. Paul was almost as tall as Max but probably weighed forty pounds less. His long jaw ended in the same square chin as his father's. This, along with his high cheekbones and aquiline nose, emphasized his flat, almost hollow cheeks. Everything combined to give him a gaunt, intense look that was added to by his straight black hair which fell over his forehead and which he had to keep brushing back from his deep-set almost black eyes. His voice, although gentle, was authoritative.

"Let's take that again, Jackie. Understand. You are not Medea. You are not about to kill your two children. You're a sixteen-year-old pagan Irish princess. It's the eighth century. While there's been a prophecy of disaster, you're young and in love. Remember, you were lying on that rock and you saw

Naisi ride by, probably bare-assed, and your little clitoris is all atwitter over him. Your problem is you've been raised to marry the king of the five parts of Ireland. And he's an old man. He's thirty-two. And that's old. Make it lighter, more lilt. Save doom and gloom for the third act." He waited.

Jackie's voice was deep and rich. She affected a touch of an Irish brogue.

I will dress like Emer in Dundaelgan, or Maeve in her house in Connaught. If Conchubor'll make me a queen, I'll have the right of a Queen who is a master, taking her own choice and making a stir to the edge of the sea . . . Lay out your mats and hangings where I can stand this night and look about me. Lay out the skins of the rams of Connaught and of the goats of the west. I will not be a child or plaything; I'll put on my robes that are the richest, for I will not be brought down to Emain as Cuchulain brings his horse to the yoke, or Conall Cearneach puts his shield upon his arm; and maybe from this day I will turn the men of Ireland like a wind blowing on the heath.

Listening to the beautiful lines and Paul's comments, Genie was filled with respect for her lover. Paul had all the natural force to be a great actor. It was this force that held his actors in line. Actors could be as temperamental as electric eels. Especially Jacqueline Bates. Genie had to admit Jackie was about the most physically exciting young woman she had ever seen. Everything about her from her natural red-gold hair and alabaster skin to her slim yet rounded body and long muscular legs exuded sex. Raw, female sex. She projected so much sensuality her working closely with Paul made Genie uncomfortable. It was easy to forget she was a fine actress who had studied for years with Lee Strasberg at the Actors Studio. She was going to be a major star. Paul had explained to Genie he didn't think he could hold Jackie for more than one or two more plays, and she half wondered if it were only Jackie's acting he disliked losing.

"Okay. Knock it off for today. Jackie, sweetie, it's better. Remember, keep it light and make it sing. Synge wrote poetry. It's got to sing." He raised his voice. "Everybody, tomorrow at twelve noon."

Paul had seen her come in as, without seeming to, he noticed everything that went on in the theater. Suddenly there he was, towering over her. Looking into his black eyes, she found herself held. His look was so bold, so provocative, she could feel herself blushing. "Paul, darling, you're undressing me in public." His look said he knew exactly what she looked like, either clothed or stark naked. Genie felt her heartbeat quicken, a small pulse beat in her throat.

"You have something in mind, sir?"

"As a matter of fact, yes. But first there's a cast party we have to look in on."

"Must we?"

"We must. It's a celebration for the beginning of the production. On West 9th Street. Why don't we stop in at O'Henry's for a bite. Then I'll pick up a bottle of champagne and we'll amble on."

"If we must, we must." She stood tiptoe and kissed his nose. "I've something to tell you."

"What, you have something to tell me?"

"Yes, I have something to tell you." Laughing, they slipped into one of their old childhood games. "I'm going away."

"What, you're going away?"

"Yes, I'm going away, but before I go, I have something to tell you."

"What, you have something to tell me?"

"Yes. My telephone number." She giggled as she ended the round robin.

"What telephone number?"

"The one at my new job. I've gotten a job."

"Wow! Great! Where?"

"Brown, Harris, Stevens, Inc."

"Our managing agents. Doing what?"

"I'm Jack O'Neil's new assistant."

Paul's expression changed. "I'm not sure I like that. I've heard the man's a devoted cocksman. Although a damn good managing agent."

"My dear Mr. Husseman, because I permit you certain liberties with the more intimate parts of my body, there is no reason to think of me as either Miss Round Heels or Catherine the Great."

He tousled her hair. "Make sure you can outrun him around the desk."

"I'll wear sneakers to work."

After picking up the champagne, they walked hand in hand up Sixth Avenue and turned east on 9th Street. It was one of the quieter streets in the Village, lined on both sides with old houses from another era of life in New York City. Genie wondered who in the cast was wealthy enough to live in any one of these houses.

They stopped halfway down the street in front of a four-story brick building of Georgian design. The building was set back from the street, and the intervening space, filled with a garden of bushes and blossoms, was enclosed by an iron fence and gate. A flagstone walk led to the outer entrance. To the left, on the ground floor facing the street, double windows set with multicolored stained glass lent a painted gaiety to the classic lines of the architecture. One of the windows was open, and they could hear the sound of someone at a harpsichord playing the Bach "Goldberg Variations."

"They're here already?" Genie asked.

"No. That's not the apartment. There are two per floor. The party's in the ground floor rear apartment. It has a garden."

Watching Paul open the gate, Genie wondered about his words. There was something odd going on. She followed him along the stone path to the front door and waited while he opened it. There was a series of bells next to the mailboxes. Genie counted eight, two to a floor. Paul fumbled in his pocket and pulled out a key. He smiled, a little crookedly, at her. "I sometimes sleep here. When the lady is out, of course."

"You sleep here?"

He didn't answer. Instead he opened the inner door which led into the house proper. The entire hallway was papered in a warm brown and white patterned paper. There was a broad staircase to the right, carpeted in a matching brown, that led to the upper floors. It wasn't deep, as Genie discovered, following Paul to the rear apartment. A jewel box of a house. He took another key and opened the door. What Genie saw was a beautifully proportioned room, not large, but with an air of spaciousness and calm. The rear wall was a series of windows very much like the front except the panes of glass were clear. She could see a kitchen to the left and a bedroom beyond that. But it was absolutely empty; there was no furniture anywhere. The walls were white and newly painted, making each room seem larger.

Genie followed Paul into the apartment. "Paul, who lives here?"

"You do."

"Me?"

"The lease is in your name."

"I can't afford it."

"I pay the rent. It's our new home. Or should I say our first home?"

"What about your apartment?"

"That's for appearances. My parents. Your parents. I had to wait until you graduated. All girls move out of their parents' home when they graduate. Rebecca's sharing an apartment on East 63rd Street with another girl."

"They move out, but not into an apartment like this. At least not on my salary. My father is too smart. He'll guess the truth. My mother will go out of her mind."

"My darling, you underestimate my ability to plan ahead. You have a roommate. Jackie Bates. You share expenses. You saw her today. She can play any part I assign her, and she knows she's on call whenever your parents are due to appear. We'll work it out."

"Jacqueline Bates?" There was something about it that she didn't like. On second thought, she knew very well what it was. Jackie Bates was too attractive. She was jealous.

Paul put his arms around her, easing his body against her. "Do you mind very much, darling? Now we'll have a home. It'll make everything much simpler. We can furnish it together."

Genie slipped out of his arms. She wandered to the rear windows and looked out. The rear yard was small, enclosed by a high picket fence, and it had a beautiful rose garden that was in bloom. She passed through the kitchen, Paul following her, into the bedroom. "You bought one piece yourself," she murmured. "The bed." Oh, how she loved him. She would have to take the risk and try to make this apartment work.

"No. Not the whole bed. The spring and mattress. You pick the frame and headboard." Genie felt the beauty of the apartment adding to her always present desire for him. The silent rooms with their thick white walls and sense of secrecy cast their own spell. She and Paul stumbled toward the bare mattress in the bedroom. They undressed as quickly as possible. They stood, naked, looking at each other. Genie's young body, perfectly balanced, had the lines of a slender woman together with an unexpected ripeness. Her waist was small which gave her breasts an even greater prominence. There was no sag, no strain to mar their perfection. Her back was as straight as a dancer's and every movement set off the rich fullness of her hips and buttocks.

Paul appeared more handsome, more compelling than even before: strong, masculine, vital. His penis was hard. She waited for him to move, but he stood still. The waiting made her body ache. She had to touch him. She knelt and took it in her mouth. As she ran her tongue over the tip, she could taste the first, slightly salty emission. Her lips moved up and down the entire length. They were entering into a world of their own.

The sound of a bell ended their sense of isolation. The bell sounded again. It was a doorbell. Their doorbell. Someone was outside ringing their front doorbell, and they were naked about to make love.

Genie looked up at Paul. She was frightened and whispered, "Who knows we're here? Who?"

"No one. Well, er, yes. I had to tell Jackie about the apartment to get her to agree."

"You told that . . . Oh, Paul. Damn! Damn! Damn! Where's the intercom? There has to be one. Probably in the hall."

"I'll look." He dashed out of the room. "Here it is. I'll send them away." She could hear the sound of a buzzer. Oh, Christ! He hadn't pushed the speaker button. He'd pushed the button letting whoever was outside into the house. She scrambled for her dress. Her panty hose would have to wait.

There was a loud knock on the door, and a female voice called out. "Let us in, oh director mine. It's Deirdre, Naisi, Conchubor, and the rest of your talented crew. We have come to help you celebrate your lady's escape from her prison north of 14th Street."

Genie could hear loud laughter in the hall. The bitch! They

were waiting for us, and she timed it perfectly. She knew, and she did it on purpose. The absolute bitch!

Paul rushed back into the bedroom. "It's the . . ." He stopped, seeing Genie trying to get her dress zipped up.

"I know. I heard them. And you have about ten seconds to get something on, because I'm about to let them in."

Before she could leave the room, she heard the front door being opened, and a voice, female of course, said, "Here we come, naked or not."

Genie managed to meet them in the living room. They were laughing and passing open bottles of wine back and forth. A young, very handsome man, probably Naisi, saw her. "Ah, the mistress of this fine establishment. We have come to welcome you and make you feel as one of us. Welcome, kind lady. Thrice welcome from all of us to all of you."

Jackie asked, "And where exactly is the master of the house? Adjusting his jockstrap, no doubt."

Genie allowed herself to be carried along with the energy and just plain fun the actors brought into the room. She and Paul would have other times.

"Ah, there he is. My God! He's dressed! Is this any way to greet your friends? With clothes on. Shame on you for false modesty."

"Cut it out, Jackie." Paul looked nervously at Genie, trying to estimate how upset she was.

"Nonsense. We had planned to be your audience. Every stroke, every sigh, every moan, every groan, every tremor, every quiver, every quake would have been subjected to the closest scrutiny and greeted with wild applause. We came to admire the majesty of your performance. The lilt and the poetry in your movement." Her voice dropped. "And here you are, dressed and ready for a party. No performance. What a loss to your lovers and admirers."

"Knock it off."

"But were we too soon or too late?"

Genie answered. "You'll never know."

"It makes no difference. We have brought all that is needed to christen your new house: wine, women, men, and pot. So I say, let the celebration commence."

The actors arranged themselves in various parts of the living room. One opened a package of plastic glasses. Everyone, including Genie, sat on the floor drinking the wine. Two actors were busy rolling marijuana joints and putting toothpicks through them. Soon, one could smell the unmistakably sweet smell of the marijuana. Voices grew quieter as the people gradually sorted themselves out into smaller groups.

At one point, Genie had a chance to have a quiet word with Jackie. "That was a pretty rotten stunt, even if it was funny. I wonder what you would have done in my place?"

"You really wonder what I would have done if a noisy group of bums broke in while I was getting fucked? I'd have killed them." She grinned. "Or suggested they join in."

Genie couldn't keep herself from sounding prim and self-righteous. "Paul and I don't go in for that sort of thing."

Jackie's emerald green eyes danced up and down Genie's body. Then she smiled, shook her head, and said very softly but with absolute certainty, "Honey, you will. Believe me. You will."

Several hours later, the party was winding down. The small amount of pot the actors could afford was smoked and most of the wine drunk. They had to get to their night jobs or to bed. Tomorrow was another rehearsal day. Genie approached Paul. "Darling, I must go home. You stay, I'll grab a subway."

"Not at this time of night you won't. We'll catch a cab, and I'll take you home." He raised his voice. "Children, it's the witching hour. Everybody out, before I turn all of you into white mice."

There were a few halfhearted groans, but the empty bottles, used and unused glasses, and small piles of ashes were gathered up and dumped into brown paper bags. Everyone left together. Once on the street, they separated. Genie looked for Jackie. She couldn't find her and assumed she left with someone.

On the way uptown, Genie told Paul what Jackie had said about her.

"Relax, honey. Jackie thinks anyone who hasn't made it with a collie is a sexual amateur."

"Ugh."

He laughed. "She is something, isn't she?"

"Something! I'm not sure what, but, yes, she's something."

The cab turned left on 71st Street. Paul kissed Genie good night in the cab and watched until he saw she was safely inside the Majestic. He said to the cabby, "Back to 9th and Sixth Avenue." During the ride he thought about the apartment and living with Genie. It was going to be the most wonderful, unendingly beautiful love affair anyone ever had. He thought about making love to her in the evening, at night, in the morning, and at high noon. The memory of their making love gave him an erection that seemed larger and harder than usual. If only he hadn't been so stupid as to give a key to Jackie. And then to push the wrong button. It was funny. Especially the way Genie threw on her clothes. He had become used to the careless ease with which some young actors and actresses exhibited their bodies. Jackie was wrong. Genie would never do that. The cab pulled up. Paul paid the tab and walked toward their new home. They would start furnishing it over the weekend. He opened the iron gate leading to the garden and stopped. A shadow detached itself from the building. He tensed for an instant, then relaxed. The shadow was obviously female. A soft, rich voice spoke. "I waited for you to come home." The voice became more enticing and added an Irish lilt. "I've put on my robes that are the richest and on this night I will turn the man of New York like the wind blowing on the Hudson."

In spite of his deep love for Genie, Paul was unable to refuse what was being offered.

16

On a wet morning in late October 1968, Andre Husseman leaned back in his limousine as Willie wound his way through Central Park traffic. Andre smoked his second Gauloise of the day and thought, with amusement, about Sara's comments that morning over breakfast.

"Andre, I don't understand why you want to do business with that man. He looks and acts like a gangster. He probably is."

"He isn't. He has an excellent business reputation."

"I don't believe he's honest. I believe he's, well, he's a wealthy scoundrel. He's not like you."

Andre basked in his wife's approval and ignored her naiveté. But he held to his point. "You're wrong. He's the perfect man for my project."

"You're a gentleman. He's crude and vulgar. That cigar is hideous." She leaned over and whispered in a conspiratorial tone, "Do you know what he once said to me in the lobby? When he still lived in the building?"

Andre restrained a smile, knowing that Gluck's humor could cut deep. "What did he say, dear?"

"He said I definitely was not a Jewish nymphomaniac."

"He said that? What did he mean?"

"He said that a Jewish nymphomaniac was a woman who would have sex thirty minutes after having her hair done. And he was certain I wouldn't do that." She shook her head. "Can you imagine?"

Andre shook his head as though bewildered, but privately agreed with Ralph Gluck. His wife certainly wasn't a Jewish nymphomaniac.

* * *

After waiting a few minutes in the reception room, Andre was ushered by the secretary into Ralph's huge office. This was their third meeting.

"How are you, Andre?" he asked, puffing cigar smoke into the room. "Have you seen Paul's latest play, *The Balcony*?"

"No. Sara read it and didn't want to go." Andre lit a cigarette partially to defend himself from the cigar smoke.

"I can understand that. It's pretty strong stuff for Sara. I saw it last night. It's a fine production. Paul's getting better with every play, and I'd sure like to know that Bates broad who played *The Pony Girl*." He nudged Andre on the shoulder. "Paul getting his?"

"I don't keep track of Paul's sex life."

"The hell you don't. I'll bet that Genie Szabo thing really pisses you off."

"We're not here to discuss Paul's affairs. Or I might ask about your son. Roy."

"That prig! Sometimes I think we're not related. He lives on wheat germ and goat's milk. He has all his integrity and a little of my money. Okay, let's go to work. I have some good news and some bad news, depending upon one's viewpoint. Which would you rather have first?"

"Always the good news."

"Fine. Since we both know I'm Sara's favorite hood . . ."

"You're too sensitive. She hasn't seen you in years."

"Quite true. But I have an excellent memory. If we become partners, she'll feel obligated to have me to dinner. And I can't stand the odor of disinfectant. It reminds me of the hospital where my wife died. That's the good news."

"Are you suggesting we will not become partners?"

"Correct. That doesn't mean your proposal doesn't interest me. It does. And I fully understand your position. 608's are long gone. Title Ones are about over. Where can an apartment house builder turn an honest buck? Condominiums of course. One hundred ten-story condominiums stretching from the Maryland shores to the Florida keys is a very imaginative idea."

"Then what's your problem? If you like the idea, is there something wrong with the building plans?"

"No. The plans are fine."

"Then what do you object to?"

"You."

"Me?"

"I don't think you've given enough thought to two vital factors in this project. First, the numbers. Second, my innate stubbornness."

Husseman put out his cigarette and sat up straighter in his chair. Sarcasm aside, if Gluck saw some flaw in his plan that was making him back off from the project, Andre wanted to know what he missed. He had to know before he contacted other prospects, although Gluck was still the most natural man for the project. "All right, Ralph, we'll go over the numbers first. There will be one hundred and fifty apartments per building. Given the average size of each apartment, about a thousand square feet, including public space like corridors, elevators, and so forth, we're talking about a hundred-and-fifty-thousand-square-foot building."

"And your projected construction costs are sixty dollars per square foot." He grinned at Husseman. "Your reputation for cutting corners precedes you."

"Damn it! I run a tight ship!" Andre exclaimed, no longer able to control his irritation. "I hire contractors at the best prices, and then I beat them down still further. Should I do less?"

"No. I'd be the last to deny your ability. It takes real talent to bring in a hundred and fifty thousand square foot, ten-story reinforced concrete building for nine million dollars. And when we add the cost of the land, the site improvements and the interest paid on the construction loan, the whole package still costs only ten million. I am impressed."

"Thank you. You are also aware the projected sale price for a typcial four-and-a-half-room apartment is a hundred and twenty thousand dollars. Buyers will be able to purchase with only ten percent down. That's twelve thousand cash. And we'll arrange with our banks to get them a mortgage on the remaining sum at seven and a half percent interest. So a hundred and fifty apartments at an average price of a hundred and twenty thousand per apartment comes to eighteen million dollars. We have a clear pretax profit of eight million per building." Gluck puffed on his cigar and listened while Andre continued, trying to convey confidence. "When we complete the hundred buildings, that's one hundred times eight million profit. We'll have a pretax profit of $800 million. On a long-term capital gain." He laughed. "Now you tell me, Ralph, what am I missing in the numbers? The big picture?"

Gluck did not answer immediately. He took a new cigar out of a nineteenth-century fruitwood humidor, clipped the end off with a silver cigar clipper, lit the cigar, and stared into space. Then he said, "No, Andre. Not the big picture. You're missing the little picture."

"The little picture?"

"You. You're the little picture. Do you have the kind of money necessary to swing this size venture?"

Andre Husseman shifted restlessly in the black leather chair facing Gluck and ran his hand through his silver hair. His mouth tightened, and his jaw extended forward. "What are you talking about? If you can take care of your end, I can take care of mine."

Many years ago, Ralph Gluck had mastered the fine art of investigating fully any business proposition. That included knowing all there was to know about both his business associates and competitors, those current and those potential. He was almost as obsessively interested in their personal lives, the lives of their families, their strengths and weaknesses, as he was in their business lives. So he knew almost everything about Andre Husseman, from Sara's disgust with their son's romance with Genie Szabo, to his approximate net worth, which Gluck estimated to be between fifty and sixty million. "In order for us to carry this through to a successful conclusion, we must start with an investment by each of us of fifteen million dollars to capitalize our Real Estate Investment Trust, the REIT. The trust will borrow the construction funds from Chase or Banker's Trust or wherever. If the projected timing of the purchase of the land, the construction, or the sale of the apartments slips to any extent, we will both have to invest another fifteen million. Can you afford to put that much into this venture? Thirty million dollars?"

Husseman, fifty-five years old, impeccably tailored in a handmade dark pinstriped suit, heretofore a man with total self-assurance, lost a fraction of his composure at Gluck's question. "I can afford it as well as you can. But at our last meeting I suggested we put together a nine-member syndicate, including ourselves, with each putting up three million. We minimize everyone's risk. You were to think it over."

"Now you're dealing with my second reason for questioning whether we should go ahead. My monumental stubbornness. I said no at our last meeting and then agreed to think it over. I've thought it over, and I still say no. I have never done business with a syndicate. I work alone or, at most, with one equal partner. So I ask again, can you afford it?"

The implication that the venture might be too rich for his blood, stung Andre's pride. He saw Gluck in a different light. He may have underestimated the size of the man's holdings. While he was a rich man, Gluck might be much richer. Rather than intimidating Andre, this made Gluck more desirable as a partner. Being a born gambler, Andre was not afraid to take huge risks to make huge profits, and this had the biggest profit potential of any project he had ever undertaken. Previous successes had proved him right often enough. He had made his own luck in business, so he decided to accept Gluck's terms.

"All right, Ralph. If you insist, we'll do it together as equal partners. Not as a syndicate. Maybe this way *is a* bit rich for my blood, but I'm still prepared to go forward. Which ought to tell you how convinced I am of the success of the venture."

Ralph Gluck looked at the ceiling, puffing on his cigar. He thought, each man is his own keeper. "So be it. Tell Sara to invite me to dinner. I'll bring my own lady and the migraine pills for her."

The first year Genie and Paul shared their apartment together slipped by so quickly, Genie wondered what happened to the time. Though their work schedules were in conflict, they always managed to make time for each other. At least on weekends they were alone in the apartment, never answering the telephone, especially those weekends when Paul had no rehearsals. Plans were cancelled, invitations declined, the world was lost for both of them. Left to themselves and their own needs, they would make love all day. In the evenings they would dress and wander around the Village until late at night, stopping to eat in small, out-of-the-way Italian or Greek or Armenian restaurants. In those months there was a curious, secret glow about them that everyone who has known physical passion would easily understand. Genie loved Paul with every fiber of herself. And as for Paul, she was the very staff of life to him. Youth and health and passion seemed to hold out an endless promise. The dilemmas of love, the sense of options denied—none of this had any meaning to them. Neither Genie nor Paul yet realized the difference between life and romance.

And then, without anything being said, something began to change, and gradually they seemed to move apart. Genie was baffled and hurt. She tried to understand. Perhaps their different work schedules were interfering? Too often she was asleep when Paul came home. And he was at work when she came home. His company was growing and some weekends had to be spent auditioning new actors. He was also taking classes toward a master's degree in theater arts. She loved him so, wanted him so; when he did come to her, she gave all of herself to him. But something was wrong.

One night she found out what it was. Paul had come in at midnight, and she knew why. The suitcase stuffed with his clothes told her all she needed to know—told her why he had been coming home so late for so long. Rehearsing actors, he'd said, or studying. Though wide awake, she had pretended to be asleep; she remained wide awake long after she heard his deep regular breathing. In the morning, she slipped out of bed and as she dressed, she decided to ask Max to have lunch with her. He could help her sort out her thoughts. Tomorrow she and Paul would have it out. She didn't dare dwell on what was coming or she'd never get through the day. And she had a very full day.

Genie left her office at 9:30 and took the subway to 66th Street and Broadway.

The Jefferson Tower Complex consisted of eight 28-story yellow brick buildings with terraces starting on the seventh floor. Brown, Harris managed the buildings, and Jack O'Neil had sent Genie to investigate tenants' complaints that some of the sidewalks connecting the buildings were crumbling, and the concrete in the small playgrounds behind the buildings were buckling. Genie thought she knew what was happening, but to make sure, she'd arranged for her father to meet her at building #3. She knew the superintendent of building #3 had gone to the dentist. There was no sense in ruffling his feathers, as she knew she would when she showed up with Zoltan. Zoltan would tell her if he saw what she saw.

He did, and much more. "Whoever built these buildings did it with spit and glue." He knelt to pick up a small piece of the cracked sidewalk. "Look. Oatmeal!" He made a sour face. "The contractor was in such a hurry to finish the job, he laid the sidewalks in the winter, and the builder let him." He crunched the piece of concrete in his hand. It fell apart. "Genie, water is used to mix the sand and concrete. If you pour the concrete in the winter and there's a freeze, the water doesn't evaporate. It freezes. That's why a good builder makes sure all his concrete work is done before it gets too cold. This was done in the winter. When the freeze set in, the water that had not evaporated froze. So only the surface concrete set properly. Under the surface is what we call oatmeal." Zoltan kicked a piece of loose concrete. "I thought so. He didn't put a cinder bed beneath the sidewalk to take up the moisture. When it gets cold, the water in the ground freezes and expands. Then the sidewalks buckle." He shook his head. "This is only going to get worse. All the sidewalks and playgrounds will have to be ripped up and replaced. The builder should be contacted along with the subcontractor."

"That's fine, Dad, but the builder sold the Jefferson Towers Complex to American Copper. Suppose they won't do it?"

"Then you're going to have a lot of angry tenants. I think these buildings must have many more serious problems than the sidewalks. Any builder who allowed the sidewalks to be done like this must have skimped all through the construction. For my own curiosity, let's see what else he did to save money."

And there was a great deal to see.

Genie had arranged to meet Max at the Oak Room at the Plaza where the captain, Robert, always welcomed him, ever mindful of Max's generous tips. Max liked the large comfortable leather armchairs. He could relax his large frame and even stretch his legs. He also liked the proximity of a plug-in telephone which he had a habit of using.

When Genie arrived and asked for Max Szabo's table, Robert gave her a guarded look. "Your name, please?"

"Eugenia Szabo."

"Ah! Miss Szabo! Your brother called earlier. He said to tell you that, unfortunately, he cannot meet you here for lunch. He would like you to go to his office. Our chef has prepared steak sandwiches for you to take along." He motioned to a waiter. "Henry, get Mr. Szabo's package from the kitchen."

The waiter hurried off, and Robert dismissed Genie's surprise with a wave of his hand. "Think of it as room service for Mr. Szabo. Only the room is a few blocks away."

Genie arrived at Max's office carrying a shopping bag containing two steak sandwiches. The whole episode was in Max's character. The switchboard girl recognized her. "Hi. Your brother's in the conference room. He said I should send you in. I've ordered coffee. He said you'd bring the sandwiches."

"I did."

"Good. The deli around the corner stinks."

Genie opened the door to the conference room. Max was seated at a round table poring over several leases.

"Boy, do I have a deal cooking! Fifty thousand square feet in the Starret-Leheigh building to a Triple-A rated tenant. Fifteen year lease. I'm almost afraid to figure the commission. I just wish we could go into business tomorrow."

"So do I, but we can't without buildings to manage. Do you know any fairy godmothers?" She put the shopping bag on an empty spot on the table.

"Robert did his bit? Steak sandwiches?"

"Room service for Fifth and Forty-eighth."

Max reached into the bag and took out the sandwiches which were wrapped in aluminum foil. "Sit down and eat. Coffee should be here any minute." There was a knock on the door. "Like now." He took the two containers of coffee and set them next to the sandwiches. "Okay. Now we won't be interrupted. What's bugging you, kidlet? You sounded like death warmed over on the telephone." He paused before biting into his sandwich. His eyes narrowed. "You're not pregnant, are you?"

"You have a dirty mind. What we do is hold hands."

"That's all right, but don't kiss. I hear that's a sure way to get knocked up." He wolfed his sandwich while Genie looked at hers. "So what is it?" Suddenly he grinned. "Of course. Stupid of me. Lover boy? He's been unfaithful?" Genie nodded. "Kidlet, that is not news. Remember those Harvard football weekends when Momma wouldn't let you go? To paraphrase Dorothy Parker, 'If all the girls he took out were laid end to end, I wouldn't be surprised.' And that one room and toilet he's now supposed to be living in. When he did live in it, don't you know he had hot and cold running actresses every time he blinked?"

"I didn't think about it."

"So think about it. Paul Husseman has done more than his share of fucking around. Why should he change now?"

"Because we're living together."

"Whoopee! So?"

"So it should make a difference."

"Kidlet, don't play dumb. It's not your style. You've heard of extramarital screwing. Consider it that. No man is faithful. And not many women. Who's the broad?"

"Jacqueline Bates."

"Bates! Every man's wet dream?"

"Is she?"

"Where, oh where are your eyes? You're one of the best looking women on Fifth Avenue, but you're no Bates. She's a professional beauty. And a professional lay. I don't mean she's a whore. Hell. I took a crack at her myself after one of Paul's cast parties. She's a pure sexual animal. I wondered how come Paul wasn't shafting her. This makes more sense."

"He's supposed to love me. I love him."

"What's love got to do with it? No man with red blood passes up a Bates. On the other hand, she won't stick around. She wasn't made for one man. She was made for a million. That kind of talent needs a big audience."

"She'll have one now. Last night a kid from the neighborhood brought over a suitcase. Paul was at the theater at the time."

"And what kind of a time bomb was in the suitcase?"

"Underwear. A belt. Socks. Handkerchiefs. All Paul's. And a note from Jackie." She fumbled in her purse and pulled out a piece of lavender stationery. "Paul, darling, since I'm leaving for Hollywood soon with a contract from Sam Spiegel Productions, I've sublet my apartment. Under the circumstances, I think I should return your . . ." Genie stopped reading. "Damn it. He's supposed to be in love with me."

"Kidlet, he's in the business of lust. Lust goes with show business the way land goes with real estate. It could happen again. Probably will. One-night stands are freebees. Even a Bates. He's like a bartender. The booze is on the house, so he drinks. It goes with the territory."

"And what about love?"

"Yeah, what about love? If he loves you so much, why

doesn't he marry you? He wouldn't marry a Bates. He's not that stupid. And she wouldn't marry him. Don't beat your breast and tear your hair out over her, but why doesn't he marry you?''

"He's not ready. We've talked about it.''

Max put down his half-finished sandwich. He took hold of Genie's hands. Once again, his deep concern for his sister showed in every motion he made and every word he uttered. "Genie, listen to me carefully. Sex is sex. It's wonderful, but don't confuse it with marriage. Marriage, to a man like Paul, is special. You know I got married, sort of, to keep out of the draft. We don't live together or work at it. It costs a little every week, and when that stupid mess in Vietnam is over, Janet will disappear with ten thousand dollars and my blessings. But Paul is different. If he married you, he'd stick. No matter who he screws behind the set. But if he doesn't marry you, no matter what he says about love, you're just another piece of ass.''

"He will marry me.''

"Okay. Put it to him. Bates really did you a favor. You've got the perfect setup for righteous indignation. So make him prove his intentions are honorable. If he marries you, he's for real. No matter who he screws offstage. Come on, kidlet. Prove me wrong. I'd like to be wrong. I really would. I'd like to dance at your wedding.''

Genie's eyes met Max's and he winked. He's challenging me. And he's right. Sexual jealousy is a useless emotion when you're married to a man in the theater. And there are many successful marriages, even in the theater. Hers would be one of those. She'd accept the risks and work with them. "You're right, big brother. I've been silly and childish.'' She walked around the table and kissed Max lightly on the cheek. "Thank you. You'll be the first to know when the date is set.''

Back in her own office, Genie could hardly wait for the evening. Paul and she would settle things once and for all. It wouldn't be the first time marriage had come up, but it would be the first time she'd take a stand. Circumstances and Max had influenced her thinking. If Paul's and her love was to survive, they both would have to do some rapid maturing. When he understood how she felt, she was certain he would marry her. He loved her. Jacqueline Bates was a business perk. From here on, she would push jealousy aside. It was not the way to think or behave. A jealous lover is a jealous loser.

She turned her undivided attention to work and walked across the hall to Jack O'Neil's office. She tapped on the door. "You have a visitor, Mr. O'Neil."

Jack O'Neil looked up. "Genie! What a relief. I'm hip deep in legalese. We're taking over the management of a new co-op on Central Park South." He looked at her curiously. "Okay, so where are the bodies buried at Jefferson Towers? We had three calls this morning from tenants. Not enough hot water."

"Yup. And yup again. And one of these days you'll be getting calls about leaky roofs from the tenants on the top floors. Providing, of course, that New York continues to have rain and snow."

"Forget my blood pressure. Give me the gory details."

"Whoever built the Jefferson Tower Complex, I'm not speaking of the current owners, I mean the original builder, nickled and dimed it to death. The sidewalks are crumbling and buckling for reasons I will detail in my written report, and that have to do with chintzing on construction costs. The hot water shortages occur and will keep on occurring because the boilers are too small. As for the roof, well, that will also go into the report." She ran her knuckles across her forehead. "Before you read it, I suggest you get yourself a prescription for those new high blood pressure pills."

"I have a prescription." He made a sour face. "Damn it! So many of those Title One projects are like that."

"Ah, yes, Title One. Weren't they supposed to be low-cost housing projects? You should forgive the expression."

"Sure. That's just another New York real estate number. Like 608's."

"You know about 608's?"

"Everyone in the business knows about 608's."

"As they must know about Title Ones. Except me. Tell me about Title Ones, kind sir."

"Simple. Title One was a federal law. Under the law, a city could condemn certain substandard areas and purchase the land for the assessed value plus ten percent. Most of the money for the purchase was provided by the federal government. Then the city sold the land to selected builders, cheap. Very cheap. The idea was the buildings were to be torn down and urban renewal projects built in their place. The tenants in the old buildings were to be relocated in comparable apartments.''

"But they weren't relocated?"

"Oh, yes, they were. Everywhere in the country but New York City. In our fair city, certain builders had a fairy godmother. Name of Robert Moses. The Pooh-Bah of New York. It was his position that New York City was not in the business of relocating tenants. That was the new owner's problem. So the owners sat on their hands and did nothing but collect the rents.''

"Doing nothing meant letting the buildings go to hell? No repairs? No maintenance?'' Genie remembered again the streets of her childhood where the small buildings deteriorated into slums. "And eventually the tenants moved out."

"You're a quick study, Miss Szabo. Except the tenants didn't get out fast enough. It took years for some of the buildings to be completely vacated. The landlords loved it. They continued to collect rent while construction costs rose. Eventually it broke their hearts to say it, but the original mortgages guaranteed by your favorite uncle—Uncle Sam—weren't big enough. They needed additional financing. Therefore they couldn't afford to build low-income urban renewal projects. They were forced—yes, forced—to build high rental apartments.''

Genie understood all too well. "The return on a luxury apartment house is much higher than one for poor folks.'' She shook her head in disgust. "Especially when along with the higher rents goes crummy construction that leads to crumbling sidewalks and no hot water.'' She had a sudden, unpleasant thought. "Jack, do you happen to have in your extraordinary filing system the name of the builder of Jefferson Towers?''

"Of course.'' Jack went to a file cabinet. "We signed our original management contract with him.'' After fingering through the folders, he pulled one out and laid it open on his desk. "Hmmm. I'd forgotten. I'll give you three guesses, Eugenia Szabo.''

"I'll take one. Andre Husseman.''

"Right! Give that little lady a pink doll.''

Genie chewed on her lower lip. She thought about Paul. Thought about Andre Husseman being his father. Andre with his aristocratic manners, his beautiful taste in wine and food, his love of painting, of literature, of music. How much of him was in Paul? For the moment, she buried the thought. "Husseman let all those perfectly sound, low-rent buildings turn into slums. Just to force out the tenants. We shouldn't manage Jefferson Towers."

"Genie, don't be naive. We're managing agents and good ones—not builders. We do not make moral judgements. If a builder pulled a number, that's not our business. It is our business to let the current owner know the condition of his property and follow orders as to what should be done to correct the problems. Now what's bugging you?"

"I was just wondering how easy it is to learn to lie and cheat."

"What are you talking about?"

"Nonsense. I'm going back to my office and write my report."

Genie wandered around the living room waiting for Paul to arrive home. She was resentful and frightened. Everything had seemed so clear after her lunch with Max. But the meeting with O'Neil and the talk about Title Ones had made her doubt her judgement. She'd been too young when she first heard Paul's stories about the 608's. She knew it was dishonest; but somehow, at sixteen, the dishonesty hadn't seemed real. Now at twenty-two, it came close to home. Andre Husseman really was a thief. Only on a big time level, but stealing was stealing. He was also a slumlord, and the knowledge sickened her. It raised questions. Like how much of his father was in Paul? How much dishonesty? How far did the apple fall from the tree?

She kept walking around the room touching this and that, touching the things that were so familiar, things that told her about him. The room was really a combination living room and work area for Paul. The concessions to their living and loving in the room were the couch and rug. The high-backed dark green corduroy couch with its wide soft pillows encouraged lovemaking. As did the heavy-pile, padded, earth-toned carpet on which they usually walked barefoot. And occasionally made love.

She looked at the little clock on the desk. It was almost one o'clock. Why wasn't he home? Was he seeing Jacqueline?

She'd better not think about that. When she heard his key in the lock, she had to sit down and hug herself to keep from shaking.

"Hello, you there," he said quietly as he closed the door. She nodded without moving or answering. He took off his jacket and hung it in the closet. And then without saying anything, he turned around and squatted on the rug in front of her so his knees almost touched her.

"I'm home," he said at last. "Aren't you glad to see me?"

"Very glad. What held you up?"

"As a matter of fact, I was talking to Jackie."

"What did you talk about?"

"You. She objects to you."

"She objects to me! I object to her."

"You shouldn't." He lifted his black eyebrows, looked up at her, and Genie had to control the rising awareness of her senses, to hold onto her fragile resistance. "She objects to the fact that I love you and live with you. And that I don't love her and live with her."

"You don't?"

"No. I like her. But love her? Oh, no!"

"Then I don't understand. Why do you sleep with her? Make love to her?"

"We don't make love. We fuck. It's different. You and I make love."

"She sent your clothes back in a valise."

"She told me all about it."

Genie turned to look out at the darkened garden so he wouldn't see her blink back tears. By the time she turned back, he had stood up. "I think I'll take off some clothes." He unfastened his belt as he entered their bedroom. When he returned, he was barefoot and wearing an old, loose kaftan. He resumed his position on the floor in front of her. "There. I feel better now. And how are you?"

"Me? Do I matter?" She was very bitter.

"Do you matter? What a silly question. Of course you matter." He put his hand under her chin. "You matter very much to me."

"Not enough to make you stay away from Jackie. She also matters."

"She matters? Why, yes, I suppose she does. In her own way."

"And what way is that?"

"Sex. Pure sex. If you're in the mood. And she's a very good actress as well."

"Then where do I fit in?"

"You're the center of my life."

"There can't be two of us in the center."

"There aren't, There's only you." He began to walk around the room. Genie sat, feeling helpless. She couldn't help being in love with him. She loved the way he walked, his body, his hands. She loved the way he dropped his head a little to the side when he was thinking. Maybe Max was right. Forget about Jacqueline.

He returned to her like a piece of iron returning to a magnet, sat again in front of her, and put his hand out to her, looking into her face. "Take off your dress," he said in a soft tone that left her powerless to disobey. He took off his kaftan. "Now come into my arms." He reached up for her, and she sank against his chest. The moist warmth of his breath against her throat wiped all other thoughts from her mind. Her fingers curled into the black thickness of his hair as his hand cupped the underside of her breast. He was so expert with her body. He knew it so well he permitted himself a dizzying, lazy seduction. His mouth moved into the hollow of her neck, kissing her shoulders, biting her, licking her. His hands parted her thighs. Then he stopped for a moment to prepare himself. Her whole body arched up to take the thrust of him, to cling to him as shudders of ecstasy raced through her. Afterward, she lay with her head on his shoulder, dazed, languorous, filled with peace, astonished at the ease with which her body had responded, her resistance evaporating as if it never existed.

So the night passed in a dreamy haze of lovemaking that flared, subsided, and flared again even more strongly. They seemed to be rediscovering each other all over again. All Genie's guards were lowered. He was the only man she had ever loved and would ever love.

Paul began to talk in their old, intimate way; to talk of secret thoughts, secret emotions. In doing this, he found he needed to tell her the truth, his truth. He was still young enough, foolish enough, even innocent enough to believe that the act of confession to one you loved and one who loved you carried with it an automatic acceptance and absolution. He had yet to be tested himself.

"I'm sorry about Jacqueline," he said, "but she could happen again. Or someone like her."

Although Genie remained motionless in his arms, she felt as though she had been struck in the face. Finally she said, "Thank you for telling me now."

He tightened the curve of his arm about her waist. "It's the only time to tell you."

"Why?"

"Because I wanted you in my arms when I told you. Like this. So I could explain how unimportant the Jacqueline Bateses of the world are to us. I'm twenty-five. It's simply part of growing up. Of becoming a man. Sowing wild oats. But you're my only love." Genie didn't reply. "I always worried someone would tell you about Jacqueline before I was ready. So I decided to break it up with her. That's why she sent you the valise. And the note. She's not going to Hollywood. Not for months anyway. It doesn't matter. What matters is you know what's going on with me. Only I had to get to the point where I could tell you."

Although Genie's body was being held by Paul, her mind ranged freely over their life together from the first time they had made love on the roof garden of his parents' apartment to their making love most of this night. It had always seemed so perfect, so completely satisfying, to her; apparently it wasn't enough for Paul. Why? Were the sexual needs of men and women really that different? She didn't think they were. So again the question. Paul's explanation about being twenty-five and sowing his wild oats, that was a cliche right out of Zelda and Scott Fitzgerald. He'd be sowing the same wild oats at forty-five, with other Jacqueline Bateses. Why? Was what Max said true? Sex went with the territory, and she'd just have to swallow it? Maybe. But there was something she was missing. Something that had to do with Jacqueline Bates. But what? A thought crossed her mind. Maybe if she understood the difference between fucking Jackie and making love to her, she might understand Paul better. There was a quality Jackie had. Something. Even she, another woman, had felt it. Max said there was a difference. Yes! That was it! She would insist Paul explain the difference between them. They were both young, they were both pretty, they both had the same standard female sexual equipment, but somehow Jackie was different. Blind to the possible pain the answers to her question could cause her, desperate for reasons to explain Paul's behavior, Genie decided she had to know.

"Paul, I have to ask you a question, and I want a complete and honest answer."

"What's the question?"

"I love you, and you say you love me. Exactly what does Jacqueline Bates give you that I haven't?"

Genie could feel the muscles in Paul's arms tense, and for a moment his whole body went rigid. His voice, usually so calm and controlled, took on an incredulous, almost frightened, edge. "You want me to tell you the details of how Jackie and I fuck?"

"I didn't say that. I said I wanted to know the difference between Jackie and me."

"It amounts to the same thing."

"If you say so, but I want to know."

"I don't think this is a good idea, and I won't do it."

"I do!" Genie put every ounce of will she possessed into her words, drew on her last reserves of strength, and for the first time in their relationship, Paul bent and broke.

"All right," he muttered. "But it's on your head." He moved away from her, put on his kaftan and sat on the far end of the couch. Genie put on her robe and sat on the other end. Both had their feet flat on the floor. "I'll put this as simply as possible. Jackie is as professional at sex as she is on the stage. And after six years of our making love, you remain a rank amateur. You don't even have a diaphragm, use an IUD, or take the pill. So, like tonight, we stop in the middle of everything while I put on a rubber."

"But I . . ." Genie stopped. When she still lived with her parents, she had been afraid one of them would find her diaphragm. An IUD or birth control pills needed a gynecologist's prescription. So, for that matter, did a diaphragm, and she didn't have a gynecologist. During the time Paul and she had lived together, she hadn't thought about it.

Paul continued. "I can only hope you're more professional in the real estate business than you are at sex."

"Since I'm such a rank amateur and you know so much, why didn't you teach me?"

"I tried to. I'm still trying. I did everything I felt I could do to get you to understand. You just weren't listening."

"Maybe your directions weren't so clear. Amazing! You can direct the entire cast of a play, and you couldn't direct one woman who wanted nothing more than to please you."

"It's hard to tell someone you love that she's not satisfying you sexually. I hoped the understanding would come from you." Paul's voice trailed off.

Genie sat with her elbows on her knees, her head resting in her hands. She realized she'd been blind and selfish, lost in her own happiness, not giving a thought to his. Assuming that because she was fulfilled, so was he. Vivid images of Jackie and Paul's sexuality raced through her brain. Totally unfamiliar with manuals on sex—she remembered the book she'd sneaked out of the Hunter High library and then had been too embarrassed to read—much of what she now envisioned had never occurred to her. At first the ideas dismayed her. Then, as she did with all new information, she decided she must think about it. At the very least, she could get a prescription for the pill. Finally she said in a voice that reflected all her suspicions and disbeliefs. "So, despite my total incompetence in bed, I'm supposed to believe you still want me."

"I told you I love you."

"Why? How could you?"

"There are many things besides sex that are a part of loving. Things no one has ever understood or been able to explain. I love you. It makes no difference why."

Genie had to battle with herself. She wanted to run away and hide. Have nothing more to do with Paul. Unless . . . Unless he . . . Genie thought about courage, the courage one needs to make wise decisions. Running away was cowardice. Instead of running away, she would do her best to carry out her original plan. He said he loved her. In spite of Jackie Bates and everything she stood for, Genie believed he did. He had to understand. She slid across the couch, took hold of both his hands, and blurted out the one request that would make her feel whole again, make her feel like a woman a man wanted. "Paul, I love you too. Let's get married. It will tell the world where we stand. As you said, sex is sex, and I will do better. But marriage is love.''

"Marriage has no significance whatsoever.'' The hard ice-cold words chilled her last hopes.

"What has significance then? Jackie Bates?''

"At this minute, nothing outside of this room. Nothing in time or space matters to me but you.''

"Yes. At this minute, me.''—She repeated his words. "But there's the future. And future Jacquelines.'' She shrank from the thought.

"Jacquelines come and Jacquelines go. We last. As for the future, the future is used up every day. The future is like a bundle of thread. When we both do some untangling, we'll get married. I love you, my darling. Please believe me. I do. One day we'll work it out.'' He lifted her face so he could kiss her mouth. She wanted to believe him. God, how she wanted to! Time was suspended in a long, exploring kiss, and Genie was caught again by the spell that bound her to Paul. She loved him. But she didn't love what had happened. And she remembered Max's words. "Another piece of ass!'' They frightened her.

17

After the Jacqueline Bates affair and Paul's refusal to consider marriage, Genie grappled silently with her fears. She tried to live each day as though the day was sufficient unto itself. She took what she could get, and accepted what she thought of as his moods. If he came in late, she pretended she was alseep. Sometimes she was. When he talked about the theater, she listened with pleasure and tried to keep the pressures of her own business life apart from their home life.

She'd persuaded Paul to help her select several sex manuals and go over them with her. Also, she now used the pill as a contraceptive. When they made love, she practiced all her new book-learned knowledge, and was surprised and delighted to discover how easily, how fully, her body responded to the sexual play. And the more she experimented, the more she looked forward to further experiments. But beneath her freed sexuality, beneath her acceptance of Paul's ways, there lay a deeper reality. She had arrived at an understanding with herself. Although her whole nature was set on marrying Paul, she knew she must not mention it. Above all, she must not show her fear of losing him.

The grapevine had it that Paul's new production would be a winner, and that Paul was a comer. It pleased Genie that Paul seemed to want her support—support she was only too willing to give. He was experiencing wild emotional swings of elation and letdown. He thought he was on the verge of a breakdown, and he was defensive about his work as he had never been before.

He told Genie, "I've lost my nerve." Then, only a few minutes later, he said, "I haven't lost enough nerve. Where do I come off doing Pirandello? I'm not even Italian."

Genie laughed. "Watch it. You'll hate yourself in the morning for showing such disrespect for your talent,'' and she rubbed his neck.

Every other Wednesday, Max and Genie went to dinner at their parents' apartment. On the last Wednesday in March, Genie tried to beg off. She'd been out of town on business Monday and Tuesday, and she wanted to have a sandwich with Paul before the next to last preview of the new production. In spite of his knowing she wanted to be with Paul, Max insisted she meet him at their parents' as usual. Something important had come up that afternoon. He would take her to the theater in a cab after dinner and tell her his news then. So Genie agreed and phoned Paul, soothing him with lies. Her father wasn't well and would be hurt if she missed the dinner.

Paul said, ''Your father is a fine man. I admire him very much. But you haven't been to one preview so get the hell down here before the curtain goes up.''

''Wild horses couldn't keep me . . .'' He hung up before she could finish.

Whenever Max and Genie visited their mother and father, Genie felt as though they had stepped back in time. Aside from the things Max had bought for the apartment, most of which Anna refused either to use or to set out on display, the apartment hadn't changed. But Max and she had changed. And, in some subtle way, so had their mother and father. Genie couldn't put her finger on it, but a distance had developed between her parents. When they had been children, Zoltan and Anna had been very close. She wondered what had happened. At least her mother should be content. She'd gotten the life she wanted. Her father's job assured him a good pension. They had Social Security and savings. When he retired, they could look forward to a reasonably comfortable life.

But something warm and very precious had disappeared. Her father's once powerful body seemed to be sagging long before it should, and his face had lost color and definition. Her mother sat rigidly and viewed the world in general, and her family in particular, with constant disapproval. They made their usual meaningless conversation, but on this Wednesday evening, Genie felt her mother's lack of approval even more than usual. During a pause in the conversation, Anna mentioned she had read in the *Times* something about Paul Husseman and a new production. She asked Genie many questions about their relationship. When was she going to stop seeing Paul? When was she going to start seeing a nice young man from her own background who would marry her? When was she . . . ? In the past, Genie had parried the questions with a smile and courteous evasions. However, tonight she struggled with a strong impulse to tell her mother the truth—a truth she knew her mother didn't want to hear.

"It's true. Seeing Paul is difficult. Our work schedules don't coincide. So we usually see each other after his rehearsals." She smiled directly into her mother's eyes and her voice dripped honey. "Of course, if it's very late, he sleeps over." She had a moment of malicious pleasure as she watched her mother's lips compress as if to stop her mouth from speaking. Then Anna rose and began clearing the table. When she returned from the kitchen, the subject of Paul and Genie was dropped.

After as short a time as was politely possible, Max and Genie prepared to leave. They apologized for having to eat and run. They were going to the theater to see a preview of the play. If her parents would like it, Genie said she could get them a pair of complimentary house seats. Anna said they didn't want the tickets. Genie followed Max out the front door. She was struck by a particular sadness in her father's face. Something in him had broken, and though he showed no outward resentment, Genie's heart ached for him. In the cab riding downtown, she burst out, "Yes, they're fine! Fine! Fine! Their health is fine! Dad's job is fine! They saw a fine movie last Sunday and had a fine dinner at Fine and Schapiro's. If they said fine once more, I think I'd have thrown up."

"They're not happy."

"Not happy? They're miserable, and I wish she'd stop bugging me about Paul."

"After what you said tonight, I think she will." He started to add something and then changed his mind. "Listen, kidlet, forget them. That's a closed book. We're the next in line, and I've got a tiger by the tail. Well, a baby tiger anyway."

"What baby tiger?"

"You know it's time we started our own business. You've learned everything you're going to at Brown, Harris. And I'm sick of splitting commissions with Alpert. Szabo and Szabo should be listed in some directory.''

"I know, but it can't be until we have some buildings to manage. As you said, it's the bread and butter of the business.''

"I've pitched five big owners in this town. Three of them own buildings where I've leased a lot of the space, and I've sold buildings to the others. But each has a reason not to put us on. Until today.''

"What happened today?''

"Pay dirt. One of the clowns has a cousin in Chicago who just bought three buildings. And for reasons I don't understand and haven't tried to, he won't use Chicago agents. He's willing to give us a chance.''

"Chicago? That's over a thousand miles away.''

"I know.'' In the last year Max had grown reluctant to speak to Genie about Paul. Although he knew how unhappy she was, she was not a woman who welcomed intrusive sympathy.

"Paul . . .'' she started to say, and so much feeling welled up in the single word that Max took a chance.

"Yes, what about Paul?'' He put his arm around her, and feeling concern, she began to pour out her doubts and her pain.

"You're asking me to give him up, aren't you?''

"Yes. You've lived with him for over two years. In two years, nothing has changed. You're still not married.'' Max was worried about his sister. "Meanwhile there's been Jacqueline Bates and who the hell knows how many others?'' He couldn't stop himself. "You've read of course that the latest sex goddess of Hollywood is returning to the scene of her first triumph. She's going to be at the opening of Paul's play.''

"I read it.'' Genie felt weary, almost defeated. "Sometimes I don't know if I can take it another day. And then I think how it would be to live without him. You know, Max, I don't let myself even think about his other women. I can't.'' She heard her own voice and wondered at the despair she heard. "But whenever I'm with him, I feel it's right for me to love him. If I can only hold on, it will work out.'' She had to continue to believe that or all was lost. "I mean something to him. A lot, I think. Someday, soon, he'll marry me.'' She hesitated. "Don't you agree?''

Max heard his sister's cry for help. The best he could manage was, "I don't know.''

"He tells me all his plans. We're very close." She added, almost gaily, "I'd make a most suitable wife."

Max looked at his sister and thought, with all her brains, her courage, she knows less about men than any broad I know. She's learned nothing living with Paul. All she knows are his hands, his mouth, his prick. She's deliberately blocked out the rest of him. But foolish or not, she was Genie, his sister, his kidlet. And he was her big brother. He had to help her as much as she would allow him. So he accepted her reality and said, "I guess what you're telling me kills the Chicago deal. I'll call them in the morning and say, have suitcase but can't travel."

The cab pulled up at the Martinique on West 33rd Street. Genie got out, leaned through the open window and kissed Max on the cheek. "Forgive me. I can't."

"I forgive you. Forget it. We'll find something else."

Genie tried to be gay. "You're such a nice big brother type." She smiled at him. "Won't you come in and watch the preview? See Paul?"

Max shook his head. If he saw Paul at that moment, he'd knock the prick's head off. "I've got a late date, but I'll be there opening night."

After the preview, they decided not to go for drinks with the cast and went home together. Paul made love to her, and she made love to him with a passion that made her marvel at the pleasure possible in her body. Later, she wondered how anyone would dare suggest to her a world where he would not be its center.

After she fell asleep, Paul lay awake staring at the dark ceiling and thinking about his life and his father. When he thought of his father, he thought of fine cotton and soft wool and supple leather. He thought about his father's shoes, so meticulously selected and cared for, with their thin soles and soft, gleaming tops, always polished to a high gloss. He thought of his father's initialled handkerchiefs and special shirts, made to order from the finest long-haired Egyptian cotton. He thought of his platinum wristwatch, a Patek Philippe, and the gold watch he'd inherited from his own father backed with a scene of peasants drinking. He thought too of how much his father had loved and dominated him. His father had taught him how to select wine, how to judge food, how to choose clothes, how to distinguish between a good string quartet and a poor one, how to recognize a real antique from a fake, and, finally, how to behave with women, how to be unfaithful. He had taught him everything there was to know about how to spend money, but nothing about how to make it. He had to learn that for himself. His father had implied, long ago, that perhaps Paul wasn't right for the real estate business. And maybe he wasn't. But more important, if this production was as good as he thought it was, if his talent for the theater was real, maybe, in a little while, he'd outgrow his father. Outgrow his need to be like him. Then he might be able to marry Genie and be faithful to her. If only she would wait, give him the time he needed to get a good hold on himself. Allow him to reclaim a key part of the identity his father had taken over so many years ago. She had to wait.

Two and one-half years after Ralph Gluck and Andre Husseman had made their decision to proceed with Andre's condominium project, Ralph and Andre were once again sitting in Ralph's office. Except for an almost imperceptible movement in Andre's eyes, it was impossible for anyone to recognize that anything had happened. But it had. The thirty months had been an unbelievable roller-coaster ride. Eighteen months straight up, during which time thirty condominiums had been built and sold and all of Andre's projected profits were realized, and twelve months straight down. The country had slid into a recession. Now everything, including the second fifteen million dollars that each man had invested, was in danger of being lost. The question Ralph had originally asked Andre—"Do you have the kind of money necessary to swing this venture?"— was a live issue. Ralph knew he could afford to carry his share. Could Andre? Ralph decided he couldn't.

"Good morning, Andre. How are you?"

"I've been better."

"Have you gone over the statements?"

"Of course. We're getting killed."

"The question is, what are we going to do about it?"

Andre lit a Gauloise, inhaled deeply, and watched the smoke rings rise toward the ceiling. He held the cigarette loosely but steadily between his fingers. "We could put on a bigger sales force and drop our prices."

"It wouldn't help. It's not the number of salesmen or the

prices that have killed sales. Even if we dropped our prices by as much as fifty percent it wouldn't do any good. The banks have no mortgage money for the purchasers of our condos.''

Andre's own studies had convinced him Gluck was correct. His suggestion had been a ruse to imply desperation. ''Do you have any ideas?''

''Several, but they're all lousy.''

''For example?''

Gluck laughed, and his laugh even had some humor in it, albeit gallows humor. ''We could tell the banks they are now the proud owners of seventy different corporations and seventy condominiums.''

Andre tapped the long ash of his cigarette into a convenient ashtray. ''I wonder if there's any way of transferring any of the money we have in the corporations before we give them the buildings?''

''Andre!'' Gluck's voice was soft. It would have taken a mind reader to know the disgust he felt at the stupidity of the question. ''I dislike losing money, but I dislike going to jail a lot more. You may think I look good in a pinstriped suit, but the broader the stipes, the worse I look. And I believe seeing the world through iron bars will rob it of a lot of its charm. Besides, Lutece will never agree to extend its catering service to Sing Sing.'' He dropped the banter. ''What you're suggesting is a fraudulent bankruptcy. I wouldn't have any part of it with an eleven-foot pole, and that's the pole you use when a ten-foot pole lets you get too close to a skunk. Better we lose everything and have it over and done with.''

''There must be another way.''

''Of course there is.'' Ralph thought, so now we come to it. ''It's simple. We pay the interest on our loans until the market turns.''

Andre had also done his homework. ''Absorb a million and a half a month?''

''A million and a half each per month.''

''On top of thirty million.'' Andre said it almost to himself.

''On top of thirty million each. Sixty million.''

''We should have followed my original suggestion and syndicated the deal.''

Ralph took out a fresh cigar, clipped the end, and went

through his usual ritual lighting it. "There's one other factor you haven't taken into consideration."

"Oh?" Andre uncrossed his legs, set his feet on the floor, and smoothed the crease in the pants of his cambridge grey suit. "What haven't I taken into consideration?"

"Me. I told you several years ago I was innately stubborn. That was why I didn't agree to your idea of a syndicate. I don't even like partners. And the only reason I finally agreed to a joint venture was I liked the concept, and you brought it to me. If it hadn't been for that, I'd have done it myself."

"And found yourself in a position where you stood to lose sixty million dollars."

"No. I'd put up the three million a month for as long as necessary. That's my decision. We make the monthly interest payments."

"Your decision? I own fifty percent of this operation. Who the hell do you think you are to make that kind of a decision?" Andre sounded angry.

"I'm a man who ususally reads contracts before I sign them." Gluck's lips tightened around his strong yellowish teeth. "Our contract states that should we fail to agree on any point, at any time, either of us has the right to purchase the other's interest for an agreed-upon amount. If we fail to agree on the price, Roger Nichelson, probably the best real estate appraiser in the county, will look over the corporation's books, estimate where we stand, and set a price. His decision is binding on both of us."

"That could take months. Meanwhile we have to keep meeting those damned interest payments and carrying charges."

"You got it."

Andre studied the tips of his polished black shoes. He looked up. His voice was thoughtful. "You said before you'd have done the deal without me. All right. Pay me back my thirty million, and it's all yours."

Ralph jabbed the end of his cigar in a huge, free-form, black alabaster ashtray on his desk. He shook his head. "If you'd done a decent job on the construction, I just might have agreed to that. But I've looked over some of the buildings. You built a bunch of shit houses. It's going to take more than thirty million to redo your fuck-ups."

"What the hell are you talking about?"

"Come off it. You're not a stupid man, so it comes down to one of two things. Either you paid no attention to the screwing your subs gave you or you got a kickback from each of them."

"Ralph, I never . . ."

"Shut up! It's over and done with. I don't care to take the time to find out the truth. The point is I know it will take at least thirty million to repair what you've done poorly or not at all. So here's my offer. My one, my only, my final offer." He leaned across his desk. His massive shoulders and huge upper torso seemed to dwarf the furniture. "One dollar, Andre. One dollar for your fifty percent. And if you refuse, we'll continue to make those interest payments together until they bleed you white. Then I'll take over."

Andre Husseman permitted his body to slump in his chair; his breath exhaled with an audible whoosh. Then he forced himself to straighten up and light another cigarette. His well-schooled face showed nothing of what he was thinking. Actually the meeting had come out just about where he had expected it to. Far from having gone into it unprepared, he'd known, even before Gluck, what their real situation was. He also knew he had no intention of handing the corporations and the buildings back to the banks. The suggestions that they might grab some cash from the corporations had been a smoke screen to deceive Gluck into believing him to be at his wit's end; if Gluck had gone for it, he'd have found reasons, not as colorful as Gluck had found but just as effective, for not following through. He had reread the contract and was equally familiar with the clause to which Gluck referred. After weeks of studying the problem, looking for possible solutions, he had come to the decision that the best chance he had was a unique gamble —a gamble he was prepared to take. He looked forward to it. All his efforts during the meeting had been spent leading Ralph up and down garden paths. Finally he'd maneuvered Ralph into making an offer to buy him out. The offer of one dollar was in keeping with the nature of the man. The insinuation that he had taken kickbacks from the suppliers neither shocked nor surprised him. He hadn't. As it now stood, Gluck could make all the accusations he pleased. He had no proof because there was no proof to be had.

One thing was true. The construction was shoddy. It had to be to bring the buildings in at the projected costs. Maybe another builder could have done better? Andre didn't know, and he didn't care. He was building apartment houses at a price, not monuments to posterity. What was first class were the site improvements, the swimming pools, the tennis courts, the health clubs. After all, they were selling the sizzle as much as the steak.

Now he was ready to spring the trap. "Ralph! One dollar? That's not an offer. That's stealing." His voice quivered in indignation.

"One dollar is my offer or you keep coming up with one-point-five million every month."

"You know I can't do that. I'd be wiped out within a year."

"I warned you I was difficult and unreasonably stubborn. One dollar is my offer."

They went back and forth. Husseman pleaded for a break, a fair deal, and Gluck, his feet propped up on his desk, puffing away at his cigar, refused to budge. Finally Husseman ran out of words and Gluck out of patience. "Andre, my first and last offer is one dollar. I'll give you thirty days to accept or reject it."

Husseman appeared to be considering Gluck's proposal. He knew every man has his flaws, and Gluck's flaw was his overwhelming ego. He believed he was smarter than Andre was, and Andre had been cultivating this belief for months. It was time for the switch. Would Ralph take the bait? He'd know in a moment. "Ralph, if all my share is worth is one dollar, then that's all your share is worth."

"My share is worth nothing. Zero. Zilch. The dollar I offered you is generous. It should have been no cash and other valuable considerations, as the lawyers like to say."

"Generous?" Andre laughed. "Suppose, just suppose' I'm as generous a man as you are."

"What are you getting at?" Gluck removed his feet from the desk.

"I'll take your offer with one change. I want the first option from you on the same terms you've asked from me. If I don't purchase your fifty percent for one dollar in thirty days, you can have my fifty percent on your terms. One dollar."

Gluck saw the trap. Husseman had been heading for this all along. But there was one difference. He could carry the interest charges by himself, and Husseman could not. Husseman would have to put together a syndicate in thirty days. He was a gambler, and he was gambling he could get the men who had made money with him in other ventures to bail him out of this one. Ralph knew they wouldn't. His continuing stream of information had told him they didn't have the cash to invest in the project. There was always a chance he was wrong and Husseman could pull it off. If Husseman did, he was a better man than he'd given him credit for being, and he deserved to win.

"It's a deal. I'll put my lawyers to work immediately. It's simple enough. A second year law student could have the agreement ready in two hours. But they'll fuck something up, and you'll probably have to wait until tomorrow morning for a draft."

Husseman nodded. "Don't get up, Ralph. Your secretary has my coat, and I can manage to show myself out."

"Thirty days, Andre."

"Thirty days and one dollar, Ralph."

Ralph Gluck watched Andre leave. He didn't move like a beaten man. Ralph wondered what he had missed? What could it be? He'd find out in thirty days. In any case, given the choice of the two positions, he preferred his.

Andre pushed the elevator button and waited. Now that he was alone, he smiled openly. For once, Ralph had overreached himself. Andre knew his past associates weren't a source for big money. But he had another source, and it was a source Ralph hadn't considered. The elevator door opened. Andre smiled. At least he'd won the first part of the gamble. Now for the second and more unpleasant part.

18

Genie and Jack O'Neil were seated in his office trying to decide where to go to celebrate. The celebration was in honor of Jack leaving Brown, Harris on Friday to start his own firm. While Genie was happy for him, she wished Max and she were in the same position. Then the dinner could be a joint celebration. But Jack had the contacts and they didn't. He'd been in the business for over twenty-three years. He had the cachet of being a senior vice president of Brown, Harris, Stevens, Inc., while Max and she were relative newcomers, almost too young to be taken seriously. Finally they settled on a small businessman's lunch and supper club, the Penthouse, which had recently opened. It was on the top of a new high-rise office building on Park Avenue and 50th Street. The decision had just been made when Jack's secretary interrupted with a message for Genie. There was a Mr. Husseman on the phone.

"Tell him I'll be right there." She stood up. "Since we'll both be out of the office this afternoon, I'll meet you at the bar at six o'clock."

"Three cheers for six o'clock." Jack watched Genie leave. Always a keen observer of women, he had become aware that some subtle changes had occurred in her over the last year. She had always interested him as all beautiful women did; but along with her natural beauty, everything about Genie was now somehow more exciting, conveying the message of a sexual female. It could be that she had completed the change from being a child-woman into a full-grown woman. Even her clothes seemed to fit her better, tighter.

After making a few mistakes at the start of his career, Jack had learned that sex and office discipline did not mix. However, tonight, Genie was no longer off limits. How would she respond to his overtures?

Genie picked up the phone in her office and said, "Hello, Paul."

A familiar, cultured voice, half laughing, said, "Sorry, Eugenia. This isn't Paul. It's Andre Husseman."

"Oh! How are you, Mr. Husseman?" Genie's voice was reserved.

"Very well, Eugenia. Thank you. Eh. I wonder, how tight is your schedule? I would like to see you at your earliest convenience."

Genie glanced at her Real Estate Board diary. There was nothing that couldn't be postponed. "How about this afternoon at three?"

"Good. I'll see you at my office at three. Good-bye."

Genie hung up and stared at her desk, her mind racing in circles. Why did Andre Husseman want to see her? Was it because of Paul? Although Genie was a woman with genuine insight, it took no special understanding to warn her this could turn out to be a disagreeable meeting.

When Genie was shown into Andre Husseman's office, he was seated behind his desk. The desk was bare of all papers and polished so that its green leather top, tooled with elaborate gold filigree, gleamed in the light. She glanced around the room and admired the office which looked more like a library in some great home than a place of business. It had a dark walnut parquet floor covered by small Oriental throw rugs, and panelled walls in matching walnut; there were floor-to-ceiling bookshelves and several magnificent paintings of the Hudson River school. There was handsome antique furniture, with extensive marquetry and bronze and brass metal fittings and trim. All in all, the room was a credit to Husseman's wallet and good taste.

He rose to meet her and offered her a Gauloise cigarette from a beautiful jade cigarette box.

"No, thank you. I believe in the surgeon general's report."

"So do I. But so much in life is a gamble, I don't feel it necessary to deprive myself of a pleasure because it would cause a slight shift in the odds. Do you mind if I smoke?"

"Not at all."

He selected a cigarette, lit it, and motioned towards a pair of Queen Anne chairs facing each other, separated by a small

Georgian table with an inlaid chessboard in oak and walnut. "Sit down, please. We have a number of things to talk about." Andre tapped the ash from his cigarette into a standing brass ashtray. He began. "I'm certain you realize I didn't suggest this meeting to indulge in small talk."

"You didn't?" Since it was apparent Husseman wanted her to ask why she was there, Genie decided to do no such thing. He would have to ask his own questions.

There were a few moments of silence, and then, almost reluctantly, Andre said, "I asked you here to talk about Paul." Genie remained silent. "To be more precise, about Paul and you."

She smiled. "Isn't that thoughtful of you."

"Thoughtful? Hardly. First, I'd like you to know I deeply regret the need for this conversation. It's never pleasant to meddle in other people's lives."

"Then why do it?" Genie knew Andre Husseman as a man who was two-faced, a Janus. One face handsome, worldly, elegant; the other hard, greedy, grasping, unscrupulous. She knew that much, but her knowledge was only a part of the man.

There was more to Andre Husseman than the two faces Genie knew. There was his self-knowledge. He knew better than anyone that he was hard, almost obsessively selfish, and, above all, corrupt. But he also knew what no one else knew. Most of the time he wished he was another kind of man. This almost romantic self-image often made him slip out of his everyday patterns. He had deliberately discouraged Paul from becoming involved in the real estate business. Paul was too much like himself with most of the same strengths and weaknesses. The opportunities in real estate to corrupt and be corrupted were too great. Therefore, despite Sara's opposition, he had encouraged their son's interest in the theater. He had been delighted to finance Paul's first theatrical ventures. There was corruption in the theater, but for a young man in Paul's position, the corruption was primarily sexual. Unlike his wife, he felt no contempt for Paul's affair with Genie Szabo. This acceptance stemmed from the same awareness of Paul's similarity to himself. He had married for money and position and was not proud of the fact. Sara was a good woman, but she lacked the physicality he would have preferred in a wife. So his life contained a long procession of lady friends and even a few full-fledged mistresses. He knew his son had been imitating him for years, and he hoped the easy availability of so many women in the theatrical world would dull Paul's need for incessant variety. Also, if Paul married a woman like Eugenia Szabo, the affairs would come to an end. She was the kind of woman who could keep a man home, and happy to be home. When he finally accepted that his only chance to prevent himself from suffering severe financial reverses was to sacrifice Paul's marital happiness and condemn him to a life similar, at least in one respect, to his own, he felt a great deal of sadness. He would have preferred another way.

Despite all this, his answer to Genie's question was blunt. "I meddle because I must. I must ask you to end your affair with my son."

"Why don't you ask him?"

"Paul is young, hopefully talented, headstrong, and foolish. He'd refuse."

"What makes you think I'll agree when he won't? Do you imagine my love for him is less than his love for me?" In spite of her resolve to maintain her self-control, she was becoming very angry.

"No, I'm sure it isn't." Husseman crushed out his cigarette. "But you've had a different life than Paul. You're more aware of the compromises life demands of all of us."

Faced with this calm, seemingly reasonable man who requested nothing more from her than that she give up what she considered the very center of her life, Genie lost her temper. Her anger at Andre Husseman had been suppressed for a long time. It started with the knowledge that he made his money through bribery when he built his 608's. Then there were the Title Ones. This was the man who had turned block after square block of the city into slums. She paced around the room so full of fury that she couldn't stop herself from telling this elegant gentleman exactly what she thought of him. And his suggestion. She finished with ". . . you're a thief. A thief who's gotten away with everything all his life. You can go straight and directly to hell."

Aside from a very slight narrowing of his lips and eyes and a mounting pallor that was hidden by his tan. Andre Husseman listened to Genie's tirade without making a move to stop her or a sign that he had either heard or understood her words. When she finally ran out of things to say, she was standing in front of him. He said, "I'm sorry to find you have such a low opinon of me. Mine is a good deal higher of you. Nevertheless, I will make no attempt to explain to a twenty-three-year-old, even a very bright twenty-three-year-old, why I do what I do. It is the way business is done. It has always been the way business has been done, and always will be. Perhaps, when you're older and more experienced, you'll understand, perhaps not. It makes very little difference. However, you are under a misconception. I am not suggesting you leave Paul as a favor to me. The chief beneficiary of your sacrifice will be your lover and my son, Paul." The last sentence was spoken in a clear, firm tone with each word receiving exactly the same emphasis.

Genie stepped back. "I'll listen just long enough for you to explain that."

"Thank you. Then sit down!" Andre had been far more surprised and deeply bothered by Genie's attack on him than he appeared, and he knew he had been on the raw edge of losing his gamble. But the lines of power had shifted again, and once more he dominated the meeting. He opened a small drawer in the table. "Before you review these numbers, I'm going to have to explain the background of the project they refer to." He spent the next twenty minutes describing Gluck's and his joint venture. Only then did he hand the documents to Genie. "Here are the annual statements for two years and the projection of losses over the next year."

Genie studied the balance sheets and statements of income and losses. Although, in a purely mathematical sense, she had no difficulty understanding the numbers, the boldness of the venture, the magnitude of the potential profits and losses, and the amount of money needed to continue operations were beyond her ability to deal with in a real sense. When she handed him back the papers, her attitude showed more respect. "Would you mind explaining to me what went wrong? Everything appeared to be going so well, and then it fell apart."

"Do you know anything about economics?"

"I took a number of courses in college."

"You are aware that Dr. Arthur Burns is now the chairman of the Federal Reserve?"

"Of course."

"And that he's a monetarist?"

"Yes."

"And that he's trying to fight our inflation with tight money and high interest rates?"

"Mostly with tight money."

Andre made a sour face. "Correct. And high interest rates and tight money are a deadly combination for builders. We pay more for the money we borrow, and worse, the banks have no money to make mortgage loans. Potential buyers of our condominiums can't get mortgages. So they don't buy. As you can see from the statements, we owe a lot of money and are sitting with a lot of vacant buildings."

"I understand. All right. What has this got to do with Paul and me?"

Andre then described his final meeting with Ralph Gluck and followed that by handing Genie a second set of papers. "This is my most recent personal statement. Also a projection of income and expenses." He waited while Genie scanned the numbers. "As you can see, I will not be ruined, but my income will be a fraction of what it has been."

"I still don't understand what this has to do with Paul and me."

"You do understand that if I can arrange to buy out Gluck's interest for one dollar in addition to finding enough money to carry the interest charges for two years, I cannot only recoup, I can carry the project through to a successful conclusion when Burns has to ease up on the money supply?"

"I still fail to see why this has anything to do with Paul and me. As you have made clear, you need a new associate. One with money. I have about eight thousand dollars in the bank." She did some mental arithmetic. "That will cover your interest charges for about three and a half minutes. Of course Paul may have some money of his own. We've never discussed the subject."

"Paul has less than you have, and he spends a great deal more." Now the game was back on track. He was beginning to enjoy seeking out, cornering, and capturing his quarry. "Are you familiar with Roseco?"

"No."

"They're the largest manufacturers of garden supplies, plants, fertilizers, grass seed, hoses, I don't know what else in the country. It's a privately held corporation, and all the stock is held by Jake Rosen. He lives in 101 Central Park West."

For the first time Genie saw where Husseman was heading. "Don't tell me. Let me guess. Jake Rosen has a daughter?"

Andre permitted himself a half smile. "He does."

"And you two gentlemen think it would be just ducky if Paul married, er . . . what's her name?"

"Joan Rosen."

"Should Paul marry Joan Rosen, Jake Rosen will bail you out." She exploded. "An arranged marriage in 1970? I don't believe it."

"Not exactly arranged. They know each other very well. Too well, as a matter of fact. Joan Rosen would be delighted t marry Paul Husseman. In fact, she's counting on it."

"What is that supposed to mean?"

Andre didn't answer her. Instead he pulled out a single piec of paper from the same center drawer and passed it to Gen She looked at it but didn't touch it. "What is it this time? 1 United States budget?"

The half smile that had remained, seemingly painted, on Andre's face broadened into a full smile. "Not exactly. It's your budget. To be more precise, this is what my accountant tells r it cost me last year to keep Paul living in the style he enjoys in the theatrical world he loves."

Genie's fingers staged a revolt. They refused to touch the pa per.

"Look at it, Eugenia. Study it. Really, young lady, the numbers won't bite."

The statement was an accountant's report. There was a letterhead: Jack Farber, CPA. And the accountant had signed the report at the bottom. Genie had never made any effort to track Paul's expenses, either personal or business. It hadn't seemed appropriate. But the total cost of the productions and their living expenses came to just over two hundred thousand dollars. By far the greatest single item was Paul's theatrical productions. She wondered how he could have lost that much on what had seemed to her to be bare-bones productions and good attendance. Yet, there they were, signed by a certified public accountant.

Andre continued in his logical way. "So you see, if my income is to be so drastically reduced, I will be unable to continue as Paul's patron. He will have to try to earn a living, either in or out of the theater. A thing he is singularly incapable of doing."

"How do you know? He's never tried."

"Precisely. To use your words, 'he's never tried.' And he won't thank you for making him have to try. You may believe in the great American dream of rising from rags to riches, but Paul doesn't. He's never even thought about it. Also, with all that free time on his hands, how do you think he'll spend it?"

Andre Husseman's question touched on Genie's deepest fears. Her voice was harsh. "I don't think that's any of your business."

"Oh, but I'm afraid it is. Next to you and the theater, the thing he loves best and does best, perhaps even better than loving you and producing plays, is making love to women. Many women. It's a talent he'll have plenty of time to exercise."

Genie's head began to swim as she saw a procession of Jacqueline Bateses passing through their life, and her horror made it difficult to think.

Andre noted the loss of some of her remarkable poise. The time was right for the final move. "A few minutes ago you asked me what I meant when I said Joan Rosen was counting on marrying Paul. I think the time has arrived to answer that question." He opened one of the doors on the side of the office. "Come in, my dear. Thank you for waiting so patiently." A tall girl with a round, puffy face, bleached blond hair, olive skin, and black eyebrows entered. She was wearing a loose paisley shift. "Eugenia, this is Joan Rosen. Joan, Eugenia Szabo."

"I remember you, Miss Szabo. Rebecca's party. Was it twelve or thirteen years ago? You did look so odd in that funny dress."

Stung by the memory, Genie struck back. "On the other hand, you look a little odd right now. Why the Mother Hubbard?"

"Because Joan is four months pregnant. It seemed proper to hide the fact as long as possible."

Genie's world fell apart with what she thought was an audible crash. "Paul?"

"Paul! It seems he does not confine his activities to the theater, where it might be considered part of the game. He extended his undeniable talents to this young lady who had every reason to expect him to marry her."

Joan took a handkerchief from her purse and wiped her eyes. Genie realized for the first time the girl's face, in addition to being naturally round, was swollen from crying. Andre took Joan by the arm. "I don't think we have to put you through any further strain. Allow me to show you out."

Genie watched them cross the room. As she did, one by one the steel bands which had bound her life to Paul's stretched and snapped. Andre Husseman was correct. It was one thing for Paul to fuck girls who accepted the casting couch as part of the business they were in. But Joan Rosen? She was a girl who assumed the sex act had some meaning beyond another conquest and some momentary pleasure. And the final band snapped when she thought about how careless, how calloused Paul had become to get this poor thing pregnant. He'd been different seven years ago. He was no longer the boy with whom she had fallen in love. Maybe he had never been that boy? It made no difference. The life she had hoped to live, the love she had hoped to have for the rest of her life, none of it would happen. For the first time Genie saw herself exactly as Max had described her, another piece of ass. The recognition of just how accurate Max had been sickened her. Another piece of ass! Another piece of ass! As the phrase echoed and re-echoed through her brain, she drew on reserves of courage she hadn't realized she possessed. No one would ever know how much she had lost this day. No one!

When Andre Husseman shut the door and turned to face her, he saw a young woman sitting in a Queen Anne chair, calm, collected, a smile on her lips. He couldn't believe it. He had a winning hand. He had played his cards perfectly. And he had lost. In spite of everything, Eugenia Szabo was not going to give up Paul. He had only one more thing to offer, and since he had been unsuccessful using far more persuasive tools, he didn't think his proposal would be given any consideration. But it was all he had left.

"Eugenia, I understand from friends in our business your brother has been looking for buildings to manage so you can start your own firm."

"Your informants keep you very well informed." Her answer was automatic.

"Not informants. Friends."

"Friends or informants. Does it make any difference? Your information is correct. We are."

Andre opened the drawer and pulled out the last of the documents he had placed there in preparation for the meeting. "Here is a five-year management contract assigning the management of eight buildings in various parts of Queens to Max and Eugenia Szabo doing business as—I've left the name blank."

"608's?"

"608's."

Genie took the contract and scanned it. It was the standard al Estate Board contract. So much had happened, it took her a few moments to understand the offer. Then she realized her struggle to maintain her composure, to retain a vestige of pride, to behave as a civilized human being had misled Husseman. In spite of Joan Rosen, of everything else, he believed she was not going to end her affair with Paul. So, thinking he had failed by one means, he was trying another. He was offering her a bribe to give Paul up. The easy thing, probably the honorable thing, would be to rip the contract in half and say something dramatic like, "My love for Paul is not for sale." It would give Husseman a bad twenty-four hours. Then he would find out that she had ended the affair, and that he had won after all. Would Andre Husseman, would Max, would the world think better of her for the bravura performance? Hardly! Max would be furious, and Husseman would think her a fool. Genie felt an emotion she hadn't felt in years, a loneliness and despair that would last beyond the moment. The grey wasteland of her childhood returned. She thought, this is not the world I expected.

She blinked her eyes to clear them. Let Husseman think what he would. She would allow herself to be bought off, but at a price. "I see you offer us three percent of the rent roll."

"That's standard." Now Andre had to struggle to maintain his poise. Was she interested in his offer?

"You're not asking a standard price. Paul is worth more than three percent." She played the scene to its hilt. "Make it five."

"Five percent it is."

"I want the five years noncancellable even if you sell the properties. We go along with the sale."

"I agree."

"Please make the changes and initial them. I still have to show the contract to Max."

"Of course." He wrote in the requested changes. "I apologize for asking, but how do you plan to break the news to Paul?"

"I'll do what I have to do." She looked at her watch. "It five o'clock." She gathered the copies of the contract and them in her large purse. "I have an appointment in an hour you have nothing else in that drawer, I'd like to leave."

"By all means." Andre showed her to the lobby. Then he returned to his office, shut the door, walked to the Sheraton highboy which had been converted into a bar, and poured himself a stiff brandy. He sat at his desk sipping the brandy and thinking. He thought about the afternoon, about himself, about Paul, and mostly about Eugenia Szabo. Nothing about that young lady seemed to be of a piece. There was her outrage at the way he'd built the 608's. Her fury about the slums he had created befo building the Title Ones. Her disgust at the poor construction. Her love for Paul. A love so strong it made her accept all his infidelities for years. Her refusal to give him up in the face of the financial difficulties she knew were coming. She even accepted the fact that Paul had gotten Joan Rosen pregnant. None of it made any difference. Then she sold out for the management of a few buildings in Queens. Why? Long ago, Andre Husseman had realized that just because something didn't make sense to him did not mean there wasn't an explanation. There had to be. He reviewed what he knew. She had an answer to every reason he gave her for giving Paul up. Oh, no! Andre's mouth fell open. No, she hadn't! When confronted with Joan Rosen, she hadn't said a word. He had seen her sitting in her chair, smiling; he, the professional, had lost his nerve. He offered her the management contract and had actually been surprised when she accepted the proposal.

He rocked back in his chair laughing at his own blunder. Of course. She accepted the contract because she was going to end the affair in any case. He had won and hadn't realized it. It was another measure of Andre Husseman that he was glad he had offered Genie the contract. And that she had accepted it. God knows, she deserved it, and much more. He looked forward to keeping an eye on the rise of Eugenia Szabo and helping her if he could. She should be something to watch.

19

Genie stood in front of 240 Park Avenue. Along with her emptiness of spirit and the void she saw in her future, she was surprised to find a small pocket of relief buried beneath all the grief. She'd spent so many days dreading the loss of Paul; now that it had hapened, part of her felt released. She'd thought she was being brave by staying with Paul. Actually she'd been a coward. Afraid to break free. Courage had to do with facing things as they are. Even things in people you love. She had stayed with Paul because she was afraid to admit he didn't love her. Not as she loved him. She wouldn't see him as he truly was, and she'd paid a high price for living so long with a counterfeit dream. Seeing the truth had been just too hard. It would have meant giving him up. Which was exactly the thing she'd been running away from all these years. Giving up Paul. Giving up love.

Genie was in front of the Union Carbide building when she realized she had to call Max. She went into the building, dialed his office, and was told he'd gone for the day. So she called his home. His answering machine was on.

"This is 688-3334. Thanks to that electronic disaster, the New York Telephone Company, you have reached the home of Max Szabo. I'm not answering the phone at the moment. Wait for the tone before leaving your name, time of call, telephone number, and message, if any. Should you talk before the tone or your message does't interest me, you will never hear from me again." It was a typical message from Max.

But Genie's reality was starting to fade. "This is your sister calling. I'm here, there, and everywhere. If you're unable to reach me by phone, try telepathy. Otherwise you will not hear my glorious news until next Whitsuntide, assuming you know when that is." She hung up the phone and left the building.

Genie watched the men and women rushing by on their way to a bus, subway, or train which would take them home. As she watched them, the people seemed to step up their pace; her eyes couldn't keep them in focus. They were in such a hurry to get where they were going, they became a blur. She had no place to go. No place she wanted to go. Until the tears reached her mouth and she tasted the salt, she was unaware she was crying. Gradually the rushing people slowed down, and she was able to focus again. She realized where she was. She also remembered that, like other people, she had a place to go. Jack O'Neil was waiting for her. He was only two blocks away, but how would she get there?

Haltingly, she moved her left foot forward and then her right. Each step took planning. She was so tired nothing, not even the simple act of walking, was either easy or natural.

A man rushed by, smiled, and said, "Hello, Genie." She nodded. The recognition by another human being helped. She realized she must have stopped crying at some point. That was good. She couldn't spend the rest of her life crying. And she was glad Jack O'Neil was waiting for her. He wasn't Paul, but he was a man. And she was still young, still alive. There had to be other men in the world, kind, loving men. Sooner or later she would meet one.

She started to hurry. Even though the Penthouse Club was only a short walk, she needed time in the ladies' room to wash her face and repair her eye makeup. The self-service elevator took her to the top floor. When she told the maitre d' Jack O'Neil expected her, he nodded and said, "Mr. O'Neil is at the bar." Before she could ask directions to the ladies' room he added, "The powder room is just to your left. If you'll give me your coat, I'll tell Mr. O'Neil you've arrived and will join him shortly."

"Thank you."

When she finished her repair job, she thought she could still see the effects of her tears so she added a touch of rouge, a trace of lipstick, and a dab of powder. After running a brush through her short curly hair, she studied herself in the mirror. The mirror gave back an image of a well-groomed young woman, sophisticated, self-contained, even happy. Genie thought. Oh, mirror, mirror on the wall, how you lie to us all.

On her way to the bar, she looked at her watch. It was 6:30! She was late. Jack was sipping a martini while glancing every few moments in the direction of the powder room. He saw her, waved, smiled and stood up. "What happened? I thought you fell in."

"I couldn't. I'm not a little girl anymore. Sorry I'm late."

His eyes ranged the length of her body, and his obvious approval caused a warm glow in the pit of her stomach. "You know, I've never seen you look better. Now what are you drinking?"

"White wine and soda, please."

"You have that at lunch. This is a celebration. I'm drinking martinis. Join me?"

Yes. It was a celebration for him. "All right. Bombay gin on ice."

"No vermouth?"

"It spoils the taste of the gin."

"Mickey, give the lady what she wants. I'll have another of my specials, and bring them over to my table." He pointed to a corner table next to a window and somewhat secluded from the rest of the room. They sat on the upholstered bench along the wall. Genie looked out the window, south toward 240 Park Avenue, now dwarfed by the Pan Am building. She tried to pick out which of the lit offices was Andre Husseman's, but since she couldn't see the street, there was no way to count the floors. Everything in that office had happened so fast. It was as if she had watched a play in which she admired the performances but hated the plot.

Jack's voice brought her back to the here and now. He was talking about his future plans. "I'm sorry to report the Mighty Majestic decided to remain with its present management. You know, Genie," he placed his hand lightly on her wrist, "if I'd gotten the Majestic, there'd be a job waiting for you."

She was about to say something about her own plans and stopped herself.

Jack missed the near interruption. "Maybe it's just as well." He squeezed her wrist slightly. "If you were going to work for me, we wouldn't be here having such a good time. Would we?"

"I guess not."

"You've finished your drink. Have another."

Genie looked at her glass. The gin was so smooth. It had gone down easily. She did feel better. "Why not?"

Jack motioned to the bartender for an encore. The drinks arrived in rapid order. "Drink up, my dear!"

Jack drained half his glass. Genie took a good swallow. She felt almost like two people, one deep in her private grief over what lay ahead this very night, and the other accepting, even enjoying, the open admiration of an attractive male. Jack returned to his favorite topic, the start of his new business. Genie listened to the details, making mental notes of things she would remember to write down and show Max. While Max and she knew a lot, Jack O'Neil knew much more about running an office than both of them combined. She sipped her drink, and on a rare occasion, when Jack paused in his monologue, asked a question. Soon they ordered another round; a martini for Jack and Bombay gin on ice for her. As Jack drank, he grew even more animated, and Genie became aware he had taken to emphasizing a point with his hands. His hand was on her wrist, her arm, her shoulder; once he patted her cheek, and on several occasions he pressed against her thigh. His hands never stayed long enough for Genie to object, but when he shifted his leg so it came in contact with hers, she realized her naiveté. Besides showing off how important a man he was going to be in the real estate business, he was making a pass. She remembered Max telling her how he had met Jack, and Paul's objecting to her working for such an avid cocksman. Paul! That bastard! The number of women he screwed! What right did he have to object to anything she did? With Jack or anyone else? She did not move her leg away.

Jack's next move was to ask, "How about another drink?"

He was trying to get her drunk. One of the oldest, best established, most successful methods of seduction. Did Paul get Joan drunk? Whatever technique he used, liquor or I-love-you, it certainly worked. How often had they been to bed? It could have been a one-shot pregnancy, but she doubted it. More likely the affair had been going on for months.

"Genie, sweetie, I lost you. Come back and have another drink."

"One more. I'm hungry. Could we order?"

"And lose the effect of the booze?"

"A bottle of wine with the meal will add to the effect."

"You're absolutely right!"

Jack was also feeling his drinks. She had an idea. "Jack, is there a terrace connected to the Penthouse Club?"

"There certainly is. The door is right over there." He pointed across her body; in doing so, the back of his hand just happened to brush lightly across her breasts.

"Let's order drinks and food. While they're preparing the food, we can walk on the terrace."

Jack motioned for the bar girl. "Please bring us another round and a menu."

"The maitre d' takes care of the food. I'll tell him." The fourth round of drinks arrived. They were sipping them when the maitre d' joined them with menus.

The terrace ran the length of the building and overlooked Park Avenue. Four Bombay gins were more than Genie had ever had at one time. Her head felt light, and she knew she had to walk with care. Jack took her arm to guide her. She could feel him pressing against the side of her breast, his hip touching hers. They stood very close together at the parapet wall looking down at the traffic. Genie remembered standing at a similar parapet long ago, the first time she and Paul had made love. Where was he tonight? Probably with some woman going through the same mating dance Jack was going through with her. She was going to have to stop thinking about Paul. There was no Paul. He was a thing of the past. The here and now was Jack. She wondered what it would be like to kiss him.

It was as though Jack read her mind. He set his drink on the parapet and placed hers alongside his. Then he took hold of her shoulders and turned her to face him. He drew her close. First her breasts touched his chest. Then her belly pressed against him. She could feel his erection pushing against her, then their thighs joined. Only when the length of their bodies were pressed together did he kiss her. Her mouth opened, and his tongue traced a course around the edge of her lips, slipping easily into her mouth. It touched the tip of her tongue and drew her tongue into his mouth. He slid his hands from her shoulders, caressing her back, and then grasping her buttocks, he pressed her even closer to him.

Genie could feel jolts of electricity spreading through her entire body. The nipples of her breasts wanted to break through her brassiere and thrust themselves into his mouth. Her legs wanted to part to accept him. And while her body was sending out strong signals her brain remained detached, making totally independent decisions. She liked Jack, but she certainly didn't love him. She loved Paul, but she no longer liked him. He had treated her cruelly. She wanted a man who would treat her well, whom she would treat equally well in return, and neither would expect more than the other could give.

Jack's hands began to roam over her body, gathering sureness as she accepted his touch. His hands became familiar with the firmness of her breasts, the soft curve of her belly, the bulge caused by the thick mound of pubic hair, the thrust of her pelvis, and the hard muscles of her behind. She delighted in his caresses. Meanwhile her hands did their own exploring. His chest, very hard and muscular, his stomach, thicker and softer than she was used to, his penis, as hard as the only other one she had ever known.

After a few minutes, they broke away, both panting, their eyes wide open in surprise at the strength of their response to each other.

"We'd better go in, Jack."

Jack nodded. At this moment, he would have gladly skipped dinner to have been in his apartment with her. He handed her her drink and took his own. As they walked to the door, his arm was around her waist and she rested against him comfortably. He released her at the door. Neither had a word to say. Both were closeted in their own thoughts.

Jack's were simple. A meal. Some wine. Coffee and brandy. A taxi to his apartment and a night of sex.

Genie's thoughts were more complicated. She was surprised and pleased over her lack of guilt at the way her body had reacted. One did not have to be in love to make love. It was almost as though her body had been compartmentalized. In one compartment was her overwhelming grief over the loss of Paul. In another was the drab empty future stretching before her like an underexposed transparency with dim and faded colors. Then there was another compartment that was temporarily occupied by Jack O'Neil. This compartment would provide her with the pleasures that men and women need. And if sex without love was not the feast making love to Paul had been, she could get by on the limited rations now available to her. But there was a practical problem. Her desire notwithstanding, she had to tell Jack she could not go to bed with him tonight. One thing had to be done first. She cast about for an excuse he would accept.

During the meal they kept their hands on the table as though afraid to touch each other and spoil what they already felt. They talked about many things, both avoiding for their own reasons any discussion of what would follow the meal.

"This swordfish is marvelous. And the wine! Thank you for the chablis."

"You know. Red with meat. White with fish. The roast beef isn't bad, either."

Towards the end of the meal Genie asked, "Is tomorrow really your last day at the office?"

"That's right. Tomorrow at 5:00 P.M. I leave the womb and go out to seek fame and fortune in the cold cruel world of New York real estate."

"Cold and cruel? Hah! How many buildings did you say you were going to manage?"

"Fourteen, to start."

"And the rent rolls and maintenance total what?"

"Sixteen million, four hundred eighty-eight thousand, eight hundred sixty-five dollars and thirty cents."

"I like the thirty cents. And your management fees come to almost five hundred thousand dollars. Some cold cruel world!" She paused, wanting to be certain she said what she wanted to say exactly the way she wanted to say it. "Jack, I have to tell you something, and I want you to understand and accept it."

Jack O'Neil had heard similar words often enough to know what they meant. He masked the crashing of his beautiful dream of a night of love with silence and a weary smile.

"In spite of what went on outside, and you must know I felt it as strongly as you, we can't be together tonight."

"Genie, that's unnatural torture."

"Tonight I have a long-standing obligation."

Jack's spirits picked up on hearing the word tonight emphasized so strongly. He tried to guess what had to happen first. "Can I assume that tomorrow night, after I officially leave Brown, Harris, Stevens, Inc., is another night? A different night?"

Genie smiled. He had made the assumption she had wanted him to make. "What's your favorite food?"

"Any kind of beef. The redder the better."

"All right. My apartment has a garden. After five tomorrow, when you are no longer an employee of Brown, Harris and my boss, you go home, change into something comfortable, pick up a bottle or two of red wine, and I will charcoal broil you a filet mignon with all the trimmings. How's that?"

"Sounds too good to be true, but don't bother with dessert. I like to claim I'm on a diet."

"Foolish man." She put her hand under the table and gently squeezed him. "Don't you understand? I'm the dessert." Her smile was oddly sad.

Jack insisted on taking Genie to her house in a taxi; after all, he wanted to make sure he knew where she lived. He kissed her good night in the cab and did not offer to accompany her to the door. Once in the house Genie put into action the plan she had finally worked out. The girl who lived in the front apartment and played the harpsichord with such delicacy was a night owl. She'd be up when Paul came in. So Genie took everything of Paul's, his clothes, his toilet articles—he could come by when she was at work and collect his scripts, scrapbooks, books and pictures, whatever he wished—and packed them in three valises. Each article of clothing was packed with loving care. She had bought him that shirt, had been with him when he bought those pants; the tear in the shorts came from her ripping them off him when he had teased her by holding back when she wanted to make love to him. Every article of clothing had a special meaning, brought back a special memory, a special delight. It was like tearing her flesh from his flesh.

After she finished packing, she took a piece of their special writing paper and wrote:

I had the bad fortune to meet Joan Rosen today. *Enough*! Your clothes are packed. Virginia has the bags. Good-bye, my love.

G.

Then she put the note in an envelope, taped the envelope on the door of the apartment, took the suitcases to Virginia in the front apartment, and turned out the lights. The last thing she did was put the safety chain on the door. Then she waited.

Shortly after midnight she heard a key in the lock. The door opened several inches until the chain stopped it.

"What the hell! Genie, open up. It's me!"

Due to the dim light in the hall he hadn't seen the note on the door. Genie started to shake. Silent tears ran down her cheeks. He rattled the door again and called her name. Then there was silence. She heard him tear the envelope from the door. Her hearing became so acute, she heard him rip open the envelope and unfold the paper. More silence. The door to the apartment slowly closed. After a minute, she saw a piece of paper shoved under the door. Genie was afraid to move. Finally the silence ended. She heard voices in the hall and Paul saying thank you, and the front door of the house closing.

She remained motionless on the couch staring at the note which was clearly visible in the moonlight. It was over! He'd gone! But it couldn't be over! He'd had to come back! Finally the dam burst, and she scrambled across the floor on her knees. She grabbed the paper. He'd written on the reverse side of the note she'd left him.

Eliot was right. This is the way the world ends; not with a bang but a whimper.

> Good-bye, my fancy,
> P.

Paul was cold sober on the opening night of *Six Characters in Search of an Author*; cold sober, although he'd been drinking consistently for the past eighteen hours. He watched the play from the rear of the theater, holding onto the rail to help him stand up. There were eight curtain calls, and he stared at the critics rushing out, trying to read something into their expressions. Especially Kerr's, the *New York Times* critic. Paul thought the performance had gone extremely well and wondered if he was happy. He remembered Jackie coming up to him and clutching his arm.

"You made it, baby! I can tell. Let's go back to my place and slip into something comfortable, like me. We can get the rave reviews there."

The night was a blur. He didn't remember where he went but he ended up at a party in a suite at the Pierre where there was a whole bunch of people drinking champagne. And he drank a lot, too, much more than he could hold. Then there was a gap in his memory and somehow he was alone in a strange bar in the Village. It was almost dawn. The papers had been out for hours. He bought them, the *Times* and the *Daily News*. Raves! He read the reviews again and thought, maybe, at last, he was free of his father.

The last years of his life had been confused and disordered, but if he could return to a certain starting point, he would recover something. He remembered that afternoon long ago and ten-year-old Genie sitting on the fire staircase, sobbing.

It made him sure that when he kissed her again and joined his new self to her, he would be free of his father forever. He would at last be his own man. They would marry. In his drunken daze he wondered where she was. Why hadn't she been at the opening? Where had she been all evening? He went to a phone booth and called the apartment. The phone rang three times and a man's voice answered.

"Hello?"

Paul listened. Then he remembered.

Genie's voice came over the telephone. "Hello, Who is it?" He could see her face so clearly she could be standing in front of him.

"It's Paul," he said. "Oh, Genie, we could have had such a good life together."

"I thought so, too."

It took Paul a minute to hang up. Then he started to cry.

PART FOUR

1970–1972

20

It was late in the afternoon a week after the successful opening of Paul's new play when Andre felt the time appropriate for his meeting with his son. Knowing what they were going to discuss, Andre had chosen his office rather than his home for the meeting. And with equal calculation, despite Paul's furious request that they meet immediately, he had postponed the meeting for days. It was tactically wise to allow the full shock of losing Genie to sink in on Paul. Andre knew his words were going to add to Paul's anger; and above all, he wanted to minimize the possibility of Paul's slamming out of the office in a rage.

Seated in the same chairs as he and Genie had sat in a week earlier, Andre was struck by the similarities as well as the more obvious differences between his son and himself. Most of the differences came from what was called a generation gap. More a matter of style than content. Paul wore a pair of chino slacks and a tweed sport coat with patched elbows. His long black hair fell over his forehead and curled down the nape of his neck. As usual he wore a sport shirt with a button-down collar, open at the throat, and his moccasins could have used a shine. Andre's white hair was cut weekly. The part never varied as much as a hundredth of an inch. He would no more wear a shirt without a tie in the city than flap his arms in an attempt to fly. But their movements, the way they held their heads, the way they stood, even the general shape of their bone structure was similar. While Andre had schooled himself to hide his thoughts behind a mask and Paul let his every feeling show in his face, Andre was certain the day would come when Paul would learn that even in the theater, where creativity permits excesses, it was wiser to conceal one's reactions from most people.

What was most alike was the cast of their minds. Their response to a given situation might be vastly different, but both men would see the situation for what it was, not allowing pride or any other self-deceiving illusion warp their appraisal. They chose to do what they did with the full knowledge of the pluses and minuses that might result from their decisions. Paul was, in effect, his father's son.

After Andre went through the routine, though genuine, pleasure of telling Paul how *Six Characters* deserved the rave reviews it had received, he lit a Gauloise and waited. When Paul remained silent, he felt compelled to speak.

"Now that you've come this far north of 14th Street, you might as well tell me what you wanted to see me about."

Paul's words came slowly. "As I understood it, you wanted to see me as well."

"That's true."

"I'm trying to decide how to start." While waiting for Paul to speak, Andre blew a smoke ring into the air and watched it rise. Finally Paul looked directly at his father for the first time. "All right. For openers, how did you manage it?" His words were more of an accusation than a question.

Andre wasn't prepared for that blunt an attack. "Manage what?"

"How did you persuade Genie to leave me? And tell me the truth."

Andre put his cigarette out. The first two parts of his gamble had been successful. Ralph had agreed to sell out for one dollar, and Genie had left Paul. This was the third and last act of the play. If it failed, his previous successes meant nothing. He'd decided his best chance of success was to attack his son directly. In fact, the truth Paul asked for was his best weapon. "Very well. I'll tell you the truth. While I realize the casting couch is an old show business tradition, you badly overdo it. Ever since you started working in the theater, you've climbed into bed with every woman who moved. And some who didn't."

"Like father, like son. You showed me how."

"Not exactly. What I did, I did with respect for the proprieties."

"What's that supposed to mean?"

"I did not insult your mother by making my infidelities public. You insult everyone who loves you, and most of all your-self, by your lack of discretion.''

Paul's lower lip tightened over his teeth and a small child-hood scar showed as a thin, white line on his lower lip. ''Any-thing else on that subject?''

''Yes. In the same vein, keeping your mother's feelings in mind, I've never made love to a woman she knew personally.''

''How does that apply to me?''

''How many of the women you took to bed were entertained at one time or another by Genie and you on 9th Street?'' Paul had the grace to flush, and Andre continued. ''Sorry. You asked for the truth. Is it so hard to take?''

Paul ran his finger around his collar. This was not the father he was accustomed to. He suspected he was seeing Andre as he behaved in his business dealings ''No. Go on.''

''Still on the subject of infidelity, I limited my affairs to women who understood the rules of the game. You know some of them. They were well paid for the pleasures they provided, and they didn't expect more.''

''What's that supposed to mean?''

''Joan Rosen is what that's supposed to mean.''

''Oh! And you told Genie?'' The scar on his lip was more ap-parent.

''Of course. How else could she have found out?''

''I assumed so and hoped I was wrong. Why did you tell her?''

''I'll come to that. Let's stay on Joan Rosen for now.''

''Joan Rosen can damn well have an abortion.''

''Joan Rosen doesn't want an abortion. She wants you. Ex-actly what were you doing with her in the first place?''

''Since she's pregnant, it's obvious what I was doing with her.''

''Stop the smart answers. You know what I mean. Joan Ro-sen should have been off limits. Even to you.''

''Why?''

''Because she's naive enough to think that marriage goes along with sex. I assume from your comment about an abor-tion, you don't intend to marry her.''

''Marry her! I'd have to be out of my skull!''

''Were you out of your skull when you seduced her?''

''I did not seduce her. She seduced me.''

"Of course, Paul. And the sun rises in the west."

Until his father's last accusation, Paul had to admit there was truth in everything Andre said. He had been constantly unfaithful to Genie. He had used the casting couch to supply himself with women. He had gone to bed with many women Genie knew. It was all true. But it was not true he'd gone out of his way to seduce a poor thing like Joan Rosen. "This time the sun does rise in the west. Joan Rosen seduced me."

"You didn't turn her down. And then, irresponsibly, to get her pregnant?"

"She said she was on the pill. How was I to know?"

"You actually believed Jake and Maxine Rosen would permit their daughter to use the pill? You're not that stupid." The longer Andre continued, the bigger fool Paul saw himself as being. "How long did the affair go on?"

"There was no affair. It was that old cliche. A one-shot pregnancy."

"All right. I'll accept your story. She seduced you and lied about the pill." Andre paused, timing his next question for maximum effect. "Why would she do that?"

"You tell me."

"It appears she wants to marry you."

"It isn't going to happen."

"Shall we move on to other truths?"

"There's more?" Paul shifted in his chair. His father's use of his knowledge of Joan's pregnancy to break up his relationship with Genie was out of character. It would be more like him to urge Joan to get an abortion, and find her an abortionist. Unless he had a strong reason for behaving otherwise.

"Do you know what your theatrical productions have cost me over the years?"

"During the first four years, about thirty-five thousand dollars a year. Last year, nothing. And *Six Characters* is doing so well there's talk of taping the show for television. If that goes through, I can start repaying you some of the money you advanced."

"I don't want your money."

"You want me to marry Joan Rosen. Why?"

"Because she's pregnant, and you're the father."

"That's not a good answer. Let's get back to the truth. Why

do you want me to marry Joan? The truth, father. It's your turn.''

"Are you aware of what's happening to the United States economy north of 14th Street?"

"About the same that's happening south of 14th Street. The company's had to borrow money on occasion. Money's tight. Interest rates are sky-high. About what you'd expect with a monetarist running the Federal Reserve. So what?"

Andre was surprised at Paul's knowledge. It would save him a lot of explanations. "Where did you learn about monetarists?"

"At college. Thank you for my excellent education. I'll ask again. So what?"

"So plenty." Andre spent the next thirty minutes leading Paul through the maze of his dealings with Ralph Gluck. When he finished, he lit another cigarette and studied his son. Paul's face was full of so many shifting emotions, Andre was unable to pick up any single, overriding attitude beyond dismay.

Paul rubbed his chin and spoke as though to himself. "You told Genie about Joan to break us up so I'd be willing to marry Joan."

"You made my job easy."

"I suppose I did. What else did you tell her?"

It was time for another truth. Andre had to gamble Paul would accept it. "I showed her a bogus financial statement which claimed that I'd spent over two hundred thousand dollars last year to support your lifestyle and theatrical productions."

"You what! Do you have a copy of that statement?"

Andre reached into the drawer in the table and handed Paul the statement. Paul scanned the numbers. His face registered astonishment. It was not the fact that his father presented someone with a false financial statement signed by a bogus accountant. It was Genie. "Genie understands numbers. How could she believe this crap?"

"She was very upset. However, it wasn't the determining factor. I also told her about my business problems. How much I stood to lose."

"And if you lost all that money, you could no longer afford to support me in the style to which I've grown accustomed?"

"Of course not."

"Naturally, I couldn't support myself. That follows from

this fake statement. Very clever. Then you threw Joan Rosen at her.''

"I had Joan waiting in the small office."

Paul winced. "They met?"

"Do you think I'd take a chance on Genie's taking my word on anything as important as Joan?"

"I suppose not." Paul sounded resigned. "What did she say?"

"Nothing."

"Nothing?" The strain was beginning to tell on Paul. "So you offered her a bribe. Eight apartment houses to help Max and her set up their own business. And she accepted the bribe."

Remembering his original mistake, Andre felt he owed Paul a truthful answer. "She was going to leave you anyway. I didn't have to offer her the buildings."

"But you did, and she accepted."

"Would you have preferred her to turn them down?" Paul nodded. "It would have been a foolish decision."

"More honorable."

"It's a type of honor she can't afford." Andre's attitude was unexpectedly understanding. "Don't blame her, Paul. Nothing made any difference to Genie Szabo except Joan Rosen. She couldn't take Joan."

"I understand that. Still . . ." He tried to suppress his anger at Genie and get to the matter at hand. "Although the answer is obvious, I'd like to hear you say it. Why do you want me to marry Joan?"

"Because Jake Rosen wants you as his son-in-law. And the father of his grandchild."

"He'll bail you out of your jam with Gluck?"

"Only if you marry Joan."

"Only if I marry Joan." Paul walked to the window and stood with his back to the office looking up Park Avenue. He studied the cars with unseeing eyes, trying to collect his thoughts. If he told Genie the truth about Joan, about the falsified financial statements, if he agreed to marry her, he believed she would marry him. That would put an end to his father's acting like Machiavelli's prince. In every business deal there are winners and losers, and in the one with Gluck, his father was a loser. He'd won enough in a lifetime of not playing by the rules. Paul thought he ought to be ashamed of his father.

But what right did he have to pass judgement on him? Andre had always been straight with his family, if not the world. He'd known since he was a teenager how his father operated. He'd known and enjoyed the way of life his father's business practices made possible. And if one wanted to put a fine point on it, hadn't his father given him his theatrical career? If Andre hadn't picked up the tab while he was learning, he had no idea if he'd have achieved the success he had. His father had been indulgent with him, never narrow, pinched, or mean. His father had given him much. It would be dishonest of him not to acknowledge the facts. He wasn't even angry at his lying to Genie. Or telling her about Joan. Andre was fighting a desperate battle, and although the loss of millions was important, there was another loss that counted far more. His father was fighting to save his image of himself. In a fight of that sort, Paul understood there was little his father wouldn't do to win. He'd given his father the weapons. Andre had simply used them.

Paul's mind returned to Genie. If he married Joan, what would it mean to Genie? He couldn't rid himself of the memory of the voice of the man who had answered her phone. She certainly hadn't waited long to replace him. Paul realized, considering his own behavior, his jealousy was irrational. But there it was. More important, what about that management contract? His father said she'd made her decision to leave him prior to accepting the contract. Was that true? If it was, why had Andre offered her the contract at all? And after he'd offered it, why had she accepted it? Didn't she realize how it looked? A clean break would have been better. He felt he'd been used, and his belief in Genie's love for him was shaken. He'd always known she was ambitious, more than ambitious, desperate for success. He remembered her cross-examining him about 608's on that summer afternoon so long ago. And his willingness to betray his father. The betrayal sickened him. He'd chosen Genie over his father then. Did he want to repeat that choice?

Now, staring out the window in the late afternoon, Paul stood face to face with his own nature. In the final analysis, the one person he had to live with was himself. And it was Andre who'd taught him to distinguish between what he really felt and what he thought he should feel, otherwise one would never learn the truth about oneself. If by refusing to marry Joan and causing his father to lose so much that was precious to him, could he ever be at peace with himself? Wasn't something owed for all that had been so freely given him? Did he really have a choice?

When he turned from the window, Andre was sitting almost exactly as he'd left him, except he was smoking one of his endless supply of Gauloises. He had the same half smile on his face—the same ease and grace as he tipped the long ash into the alabaster ashtray. For all the tension Andre showed, they might have been discussing whether they should walk home on this balmy evening or have his chauffeur drive them. Paul wondered if he'd ever be able to maintain that kind of public face.

Andre had been waiting. As the minutes passed and Paul continued to stare out the window, he'd grown more confident. It had been a matter of allowing Paul to think of the reasons for doing what Andre wished him to do. Given time, Andre was certain he would.

"Exactly what are the terms of the deal you cut with Rosen?" Paul asked.

"The terms are simple. You marry Joan. Jake picks up Ralph's shares and puts up the money to carry the interest payments for three years. Three years will be long enough for the economy to change."

"What guarantees do you have that Jake will live up to his end of the deal? After my experience with Joan, I don't trust the Rosens. She had to learn from her father."

"We've agreed on a simultaneous marriage and contract signing."

"Sounds like feudal times. Do we need pig's blood to stain the sheets? I can see waving them out the hotel window the morning after the wedding. It would stop traffic."

Andre chuckled. "I don't think bloodstained sheets are necessary."

"How do you know Rosen won't back out even after signing?"

Andre stopped smiling. "If he does, our lawyers will be all over him."

"He has more money than we do. So his lawyers will be at our lawyers. And in the meantime, who pays the interest?"

Andre had considered the same problem. There was only one safe answer. The total sum should be put in escrow—over one hundred million dollars. Would Jake agree to that? Although he would try, he didn't think so. He hedged his answer. "We'll try to protect ourselves as best we can. That's all we can do."

Paul remained doubtful. He only hoped Andre's lawyers were smart enough. "One final question, father. Am I correct in assuming Jake and you have already worked out when and where these momentous events will take place?"

"No, you're not. Are you aware, Paul, I'm a superstitious man?"

"No more than most people. Ladders, black cats, and the like."

"Well, I am. And one of my superstitions is never to plan for an event until I'm certain it will take place."

"Did you think there was a real possibility I'd turn you down?"

"I'd like to say no, but since this is a truth-telling session, the answer is, yes. I thought you might turn me down."

"Doesn't say nice things about either of us."

"I don't know. What's wrong with being realistic? I watched you at the window. It was a close thing for a while."

The thin white scar on Paul's lip reappeared. "True. There was a moment . . ."

"That's all it takes."

"Anyway, now that you know I won't let you down, I have a suggestion and a favor to ask. Make as tough a contract with Rosen as possible. And make it as small a wedding as possible."

"The wedding is out of my control. Your mother and Mrs. Rosen will make that decision, and I'm afraid neither will understand a small wedding."

"Then make it quickly or the bride might have to wear a maternity wedding gown."

"You'll be a husband within weeks."

"I assume mother is expecting me for dinner?"

"She isn't. You must realize I couldn't tell her about our meeting."

"Of course. Foolish of me. Since I'm north of 14th Street, call her. Tell her I dropped in, and you're bringing me home to dinner. I'll break the news about Joan to her. She'll love it."

Andre shook his head. "She won't, you know. She really won't."

* * *

It took three days to work out the final terms of the family/business merger, which was the way Andre thought of the proceedings. As he'd expected, Jake Rosen refused to place over one hundred million dollars in escrow. They had settled on one year or just over thirty-six million, and in order to get Jake to agree to that, Andre had to make a potentially disastrous concession. If the original money was used up and more required to cover interest payments, Jake had an option to buy Andre's interest for Andre's original investment of thirty million dollars. Rosen claimed that was only fair since he would have more money invested than Andre. Andre chose not to tell Paul of this takeover clause and hoped he would never have to.

He arranged to have a silver dollar encased in a Lucite square and delivered to Ralph Gluck. A photocopy of the one-page agreement which assigned Ralph's holdings to him was on the bottom of the Lucite. The print was small but quite legible. Andre would have given a good deal to have seen Ralph's face when he received the package. He would have enjoyed Ralph's rage. However, Andre miscalculated his man. Gluck had so seldom been beaten in anything, he believed Andre was entitled to his full triumph. He'd found out about the coming marriage, and it wasn't very hard to deduce what Andre had done. In fact, he was pleased with the Lucite square. He placed it on his desk as a constant reminder never to underestimate an opponent at any time. He'd underestimated Andre's need to beat him and the extent to which he would go to satisfy that need. Not having a warm relationship with his own son, he had also left Paul's love and feeling of obligation to his father out of consideration. He thought briefly about calling Genie Szabo now that she was free and decided against it. Thirty years' difference in their ages was too great.

The mothers agreed to a short engagement, and the wedding was scheduled to take place in four weeks. In spite of Paul's wishes, it would be a huge affair at the grand ballroom of the Plaza. Joan was the Rosens' only child and deserved a wedding she could remember as one of the most beautiful events in her life.

Genie sat up and blinked at the early morning sun shining into her eyes as it reflected off the glass covering a Picasso print. She looked around the apartment, which was a testimony to the last few months of her life, being both full and empty at the same time. Although Paul had done as she requested and collected his belongings while she was at work, the apartment still resonated with his presence. It would always be that way. The bed she was sitting on had been bought by him. The bookshelves had been built by him. Even the books he had left—everything that did not relate directly to the theater—had been bought by both of them. The rug and the couch upon which they had made love remained. With the exception of his clothes and the corner of the living room which had been reserved for his work, everything was the same. Only Paul himself was gone.

Though it meant far less, Jack O'Neil was gone, too. Last night he had taken her home, made love to her, and left for good. Although his reasons were not discussed openly, Jack and Genie understood and agreed it was for the best. Jack had started to take her seriously, and while Genie was flattered, she was not in love with him. She was the wrong woman for Jack, and Genie knew all too well the heartbreak that comes from loving the wrong person. So they agreed to stay in touch—after all, they were in the same business—but the affair was over.

Thinking back, it seemed to Genie the last three months had passed in a blur. After the first exultant explosion when she told Max her news about their managing the Husseman buildings, they went to work to plan for the future. First they had to pick a name for their company and organize it as a corporation. Szabo & Szabo, Inc., was formed by a lawyer friend of Max's and filed in Albany. After incorporating came the matter of selecting an office location. It had to be convenient and inexpensive. They chose Queensboro Plaza, an area just over the 59th Street bridge in Queens. A small suite of offices was available on the top floor of a two-story block-long building. It was convenient to all the subways. Since the IRT and BMT both became elevated lines at Queensboro Plaza, Max had an advertising idea which he convinced the landlord to insert in their lease. A one-hundred-foot-long sign in white with red letters that read Szabo & Szabo—Real Estate now faced the elevated subway stations.

Remembering the morning it had been finished, Genie smiled. Max and she stood on the curb craning their heads skyward trying to read the sign. No matter how far they leaned back, it was unreadable.

"I don't think we'll grab the sidewalk traffic," she had teased Max.

"I told you that's not the point. Come on! Let's contribute to the solvency of the New York subway system and find out how it reads from the IRT platform. That's the test." When they stood on the platform, the sign stared them in the face. "See what I mean?"

"Can you arrange to have the car windows cleaned so the riders will be able to read our sign?"

"Don't need to. While you were running around looking at the buildings, your innovative brother spent some time during the rush hour standing where we are now. The platform was mobbed with people changing from the IRT to the BMT or vice versa. Those folks have nothing better to do than read our sign."

"At least they'll know we exist, and who knows what might come from that?" She felt a deep satisfaction and added, "The office furniture and files arrive tomorrow, including all the agents' records we need for operating the buildings. Max, do you realize we're actually in business?"

"Yeah. I know. Any trouble with the previous agents?"

"No. Mr. Husseman saw to that."

"Kidlet, I admire your nerve. That was some trade you made. Paul for eight buildings."

Genie tried to pass it off. "Don't admire me too much. It wasn't cut and dried. I omitted some of the finer points of the deal."

Max caught something in her voice and backed off. "I figured as much. Don't fill me in. I'm just proud you had the guts to go the distance." He gave her a hug. "With Paul marrying someone named Joan Rosen, as the *New York Times* announced, picture of the bride and all, he's past history. Let's look at the future. Our new offices."

When Max took her hand, Genie steadied herself and nodded. He led her down the stairs, across the street, and into the building that would house the new firm of Szabo & Szabo, Inc.

Their offices were the best she could do on a limited budget, but they would do. The walls and ceiling were painted an off-white, and the white asphalt tile floors were washed and waxed. A fake Oriental, bought in Macy's, for the outer office and two navy blue carpets, purchased at Woolworth's, covered Max's office and what eventually would be hers. All the office furniture, including the typewriter, was secondhand. The only extra she'd permitted herself was new file cabinets. Files were the lifeblood of their business. They'd borrowed another of Jack O'Neil's ideas and took pictures of the eight buildings they were going to manage. When they could afford it, they planned to hire a secretary-receptionist. That was when Genie would move into the second inner office.

She was grateful for the way Andre Husseman had cooperated. He'd provided them with the operating records of all the buildings for the past five years, had informed the superintendents of each building of the management change, and had personally instructed the supers to provide her with any information she required. If the supers had any objections to working for a woman, they never surfaced. Max and she gave the usual two weeks notice and both had the satisfaction of refusing requests from their employers to stay. It was nice to be wanted.

The other day they'd tossed a coin to decide who would be president and who secretary-treasurer. Max lost and was stuck with the unwanted title of president. He explained to her it was excess baggage. There was no way he could canvass a loft building or show space to a customer with a business card that identified him as the president. "President of what?" they would ask. What was Szabo & Szabo, Inc.? If his card read "sales and leasing," a landlord might think he was one of a number of salesmen working for the firm and be more willing to list space with him. A client, having the same idea, would be more inclined to look at the space he suggested. Genie agreed with Max's logic and had her cards printed managing agent. Who cared that she was secretary-treasurer of a firm with two employees?

Today was the day Max and she were officially opening their doors. They were to meet at the office at nine o'clock. For a moment she stared at the ceiling remembering another day when she'd met Andre Husseman at his office, and struggled again with her sense of loss. While she accepted the reasons for Paul's marrying Joan—it was the only thing he could do given the circumstances—she bitterly resented it and everything the marriage stood for. Then, slowly, she gathered herself together, losing patience with her self-pity. This was the life she'd chosen. She would go on from here. On and on, and with luck, up and up. Max and she, working together, would show them all how far the super's kids could go.

21

Andre Husseman left his office early, having decided to walk home, something he did occasionally when he needed solitude to sort out his thoughts. Despite the crowded New York sidewalks, it was the one place where the telephone could not ring, there was no mail to open, and Harriet Greenspan, his secretary for more years than he cared to remember, could not interrupt, no matter how great the emergency. He planned to be home ahead of Sara, who was visiting Joan and the baby in Joan's suite in the Rosen apartment. He assumed Sara would be in a state. She usually was after visiting Joan, and he considered it his husbandly duty to be at home to comfort her.

Sara was disturbed that Joan had given birth seven months after Paul and she were married. Added to that, the fact that the premature baby was fully formed and as large as many a baby carried nine months raised serious, if unvoiced, questions in Sara's head. Andre had briefly considered telling her the details of the deal he'd made with Rosen, then dismissed the idea as a mistake. Sara had led far too sheltered a life to accept the connection between business, sex, and feudal marriages. It would shake her faith in Paul as a decent upright young man to say nothing of what it might do to her trust in him.

Sara had been born in 101 Central Park West and had moved to 115 Central Park West after she and Andre married. In spite of the summers they'd spent in Europe and winter vacations in the Caribbean, Mexico, and other warm climates, Sara's real world was bounded by 70th Street on the south, 72nd Street on north, and Central Park West and Columbus Avenue on the east and west. She hoped once Paul was married he would give up the Village and move uptown to Central Park West. Certainly Joan was prepared to live in 101 or 115. However, Paul refused to accept a loan from Andre or Jake Rosen to buy an apartment.

His position was simple. Either the Rosen or Husseman apartment was large enough to provide a suite for Joan and him. And if Joan wasn't satisfied, she could buy any apartment she chose. As for himself, he would keep his small flat on Bank Street in the Village. In fact, at the start of their marriage, he'd spent many a night in the Village, explaining that the late hours he put in at the theater made it difficult for him to take a taxi uptown to be with his wife. Faced with that situation, Joan chose to move into a separate wing in the huge apartment in 101 owned by her parents. If and when Paul did appear, it gave her privacy, and it had several rooms which were turned into a nursery for the baby and a room for the full-time nurse. This design for living further outraged Sara's idea of what was fitting and proper.

As he walked home, Andre's mind turned from Sara and her indignation to Jake Rosen. Unlike Ralph Gluck, lacking Ralph's sense of humor or Ralph's knowledge that there was a wider world than the one of amassing money, Jake was rude and crude. He irritated Andre far more than Ralph at his worst ever had. Originally their meetings consisted primarily of Jake's complaining to Andre about Paul's behavior towards Joan, with the outright threat that if Paul didn't change, he would execute his option at the end of the year. Then, abruptly, Paul did change. He became a model husband, spending every night with Joan, and Jake quieted down. But it was Andre's guess that if the economy didn't turn around, what Paul did was irrelevant. Jake, being Jake, would take over the properties. Andre's major concern was how to explain it to Paul since Paul knew nothing of the takeover clause in the contract, and undoubtedly would never have married Joan if he had known.

Over the last six months Andre had spent sleepless nights examining his motives in having Paul marry Joan. Originally he thought he had no choice, but something within him was deeply troubled by the immorality of his actions. He'd sacrificed his son's happiness, played on his loyalties, in order to make a business win. A big win, inspired by his obsession for big money. He'd made a million—made ten, even thirty million. But he wanted more. He wanted the hundreds of millions he now realized Gluck was worth. He remembered something his father once told him. The first million is very hard and very important. It gives you freedom. Five or six million can buy you extraordinary luxuries. After that, it's a game. And the name of the game is power—or pride. Since Andre knew power did not interest him, he had to accept that his motivation had been pride. But the reality was, the times had gone against him. Gluck had been prepared. He hadn't. It was difficult to accept that he wasn't up to the big game. And to save his face, save his pride, he'd bartered Paul. He'd always had his own double standard of suitable behavior. Different for business than for private life. And he'd had the the confidence of one who lived according to those standards. When immersed in the realities of business, when building 608's or destroying a neighborhood to construct a Title One project, he'd accepted his actions as those of a businessman. This made it possible for him to ignore the pain and the suffering his actions had caused other human beings. But now he'd betrayed his own private code of ethics. It astonished him how far his pride had taken him. It had driven him beyond his business code and compromised his private standards.

He couldn't remain indifferent to this fact. His love for his son was deep, tenacious, and more spontaneous than any other feeling he'd ever had. And he had damaged Paul by his indifference to everything but his pride in winning. For many months now his pride had been fighting with his conscience— fighting his many doubts about Paul's marriage to Joan. Deep in a secret part of his soul, he almost welcomed the prospect of losing the condominium project. He didn't deserve to win. Pride, which had led him so astray, was finally giving way to the other side of Andre, the side of him that cared what happened to people, that wished he'd been other than a destroyer of lives. He doubted very strongly, no matter how the REIT finally came out, that he would ever start another building project. How he would spend the rest of his life was something he'd have to think about.

When Andre arrived home, Sara was waiting for him in the library. That she still had her coat on was strange enough. But that her hair remained uncombed was even stranger. He wondered what could have angered her so much she'd neglected to comb her hair. Even when they made love, Sara's first action afterward was to rush to her vanity to comb her hair. As Gluck said, she was not a Jewish nymphomaniac. He waited for her to explain her distress. Was it the premature baby? Was it where Paul chose to live? It was neither.

"Andre, I've just been to see Joan and our granddaughter. And by misfortune I ran into Jake and Maxine. The language Jake Rosen used when speaking about Paul made me so angry I almost slapped his face. When I told him never to use such language in front of me, or about my son, do you know what he said?" She paused in embarrassment, then gathered herself. "He said, 'Sara Husseman, tough sh—sh . . .' " Sara gulped and blurted out the words. " 'Tough shit!' " She stood in front of Andre, her feet planted wide apart in indignation. "I will not have those people in our home again, nor do I ever wish to visit them again. They are vulgar, disgusting people. I was against the marriage, and now I know how right I was."

Jake's crudity was well within his character, though a little raw, even for him, in front of Sara. Andre had to placate his wife. At least for the time being. "I agree with you. But if you won't have them here and you won't visit them, when will we see our granddaughter?"

"You will insist Paul purchase an apartment in the Majestic. His wife and child will live there, and we'll see the baby in their home."

"I don't think Paul will agree to buy an apartment."

Sara was more adamant than Andre had ever seen her. "He'll have to." She chewed on her lip. "Andre, do you know why Jake Rosen behaved so disgustingly?"

"No."

"I'll tell you. Although I despise the man, I have to admit he was in the right. He was furious because Paul refused to help Joan pick a name for the child."

"I see." Andre thought about this. It was one thing to ignore your wife. It was another thing to ignore your own child. Much as he disliked the prospect, he would have to talk to Paul.

Then Sara let loose her thunderbolt. "Andre, I know my son. If Paul doesn't care enough either to live with or name the child, then he's not the father of the child. That was no seven-month baby! Joan was months pregnant when Paul married her."

Andre was struck with Sara's insight. Given mother love, it never occurred to her that her upstanding son could possibly have caused Joan's premarital pregnancy. And because it never occurred to her, she'd come up with a remarkable bit of intuition. Suppose Paul wasn't the father? He mentally reconstructed the timetable of events. Paul and Joan had been to bed in November. If Paul's story was true and it was a one-shot pregnancy, then the baby would be an eleven-month baby. Was there such a thing? He'd check with the obstetrician. And recheck Paul's story with Paul at the proper time. The more he considered the possibility, the more logical it seemed. It explained Paul's unusually callous behavior. Paul had done the same arithmetic and come to the same conclusion. He was not the father of the child.

Sara had one last word on the subject. "If Paul isn't the father, I want to know. And if he is, he will have to find a way for our seeing the child."

Andre rubbed his chin. "It won't be easy for me to find out what Paul thinks. It will take time and tact. In the meantime I suggest you make the best of the Rosens. We have no choice."

It was a few weeks before Andre and Paul were able to meet privately. They sat in the same seats they'd sat in almost a year before. After several minutes of polite conversation, Andre made a blunt statement. "Paul, you've been living with Joan more than you did during the first months. But we know you've refused to have anything to do with naming the baby. When did you realize you were not the father?" He watched for Paul's reaction and was pleased to see almost none. The usually mobile face was still.

"Are we still playing the truth game?"

"Yes."

"Why didn't you tell me about the takeover clause in your agreement?" Suddenly Andre felt foolish. How could he have missed the obvious? Jake would tell Paul to make him toe the line. That explained his switch to a model husband role. Paul's next words verified his guess. "Jake told me. He warned me if I refused to conform to his idea of a husband, he would buy you out as per the contract. When I said I didn't believe he could, he showed me the agreement."

"What did you say?"

"I said I'd do my best. Providing he eased off you. And I have tried. The other day he started leaning on me. He said I should get out of the theater and go into his business. 'Be a man. Not a fucking pansy! Be a Rosen.' A Rosen! I told him to take his business and shove it. I agreed to be a husband. Not his

water boy. So I thought I'd better warn you." Paul continued.
"I was so mad I suggested I might go to court and prove I
wasn't the father of Joan's child."

"He must have relished that."

"He was apoplectic. But if it comes to a choice between
Joan's reputation and your condos, he'll opt for the condos."

"When did you find out about the baby?"

Paul considered the question. He had an opportunity to strike
a devastating blow at his father. If he told Andre he'd known all
along and only agreed to save him, Andre would be forever in
his debt. Did he want his father owing him so much? Wasn't it
enough that he'd paid his debt? Was it necessary to collect a
bonus in return for meeting his obligation? No! He owed his father an honest answer.

"The truth. I didn't figure it out until after we were married.
Dr. Berman told me when he expected Joan to give birth."

"What did he say?"

"I ran into him at the theater. He congratulated me and made
some stupid crack about seven-month babies being the rage in
the theater. Then I did the numbers. Eleven-month babies are
not the rage anywhere."

"Do you think Jake put her up to it?"

"Yes. She's not very bright. He is. The Husseman name is a
good one, and he wanted her married and off the streets. Joan is
an easy lay. She was a long way from being a virgin when we
made it."

"If Jake runs true to form and exercises his rights under the
contract, will you follow through and take Joan into court?"

"No. It isn't fair to the baby and would accomplish nothing.
Revenge for the sake of revenge isn't my idea of human behavior."

Andre looked down pretending to study a fleck of dirt on the
tip of his shoe. When he raised his eyes to meet his son's he
said, "So in spite of everything I've done wrong, somehow
you've turned out to be a man."

"You did the best you could. I wish you'd told me about the
takeover clause. I believe I'd have married her anyway. I owed
it to you. To give you your chance." He said it matter-of-factly
but with a trace of sadness. "I just wish you'd trusted me
more."

"I wish I had it to do over. You wouldn't have married Joan."

"What's done is done. I'll stick the year. Then we'll see what Jake does." He frowned. "Father, if he leans on you, the buy-out is thirty million, right?" Andre nodded. "So at the worst, my marriage will be worth thirty million. That's not nothing. Either way we're square."

"Square." For a moment Andre was silent. Then he decided to risk it. "Would you like me to speak to Genie? I could explain everything."

Paul didn't hesitate. "No. There's a time for all things, and the time for Genie and me has passed. I did sleep with Joan and all those other ladies." He chose not to mention the doubts about Genie he'd been feeling. "We'll see what the future holds. But for now, no."

"As you wish."

"As I wish." Paul rose to leave. Andre put his arm around his son's shoulder and walked with him to the door. Looking at his son he thought, if they'd been luckier, if events had not taken hold of them, his love for Paul would not have shown its flaw. He was too realistic not to realize that their intimacy had been damaged. Andre knew he'd never find another relationship as deep and important as the one he'd had with his son. Maybe, in time, Paul would again feel as he'd once felt toward him. Then there was Genie. He would think about Genie and see if there was something he could do.

The winter had come and gone, and it was spring. Szabo & Szabo was almost ready to celebrate a year in business. While Genie attended to the routine building management—collecting rents, repairing a boiler in one building, finding a qualified super in another building—Max had devoted himself to trying to sell or lease office and factory space. Although he'd closed a few small leases, it hadn't gone as he'd expected. Much to his chagrin, he'd found the transition from being a successful salesman for Robert Alpert & Company to being the same for Szabo & Szabo was not that easy. Landlords were not inclined to list space with him, and clients seemed to prefer doing business with a more established firm. Max was going through a dry spell, and it increasingly depressed him.

"It's a damn good thing you got us those Husseman build-

ings. We sure need that income to pay the rent and our salaries.
I'm beginning to feel like a fifth wheel.''

"Quit it, Max. It's never easy for the new kids on the block.
Something will break for you. Managing buildings was supposed to be our bread and butter. Leasing and selling is the
icing. You read me the bible yourself, and see how right you
were." Genie was doing her best to bolster Max's spirits.

"Yeah, sure. Max Szabo, man of vision." He cocked his
head to one side as though weighing an idea. "I might have a
lead on something, but I need your help."

"What is it?"

"Sheila Roth's parents have invited us to dinner Friday
night. They live in Jamaica Estates."

"Sheila Roth? Us? Isn't she your latest model type?"

"She's a good kid. She doesn't pester me about marriage."

"She wouldn't. You're not an eligible husband."

"Like you with Paul?"

"Same reasons, more or less." Genie managed to hide her
dismay at Max's reminder of Paul and what had happened to
them.

"Even if it turns out to be a fizzle, we'll get a good meal."

"Don't sell me. I'll go. But why do they want to meet me?
You I can understand. More or less, anyway. They want to
make sure your intentions are, if dishonorable, at least not serious."

"Why you? I don't know. Sheila's father sells sportswear for
Oak Ridge Fashions, and Sheila thought Oak Ridge might be
looking for more space. Ready for this one? Her father saw our
sign on the subway to work, and he asked her if the Szabo she
was dating was the real estate Szabo. So we're invited."

"Anything to make a buck. Especially if her mother's a real
Jewish cook."

Mrs. Roth was, and the way Genie ate pleased her. "I can
tell you like Jewish cooking."

"Oh, I do! We grew up a block from Fine and Schapiro's, a
great kosher deli." Genie took another bite of a matzoh ball.
"I'm a chicken soup and matzoh ball freak. Chicken soup is
Jewish penicillin."

Sam Roth had thick black hair streaked with grey and a handsome lined face that showed a Slavic heritage in its width and

heavy bone structure. He was short and sturdily built. Genie wondered why, given the amount of food he ate, he wasn't fat. She liked the man. His love of good food was equal to hers and Max's. He ate so continuously he hadn't time to join in the conversation. However, when the main course was eaten and they'd settled down to apple strudel and tea in a glass, he saved Max the trouble of finding a tactful opening by introducing the topic of Oak Ridge's need for space himself.

"Sheila tells me you lease factory space, Max."

"Factory space, office space. She tells me your firm might be looking for some additional loft space."

"Might be . . ." He glanced at Genie. "I understand from Sheila you manage a number of apartment houses."

Signals began to flash in Genie's mind. "Yes. I'm the inside man of Szabo & Szabo. Max is the outside man."

"How many buildings do you manage?"

"Eight in various parts of Queens. Six-story, red brick, rent-controlled buildings. In good condition." She smiled at him, encouragingly, giving him the additional information to spare him asking questions.

Sam answered her smile with a grin of his own. He knew she'd picked up his thought. "Any vacancies?"

"How soon do you need a place?"

"Six months at the most."

Max looked around the pleasant dining room. The Roths rented the ground floor of a comfortable, well-kept, two-family house. According to Sheila, she'd grown up in the house. Now he understood too, and his professional mind went to work. "How much is going to be torn down and what's going up?"

"The entire block is going. They're putting up a high-rise apartment house. A hundred dollars a room. We can't afford it."

Sheila was not as good as her parents at containing her emotions. "I grew up in this house. Daddy thought Mom and he would live here forever. Or at least until they retired and moved to Florida." She showed her concern. "They don't deserve this to happen."

"Sheila, dear, it's not the end of the world," said Mrs. Roth.

Genie watched the young girl, fascinated. Sheila reminded her so much of herself all those years ago when the same thing had almost happened to their family because they didn't own their own home. They weren't even renters the way these people were. And now it was happening to them. Her face became thoughtful and then smoothed over. "I won't make any promises, but . . ."

"We only need four rooms," Mrs. Roth said, hopefully. "Now that Sheila lives in Manhattan."

"I'll see what's possible." All at once Genie couldn't help herself. Even if there was no factory space deal for Max, she couldn't allow these people to hang by their thumbs. "Could you afford one-eighty-five a month for the four rooms?"

"Oh, yes!" Relief flooded Roth's face, and Genie realized what an effort he'd been making to appear unconcerned. "We've been scouring Queens for something like that. But there's always someone ahead of us. You see, I have to live near a subway. I open the place at seven-thirty."

"I know of a sunny four-room apartment on Queens Boulevard right near the Forest Hills station of the IND that will be available in three months." Genie was bent on allowing the Roths to maintain their pride by being offhand herself. "The couple living there is moving to Dallas."

Involuntarily, Sam Roth reached out and patted Genie's arm. Then he turned to Max. "What's the opposite of an eye for an eye? A loft for a bedroom? Call Sandor Kaplan Monday morning. Say I told you to call and tell him about the loft space you have available."

When Genie and Max met the following Monday morning, they had their usual business discussion over coffee. No, there was nothing unusual to report about the buildings. Yes, she'd double-check the superintendent in the building she'd mentioned to the Roths to make sure of the coming vacancy. Max was anxious to call Kaplan which he did as soon as he finished his coffee. An appointment was set up for that afternoon. Then, much to his surprise, a call came in from a client with whom he'd been working for the last six months. The man had finally made a decision, and Max would receive an offer tomorrow.

"It never rains but it pours!" Max said after he'd hung up.

"I told you your luck would change." Genie was delighted. Not only because of the commissions, which might be large, but because of the ego boost it gave Max. If he could close a large deal, it would make up for a year of disappointment. And

it was further proof to Genie that her confidence in their ultimate success was not misplaced. But beyond what they were
doing, she'd had a genuinely original idea over the weekend.

Max noticed her preoccupation and prodded her. "I don't
want to sound nosey, but I am. You've got something germi-
nating in that fertile brain of yours."

Genie sipped her coffee. "I'll tell you just as soon as I get it
straight in my fertile brain." But she couldn't keep the excitement out of her voice. "Anyway, don't you have an appointment with Mr. Klein at 333 Seventh Avenue to show some
space?"

Max looked at his watch and reacted immediately. "I'll have
to take a cab to be on time."

"The subway's faster. Especially this time of day."

"And cheaper?"

"And cheaper!"

Max finished his coffee and tossed the paper cup into the
wastepaper basket. "See you, kidlet. If you have to leave,
check in with the answering service. I'll leave messages, too."

After he left, Genie cleaned up the remains of the coffee and
went to the files. The evening at the Roths had disturbed her
deeply. It made her bitter and a little sick thinking how vulnerable families such as the Roths were. But the evening had awakened something that had lain dormant for many years. What
was happening to the Roths was happening because they were
apartment renters, not owners. Apartment owners could not be
forced to move.

As she'd turned this idea over in her head, a young long-ago
dream that had been vague, nebulous, undefined, began to take
shape. It stayed with her through the weekend and grew so
strong that she could hardly wait for the weekend to become
Monday so she could get back to the files in the office. She actually started to go to the office on Sunday and decided at the
last minute not to, electing instead to give herself time to think
through her plan in a logical step-by-step sequence.

Now with Max off to see Kaplan, she started pulling folders
from the files. She knew exactly what she wanted to do, if it
could be done. She wanted to sell apartments to middle-income
people. People like the Roths and her parents. It was a new
idea. A big idea. No one had ever thought of converting

middle-income, rent-controlled apartments into cooperatives. But wasn't there a first time for everything?

The first question that needed answering was simple and absolutely crucial. Was it possible to turn rental apartments in middle-income buildings into co-ops that the renters could afford? Or was owning your own apartment only the privilege of the wealthy?

Since she could not devote full time to the question, it took most of the week for Genie to come to a decision. She'd arrive at the office an hour earlier, then put in a full day doing the routine business of managing their buildings. At the end of an eight-hour day of management problems, she put in another two hours on her own project going over the facts and figures.

"What are you doing here so late, kidlet?" Max asked one evening when he dropped by the office to pick up additional information on some space for Kaplan. Kaplan was looking more and more like a buyer.

"I'll tell you when I'm ready, and don't try to read upside down."

"You're acting like a secret agent."

"Only my secret isn't the formula for a new weapons system. It's a formula for living happily ever after. Wait and see."

"I'll wait. With bated breath." Max picked up his folder and left.

Genie analyzed each building they managed—its mortgage, taxes, maintenence, and exactly how much income Andre Husseman had received over the past years from the buildings. She tried to establish a hypothetical purchase price for an apartment as well as how much it would cost a tenant on a per room basis to buy the apartment, and what the monthly maintenance would be. To arrive at a price she used the classic real estate formula for selling apartment houses. A total price of six times the rent roll. She divided this figure by the number of rooms in the building and allowed for individual apartment differences, such as the floor the apartment was on, what the view was, and other variables.

When she finally finished her calculations, she stared at her numbers in disbelief. The building on 43rd Street off Roosevelt Avenue, for example, contained 125 apartments and had a rent roll of $165,000. If that building went co-op, the average apartment could be bought for less than $8,000, despite the current rate of inflation. Genie was astonished. For a well-maintained building, convenient to the city, in a decent neighborhood, it was a low purchase price. And since she'd figured the mortgage in the total price, the actual cash each tenant would have to pay would be considerably less. Her instinct had been correct. From the tenant's point of view, it was both practical and prudent. Actually it was an ideal investment. It would provide families like the Roths and the Szabos with the safety net that comes when one owns one's own home. Max could use his considerable selling ability to persuade the tenants to buy their apartments. She was not so naive as to think all tenants would see the advantage of owning their own home. Some would think they were being conned, but Max would convince them, and Szabo & Szabo would make sizeable commissions selling the apartments. If making money was something she wanted desperately, making money by doing what she believed in was even better. Of course, Max would have to be careful. Genie still remembered Mrs. Robbins' suicide when the Majestic went co-op. There might be a few tenants who simply could not afford even the few thousand dollars required to purchase their apartments. Very well. They could remain tenants.

There was only one thing to do. Convince Andre Husseman to convert his buildings into co-ops. To sell them to the tenants. At this point Genie stopped. Her brain raced in a new direction. Suddenly another thought burst forth and lay before her, shining and clear. Why should Szabo & Szabo simply make a commission on selling the apartments in the buildings that Husseman co-oped? The commissions would be nothing compared to what they'd make if they owned the buildings themselves and sold the apartments to the tenants. The idea was so compelling, so powerful, she had to force herself to sit calmly and consider it from every angle. Why shouldn't she propose to Andre—it was so audacious Genie had to pause before she dared continue—that he sell the buildings to Max and her? She gasped at the thought. In her mind's eye she saw the harsh, disapproving face of her mother staring at her. Buy Andre Husseman's buildings? You? The daughter of a superintendent! Have you taken leave of your senses? Genie nodded. Yes, she had. Maybe she was drunk with her idea. But drunk or not, all she wanted to know at this moment was how high a price he would ask. If the price was too high, Szabo & Szabo would not be able to resell the apartments to the tenants at a reasonable price, and her whole idea would go down the drain.

Hoping against hope, Genie went back to her numbers. Andre was a businessman. He was practical. If he would agree to sell them at all, he would not ask a crazy price. Suppose he asked seven and a half million for the eight buildings? That was more than six times the total rent roll. At that price could they— her mind was flying at top speed, adding, subtracting, multiplying the numbers—could they still afford to resell the apartments at affordable prices? They could! When she came to the end of her calculations, she was breathless and flushed with excitement, as if she'd been running a race. Unless she was wrong about Andre and he asked a totally unreasonable price, it was all possible, and it would be profitable to Andre. Max, and herself, as owners, and to the tenants, who would benefit from the best possible investments they could make.

Genie's hand shook as she poured herself a cup of coffee and slowly sipped the hot black liquid. Sitting quietly, trying to regain her composure, she thought about the next obvious question. Why should Andre Husseman sell his buildings? He'd owned them over twenty years. He didn't need the money. And they provided him with an income on one hand and protection against taxes on the income on the other. She was concentrating so hard that the ringing telephone jarred her, almost causing her to spill her coffee. It was Jack O'Neil.

"Genie! How did I know you were working late?"

"You know human nature. That's why you're a first-class building manager."

"Flattery will get you everywhere. How about a celebration dinner? Hasn't Szabo & Szabo been in business a year today?"

"A year next week. Max and I are planning a small celebration."

"Okay. How about a preanniversary dinner tonight? We're both working late. I could use a pretty woman who likes to talk shop."

"You sound harassed."

"Mildly. You want to buy a sixty-million-dollar building?"

"Ooops. That's a little steep. You're a few years ahead of my schedule. Who's selling?"

"The Ferris Brothers have put the Excelsior on the block—

their forty-story apartment house on 56th Street. You could get in with only fifteen million cash.''

''Only fifteen million. Cheap at twice the price. Oh! I see your problem. Suppose the buyer has a cousin who's a managing agent?''

''Right! I need a buyer who thinks of me as a cousin. Or there goes a hefty commission and a beautiful monthly management check.''

''Why are they selling? That building is a money machine.''

''Was a money machine. The Ferris boys are big builders. Unlike Christopher Wren, they are interested in money, not posterity. They'd have sold Canterbury Cathedral if they didn't make at least a ten percent return on their cash.''

''So? They must make that on the Excelsior?''

''Child, they did better. Their accountants took advantage of that neat tax gimmick, double-declining depreciation. You know the stunt. But in a year the depreciation of the building will no longer offset the amortization of the mortgage. And, forgive the obscenity, they will have to pay taxes on cash they won't receive. I think that will give Larry Ferris a stroke.'' Genie stared at the telephone, scarcely breathing. ''Genie, are you there?''

''I'm here.''

''Soothe my shattered nerves and meet me at the Pen and Pencil. Take a taxi. I'll pay.''

''Jack!'' Genie could hardly speak coherently. It was as though she'd been struck by lightning. ''Jack! Listen!''

''I'm listening. What's the matter?''

''I just had an idea. I can't have dinner. I have more work to do.''

''You have to eat. To keep up your strength.''

''How about keeping up my strength tomorrow night? I absolutely have to work tonight.''

''All right. I know a fanatic when I hear one. Tomorrow night. The Excelsior will probably still be available if you happen to change your mind about buying it.''

''See you tomorrow.'' Genie hung up the phone and stood up slowly. Almost on tiptoe, she walked to the files and took out the accountant's statements on the buildings for the last five years. As she studied them, she held her breath. Did he? Yes! He did! She let out a great ''wheeee!'' Andre Husseman, builder, had also used double-declining depreciation. Three of the buildings had already been depreciated to almost zero, and the other five weren't far behind. He'd been paying taxes for the last two years on nonexistent cash flow. Genie held the statements tightly to her breast and kissed each and every one of them. Andre Husseman had a good reason to sell the buildings—and sell them right now.

She met Max as usual the next morning. He was full of news, and she tried to pay close attention. Yesterday had been a big day for him.

"I did it, kidlet. Almost, anyway."

"You almost did what?"

"I got my offer on the big deal yesterday, and the landlord accepted the offer. We close today at three-thirty. Fifteen thousand square feet, office and showroom space, at $9.50 per square foot. Ten-year lease with a five-year renewal option. Our commission is a snappy $13,500."

"Wow!" Genie was as enthusiastic as Max. She understood how important this deal was for him. "Isn't that a quick closing?"

"You bet! One thing I learned from Alpert is don't allow a deal to go over a weekend. The guy's wife or girl friend might get sick in the elevator. Anything can happen. So we close at three-thirty. And there's more."

"More? Tell me."

"Kaplan's a definite maybe. He likes two locations."

"That's wonderful!"

"And remember my subwaying to 333 Seventh Avenue? He wants to see the space again. Office, showroom, and special storage space. I think I'll get an offer on Tuesday. He's the biggest dealer in mink coats in town. How would you like a mink at a wholesale price?"

Genie shook her head. "Wait until I can afford to buy one at Bergdorf Goodman. Then you'll get it for me wholesale."

"Like the subway?"

"Like the subway. When we can afford a limousine, we'll take taxis." Genie sipped her coffee trying to contain herself. Her enthusiasm for Max's success was tinged with impatience. She had much bigger news to tell him, and it was hard to hold herself in check.

Watching her as he always did, Max saw something in Genie's face. He remembered her night work. "All right, kidlet, you've sat through my song and dance. Now what's your scoop? You look like you're about to burst."

"Oh, Max!" Genie burst out. "I am. My night work. It paid off."

"It should. Time and a half for overtime. What's the story?"

"I was trying to work out if we could buy the buildings we manage."

Max stared at his sister wondering if she'd suddenly freaked out. Or was this some kind of joke? "Yes? Go on."

"Go on? Didn't you hear what I said?"

"Something about buying the buildings we manage. I'm waiting for the punch line."

"That is the punch line. I mean buy the buildings! Listen!" Point by point, Genie went over the project. Max's expression gradually changed from polite interest to amazement and finally to incredulity.

"I'll say one thing for you. You do not think small."

"Neither do you. We have the energy and brains to do it. Why shouldn't we?"

"Just so I understand the rules of the new game you've invented called, let's see, Own Your Share of the American Dream. The first step is for us to buy the buildings from Husseman?"

"That's the first step."

"And then we convert them into co-ops. Resell them to the tenants?"

"Go to the head of the class."

Max leaned forward. "And how much do we make from this fandango?"

"I don't know. It depends upon how much Husseman asks for the properties. And how much we can get for the apartments."

"But you're talking about big money!"

"Big, big money."

Max was silent, brooding, for a moment. Finally he asked, "Since we don't have enough money for taxis, where will we get the money to buy eight apartment houses?"

Genie's confidence was unshakable. She knew they would get the money some way. "I don't know where we'll get the money, but I know we'll get it.'' Her belief in the success of her dream was absolute.

Genie's enthusiasm was contagious. In spite of his doubts about their ability to make her idea work, Max was caught by its potential. Unlike Genie, he had no commitment to her vision of the average American family owning their own home. What he had was a strong commitment to making money. And Genie's idea could very well be the fastest road to reach that goal. He believed Andre had traded the buildings for his son. What was her trading card this time? ''The next step, I suppose, is to call Husseman and find out if you can strike a deal?''

Genie made a pretense at considering the suggestion. But she'd only been waiting for the green light from Max to signal her on. She picked up the phone, dialed, and reached Andre's receptionist, secretary, bookkeeper, Harriet Greenspan. ''Harriet, Eugenia here . . . I'm fine. And you? . . . Good. Is Mr. H. available? I'd like to talk to him . . .'' While she waited, she winked at Max. ''Mr. Husseman? . . . I'm fine . . . and you? Ah. Something has come up that I'd like to discuss with you. In person. No, the buildings are fine. It would be easier if we met . . .'' There was a short pause. ''Nine-thirty Monday morning would be excellent. I'll see you then. Have a pleasant weekend. Good-bye.'' She hung up and turned to Max. ''Done! We'll know half of what we have to know soon enough.''

Max finished his coffee. ''I'm off to pick up a check. We'll celebrate our anniversary next week no matter what Husseman says.''

''The timing is perfect. With some persuasion, he should see things our way.''

''I gather you have the persuasion in mind?''

''You gather correctly.''

Max grinned. ''Knowing you, it's a beaut!''

''It is.'' The ease with which Genie answered Max's questions hid a genuine concern. If anything, her persuasion was too good and her numbers too compelling. That in itself could end up by working against her.

22

Genie arrived at Andre Husseman's office about five minutes early. She'd spent the weekend going over most of the numbers which would support her idea. While waiting she felt a mixture of eagerness and anxiety. To help maintain her composure and not overthink the meeting, she examined the outer office in detail. There was one important change in progress. A wall which had previously been devoted to plaques, mementos, framed scrolls—evidence of the time and energy Andre Husseman devoted to charitable organizations he belonged to—was being altered. Miniatures of theatrical posters advertising Paul's productions were replacing them. In the last year, Paul had produced two plays, *Henry IV, Part I* and a version of Ibsen's *Enemy of the People* adapted by Arthur Miller. Both productions were well received by the critics and ran their allotted four months. Genie had recently read an interview in the *Village Voice* in which Paul explained his philosophy. He ran a production for four months regardless of the reviews and the attendance. The last month of the run was spent planning for the next production. After a play closed, two months were allotted for rehearsals and previews. Then the cycle repeated. The reporter asked if Paul ever thought of Broadway, and Paul answered of course. But he wanted the right play, the right cast, and the right production before he took that step. In any case, he had no intention of giving up Off Broadway. There were too many plays which deserved to be produced but were not suited either for a large theater or the audiences who attended Broadway productions. It was obvious to Genie that Paul was building his career in the sanest, most sensible manner possible. In spite of the misery she still felt over their breakup, she retained an active interest in his career. Andre's posters gave her an idea. She would buy a scrapbook and keep track of his work. Reviews, interviews, and ads would be enough. She'd noted there was nothing about his wife in the article, and Genie wondered if he was still married. He must be. Paul was now too important for the theatrical columns not to have picked up a divorce.

Harriet interrupted her musing. "Mr. H. is ready for you, Genie. Go on in."

Genie opened what was by now a familiar door. No matter how often she'd been to the office to discuss the buildings, she was always struck by the beauty of the various pieces of furniture and the care that had gone into their selection. Andre rose to greet her.

"Good morning, Eugenia. Would you like a cup of coffee?"

"Yes, thank you. Black as usual. No sugar."

"Shall we?" He gestured to the small table by the window where they always sat. After finishing their ritual cup of coffee, Andre asked, "What can I do for you today, young lady? Has something come up with one of the buildings?"

"Yes. Although as I told you Friday, it doesn't relate to management. I've an idea I'd like you to consider."

"By all means. What is it?" Having arrived at the moment of truth, Genie's courage deserted her. Andre saw her hesitation and prodded her. "Out with it, Eugenia. If I don't like your idea, the worst I can do is say no."

No, she thought. That was not the worst. The worst was he'd like the idea and do it himself. She forced herself to speak. "You must be aware you're about to run out of depreciation in most of the buildings. You already have in three."

Andre shrugged. "My accountants warn me about that every year. But it's a fact of tax life. What can one do?"

"Sell the buildings and use the money to buy other buildings, or to make an investment which would give you a higher after-tax income."

"Do you have a buyer in mind? The commissions you'd earn would be quite large."

"I have a buyer in mind."

"Who?"

Genie fiddled with her cup, swallowed, and, with a flash of bravado, answered, "Max and me." She was surprised at how confident she sounded.

"Max and you?" Andre had expected anything but that. "Eugenia, we both know those buildings are essentially a rich man's investment. The way the tax laws read, he gets to keep most of the income." Andre's words became self-mocking. "Except for those eccentrics like myself who run out of depreciation. Unless I've missed something, neither Max nor you are that wealthy."

"No. We're not wealthy at all. Not yet. But believe me, we will be."

"I'm sure you will be. My point is you aren't at the moment." He realized he'd ruffled her feathers unintentionally, and he wanted to soothe her. "The buildings are good examples of 608 construction. Better than some and not as good as others. Why do you want to own them?"

Genie parried the question. "We know them. After a year, I know where all the warts are. What needs work or will in the future."

"True. But you haven't answered my question." He saw she was very tense, and he was prepared to be as patient as necessary. He was now more curious than ever to know what she had in mind. "I still don't know why you want to own these buildings."

Genie had puzzled all weekend for an answer to his question. Why? After long hours of thought, she'd not been able to come up with anything better than the truth. Still in a quandary, she continued to stall. "We don't plan to own the buildings. At least not for long."

Andre was both amused and saddened. She still wasn't ready to tell him the truth. He realized it was because she didn't trust him. It wasn't a matter of his saying no. She was afraid the idea was so good he'd steal it. He remembered the tongue-lashing she'd given him over his 608 and Title One construction. From her point of view, she had good reason not to trust him. The silence grew heavy. Finally Genie reached the point of no return. Like it or not, she had no choice but to tell him. If he stole her idea, there was nothing she could do about it. Andre had been waiting with what was, for him, a mischievous look. He realized she needed some direct encouragement. "Eugenia. I like imaginative people, and I have a notion you have an imaginative idea."

"Do you like such ideas when they come close to you?"

"I'm imaginative myself. Haven't you seen that?"

"Yes, I believe you are." She remembered his deal with Ralph Gluck.

"Since you understand that much about me, you're withholding your reasons not because you're afraid I'll say no. It's because you're afraid I'll take your idea and do it myself."

His candor took Genie aback. What could she say?

Andre continued. "If you had any other choice, you wouldn't be here. So risk it. Trust me."

Genie smiled. "Under the circumstances, it does seem I have to. She sensed something new about Andre Husseman, and it made her more hopeful that it was safe to proceed. "You asked me why Max and I want to buy your buildings. As you so rightly put it, we're not wealthy and can't use the tax benefits owning them would provide. As I told you, we don't intend to hold them very long."

"You have a buyer who'll pay you more for the properties than the price for which I might sell them to you?" Andre didn't believe this, but he felt it was worth asking.

"Not quite. Not one buyer. Over eight hundred buyers."

"I don't understand. Eight hundred buyers?" He sat still, thinking about the number. Then he almost rose from his chair as he leaned toward Genie. "I see! How clever! You buy the buildings and sell them back to the tenants. Middle-income cooperatives." Andre looked straight at Genie. "It's brilliant. The tenants will pay much more than any single buyer might. The apartment is their home, and who doesn't want to own their own home?"

Genie's heart sank. His enthusiasm was too high. With such a quick grasp of the potential, why shouldn't he do it himself?

"Have you worked out what you might pay for the buildings and how you'd price the apartments?"

The blood started flowing again through Genie's body. Did that question mean Husseman had said yes? He would not steal her idea? He would take her proposal seriously? "I thought it would be up to you to set the price. That determines what we have to get for the apartments."

"True." Andre leaned back and lit a cigarette. It gave him time to consider his next move. "How much cash do you think you can raise to pay me for the buildings?"

"I don't know. It depends on the banks and the terms of the deal."

"Of course." Andre tapped his ash into the tray. He remembered Gluck's statements that he didn't think much of Andre's integrity. Was Gluck's that much higher than his? Andre admitted that in the past the answer was yes. But the experience he'd had with Gluck, Paul, and Jake Rosen had altered him forever. What he might have done five or even two years ago, he was not prepared to do now. He made his decision. He'd be more than fair in his price. It was the least he owed Genie for Paul. "Eugenia, I'll sell you the buildings for—" and he paused while her heart pounded. "Would five times the rent roll be reasonable?"

Genie almost said wow! The rent roll totaled about $1.2 million. At five times the rent roll, Andre was offering her the buildings for $6 million. Practically making her a gift of more than a million dollars. "Mr. Husseman, we both know the price is more than reasonable." Now for the next hurdle. "What about the cash? How much do you want?"

"Do you have the most recent statements with you?"

"Yes." She handed him the papers.

Andre picked a single number off each statement and totalled them up. Genie assumed he was adding up the mortgages on the eight buildings. She studied his face trying to guess how much he would ask. The cash payment was as important as the total price. If he wanted all cash over the first mortgages, he would ask for more than three million dollars. There was no way they could raise three million dollars.

"Eugenia, I think we want to make this fine idea work." Genie held her breath again. "Suppose we say ten percent of the total price in cash. For the balance of the purchase price, I'll take back a series of thirty-year, self-liquidating mortgages at eight percent interest.

Genie gasped. "Six hundred thousand in cash?" Her voice dropped. "That's all?"

Andre shrugged. "You'll have enough trouble raising that. If I ask for much more, there would be no point in this discussion. And the second mortgages will be a nice annuity for Rebecca in case anything happens to me."

"We'll need time to raise the money."

"Would a three-month option for one dollar be reasonable?" He'd done it again. If they couldn't raise the money in three months, they'd never raise it. "More than reasonable. Generous."

"I'll have my lawyers draw up the contract. In fact, unless you object, they can represent Max and you as well. That way you can be sure the contract will be fair, and it won't cost you any money."

Genie's head was spinning. "What can I say? Thank you doesn't seem enough."

"Later. Assuming you're able to raise the money and close the deal, I'll explain exactly how little selling the buildings to you under these terms will cost me in after-tax money."

Genie realized that was the first thing Andre Husseman had said today that was a lie. She knew how much it would cost him, and it was plenty. Over a million dollars. And that trust for Rebecca was nonsense. She was already well taken care of. She thought, he wants me to think he's being all business when he's being Santa Claus. Maybe some day she'd find out why, but in the meantime, she wasn't going to question his generosity.

Andre stood up. "It will take my lawyers a week to prepare the option and contracts. Suppose Max and you meet me here a week from today, same time, for the closing?" He smiled. "And don't forget to bring a dollar. It won't be legal without that dollar."

"I think I can remember that."

"We're finished for today?"

"Yes. Unless you have something else to give away?"

After Genie had left the office, Andre buzzed his secretary. "Have you sorted the mail?"

"Yes, Mr. Husseman. All ordinary. Except for one registered letter for you marked personal and confidential."

"Bring it in." He waited until Harriet had left before looking at the envelope. The return address was printed in several colors on the upper left-hand corner. He'd been expecting this letter for about a month. He buzzed Harriet. "Will you please hold all calls for ten minutes?"

He opened the letter. Inside was a copy of the takeover clause he'd signed with Jake Rosen. He read the short formal note attached.

Dear Mr. Husseman:

In accordance with our agreement dated May 4, 1971, I
hereby choose to exercise my option as stated in Paragraph
3, Section A. My attorneys will be in touch with yours to
set a time and place for a closing. At that time you will receive a certified check for $30 million, and you will turn
over to me all stock, records, and any other documents
agreed upon by our attorneys. This will give me total ownership of our venture.

Very truly yours,
Jacob I. Rosen

JIR/bb

In addition to the formal notification, there was a handwritten note. Jake's handwriting was so illegible that Andre had to
struggle to understand it. When he finally figured out the message, he shook his head in disbelief. Joan was going to sue Paul
for a divorce on the grounds of mental cruelty, desertion, and
infidelity. She would demand total custody of the child who
would be renamed Amber Rosen. Paul would have no visitation
rights. Obviously, Jake believed the best defense is a good offense. He ignored Paul's threat to take Joan to court and prove
he wasn't the father of the child. He behaved as if Paul was the
father, and emphasized that if Paul contested Joan's action,
Jake would show he'd been duped by Andre's false statements
into making the real estate investment. While Andre defended
himself, Jake would stop making the interest payments to the
banks. He was prepared to lose his money to get rid of Paul,
and he'd see to it Andre lost his money as well. How could a
successful man be so stupid as to put such a threat in writing? If
Rosen's lawyers knew, they'd have a hemorrhage.

At that moment, Harriet buzzed him. "Mr. Husseman, your
son is calling."

"Paul? You've heard?"

"I was just served with divorce papers at my place on Bank
Street." He started to laugh. "What a crock of shit! Can you
imagine me contesting that divorce? Or refusing to give up custody of someone else's kid?"

"That's Jake. Covering his bets."

"He needn't have bothered. They can keep their Amber."

Paul's voice changed to concern. "I assume he's exercised his takeover clause?"

"He has indeed."

"Will you fight it? Can you?"

"Jake added a note. A stupid, threatening note. With this note I can, but I won't. While I haven't made a career of losing, I've lowered my sights. I think it will be good for my soul to let go of the project."

It was Paul's turn to be quiet as he searched for some way to phrase his regret. Finally he settled for, "I'm sorry, but I think your decision is the right one." When Andre didn't reply, Paul prodded him. "What are you thinking, Dad?"

"I've been thinking about how I spent my life. And what I ought to do with what's left of it."

Paul laughed, nervously. "You'll do what you've been doing. Or something that interests you more."

"I suppose so." Then, wishing he'd never brought up the subject, Andre said, "I'd like you to come to dinner. Your mother hasn't seen you in weeks. Now that Rebecca's in Europe, she misses you even more."

"Who would have thought that my playgirl sister, who barely graduated from college, would leave a good job at *Vogue* and take herself to Paris to get her doctorate in medieval history?"

"Certainly not I."

"Have you heard from her recently?"

"Three weeks ago. She loves France. Hated the United States and may never return."

"Yes. I see how mother could use some comfort. No matter what, I'll be there at six."

After Andre hung up, he thought about the morning. First Eugenia, and then Jake Rosen. With luck, the afternoon would be dull. He had to tell Sara about the baby not being Paul's. That would be easy. She expected as much. What was harder and what he disliked more was the prospect of explaining the financial link between Paul's marriage and his venture with Jake. She should know, though it might shake her image of him rather badly. For him to live in peace with her for the rest of his life, she would have to accept him as he was. All his life he'd acted with cynicism, pride and a drive for success. Now he'd taken another road, and he did not know where it would lead.

Although he felt somewhat fearful, he hoped for the best. After all, he might still find a little luck somewhere along the way.

Genie floated rather than walked to the IRT, and took the train to her office. Max was waiting to find out how her meeting had gone. She still couldn't believe what Andre Husseman had done. At one point she'd thought of asking him why he was being so magnanimous, then she decided she knew why and didn't want to hear him say it. Although she had no illusions about the difficulty Max and she would have in raising even the amount of money Husseman had asked, in her euphoric state, Genie refused even to consider the possibility that they might fail.

23

Genie had waited all week, hoping, praying for a telephone call. Then on Thursday morning she saw a large manila envelope with the name Bankers' Trust on it. She knew the call would not come. Bankers' Trust had been her last hope among the large New York banks. It was the only bank which had shown any real interest. The Mr. Bailey she'd spoken to had been interested and spent an hour discussing the project. He said he would present the proposal to his committee and be back to her within a week. She knew a yes would come in the form of a telephone call, and a no by mail. The envelope would enclose her proposal for buying and co-oping the buildings along with a polite letter giving the reasons for the bank's rejection. She stared at the envelope, unwilling to open it.

Originally, her best hope had been the Bank of New York where they kept their account. "It's unfortunate," the branch manager said. "Though your idea is excellent and we trust Mr. Szabo's and your business sense, money is too tight for this kind of loan now." That was their first rejection, and the tune never changed.

One morning Max said, "Stop fooling yourself, kidlet. No bank vice-president's got the brains or guts to see the size of this idea. And besides, they think we're too young, too inexperienced, and you're a woman. It stinks, but that's the way it is no matter what they say about tight money."

Genie dug in her heels. She refused to accept defeat. The city was full of banks, and she meant to find one that would make the loan. Now that Bankers' Trust had said no, she'd have to dig up introductions to smaller banks. The introduction was almost as important as the proposal. She began to make a list when the phone interrupted her.

"Szabo & Szabo."

"Good morning, Genie." It was Harriet Greenspan. "Mr. H. wants to talk to you. Hold a minute."

Andre picked up quickly. "Good morning, Eugenia."

Genie marveled how his voice never changed. No matter what she'd read in the real estate section of the *New York Times* about how he'd been forced out of his condominium project by Jacob Rosen, he sounded as calm as ever. Neither the loss of his great project nor Paul's impending divorce—Genie had the newspaper clipping of this in her scrapbook—marred the surface of his charm. "Good morning, Mr. Husseman. What can I do for you today?"

"Not having heard from you to the contrary, I assume you've not yet raised the cash for the buildings?"

"Not yet, but we still have thirty days." Her tone was more buoyant than she felt."

"I have a lead for you. I ran into an old acquaintance, Raymond Brenner. He's vice-president of the Queens-Manhattan Trust. They have an office in Flushing, not too far from you. I took the liberty of telling him about our agreement, and he expressed an interest in seeing you."

"Do you have his number?"

"Harriet does. I'll put her on."

"Thank you, sir." It seemed to Genie that Andre Husseman was in a hurry to get off the phone. Unusual.

Harriet picked up, and Genie wrote the name and number in her diary. Later, staring at the number, Genie had an impression something was wrong, wrong with Andre's tone when he mentioned Brenner. And his rush to get off the phone. She'd wait to talk to Max before calling.

Waiting was hard, and Genie had to force herself to keep away from the phone. Max was showing space this morning and would call in for his messages. At 11:45 he did. After giving him his messages, Genie asked him to meet her at the office.

"Is it important, kidlet? You know canvassing for space and clients brings in the bacon."

"I think it's important. Andre Husseman called with an introduction to a bank loan officer. Although it's a bank I've never heard of, I don't know many of the smaller banks."

"Okay. What's the bank's name?"

"The Queens-Manhattan Trust."

"Oh, Christ! I'll be there as soon as I can. Order me a roast beef on rye and a beer."

After placing the order with the local deli, Genie waited for Max, wondering. Why the strong reaction to the Queens-Manhattan Trust? Max had paid no attention to her search for a bank. He was on a hot streak of his own. After the first large commission, he'd closed almost a deal a week. Some commissions were large, some small, but they all added up. Leasing space was a business he understood, and now that the deals were coming in, while he sympathized with Genie's problems, he was too pleased with himself to share her frustrations.

When Max arrived, he sat down and began eating his sandwich. Between chewing and swallowing his beer, he said, "Tell me."

"I told you. I got this call from Husseman about the Queens-Manhattan Trust. The reason I wanted to talk to you is the more I thought about it, the more I got the feeling Andre really was concerned about making the introduction."

"He should be. It's a Mafia bank. They launder Mafia money."

"The Mafia? They're into banking, too?"

Max looked at Genie impatiently. "Sure they're into banking. They have to be. The Mafia takes in large amounts of cash. Drugs and loansharking mostly. The amateurs have spoiled prostitution, and the blacks run what's left. Gambling isn't what it used to be though the take is still pretty good. And everything they do is on a cash basis. No checks or credit cards accepted. They launder it through their banks. Smarter than freezing it in a safe deposit box."

"I don't follow you."

"They have to do something with all that cash. So they feed it into certain banks, and it comes out clean in the form of loans to people or businesses they don't control."

"Isn't that illegal?"

Max laughed. "Sure, it's illegal. But it works. You'd be amazed how many five hundred and thousand dollar cash deposits appear at certain banks. You see, more than a thousand dollars deposited in cash has to be reported to the IRS. And the bank examiners will pick it up."

"Why doesn't the government go after them?"

"Don't be silly. They try. Do you think it's easy to get proof of where a deposit comes from that will stick in court?"

It took a moment to sink in. Andre Husseman suggested she call this bank. Did that mean Andre Husseman was owned by the Mafia? She asked Max.

"No. And he doesn't bank with them either. He doesn't have to. But you can bet your ass he's done business with plenty of companies that are owned by them."

"Why would he deal with such companies?"

"Genie!" Max was becoming exasperated. "Where have you been the last years? He's a builder. He uses subcontracters to pour concrete and to install on-site water, sewer, and gas lines. You spent your life in real estate and you don't know that the industries that pour asphalt and cart away garbage during construction are riddled with Mafia-owned companies? He couldn't construct anything without doing business with the boys. He's not owned by them, but he certainly knows them. He'd have to."

Now Genie understood Andre's behavior. Much as he wanted her to be able to raise the money, he didn't want her to know that he'd dealt with organized crime. "And exactly how did you come to be such an expert on the Mafia?"

"Two ways. I told you years ago Alpert was in trouble. Not enough deals to cover his overhead. And no management contracts to carry him. What's kept him alive is Mafia money. They own him. Also, the boys like women. Like with Jack O'Neil, I happened to share a girl with one of the troops."

"Isn't that dangerous?"

"No. You leave them alone, and they leave you alone. Besides Arturo and I get along. If the broad were his daughter, that'd be trouble. They can be very strict with their daughters. But this broad is a broad."

"How do you feel about doing business with the Mafia?"

"If the business is legitimate, I couldn't care less. It's not my job to control their operations. If you ask me would I borrow money from a loan shark, the answer's no. If you ask me would I borrow money from one of their banks that I wasn't damn sure I could pay back, the answer's the same. No! But this loan is different. How long do you figure it will take, once the contract closes, to file the necessary papers and co-op the buildings?"

"If you don't run into strong opposition from the tenants, six months at the most."

"I'll sell the tenants. Don't worry about that. So we'll owe the money for six months. You only get into trouble with a Mafia bank if you can't repay the loan. That's what happened to Alpert."

"I still don't like it."

"No one does. If you have another idea, I'm listening. As a matter of fact, it was damn decent of Husseman to make the introduction. They won't talk to anyone who walks in off the street about six hundred thousand dollars."

"I guess not. Then you think I should call them?"

"Let me make a call first. What'd you say his name was?" He reached for Genie's phone and started dialing.

"Raymond Brenner."

"Brenner. Good. He's not Italian." Max's hand was over the mouthpiece.

"Why good?"

"If he's not Italian, he's not that high up. Too high could be dangerous. He might even be a straight banker who happens to work for a Mafia bank." Max took his hand off the mouthpiece, and his voice became warm. "Hello, Elsie. This is Max Szabo. Can I talk to your boss? . . . Sure. I'll hang on." Genie waited, nervously. "Arturo! How are you, old sport? . . . Yeah . . . I'm fine . . . Sure. Anytime. Just say the word, and I'll set you up. Absolutely . . . Listen. I know you're busy, and I won't hold you up. I just have one question . . . Naturally, if you don't feel it's your business, you'll say so . . . Look, I've a relative doing business in real estate . . . Yeah. Strictly legit . . . Needs a six-month loan. No. It's six months and out . . . A friend suggested the Queens-Manhattan Trust. Oh! . . . It's out of your area? Too bad . . . No. What I hoped was you might be able to tell me something about one of the loan officers . . . Yeah. His name's Brenner. Raymond Brenner . . . Oh, you do? Yeah . . ." Max listened, grunted, and at one point broke into a loud, hearty laugh; the more he laughed, the quieter Genie became. Finally Max said, "I see . . . I got it. . . . And thank you, Arturo, for the info. Anytime I can do something for you, just ask. Yeah, I'll be seeing you." Max hung up the phone and took a deep breath. There was a thoughtful expression on his face.

"What did he say, Max? What was so funny?" Genie had come back to life.

"I guessed right. Brenner's their front man who handles the legitimate loans. He's a smart banker. They trust him, and he can make loans without clearing it with the boys."

"That's wonderful. I'll call him now."

"There's more."

"More? What?"

Max hesitated. It was obvious he didn't like what he had to say. "Arturo also made a joke. He mentioned in passing that if my relative happened to be a woman, an attractive woman—ha! ha!—it might go even more smoothly. Brenner's known to like attractive women."

"What's that supposed to mean?"

"Genie!" Max was angry. "didn't you hear me?"

"I heard you. He likes women. Don't most men?"

"It hasn't occurred to you that as an attractive woman, you may go along with the loan?"

Suddenly Genie understood. "Are you saying Brenner will want to sleep with me before he'll grant the loan?"

"It seems a distinct possibility."

"I won't do it."

"That's okay with me. In fact, you know I'd prefer it." He smiled. "It's sort of funny. Bankers even have a special name for this kind of loan. Would you believe they call it a legs loan?"

Genie was furious. "I've got a straight business proposition, and you tell me I'll have to whore for it!"

"Stop yelling. I'm not telling you you have to do anything. You make up your own mind."

"Make up my own mind. About wading in shit?"

"There's plenty of that in the world."

"Not in my world."

"If you say so, it's not in mine either."

"Oh, Max!" Genie felt sick. She thought she might throw up. "What should I do?"

"I don't know. This whole project is your dream boat. How can I tell you?" Then he became more matter-of-fact. "In any case, I'd call him and present our project. Right now it's the only game in town. He might say yes without any funny business."

"And he might not?"

"And he might not. Then you tell him to shove it you know where. You don't need it." As always, Max's love for his sister was stronger even than his desire for money. "Look, I planned to call on some old clients this afternoon. But if you'd like me to stay, I will, and we'll talk some more about what you should do."

While Genie recognized the depth of Max's feeling about her, she also knew her dream of everyone owning their own apartment didn't mean a thing to him. She felt peculiarly alone. She had thought she would find joy in her ability to meet the challenge of her dream. Instead, she felt a violent protest against what was being asked of her. Then, suddenly, she felt nothing, and she knew the decision was hers to make. "No." Her voice was steady. "You do whatever you planned. If I decide to call, I'll call. Or I won't. Anyway, even if I do call, nothing can happen on the phone."

She saw Max's huge body tense. His words were forced. "Whatever you do is okay with me." Awkwardly, he put his arms around her shoulders. "I'll check in at the end of the day for messages."

"Right! And I'll bring you up to date on the Perils of Pauline."

After Max left, it took Genie over an hour to decide she might as well call Brenner. When she finally got up the courage, his response was hardly menacing. Yes, Andre Husseman had spoken to him about her proposal. Yes, the bank might be interested in lending her the money. No, he didn't want to meet at the bank.

"Miss Szabo, first loans are rarely made purely on the numbers. They're made by a banker who has faith in the borrower's ideas. And integrity. No balance sheet or cash flow projections can supply that faith. And we are speaking about a substantial amount of money. I have to make a judgement about you. How hard will you work to succeed? How much does it mean to you? I find a bank office can be intimidating. It interferes with the necessary open exchange of information." He paused. "Are you free for dinner tonight?"

Genie slumped over her desk. She was free for dinner, but would it end with dinner? Should she even start down that path? She wanted to say she was busy for the next three months. The words wouldn't come. Instead she said, "I'm free. What time and where would you like to eat?"

"Do you have a car?"

"Yes. The buildings I manage require a lot of driving."

"Would six-thirty be convenient? At Carl Hesse's? Do you know the place? It's a steak house on Northern Boulevard close to the city line."

"I don't know it, but I'm sure I can find it. Six-thirty is perfect. How will I know you?"

"The headwaiter knows me. I'll be waiting. Good-bye, my dear."

Genie hung up and ran out of the office to the ladies' room where she threw up what was left of her lunch. The "my dear" had done it. In spite of her revulsion, she knew she must meet the man. After that she'd decide what to do.

Max called in as promised at five-fifteen. He didn't ask about Brenner. After giving him his messages, she said in a quiet voice, "I'm meeting Brenner at six-thirty. At the Carl Hesse Steak House."

"Very classy Mafia hangout. Great food."

"Wish me luck, Max."

"Kidlet, don't . . ." For an instant he faltered and then recovered himself. "Luck, kidlet. Luck!" He hung up quickly as though he couldn't trust his voice any further.

The Carl Hesse Steak House was not what Genie expected. It appeared to be more conservative than an expensive Manhattan steak house. The restaurant was large and constructed on three levels. The entrance level where she was standing, and where the bar was, led to two broad staircases. One descended to what she could see was a series of booths with high wooden panelling separating each booth from its neighbor. The other staircase went upstairs to what appeared to be a more open area for those who neither desired nor rated privacy. The walls were panelled in oak and the waiters as well as the maitre d' wore black ties, dinner jackets, and white cotton gloves. While she waited to get the maitre d's attention, two couples entered. The women wore heavy gold jewelry and summer furs. The men wore custom-made dark business suits. Genie realized they explained the number of chauffeured limousines in the parking lot. They were newer models of the hearse she remembered from the Costello shooting all those years ago. The first contingent of jeweled women and custom-tailored men were followed by others, and they all appeared to know each other. The maitre d' seated each party, with respectful reverence, in different sections of the downstairs area. He understood they were to be separated.

After seating what appeared to be the last group, the maitre d' returned. "Do you have a reservation, Miss?"

"I'm meeting Mr. Raymond Brenner."

He nodded. "This way, please." Without any hesitation, he led her, as she'd expected, downstairs toward the booths. As they walked down the near aisle, Genie surveyed the room. There were only two rows of booths against what she assumed were the walls of the building, and the entire center section of the long room was devoted to a series of tables upon which were set bowls of fruit and salad, boards of cheese, and racks and rows of pastry. Opposite some of the booths were wheeled carts which could be used to flambé any number of delicacies. Genie decided if the food measured up to the atmosphere, the owners of the Carl Hesse Steak House must work very hard to maintain their obscurity and avoid any publicity.

The maitre d' stopped about three quarters of the way along the row of booths. "Mr. Brenner, your guest has arrived."

"Thank you, Guido."

A short, slim man with a pleasant face, thinning brown hair brushed straight back from a sharp widow's peak, and dressed in a typical banker's dark grey three-button vested suit rose to greet her. "Miss Szabo! This is a pleasure."

Shaking hands with him, Genie was relieved to note that he was rather attractive in a civilized way; neither gross nor crude. Except for the fact that she noticed he had unusually large hands for a man his size, he looked quite conventional. Then his eyes ranged over her, and though Genie shivered inwardly, she was glad she'd dressed with more attention that morning than she usually did on a working day. Originally she planned to take herself to a Broadway show to get her mind off her banking problems. Now her latest banking problem was smiling at her.

"Sit down, my dear." Genie slid into the banquette seat opposite Brenner and leaned her briefcase against the wall. "What would you like to drink?"

"A Bombay martini, please. Extra dry, straight up."

The maitre d', who had been waiting for the drink order, left. "It was kind of you to join me on such short notice. I don't often have dinner with a young lady as attractive as you. Andre didn't do you justice." Genie realized that while flattery was a standard approach to seduction, Brenner actually seemed to want her to like him. Other men in his position might not have made the effort. "And I understand you're as bright as you are beautiful," he continued.

He certainly was making an effort, and it threw her off balance. "Thank you. It's nice to have a good advance PR man." The idea of Andre Husseman doing public relations for her made Brenner and Genie smile.

A waiter appeared. "And here's your drink. Nick, the bartender, makes an excellent martini. As easy to swallow as you are on the eyes."

"Please. Your compliments will turn my head." She sipped her martini wondering when the other side of his personality would show. There had to be another side. A man who would work for a Mafia-controlled bank, and was well known for making sexual demands on young women who needed money, had to have a darker side. She noticed he wore a wedding ring. Why should marriage make a difference? It hadn't to Jack O' Neil. Or Paul. Occasionally, she'd seen pictures of Paul in the newspapers attending an opening night with one or another stunning woman on his arm. He'd been no more faithful to Joan than he'd been to her. Less faithful, if that were possible.

Brenner and she chatted about this and that, and by the time she'd finished her martini, a second one arrived as though previously arranged. Genie thought, he may be a gentleman so far, but his technique is cliché. Liquor is another of the oldest and best established methods of seduction. Undoubtedly a third martini would follow in short order.

When he asked for menus and a wine list which clearly indicated an end to the martinis, she was surprised. "I limit myself to two drinks before a meal," he said as though reading her mind. "More spoils the taste of the excellent food they serve here." His smile was agreeable. "And they have a first-class wine cellar."

After glancing at the menu, he turned to Genie. "I can recommend everything on the menu. Do you prefer fish or meat?

On the other hand, would you prefer to get the business out of the way before we order?''

Now that the time had come, Genie suffered a temporary loss of self-possession. She'd promised herself to pitch Brenner and worry about the cost if and when the bill was presented. "I think business before pleasure."

"As you wish. Andre only outlined your plans. He said you would make the best case for them."

"I've brought the projections for you to study at your earliest convenience." She opened her briefcase and handed Brenner a nine-by-twelve-inch manila envelope. "They will give you the current status of the buildings, the price Mr. Husseman is asking, and the proposed sale price of the apartments. Once you study the numbers, you'll realize how sound the proposition is, and what a great buy it is for the tenants."

"Not to mention the amount of money Szabo & Szabo presumably will make from the sales." He gave a short laugh and then went on. "I will study your figures carefully. It certainly is an imaginative idea, co-oping apartments for middle-income families. However, as with all loans, a banker has to make a decision not simply on the merits of the proposition but on the person being granted the loan. How thoroughly have you analyzed the probable success of this venture?"

"You'll see. Down to the last detail. I know we can sell the apartments to the tenants. Everything I've seen tells me the single most important investment a family can make, the one that contributes most to their security, is the purchase of their own home or apartment."

"You sound as if you're in this solely for idealistic reasons. I can't believe that. From what Andre told me, if your numbers hold up, this will make you a very wealthy woman."

His view of the venture ended any further comments Genie might have made as to its value to the tenants. "You're right. I can hardly claim not to be interested in making money. And you'll find, after studying the numbers, that this is a very solid business proposition. For everyone, including the bank, Mr. Brenner."

"Call me Raymond, please. And if I may, I'll call you Eugenia?"

Genie smiled. "Max and I plan on being rich. Very rich. Co-oping these buildings is a good way to start, Raymond."

"I'm relieved to hear you say that. As a banker, I find people who want to make money far better risks than idealists. They're more realistic."

"Szabo & Szabo is a realistic operation."

"I hope so. A banking relationship is somewhat like a marriage. In a marriage, both parties tend to start out with the best intentions. And presumably a realistic approach to each other. Then things often change. It's the same in a banking relationship. The realistic man, or woman, knows the value of keeping the banker happy. Just as in a good marriage a wife knows the value of keeping her husband happy. I speak from experience."

Listening to him, Genie realized she was approaching the point where it would be now or never. Either she turned the conversation back to purely business channels, thus accepting she'd lost the loan, or she swallowed her outrage and followed his lead, wherever it took her. She heard herself say, "What an interesting analogy!"

"Isn't it? And accurate. Idealists are poor banking risks. And a marriage based upon an idealized, unrealistic appraisal of one's mate, by either party, is a poor marriage risk. Again I speak from experience."

Still unwilling to face the inevitable, Genie asked, jokingly, "Your wife defaulted on a loan?"

"The metaphor is apt. My wife defaulted on our marriage. I married a beautiful woman whom I loved deeply. What I didn't know was, like many beautiful women, she was also highly narcissistic and regarded the sexual act as an invasion of her body—a marring of its perfection. Consequently, it had no pleasure for her, and as a result, soon ceased to have any pleasure for me. It approximated legal rape."

Genie held herself still, clenching her stomach muscles to prevent any movement. In a series of flickering images—like an old movie speeded up—she reviewed the long procession of bankers to whom she'd spoken. And the equally long procession of noes she'd received. All the doors were closed. She forced herself to smile. "And you enjoy the sexual act?"

"Yes. I'm an ordinary man." He cleared his throat. "So I must find my sexual pleasures elsewhere."

There was no mistaking his meaning. Genie's automatic rejection of everything Brenner was asking of her was stopped by the knowledge that if she was to have her loan, this was what he required of her. "You have women friends?" she asked.

"I have carefully chosen women friends. Attractive, sometimes beautiful women. Often women I meet through my business dealings."

"Such as myself?"

"Yes. Such as yourself."

Genie exhaled sharply. Her stomach unclenched, and she finally accepted what she'd known to be true ever since she'd made the phone call and agreed to meet this man for dinner. The possibility that Brenner might make the loan was too overpowering. Trapped by her own needs, she was going to agree to anything he wished. "I'm flattered by your interest."

"You needn't be flattered," he said softly. "You're a beautiful young woman. That fact gives you an obvious advantage in anything you wish to do. You also need to borrow money. I have money to lend. So I have an arrangement to propose. One that will facilitate our having a good banking relationship."

"What are the terms of the arrangement which will make my banker happy?"

"I suggest we see each other one or two nights a week, depending upon my schedule, for as long as you owe the bank money. It will help us maintain a sound banking relationship." He looked at her with his steady, stocktaking eyes, making her feel like a piece of human merchandise. "Once you've repaid the loan, all my rights cease. I should add what you do on other nights is none of my business. Also, I will try to give you as much advance notice as possible so as not to disrupt your usual social activities."

"When would this arrangement begin?"

"After the loan is granted, and you have your money. There's no reason for you to accept my word, or me, until you have the money."

Genie had lost her capacity for outrage. Then, too, despite her original fears, this man was not the monster she'd imagined. He was a man who wanted something he couldn't get at home. In a way it reminded her of the reasons Paul had given her for his affair with Jackie Bates. Jackie gave Paul sexual pleasures she couldn't or wouldn't give. A thought flashed through her head. Why did Brenner stay married to his wife? This was not something she'd ask. Meeting his eyes, she said carefully, like a tired runner taking breaks between each word for breath. "And suppose you fill your part of the agreement, lend us the money, and I refuse to perform my part?"

Brenner's expression remained fixed. "That's one of the reasons I wanted to meet you. Why we're having dinner. I'm a student of human nature. It's made me a good banker. If you agree, you'll keep your word."

He was correct up to a point. If he kept his word, she would keep hers. That is, she would if she could. Despite her craving for the loan and her willingness to pay his price, the question remained, could she pay his price? Could she make her body something which so violated everything she'd always considered basic to her nature? Brenner had put his proposal in terms of a business relationship. Give a little, get a little. It certainly simplified things to view it that way, but it was not that simple. When Genie faced the fact, unsoftened by shading or color, it was what it was. In return for a substantial amount of money, she was to allow her body to be used sexually by this man. If the money had been fifty dollars, she'd be a whore. That reality must somehow be handled.

"I see you're having difficulty coming to a decision." He seemed almost pleased by her hesitation. "Am I that unattractive?"

"Oh no! You're very attractive." Genie was startled at her own vehemence. "I mean . . ." She groped for words.

"You mean if you met me under other circumstances, you might be less reluctant?"

He was correct. If she'd met him at a party and he'd asked for her telephone number, it was possible they'd eventually have ended up in bed. That thought gave her an idea which seemed to her to be more in keeping with her nature—with what might be possible for her to do. "I'd like to suggest a change in our arrangement." She paused to reconsider and then decided it was the only way for her to proceed. "Hold off reviewing our loan application. If you're free, come to my apartment tomorrow evening."

"I'm free."

"Then come to dinner, and we'll see what happens. Depending upon that, you can review our loan and decide on its merits."

"But even if we do make love, how do you know what I'll do about your loan?"

"I'll have to take my chances. Like you, I try to judge people. It's my opinion, if you think the loan worthwhile, you'll make it."

He signalled his acceptance of her terms by clasping her hand and brushing his lips against it. A shiver ran through Genie's body. Maybe it would work out? She withdrew her hand and placed both of them on his face. The dry skin and slight roughness of his day-long growth of beard pleased her. She leaned over and kissed him lightly on the lips. The kiss sealed the bargain.

Now it was Brenner's turn to breathe deeply. "Tomorrow night, then. At eight."

Genie colored slightly—a blush in which all the humiliation at what she had agreed to and a hope that it would be possible for her to carry out her agreement were mingled. "At eight."

Brenner sat silent, his hands clasped on the table, his puzzled eyes staring directly at her. "You are an unusual woman," he remarked. "And now that our business is settled, let's order."

24

Instead of meeting Genie the next morning at the office as usual, Max called in claiming he had an early appointment to show some loft space. Genie wondered if it was true. He asked only briefly about the dinner.

"It went well. Nothing's settled yet. I'll know more tonight."

"You'll tell me when you're ready?" Genie could hear the pain in Max's voice and understood he didn't want to know more than was absolutely necessary. "When I know, you'll know." He hung up without saying good-bye.

Genie questioned herself as to what she might have said to her brother to make things easier for him. She knew how he felt, and she respected his feelings. She also knew how important this loan was to her, and she asked herself another question. If the banker had been a woman and the woman expected Max to sleep with her in order to get the loan, what would Max do? She laughed at herself for asking the question. He'd sleep with her even if she was the Witch of Endor. Why then was it different with her? Like most men, Max had a double standard, things a man could do and a woman could not. She remembered her fears, as a teenager, of what Max might do to Paul if he found out about their affair. Max had been right about only one thing—Paul, her love, wouldn't marry her. She wasn't good enough. But he'd marry Joan Rosen for her father's money. He'd whore for his father, and he wasn't ashamed of what he'd done. It was the honorable thing for a man to do. Yet, if Paul knew what she planned, he'd agree with Max. She was a whore. The hell with Paul! The hell with Max! Their honor was no different than hers. Anything they could do, she could do. Genie's agitation was such that she was unable to grasp the entire truth that lay behind Paul's marriage. She saw what she wanted to see and refused to look for the other, more complex motives that had played a major role in Paul's decision. She'd damn well see Brenner and put an end to that double standard, at least as far as Max was concerned. And the same went for Paul Husseman. It was time they understood that a woman's body was hers to use as she saw fit, and the only person to whom she had to answer was herself.

Despite her refusal to accept what she saw as the male view of women, Genie lived through a long day of conflicting emotions. Although most of the time she managed to bury the shame she felt at the connection between sex, Raymond Brenner, and money, there were enough moments when the reality of the trade-off caused her to choke, swallow hard, and fight the urge to rush to the ladies' room to throw up. She knew her small change in Brenner's arrangement was a joke. Sex before or after his decision on their loan? What difference did it make? The two were still linked.

She was getting ready to leave the office at the end of the day when Brenner called. He explained he had a late afternoon meeting and having dinner might be difficult. Instead, he would catch a bite on the run and be at her apartment by eight-thirty. Genie agreed, concealing an upsurge of resentment. Did he expect to walk in and leap into the sack?

After hanging up on Genie, Max attempted to busy himself with the day's work. He showed space to three clients and finished the day by meeting with the owner of a large, empty, seven-story factory building on Northern Boulevard. Had he not been obsessed with other matters, he would have called the office any number of times to report to Genie. It was the most successful day he'd ever had in the real estate business. Two of the three clients made offers to lease space which were accepted. One offer was for five thousand square feet of office space in the most prestigious building in New York City, the Seagram Building at 375 Park Avenue, and the other was for sixty thousand square feet of manufacturing space in the Bush Terminal in Brooklyn. His commissions would total thirty thousand dollars or more. As if that weren't enough, the owner of the factory building agreed to give Szabo & Szabo a six-month exclusive, either to lease or sell his building. This was the first exclusive Max had ever obtained.

He'd actually picked up a phone several times to call—maybe the commissions were enough to convince Genie she didn't have to buy Husseman's buildings, that she didn't need the bank loan, that she didn't have to . . . And each time he'd slammed the receiver down without dialing. Genie wouldn't listen, and he didn't want to hear anything further about Brenner.

The owner of the factory building had an office at 60 Broad Street in lower Manhattan. After signing the exclusive, instead of taking a subway home, Max started walking uptown. The sun was setting, and the gathering gloom of dusk matched the dark sickness in his heart. What kind of a man was he to permit his sister to do what she was going to do to get a bank loan? He wasn't a man at all. He felt the same way about himself as he'd felt many years ago about his father. Men are able to protect the people they love, especially their families, especialy his kidlet. The sense that he was less than equal to others, which he felt so often as a child, returned. There was a phone booth. He had to make one last effort to stop her. Max's hand shook so badly it took three efforts before he was able to dial the office number correctly.

"Szabo & Szabo."

"Genie, I . . ." He recognized the answering service. "This is Max Szabo. Miss Szabo isn't answering?"

"She left a little early tonight. Do you want your messages?"

"No. Hold them." He hung up and dialed Genie's apartment. After ten rings, he gave up and slammed the phone down so hard the cradle broke in half, and with that, Max's need to do something, anything, exploded. He attacked the offending phone which had refused to permit him to talk to Genie. In a few minutes the booth was a mass of broken glass, twisted aluminum, and tangled wire. Even the coin box had been smashed open.

Leaving the carnage behind him and oblivious of several boys scrambling among the wreckage to pick up the loose change, Max entered the nearest bar. Normally Max's drinking consisted of a martini or two before dinner and a beer with dinner. Now he sat in a booth in the rear of the bar, placed a twenty-dollar bill on the table and ordered a double scotch with refills to be brought just as soon as he'd finished the drink in front of him. Four doubles did nothing to dull his feelings of inadequacy. However, they did something else. They reminded him of the time Paul Husseman had gotten drunk, and he'd found out about Genie and Paul. Paul Husseman had seduced his kidlet when she was too young to know what she was doing and later refused to marry her. Max had been promising himself for a long time to do something about that. After finishing his fifth double and paying the tab, he went looking for Paul. The first stop was Paul's theater on Fourth Street.

"Paul around?"

"No. You missed him by about fifteen minutes."

"Any idea where he is?"

"I think he's having dinner at the Blue Mill."

Max knew where the Blue Mill was—on Commerce Street. He started running toward the West Village. The actor who'd given him the information watched him. There was something about Max that alarmed him, and he considered calling the restaurant to warn Paul. Just then the girl he'd been waiting for arrived.

"Sorry I'm late, hon. My boss, the bastard, kept me overtime."

"Yeah. Sure. I think I'd better make a phone call."

"Ah, gee! Do you have to? I've been dreaming about you all day. Come on, hon. Do you have to call?"

"No. I guess not. Paul can take care of himself. Let's go."

Max stood at the entrance to the Blue Mill. He didn't look or act drunk. But he was—murderously drunk. He ordered a double scotch at the bar. There was Paul, sitting in a booth near the side door with a girl and another couple. Max finished his drink, scribbled a note on a pad he always carried and gave it to a passing waiter. The waiter handed the note to Paul who read it and looked towards the bar. He saw Max, excused himself and joined Max at the bar.

"How are you, Max? It's been a long time."

"Has it? Come outside for a moment, Paul. It's too crowded and noisy in here. I have something I want to tell you."

"Sure." Paul had no reason to refuse. He'd known Max for almost twenty years.

Once outside, Max guided Paul into a narrow alley next to the Cherry Lane Theater. There was no play running in the theater, and the alley was dark. Max held Paul's arm. His voice was unnaturally emotionless "You know what Genie's doing tonight, Paul?"

"No. I haven't talked to her in over a year."

"She's whoring tonight, Paul."

"Genie? Whoring? Come on, Max. What the hell are you talking about?"

"You heard me. Genie's whoring tonight to get the money to buy your old man's buildings."

"I don't believe you."

"Why not, rich boy? She's only doing what you taught her when she was a kid."

Paul realized too late what was about to happen. Although he knew he was no match for Max, he refused to try to run. Instead he hit Max as hard as he could in the stomach. It was like hitting concrete. Then Max was on him. A left to the belly doubled him over. A right straightened him up. Another left to the head and a right to the jaw knocked him down. Max's punches were so fast his fists blurred. Paul saw Max standing over him. He got to his knees and then to his feet. A right to his ribs. Something cracked. Another left and a right. He was flat on his back. His nose was broken and bleeding, and he'd bitten his tongue. Over on his stomach, on his knees, and to his feet. Max's face was a mask. More punches. Paul's head hit the brick wall with a sickening thud. He was down again. From a distance he heard a voice. "Stay down, you bastard. Lie there!" But the voice was sobbing. "My kidlet's whoring because of you." Kidlet! That's what Max called Genie. Max was beating him up. Why? Paul's head hurt so badly he couldn't remember. He couldn't lie there. He had to stand. Max said Genie was whoring. He'd find her and stop her. He had to stand up.

Paul leaned against the wall waiting to be hit again. Nothing happened. When he was able to see, he saw Max standing in front of him, his closed fists hanging by his side and tears streaming down his face. There was a silence broken only by the sounds of Paul's swallowing blood and coughing it up and the bitter sound of Max's crying.

"What do you want, Max?"

"Nothing." The outlines of his powerful figure kept swimming in and out of focus. "Nothing. Neither of us can stop her."

Stop her from what? Paul wondered. Then he remembered,

and his coughing became mixed with his own tears. He felt Max's arm around his waist, lifting him, helping him to walk.

Once in front of the restaurant, Max released him. Max's voice was reduced to a dry rasp. "Get your friends to take you to a hospital. I broke some ribs, and you may have a fractured jaw and a concussion." Then Max ran down the street towards Seventh Avenue. Paul understood why. Max had to run away or Max would have killed him.

Paul's friends, having become concerned, finally found him sitting on the sidewalk, leaning against the building. His nose was bleeding, his eyes were cut, one side of his jaw was swollen, and he had a large lump on the back of his head which was also bleeding profusely.

"For Christ's sake! What happened?"

"I got mugged."

"The big guy who sent the note?"

Paul shook his head. "No. He wanted to tell me something about his sister." His next words, "Two or three kids jumped me," were spoken in a choked, broken voice. It was no one's business that Genie was—what did Max say?—whoring to get the money.

"We'd better get you to a hospital."

"Yeah!" Paul choked and coughed up a mixture of phlegm and blood. He remembered his father's suggestion that he call Genie. After giving his father a quick no, he'd thought long and hard about how deeply he still loved her, and had only been waiting for Genie to complete her business deal with Andre before calling and asking her to take him back. They would marry. Now all his original reasons for rejecting the suggestion returned. As intelligent and sensitive as Paul was about most things, he'd neither understood nor accepted the harsh realities that had ruled Genie's world as a child and continued to rule it as an adult. What was often required from an actress, what he had required from actresses in return for a role in one of his productions, what was so much a part of his life, was unacceptable, even unbearable, when it came to Genie. Max had called it whoring, and he was right. Paul knew no matter how much he loved Genie and would continue to love her, it was impossible for him ever to see her again.

* * *

Genie lay soaking in a tub full of hot water and soap suds. She was trying to calm her nerves. As she entered the hall, she'd heard her phone ringing. She suspected it had been ringing for a long time; just as she reached it, the ringing stopped. She hoped it wasn't Brenner calling off the evening. She did hope he'd show up, didn't she? Her mind was galloping off in all directions. Finally the water began to cool and the skin at the ends of her fingers to wrinkle. She had to get out of the safety of the tub, dry herself, and decide what to wear. Her favorite clothes were all outfits she'd either worn with Paul or bought to please him. She was unwilling to choose among those. What she finally selected was a dress she'd never worn, the dress she'd bought to wear to the opening of *Six Characters*. It was a simple brown silk wraparound held together by a series of snaps and a belt and could be as revealing or conservative as she wished.

Sheer flesh-toned panty hose, a brown brassiere, and brown high-heeled pumps completed her selection of clothes. A dab of perfume here and another dab there, eye makeup and mascara to emphasize the size and depth of her eyes. She closed the snaps and tied the belt of the dress as though she were going to a restaurant. After all, she didn't know for sure what was going to happen. It was possible that on second look she wouldn't like Raymond Brenner. She'd look him over and make her decision, just as she would with any other date. It was still her decision to make.

At 8:25, Genie put the ice in the ice bucket, arranged the cheese and crackers she'd bought on the way home, and opened the bottles of gin and whiskey. At 8:40, she made herself a stiff martini. Where was he? Had that been him on the phone? Why the hell hadn't he hurried to answer it? If he wasn't going to come, why didn't he call? Then she heard the buzzer. It sounded so loud she almost dropped her drink.

"Hello?" she said into the grill.

"It's Raymond, Eugenia. Sorry I'm late."

"When you hear the buzzer, push the door, and come straight back. I'm on the ground floor, rear."

She pushed the button and opened the door to the apartment. "I'm here, Raymond. Back here."

Raymond Brenner appeared under the dim hall light wearing what seemed to Genie to be a twin to the suit he'd worn at the restaurant. He was carrying a slim attaché case. She stood aside to allow him to enter and realized that, in high heels, she was taller than he was. He was so slender, almost delicate. Except for those hands which seemed to belong to a much larger man. She watched him glance around the room.

"My compliments, Eugenia. You live in a charming neighborhood and in a lovely apartment." He turned to look at her. "And you look even better than I remembered."

"I have drinks ready in the living room."

"I could use a drink. My president had nothing better to do this evening so he decided to spend two extra hours reviewing the bank's loan portfolio. At least it ended well."

Genie was amused. Even a Mafia bank had to make money. Then she realized she was being silly. Why launder money if they lost all those nice clean dollars in bad loans? "You drink Canadian whiskey. Have you ever tried Crown Royal?" When he shook his head, she said, "You have a treat coming. It's sippin' whiskey."

"Do you mind if I take off my jacket, vest, and tie? Sometimes I think bankers' clothes are an invention of the devil, or at least one of his more sadistic friends." He handed her the garments and his attaché case which she carried to the closet, all the while feeling the pressure of his eyes on her as she moved. Her skirt was tight enough for him to notice the telltale signs that she wore panty hose. And Raymond Brenner was a man who would notice such things. That should tell him everything wasn't settled yet. She wasn't going to be a pushover. When she returned, he'd taken off his shoes and was standing at the rear window looking out at the garden.

"What a lovely garden. We have a rose garden at home."

Genie didn't want to talk about roses or his life at home. "Would you like your drink?"

"Please." She handed it to him, and he sipped it, rolling the liquor around on his tongue. "This is really good."

"Some cheese?"

"No, thanks. I grabbed a bite with the president in the office, but I could use another sample of that sippin' whiskey."

"Coming up." Genie hurried to the table and poured a double shot. Her hand shook, and a small amount sloshed over the edge of the glass. "Damn! Here." She handed him the drink. "I'll wipe that up."

"May I help?"

"No! I can do it myself." Genie heard the edge of hysteria in her voice. So did Brenner, and he contented himself with enjoying the whiskey which gave Genie the time she needed to bring her nerves under better control. She made herself a second martini, managing not to spill any. As they sat on the couch like the strangers they really were, Genie cast about for something to say.

Their words came at the same time. "How was your .."

"Ladies first," Brenner said, smiling.

"Tell me about your day. How does a banker spend his day?"

"Let's see." He counted on his fingers. "One, two, three, four in all. We foreclosed on the houses of two widows, very old ladies, and on two orphans, very young children. Threw them into the street."

"You what?"

"They were seven days late in their mortgage payments. Nothing else we could do. Bankers have to maintain their reputations, you know."

"Mortgage payments? What on earth are you talking about? You're a commercial bank. You don't give mortgages."

He sighed. "Oh, dear! What a blunder! How was I to realize you'd know the difference between a commercial bank and a savings bank? Let me think. Yes! We gave the City of New York twenty-four hours to pay back its loans or we'd take over the collateral—City Hall and the mayor's mansion at Gracie Square." Brenner stretched. "That was a decent morning's work so I went to lunch."

"Bankers take time off from doing charity work to eat lunch?"

"This banker does. I had a splendid piece of filet of barracuda, amandine."

Trying not to giggle, Genie sputtered, "Stop it! Enough!"

"Then I dreamed of a beautiful dark-haired woman I was going to see tonight and wondered if my fantasies would come true." He set his drink on the table and placed his hands on her face drawing it towards him. Genie didn't resist and soon their mouths touched. His tongue traced the outline of her lips, pleasing and exciting her, and she moved her body closer. Now his hands slipped down to her breasts, and as her arms went around his neck, he kissed her until her mouth burned, until it was as though all her erotic sensations were concentrated in her mouth. Only then did his tongue slip between her open lips, exploring, teasing, going round and round hers until it touched the tip of her tongue. She trembled as she slid her hand down to feel his erection. He was hard, and the size of his sex awed her. Like his hands, it seemed to belong to another, more powerful man.

Then he began to undress her. In a moment, she stood before him in her panty hose and brassiere. She wondered why she'd bothered to wear them. He unhooked her brassiere and looked with obvious delight at her bare firm breasts with their pouting nipples. Then he moved away from her and began undressing himself. His skin was smooth, and his sex, huge and firm.

"I've never been able to cope with panty hose without tearing them. You take them off."

She did, and they faced each other, naked. He passed his hands along the curves of her body to become familiar with them and kindle each special part with his touch. His caresses aroused him as much as they did her, and taking her by the hand, he led her to the bedroom. He bent her back on the bed and leaned over her, kissing her into a reclining position. As her eyes blurred with passion, her legs opened wide. He lay his full length over her, and she loved his weight on her, loved being crushed. Shivers ran through her body as he excited her further with words, with his hands, with his mouth. Involuntarily, she began to move, and it became like a dance in which their bodies turned and twisted into new shapes, new designs. Now they were cupped, like twins, spoon fashion, his penis against her behind, her breasts undulating like waves under his hands. Now he was crouched over her like some great animal as she raised herself to meet him. When he entered her, they shuddered as they came together. Genie cried out with a half-sob of joy at the flow of pleasure through her body.

Later they sat on the couch sipping their drinks. Genie wore a light kimono and was amused as Raymond, with true banker foresight, produced a silk robe he'd packed in his attaché case. They chatted comfortably like lovers who'd known each other for years. At one point, Raymond remarked offhandedly, "I gather I wasn't the beast you expected?"

"No. You're incredible."

"That reminds me." He rose from the couch and walked to the closet. "I have something for you." He returned in a minute, beaming. "Here it is." He handed her a sheaf of papers. "All it needs is your and your brother's signatures."

"The loan for the buildings?"

"Yes. Look at the papers."

Genie scanned them and stared at him. "I don't understand."

"Let me tell you something, my dear. I lied. I reviewed your proposal this morning. It stood up very well. So I presented it to the loan committee with my recommendation that we proceed. That's why I was late. I had to prepare the papers." He grinned. "If I hadn't decided to make the loan, or if the committee hadn't agreed with me, I wouldn't be here."

"You wouldn't?"

"I wouldn't. I know I have something of a reputation, but it's only partially deserved. I'll tell you how I acquired my fame. It's like the story of the Vassar honor student who becomes a prostitute. When asked how she got into the business, she replied, 'Just lucky, I guess.' " Genie giggled and Brenner continued. "I suppose the same could be said of me. Early in my banking career I discovered that many women who came to see me for loans assumed it would be easier to persuade me if they used their bodies to collateralize the loan. I was propositioned regularly."

"You were!" Genie was appalled.

"I was and still am. Many women take it for granted that the way to a banker's purse is through his penis. And since there's no longer a stigma attached to casual sex, they see it as an added trading card. Being a simple Iowa farm boy, this came to me as a shock. But being a simple Iowa farm boy, I saw no reason to disappoint them. If on its own merits I decided to make the loan, I took up the woman's offer. But if I didn't, then I didn't. No loan, no sex."

"Suppose the woman didn't make an offer? I mean didn't proposition you?"

"If she was good looking enough, I'd proposition her. As I did you."

Genie swallowed her drink. "And suppose she said no? Suppose I'd said no?"

"You'd have gotten the loan. It's a good loan. Remember, I never said you had to sleep with me to get the loan. I merely suggested we have an arrangement. You made your own interpretation of what effect your answer would have on my decision. I'm a banker first. Pimping for myself comes second."

"I'll be damned!"

"No. Blessed. Look at what happened."

"I feel like such a fool."

"Don't. You acted out of an ancient tradition. That a man is a sucker for a roll in the hay. Some men are. I'm not."

"And I'm a cliché come true." Genie blushed. "Then we have no arrangement?"

"Not unless we both want one."

"Tell me, was that story about your wife true?"

"Unfortunately, yes. That part of my song and dance is true."

"Then I want you." And she did. She drew him to her and sealed their new arrangement with a long, passionate kiss.

The next morning Genie took the subway to the office, clutching her briefcase containing the loan agreement tightly under her arm. As usual, she passed the time catching up on the news as reported in the *New York Times*. A short item in the theatrical section made her turn pale and exclaim out loud, "Oh, no!" Heads turned toward her, and she covered her embarrassment by burying her face in the paper and rereading the item. Paul Husseman had been attacked by a gang of three young muggers. Despite a number of broken bones, bad bruises and a mild concussion, St. Vincent's Hospital listed him in good condition and expected to release him in a few days.

When she arrived at the office, Max was waiting for her. This was unusual in itself, but something in his face, a submission to forces beyond his control which she'd never seen before, warned Genie not to ask any questions. She restricted herself to business and tossed him the loan documents. Max looked at them without reading their contents.

"You got the loan." It wasn't a question. It was a joyless statement acknowledging the realities that stood behind the loan.

Genie refused to permit Max's attitude to affect her. "We got the loan. All you have to do is sign in the proper places."

"Uhuh. Will there be a formal closing?"

"Would you trust the U.S. Mail with a check for six hundred thousand dollars?"

"I guess not. Do I have to be there?"

Genie understood. Unless it was absolutely necessary, Max would never meet Raymond Brenner. And maybe it was better that way. "No. Once you sign, I'll pick up the check."

"Where do I sign?"

"The places are marked with a red X."

Max fumbled in his pocket for a pen. The movement was clumsy, and he dropped the pen. Genie stared at him. Max was never clumsy. Then she saw his hands. His knuckles were raw and swollen. Involuntarily, her hand flew to her mouth. Paul! The story in the *Times* was wrong. Paul hadn't been mugged. Max had beaten him up.

Max saw her gesture, looked down at his hands, and knew she knew what he had done last night. The only escape for either of them was silence and a mutual acceptance, of what had happened, since neither of them could alter it.

Thus, Max and Genie reached an unspoken agreement. Max would avoid anything involving Genie and Brenner, and Genie would ignore anything connecting Max with Paul. It remained as it had always been, Szabo and Szabo against the world.

It took five months in all for the apartments to be sold, checks collected, and the final transfer of titles of ownership from ConVert-Co, Inc., the new subsidiary of Szabo & Szabo, to the eight building corporations. The Roths were among the first to sign, and Sam Roth went out of his way to help Max convince a few reluctant tenants that owning their own apartment was a damn good thing. Once the sales were completed, the lawyers released the proceeds of all the transactions to Max and Genie in the form of a certified check made out to ConVert-Co, Inc. The check was deposited in a new account opened in the Queens-Manhattan Trust. After repayment of the bank loan, disbursements to the lawyers, accountants, state filing and transfer fees, and a special account set up to cover ConVert-Co corporate taxes, Max and Genie sat in their office in Queensboro Plaza and stared at the net figure remaining in the corporate checking account. The size of the figure frightened both of them.

"How much does it come to?" Max asked.

"I've told you three times. The number won't change."

"Indulge me just once more."

"After all expenses and provision for corporate taxes, we're worth one million, five hundred and twenty-six thousand, six hundred and eighty dollars and eighty-eight cents."

"My God! We're millionaires! You're twenty-five, I'm twenty-seven, and this is only our first deal." Max finally noticed Genie's worried expression. "What is it, kidlet? We're so rich, I'll splurge. A dollar for your thoughts."

"For free, big brother. Do you realize we're what Momma would call aristocrats? This very moment we're American aristocrats. I wonder how Momma will feel about that?"

25

Even though, in a half-joking fashion, Max and Genie spoke of themselves as American aristocrats, the success of their first venture did not actually seem real. How was it possible for the super's kids to climb so high and so soon? It would take many more successes before either of them would fully accept their new status in the business world and the world at large. The psychological baggage they'd carried since childhood was not so easily laid aside.

Although they continued to see their parents for the ritual supper on alternate Wednesday nights, by tacit agreement they never mentioned their co-op venture to either Zoltan or Anna. Now that it was completed, Max was anxious to share their success, while Genie was no longer sure it could be shared. While riding in a cab from their office to the Majestic, they discussed the best way to break the news.

Max's position was typical of Max. "We'll just tell 'em, that's all."

"If there was only Dad to tell, you'd be right. But there's Momma."

"She'll be proud. We've proved ourselves. What's wrong with that?"

"I've thought about it. Momma's idea of aristocracy isn't money. It's something one is born to."

"That's old hat from Hungary. She'll see that now."

"She doesn't have to see anything. But you're right. We can't keep it a secret forever." Genie felt tired. The prospect of telling her parents, which should have been a celebration, not a strain, was depressing. That, on top of everything else that had happened during the last months, made her shrink from the dinner ahead.

* * *

Dinner was a solemn, cheerless affair. Searching for some way to bring a hint of life to the table, Max fell back on the family staple, the Majestic.

"What's new, Dad? Still having trouble with water leaks?"

"Yes. We're working on waterproofing the north tower. It won't do much good. The building was built without counter flashing so the water keeps coming in."

"If you'd taken a proper job years ago, by now you might be working here and not have to ask your father such questions."

Anna had been saying the same thing for years. Max glanced at Genie. Was this the time to tell them? She shook her head so Max said nothing.

All through dinner Genie had watched her father. Zoltan's physical appearance troubled her. A decline, which had begun years ago, was accelerating. She tried to remember how old he was. Although she'd always known his birthday, the actual year kept slipping away. She thought it was 1910, which would make him sixty-two. A sixty-two-year-old man could not be considered an old man. Still, her concern made her ask, "Have you had a checkup recently, Dad?"

"No, Genie. Why should I spend money foolishly on a doctor?"

"It's not foolish. Everyone over forty should have annual checkups."

Anna's voice cut in, harsher than usual. "It is foolish. People live as long as they're supposed to live. And we must save every penny for your father's retirement. He has to retire in less than three years, and I don't know where we'll live. If Max knew enough, he could be the new superintendent, and we wouldn't have to move."

"Momma! Even if I was the super, you'd have to move. Or where would I live?"

"In your old room the way a good son should." She turned to Genie. "And you should still be living home. Not like an orphan without a family. Good girls live home until they're married."

"Do you honestly think a grown man should live with his parents?" Max was trying to be diplomatic.

"Yes, I do. The apartment is big enough. And when you marry, there's room for your wife. We could cook together, clean the apartment together. That's the way things should be.''

''Is that the way things were in Hungary, Dad?''

''Sometimes, Max. If the house was large enough.'' Since Zoltan, as usual, wanted to please everybody, he added, ''Not always, though.''

''This apartment is large enough. It's the proper way.'' Anna was becoming angry.

Hoping to head off any further disagreements, Genie said, ''I'll clear the table, Momma. You and Dad go into the living room and relax. Max and I have news to tell you when I'm done.''

''You don't live here, and I don't need your help cleaning up. Your father and I will do what we always do.''

''I'll take your place tonight, Dad, and help Momma. You and Max go into the living room.''

''I said I don't want your help.''

Genie could be as stubborn as her mother, and that stubborn streak was reinforced by the exhaustion she saw in her father's face. He'd long since given up opposing Anna and was getting ready to do as she said. Without waiting for further discussion, Genie began to stack the plates. As she stacked, she said, ''Max, take Dad into the living room. I'll help Momma.'' The words were delivered in an evenly measured voice with equal emphasis on each word. It told Max she meant what she said.

''Come on, Dad. Let's let the women do their thing. I want to hear more about the counter flashing.''

Zoltan allowed Max to drape an arm over his shoulder and lead him away.

Anna glared at her daughter, silently, while Genie stacked the dishes neatly in the sink. When Genie turned to face her, she gave her a stinging slap across her face. It was so hard, Genie had to step backwards to keep her balance, and the second slap missed her completely. ''You will remember this is my home, and when you are in my home, you will do as I say.'' Although the words were spoken so softly they barely reached Genie's ears, the lack of volume in no way lessened their impact. ''You have never learned your place. I tried to teach you when you were children. Max and you. But now, in my home, you will behave as though you learned proper behavior.''

Genie struggled to gather her wits together. She could remember an occasional spanking as a child, but this was the first time her mother had ever struck her across the face. "Oh, Momma!" she cried. "Momma!"

Anna sank into a chair next to the kitchen table, put her head in her hands, and rocked back and forth. Her voice was choked with tears. "If you had been a proper daughter and Max a proper son, we would all be living together now. Your father and I would have our home. No one would take it away from us."

Genie sat in a chair next to her mother, her own tears running down her cheeks. She understood that while some of Anna's sobs were due to Anna's feeling sorry for herself, most of her mother's suffering came from a genuine despair because she had failed to teach her children her own standards, to believe as she believed, and she was terrified that God would punish the Szabo family for her failures. She could not accept the fact that her beliefs had no basis in the real world. They were her fears, her failures, and they'd become a part of her.

The shattering slap and the sight of her mother sobbing affected Genie's judgement. She wanted desperately to please Anna. In her eagerness to do something, she allowed hope to overcome her usual hardheaded good sense, and she chose this moment to tell her about the co-op venture. She thought, perhaps when her mother understood the success her children had achieved, she might begin to glimpse the possibilities in the United States which were open to everyone. With that understanding might come a lessening of fear and more trust in Max and her.

"Momma. Stop crying. It's all right." She reached for her mother to console her.

Anna violently drew away. "It's not all right. Leave me alone."

"Momma, come into the living room. Max and I have some wonderful things to tell you."

Anna looked at her daughter, her face showing all the distrust and disapproval she felt. Then she saw the red mark on Genie's cheek beginning to fade, and her shame at having struck her daughter, more than any desire to hear the wonderful things, made her allow Genie to help her from her chair and guide her to her usual place next to Zoltan.

Max and Zoltan had been talking in low voices. As soon as

Anna and Genie entered the room, their conversation ceased. Always attuned to violence of any kind, Max saw Genie's face and knew immediately Anna had hit her. He clenched his fists and his knuckles turned white with the effort he made to keep himself still. What was the matter with their mother anyway? Zoltan knew something unpleasant had happened in the kitchen, but as usual, he hoped no one would tell him. That way he would not be forced to choose between his wife and his daughter.

Genie spoke first. "Max, I told Momma we have some wonderful news. Do you want to tell her or should I?"

"Do you think this is the right time?" Now Max was uncertain, but Genie's nod was emphatic. "Then I think I'd better."

Using the shortest sentences and simplest language possible, Max described how they'd borrowed money to buy the apartment houses from Andre Husseman and turned them into cooperatives. As he told the story, Genie studied first one parent then the other. She saw understanding, approval, and astonishment in her father's face. Her mother's face was unreadable. It was absolutely still, her lips thin and the corners of her mouth turned down.

Max finished by giving them the financial results of the venture. "Our new corporation, ConVert-Co, has over one and a half million dollars in the bank. The money is all ours. Genie's and mine. And this is only one conversion. We're just beginning."

Zoltan remembered how when Max had finally accepted his not becoming a builder, he'd said it was now up to them. They'd done it, and he felt as proud as if he'd done everything himself. "Anna! Did you hear? Max! Genie! They're millionaires!" There was a silence in the room. Zoltan continued in a weaker voice. "Say something, Anna. Say something!"

"What should I say?" She couldn't understand how Max's story was possible. "It's wrong. All wrong. It's against God's will. God will punish us, and now Max will never come to work here. Should I be happy because we will lose our home?"

"Momma!" Max tried to ease his mother's fears. "We'll buy you an apartment so you'll never have to worry again."

Anna didn't hear him. She was lost in the final realization that Max would never replace Zoltan and be the superintendent of the Majestic, a dream she'd kept alive through the years by ignoring all the evidence to the contrary. Now she cast about for a reason to explain why her dream had failed. And she found one—the Hussemans. Although her reactions were warped, even half-demented, they were curiously accurate. She muttered, more to herself than anyone else in the room, "If Genie hadn't known Paul Husseman, Mr. Husseman would never have given them the buildings."

"He sold them to us, Momma. He didn't give them to us."

"Quiet, Max. I want to hear this." Genie had an awful premonition of what was coming.

"We should never have let them meet. No matter what Mr. Husseman wanted. Remember Rebecca's party? Genie should not have gone. I thought, at least if she wore that dress, it would end it once and for all. I was wrong."

Genie now knew that what she'd long suspected and avoided facing was true. Her mother had meant her to look ridiculous at that long ago children's party. It was deliberate. And she'd succeeded, but her success had only brought Paul closer. Thinking about it, Genie felt more sadness than anger.

Max and Zoltan were appalled. "Anna, are you saying you made a dress for Genie to make her look foolish? You did it on purpose?" Zoltan asked.

"Yes!" Anna screamed her defiance around the room. "She should never have gone to the party. Genie did not belong with those people."

Max whispered to Genie, "She's crazy. What'll we do?"

"Nothing. She's been sick a long time. Now it's coming out."

Zoltan stood in front of his wife. "You wanted our daughter to be laughed at?"

"They'd have laughed at her anyway. I wanted to make sure."

"Why would they laugh at her?"

"Because she's the superintendent's daughter, and aristocrats always laugh at foolish peasants trying to rise above their station."

Listening to her, Genie closed her eyes in deep grief. Unwillingly, she accepted that her mother had become irrational. What had started as a belief in the rightness of a certain way of life, a life which rested on a strict caste system where one never moved from the social position into which one was born, had become a blind hatred of anything and anyone who might think this idea wrong or oppose it. This hatred was so strong it blotted out all the love Genie was certain her mother still felt for Max and for her.

Opening her eyes, she heard her father say, "Anna, you're wrong. You've been wrong all along. And I was wrong to listen to you. I should have become a builder as I wanted to."

Anna started screaming at her husband, and under the cover of her raised voice, Max whispered, "Genie, did you hear him? Dad wanted to build the 608's!"

"I heard. I know. It was Momma who stopped him."

"But he wasn't scared. He would have done it!" Max was elated. The rebirth of his faith in his father as a brave man was vital to him, vital to his own self-esteem. He wanted to put his arms around his father and tell him how sorry he was for not understanding. It would be different from now on. Zoltan would work for ConVert-Co with Genie. They needed a managing agent.

Genie saw Max start to rise and restrained him. "Wait, Max. Let them work it out."

As Zoltan and Anna continued to argue, Anna's rage turned back to her children. They were the guilty ones. If she could, she'd have struck Genie again. As it was, she said, "I order both of you out of my house. I never want to see or hear from you again."

Max refused to believe her. "Momma, that's silly."

"Silly!" Anna shrieked. She half ran towards Max and tried to hit him. Max's reflexes were too fast. He caught her wrists and held them.

Zoltan grabbed her by the shoulders and swung her around. He shouted, "This is not your home. This is *our* home. All of us. And our children are always welcome in their home."

This was the first time in their entire lives Max and Genie had heard their father raise his voice.

"It's my home," Anna screamed, her two fists beating on Zoltan's chest.

The sudden violence of Anna's actions paralyzed everyone. Before Max could reach his struggling parents, Zoltan crossed his arms over his chest, a choking sound came from his throat and he crumpled to the floor. Anna stood over him, erect, implacable. Zoltan's fall had proven her right. She spoke for God who had taken vengeance on the Szabo family.

Max knelt close to his father. He tore open Zoltan's shirt and put his ear against Zoltan's chest. Then he felt his pulse.

"Call up front, Genie. He's still alive. There may be a doctor in the building with evening hours. And call emergency at Roosevelt Hospital."

Zoltan's eyes opened. As he looked at his son, they were full of admiration and love. His voice was very weak. "I'm sorry to spoil your wonderful news. The doctor said my heart wasn't too good. It seems he was right."

"You'll be fine, Dad. I'm so proud of you. And if you couldn't be a builder, you can work with us at ConVert-Co."

Zoltan smiled at hearing his son's words. Thank God, in the end, he hadn't failed. Max loved and honored him again as a son should love and honor his father. Then his face became grey and contorted with pain. He clutched himself again. "There's a band crushing my chest. Bad! Bad!" He gasped as though trying desperately to force air into his lungs. Suddenly his arms slipped from his body and his head rolled back.

Max grabbed his wrist. There was no pulse. He straddled his father's body and breathed into his mouth, forcing air into his lungs. Breathe in. Pump out. Breathe in. Pump out. Don't stop! Don't give up! He became aware of a hand shaking him and a voice screaming, "Leave him alone. He's dead. Leave him . . ."

"Genie," Max shouted. "Get her away from me!" He continued. Breathe in. Pump out. Breathe in . . .

Genie used her full strength to force her mother into a chair. All the while Anna raved wildly. "I was right. This is my home. All mine now. Not his. Mine!" The front doorbell rang, and Genie stared at her mother who was suddenly quiet, sitting calmly, even contentedly, in the chair. She rushed to the door. John, the doorman, was there with an elderly man in a white coat.

"I'm Dr. Weinstein. What's happened?"

"My father's had a heart attack." Her voice broke. "I think he's dead."

The doctor brushed by her and hurried into the living room. He tapped Max on the shoulder. "Let me examine him, young man!" Quickly he replaced Max and tested Zoltan for signs of life. Max and Genie waited. Dr. Weinstein's final actions told them everything. Carefully, he placed a forefinger on each of Zoltan's eyelids and closed them. "I'm sorry. There's nothing I can do."

Max knelt. "No! I can keep him alive. I can . . ." His voice trailed off.

"There's nothing you can do. Has anyone called a hospital?"

"I called Roosevelt Hospital. They should be here any minute."

Dr. Weinstein turned from Max and Genie to Anna. "I'm so sorry, Mrs. Szabo. I'll stay until the ambulance arrives." Anna remained seated, immobile. There was no indication she was in any way aware her husband of thirty-five years had just died, and his heart attack might have been brought on by her. Her face was frozen. Seeing this, Dr. Weinstein passed his hand in front of her eyes. There was no response. Then he placed both his hands on her face. Anna's reaction was immediate and violent.

She screeched, "Get out of here! Out! And get him out too! He had no right to die! Now I will lose my home! Get him out of here!"

"What is she talking about?" Dr. Weinstein incredulously asked.

With a great effort, Genie answered the question. "You know our father was the building super. This apartment goes with the job. The apartment is important to our mother."

The doctor glanced at Zoltan's body and shook his head. He'd seen grief in many forms, but this was a new form—grief for an apartment, not a husband. "Do you know where your mother keeps the sheets? I'd like to cover the body."

Anna answered. Her acceptance of Zoltan's death was more frightening than the wildest weeping and tearing of her hair would have been. "This is still my home. I will get the sheet." She looked at Zoltan. "You don't want a large sheet. One from a twin-size bed will do?"

"Of course, Mrs. Szabo. Of course."

They waited in silence until Anna returned with a white sheet. It was old and the tears had been neatly sewn together in a number of places. Dr. Weinstein placed the sheet over Zoltan making certain it covered him completely. "The ambulance will arrive shortly. At the hospital they may decide to do an autopsy. Unless your family doctor will sign the death certificate."

"We do not have a family doctor. We do not have the money to waste on such things. There was nothing wrong with him."

Max realized he was the only one who had heard his father's dying words. "That's not true. Before he died, he said something about a doctor telling him his heart wasn't in good shape."

"Do you know the doctor's name?"

"No. But I'm sure he's in the neighborhood."

"Find him as quickly as you can. If your father had a bad heart and the doctor will sign the certificate, it will spare you the autopsy. Mrs. Szabo, I would like to give you something to help you sleep. I think your son and daughter should stay with you tonight." He looked at Max and Genie who nodded their agreement.

"I do not need anything, and I do not wish them to stay." Anna said sharply. "They know how I feel. Their ideas killed their father. They can leave when you leave."

The shattering death of his father and what he saw as his mother's sudden madness temporarily blinded Max to the world around him. He squatted down next to his father, pulling the sheet back from the still face. He stared at Zoltan with pride, without hope, and with infinite regret. He was so lost in his grief it took a moment before he felt Anna's grasp. She seized his shoulders and pulled him away from his father. Taken by surprise, Max was thrown off balance and sprawled backwards, having to prop himself up on his elbows. His mother had spoken of blasphemy, and Max had not known what she meant. Now, watching her replace the sheet over Zoltan's face, he knew.

"He's dead because of you. Leave him alone."

Max slowly rose to his feet and faced his mother. His mouth was a pale slash from words he could not say, and the muscles of his neck stood out from actions he could not take. Helpless, he turned to Genie. "You heard him. He said this is our home. We don't have to leave."

Genie put her arms around her big brother. She knew she had more resilience, more ability to bend and absorb great blows. She held him, trying to quiet his shattered spirit, and the physical contact helped Max regain some of his self-possession. "It's true. We don't have to leave, but . . ." She looked at her mother who was now seated in what they'd thought of since childhood as their father's chair. She knew Anna's choice of that particular chair was deliberate, and the symbolic gesture was not missed by Genie. "But I think we should. Maybe tomorrow or the day after . . ."

Max accepted from Genie what he'd refused to accept from his mother. Like Genie, he hoped that when Anna had more time to absorb the reality of Zoltan's death, she would look to them for help, and they would unite to restore what was left of the family. But for the moment, all they could do was wait for the ambulance.

The next day, as he'd expected, Max found Zoltan's doctor in the neighborhood. Dr. Warren Hurley, on West 71st Street, had examined his father about three months earlier.

"Yes, Mr. Szabo. He'd had a minor heart attack before he came to me. His blood pressure was too high, and his cholesterol count was well above acceptable levels. I gave him a prescription for his blood pressure and warned him about his work."

"His work?"

"The job at the Majestic was too demanding for a man in his condition. I suggested he rest or take early retirement. He said he couldn't. Something about his wife and the apartment. Then he called to cancel his next appointment. I assumed he went to another doctor."

"He didn't. He simply ignored your advice. There's a question about a death certificate. Will you sign it? We don't want an autopsy."

"How did he die?" Max made up a story about a simple family dinner at the end of which Zoltan collapsed and died. Dr. Hurley agreed there was no need for an autopsy. He'd sign the death certificate. "Your father died of a second heart attack."

While Max searched for the doctor, Genie spoke to Jim Blake at Brown, Harris, Stevens, Inc. He was Jack O'Neil's successor. Blake's looks reminded her of Jack—both from California, both large handsome men, although Blake was a good deal younger. He'd heard about Zoltan's death and was most sympathetic.

"We will need a new superintendent, and the apartment does go with the job. But, naturally, we'll give your mother all the time she needs to find another apartment. Your father was a fine man. Please give your mother my deepest condolences. And the same to you and your brother."

"Thank you, Mr. Blake. We'll find something as soon as we can, and will be in touch with you shortly."

The funeral took place in a small cemetery in northern Westchester County that was owned by the St. Elizabeth of Hungary Church. It was a family affair, with the church supplying the priest and pallbearers. A cloth of gold was draped over the dark wooden coffin. Although Max kept dabbing at the corner of his eyes with a large white handkerchief, Genie made no attempt to stop the flow of tears which streamed down her cheeks. As for Anna, she seemed a stick figure in a plain black dress, her face placid and empty of all feeling. After Max poured the first shovel of dirt over the coffin, she turned and walked to the rented limousine.

On their way back to New York, Genie, choosing her words carefully, told her mother she needn't worry about moving. She had time. "The people at Brown, Harris were very understanding."

"They don't have to be. I will be moving out in two weeks."

"Where? How did you find an apartment so quickly?"

"Momma," Genie said. "We were going to buy you an apartment in one of our buildings. And give it to you."

"I don't wish to own an apartment in one of your buildings. People like us are not meant to be owners. And God has punished us because of the two of you." Anna continued. "Mrs. Sagi's husband died last year. You may remember her. She lives on 72nd Street and needs a housekeeper and companion. I will move in with her and share the expenses. It won't be the same as having my own home, but it will have to do."

Genie tried again to reach her mother. "If you'd let us buy you an apartment, you'd have your own home."

"No! Do not forget what I said the night you killed your father."

"Stop that, Momma!" Max was furious. "I haven't told

anyone how you beat on his chest. That's Szabo family business. If anyone killed our father, it was you. You and your crazy ideas about your home. Did you know he'd had a heart attack months ago and refused to retire? He was so worried about you and your damned obsession with that apartment. We did not . . ." His voice broke, and he stopped.

Anna finished the sentence her own way. "Kill your father? Yes, you did. You killed your father. And this country did with its crazy ideas. If I could, I'd return to Hungary. But there's no one left. I'm moving in with Mrs. Sagi, and we will speak no more about it."

"Then give us your telephone number. Once you've settled in, we'll go out to dinner. Maybe next Friday evening."

"No. Genie, you may not take me out to dinner next Friday evening. Not then or ever. I do not want to see either of you again."

When Anna left the limousine at the Majestic, Max and Genie watched her walk through the front door, and they wondered if their mother would ever be their mother again.

PART FIVE

1972-1982

26

The phone rang continuously. It was the day after the article about the co-oping of eight middle-income apartment houses in Queens by the Szabos' new corporation, ConVert-Co, Inc., had appeared in the *New York Times* real estate section. Among the calls was one from Mr. Edward Bailey of Bankers' Trust who suggested that Genie and he have lunch. It seemed the branch manager was now more favorably disposed towards the Szabos and middle-income cooperatives. Perhaps they had something to talk about? Genie's eyes opened wide as she thought, yes! A line of credit. After setting a date, she hung up the telephone.

As soon as she did, it rang again. It was Jack O'Neil.

"Hi. I was just going to call you."

"A likely story. In any case, I saved you a dime. Listen, I've got a great apartment coming up at 40 Central Park South. Remember, you asked me to keep you in mind. Well, ask and thou shalt receive. It's a large, three-and-a-half-room, one-bedroom apartment on the twelfth floor. Both the living room and bedroom face the park. It's a steal."

"Central Park South is never a steal. How much?"

"A pittance. Five-seventy-five a month. Three-year lease. And for you, we'll paint and throw in a new refrigerator and stove."

"That's a lot of money, Jack. Most of what we made is supposed to be plowed back into the business for operating capital."

"You have to sleep somewhere between deals. And you said you wanted out from 9th Street."

"I do. But that rent? Let me talk to Max. If he agrees, I'll look. I'll call you back later."

Genie leaned back and toyed with the idea of moving to Cen-

tral Park South. Her lease was running out, and she wanted
badly to move. She'd called Jack O'Neil several weeks ago and
asked him to keep her in mind if a reasonable vacancy came up
in one of his buildings. Because, for all its charm, the 9th Street
apartment was a constant reminder of her life with Paul. A year
and a half without him had not eased the pain. She felt the
apartment wasn't hers, it had never been hers, it was part of a
life that no longer existed. Sometimes, lying alone in their bed,
Genie was certain she could feel Paul's body next to hers
weighing down his side, the way a person who has lost an arm
or a leg will swear they can feel the missing limb. Half asleep,
she'd reach over and be shocked to discover he wasn't there.
The result was she tried to spend the night in the apartment of
whomever she was seeing. And if the evening ended in her
place, and they made love, she always insisted the man leave
afterwards. Paul's presence was too real. Sometimes she heard
his key in the latch and knew, any minute, he'd walk in and find
her with another man in their bed.

The phone rang again, interrupting her musing. To her surprise, it was Max. "Where are you? You should be here. We
have to make plans."

"I'm at 299 Park Avenue. I've just looked at a beautiful,
small suite of offices on the thirty-sixth floor."

Genie was exasperated. "You're no longer in the business of
leasing office or loft space. Our new corporation is called
ConVert-Co, Inc. Remember? And we convert rental apartment houses into co-ops or condominiums."

"I'm not looking at the space as a broker. I'm looking for
us."

"For us? What's wrong with here?"

"Look around you." Genie looked at the used furniture, the
cheap imitation Oriental rug, and the carpets she'd bought at
Woolworth's. After a long moment of silence, he asked, "See
what I mean? There was nothing wrong with here as long as we
were managing buildings in Queens. And as a broker, I never
had to bring clients or owners to the office. But, kidlet, we're
going into the business of buying apartment houses. That takes
chunks of money, and most of the money will come from the
banks. How many bank vice-presidents will lend big money to
an outfit with offices like ours? In Queensboro Plaza?"

That was a long speech for Max. Genie wondered if the address on her original prospectus had had some negative effect when she'd first tried to raise money. The sizzle was almost as important as the steak. Although it hadn't affected Raymond Brenner, Genie couldn't laugh it off where others were concerned. "All right. When can I see the space?"

"Now. Grab a cab and meet me in the lobby of 299. It's between 48th and 49th on Park."

"I know. I'll take the subway."

"Think big, Genie. Take a cab." Max hung up.

As Genie sat in the taxi on the way to meet Max, she considered the move. It seemed to her the new office space was like leaping from a basement apartment to a penthouse. And wasn't that exactly what they'd expected their father to do years ago when they suggested he become a builder? He had Momma holding him back. Nobody was holding her. Why was she having so much trouble accepting their new status? Obviously there was more of her mother in her than she liked to admit. That settled it. After she saw the space, she'd talk to Max about the apartment Jack had offered her. If he didn't object, she'd look at it in the afternoon.

Two months later, ConVert-Co, Inc., moved from Queensboro Plaza to the thirty-sixth floor of 299 Park Avenue, and Eugenia Szabo moved from 9th Street to 40 Central Park South. Instead of an imitation Oriental from Macy's and carpets from Woolworth's, they hired Billy Bayberry, a decorator, who spent what Genie considered an outrageous amount of money on special wood flooring and real Orientals bought at Haratoorian. The furniture was all steel and leather and glass with occasional fine copies of antiques to soften the ultramodern look. The only real conflict came when Billy wanted to cover the walls with abstract paintings. There was a scream out of Max. If he couldn't tell what the subject of the painting was, it wasn't a painting. It was a splash and smear any child could imitate. Genie knew when to quit. The paintings were purchased at galleries which specialized in fine painters painting in the style of Andrew Wyeth. For all the wrong reasons that went into the decision, Max's choice of art turned out very well. The scenes of barns, wooded areas, and sand and sea, all done in beautiful detail, were the perfect foil for their ultramodern office.

When Genie moved into her new apartment on Central Park

South, she hoped the move would help blur her memories of Paul. But standing at the window at night, looking at the lights of the cars in Central Park and the four twin-towered buildings that dominated Central Park West, she was reminded of her evenings looking at the Park, evenings when she and Paul had made love on the rooftop of the Majestic. She could even see the Majestic and had no trouble picking out the Husseman apartment. Sometimes she thought she should have moved further east. But there was one marked improvement—the apartment contained nothing she had shared with Paul. From the king-sized bed to the L-shaped couch in the living room, it was all new. She went so far as to give all the clothes Paul had bought for her to the Salvation Army. Then she went on a buying binge. She opened charge accounts in every major store in Manhattan, from Bergdorf Goodman to Henri Bendel, from Saks Fifth Avenue to B. Altman to Bloomingdale's. While she found she had a taste for high fashion and a somewhat extreme look that went with her striking face and figure, for business she chose clothes along more conservative lines. They were casually elegant clothes such as she'd always worn, but now they were made of superb fabric, with superb cut and line. Like the proper office space, wearing the proper clothes was part of the reality of business life.

On the second Monday in October, after all the paintings were hung, the Orientals on the floor and the ashtrays and furniture in place, Max and Genie sat down to business. They met in Genie's office, and Max poured them both a cup of coffee from the brand new Coffee-Mate machine, using coffee bought in Zabar's and prepared by their brand new, straight out of Katharine Gibbs Secretarial School secretary, Helen Bradley.

"What we need is merchandise. We can't sell what we don't own."

"Agreed. We need stock for this store." Genie shrugged. "I guess I have my work cut out for me." The division of labor they'd worked out called for Genie to find the properties and negotiate to buy them. That included working with the banks to develop the financial package. Max's job was to sell the apartments to the tenants. Each depended on the other for success.

"Yes, you do, kidlet. But this once, since I don't have anything to sell at the moment, I'll pitch in, too. It may help us get off the ground faster."

"All help will be greatly appreciated. You make a list of prospective owners who might have a building to sell, and I'll do the same. We'll reconvene on Friday. Same time, same place."

That evening, Tom Sword, Genie's latest, took her to the theater. He was thoroughly pleased with himself for having been able to get seats for the hot ticket in town, Paul Husseman's latest Off Broadway musical, *Beard*. At first Genie had reservations about going, but she finally decided this was a hang-up she'd better get over. Besides, this was the fourth month of the run, and Paul was probably busy working on his new production, not standing in back of the theater.

Genie enjoyed the play. During the intermission, while she waited for Tom who was in the men's room, she saw Edgar Redford, their former banker from the Bank of New York.

He greeted her. "Miss Szabo, we at the bank are very impressed with your Queens project. I want to congratulate you."

"Thank you, Mr. Redford."

"In fact it's been on my calendar to have my secretary call you to set up a lunch date for us."

"Money has grown less tight, Mr. Redford?"

He gave her a sheepish smile. "There's always money for the right borrower."

"By all means. Have your secretary call me for lunch." Watching the banker wander back to his party, Genie thought again how nice it was to be appreciated. Edgar Redford might not be only a source of money; the Bank of New York, being one of New York's oldest and most prestigious banks, must have many clients who owned apartment houses. Little old ladies in running shoes who kept tens of thousands of dollars in their checking accounts.

When Max and Genie met on Friday morning to compare lists, they both had done extensive homework. Having had lunch the day before with Redford confirmed an idea Genie had. This time they met in Max's office, and after Genie poured the coffee, he waited for her to begin.

"You have your list?" she asked.

"I do indeed. Ready when you are, E.S."

"Okay. I have twenty-three names, telephone numbers, and addresses. And on the top of the list is guess who? And don't laugh." Max tilted his head back, questioningly. "Won't guess? All right. Ralph Gluck. Remember him?" She glared at Max who was holding his hand over his face trying not to laugh. "Why are you laughing at me? What's so funny?"

"I'm not laughing at you. I'm laughing with you. Here." He handed her a sheet of paper on which there was a long list of carefully handwritten names. On the top of the list was Ralph Gluck. Then there were a lot of names she recognized from Robert Tishman to the Minskoff Brothers to Harry Helmsley as well as other real estate tycoons.

"Okay. I'll call Gluck."

"Yep. Now it's in your ball park."

"Is there a telephone directory in this office?"

"Don't need one. Watch." Max's desk was a piece of stainless steel set on a stainless steel base. What was unique was the L-section. It was a slanted piece of stainless steel containing enough buttons and lights to make a small Christmas tree. There were three phones. One was his private line, the second a special phone which he used to dictate directly into a tape recorder, and the third phone was the regular office phone. Each phone had three lights next to it to represent the type of incoming calls. It was Genie's private opinion that red was for "pick up now!" orange for "pick up when ready," and green for "pick up if you've nothing better to do." Another set of buttons operated a wooden panel which concealed a fully equipped bar. Max pushed a button and a large Rolodex began to turn. "Let's see. Gluck? Gl? Here we are." He pulled out a plastic card and placed it in a slot near his private telephone. He pointed to a phone next to Genie. "When the light goes on, push the button and pick up."

"What on earth is that?"

"I had the phone company put the fifty most important real estate owners in Manhattan on plastic cards which dial the number automatically."

"Oh, Max!" Genie waited for the light to go on and picked up the phone.

"Ralph Gluck and Company," a woman's voice said.

"This is Eugenia Szabo. I'd like to speak to Mr. Gluck, please."

"Oh, Miss Szabo. Mr. Gluck said when you called to tell

you he was available for a meeting Monday morning at ten o'clock or Thursday afternoon at three-thirty.''

Genie stared at the telephone, dumfounded. Making a major effort to keep the astonishment out of her voice, she said, ''Monday at ten will be fine.'' Then she hung up the phone, feeling slightly dazed.

''What was that all about?''

''Beats me. Would you believe he expected my call? He had two possible times for a meeting scheduled.''

''From the things I've heard about that operator, I'd believe anything.'' Max frowned. ''Do you think it's a good sign or a bad sign that he expected your call?''

''I think it's a good sign. If he knew I wanted to see him, he also knows why, and he could have had his secretary say he was unavailable.''

''Unless he's a sadist. I've heard he's a tough bastard.''

''I've heard that, too. We'll see.''

Genie arrived at Ralph Gluck's office promptly at ten o'clock. She was received by a tall well-dressed woman who had answered the phone the week before. Apparently Ralph Gluck had no use for an organization. The woman was a combination receptionist, secretary, and bookkeeper. Judging from her clothes and general appearance, she was well paid and worth the money. She had to be, or Gluck wouldn't employ her.

The young woman buzzed an inner office and said, ''Miss Szabo is here.'' Then she turned to Genie. ''Make yourself comfortable for a few minutes.'' She gestured toward one of several empty chairs. Ralph Gluck was as good as his word. Within five minutes his secretary ushered her into his office. Ralph was not waiting in his usual position with his feet on his desk puffing on a cigar. Instead, probably as a chivalrous gesture, he was seated in one of the low chairs that faced his desk. Genie was struck by the originality, beauty and elegance with which the office was furnished. She realized immediately there was far more to Ralph Gluck than being merely another rich man. When he saw her, he rose to greet her. The last time Genie had seen him she was thirteen, and she dimly remembered a short stocky man always puffing on a thick cigar. He was still short. In her heels she was taller than he. And he still puffed on cigars, judging from the one in the ashtray next to where he'd been sitting. But stocky was not an adequate description. He must be sixty, she thought, and he's massive. Almost as powerful as Max.

"Good morning, young lady. Have a seat. I understand you're interested in buying property from me."

Genie had been prepared for a blunt approach and had decided to be equally direct. "I am. But first, tell me—how did you know?"

"The article in the *New York Times*. And then Redford, one of my bankers, called me after your lunch the other day, and told me you were looking for available buildings to buy and convert. He thought I was high on your list of prospective sellers."

"You are. Very high." Genie couldn't help smiling as she realized everyone knows everyone, especially bankers. "My brother and I might be interested in buying an apartment house from you providing the price and general condition of the building are suitable for our purposes."

Without asking, Ralph relit the end of his cigar. Genie was reminded of Andre Husseman who had always been careful to ask whether she minded his smoking. Gluck would never ask. He puffed on the cigar and blew the smoke toward the ceiling. "I may have two buildings for you."

"Where?"

"Philadelphia."

That fit into the geographic limits Max and she had set. "What kind of buildings?"

"Apartment houses, naturally."

"Naturally. Tell me about them."

"They were built with cinder block but without the usual brick facing. The builder used Cyncrete over the block. Very colorful."

Genie's brow furrowed. "I'm sure they are, but if he did, we wouldn't touch the buildings. Given the weather in the northeast, the Cyncrete will crack, if it hasn't already. Water will pour through those walls."

Gluck gave her a broad grin. "You know a little something, don't you? Relax. The builder didn't use Cyncrete."

"Mr. Gluck, I don't enjoy your humor. You knew my father. You must realize I grew up in the real estate business. I also worked for several years as an assistant to Jack O'Neil. And for the last year and a half I've managed a number of apartments for our own firm. I know more than 'a little something.' "

Her response didn't faze Gluck. He continued to smile. "All right. What I'm offering is two twelve-story buildings with penthouses. Reinforced concrete construction." He looked at her questioningly. "You do know what reinforced concrete is?"

That did it. Genie stood up. "Would you like my lecture 32B on reinforced concrete and how Frank Lloyd Wright invented it? I call it my skin and bones speech. Either you start treating me as a professional, or you're about to be talking to an empty chair."

Gluck's face showed a shade more respect. "Sit down. If you leave now, you'll never know what a gem I'm offering."

Genie sat down. "Just tell me about the buildings, and I'll do my own Tiffany appraisal of your gems."

"Each building has twelve thousand square feet per floor, three automatic elevators, and a sizeable underground garage between the buildings. They're located just north of the Society Hill restoration area near Independence Hall."

"Why do you want to sell them?"

"I'm in the business of buying and selling buildings. But these are dogs. And since you're so smart, you figure out why."

Genie laughed. "The gem is now a dog." It was either the city making problems or the tenants. "This intrigues me. Do you have any operating figures available?"

"Gerry will give them to you on the way out."

"Are you suggesting I leave?"

"Do we have anything else to talk about?"

"The price and the terms."

"All included in the papers."

"And the operating expenses can be verified by actual bills?"

"By actual bills." There was a touch of scorn in his voice.

"If we're interested, I'll be in touch."

Ralph watched her leave, thinking again, it's a pity I'm too old to take her on.

When Genie reached her office, Helen Bradley gave her her

messages. Max would be in at about eleven o'clock. She got a call from Tommy Sword: "Pick you up at eight for dinner." For an instant Genie considered the number of men who had passed through her life since Paul. At least, thanks in part to Raymond Brenner, she was enjoying herself without any of the sexual guilt Anna had instilled in her. But with this project in the offing, she'd have less time to enjoy her private life. She'd have to put Tommy on ice for a while. The last message was from Jack O'Neil: "Call me when you're free." She would, when she was free. Right now all she wanted to do was pore over the details of Ralph Gluck's buildings.

"Helen, hold my calls. And tell my brother I want to see him when he comes in." She glanced toward the supply room. "By the way, is our Xerox working? Or do I have to kick it again?"

"The repair man was here at nine-fifteen this morning."

"Good. I'll have some papers for you to Xerox later."

Genie hurried to her office, tossed her jacket on the couch, and went to work. She tore open the thick package and ran a knowing eye over the contents. There was a series of eight-by-ten-inch photographs of the buildings and the huge gravel roof over the garage. The buildings appeared to be clean, modern and well kept. One picture was a close-up showing the details of the white Roman brickwork. She looked carefully. No water stains. Then she turned to the numbers. They seemed to be too good to be true.

Gross rentals of $1,652,386. That was more than the combined rent rolls of the eight buildings they had owned in Queens. Operating expenses under a million before mortgage interest, and amortization payments of about half a million. A pretax income of $214,975. The more Genie studied the numbers, the more she liked them. She went to her files and checked the operating expenses against photocopies she'd taken from Brown, Harris of the expenses of similar buildings. Allowing for differences in wage scales and real estate taxes between Philadelphia and New York, the numbers checked out. That also checked out with her estimation of Ralph Gluck. He wouldn't give out phony operating expenses. The only number she questioned was the one for repairs and maintenance. It seemed low, but the buildings were barely five years old and that might explain it. In any event, she would ask to see the invoices.

Genie turned to the page detailing Gluck's asking price. The total price was $9,075,000 or about five-and-a-half times the rent roll, below the price for New York buildings, but in line for Philadelphia. He wanted $1,275,000 in cash. Genie was confident they could knock $75,000 off the total price and the same off the cash, and Gluck was prepared to take back a second mortgage for ten years at a rather low interest. Time passed as Genie pored over the figures and then retraced her steps. Unless she was doing something crazy, much like their first deal, reselling the buildings to the tenants could be a great deal for the tenants and highly profitable for ConVert-Co. What was she missing? Why were these buildings dogs? They really were gems.

She played with the numbers. If they asked $1,500 a room, a tenant could buy a four-and-a-half-room apartment for a total payment of $6,750; and their cash investment, on top of the mortgages, would be less than half of that. A little over $3,000 was not much for a family to own their own apartment. At the same time, the monthly rent of $310 would be reduced to a maintenance of $270. Not a big deal, until one considered the tax benefits. Since half the $270 was interest on the mortgages and real estate taxes, a tenant in the thirty percent tax bracket would save close to an additional $40 per month after taxes. That brought the real monthly cost down to $230. Easy to swallow as butter. Eighty dollars per month savings, or $960 a year, was money.

The tenant's gain would be ConVert-Co's gain. They'd gross about $3,180,000 on the deal, almost $2,000,000 over their cash investment of $1,200,000. Naturally, there would be additional expenses such as legal, auditing, interest charges on any money they borrowed to swing the deal, and so on. But after the smoke cleared, ConVert-Co would make a huge profit.

Trying to contain her enthusiasm, Genie rechecked her numbers using a calculator with a tape printout. No matter how she juggled them, the results were the same. They could ask a reasonable price for the apartments and still make a healthy profit. That left her with two problems. What was the actual condition of the buildings? Genie thought about her father and how much she missed him. Had Zoltan been alive, she'd have asked him to come with her on the inspection tour. He'd known so much, and suddenly she found herself fighting the impulse to weep over her loss, of both her father and her mother. She stopped herself. What was, was. The second and more important question was why did Gluck call these buildings a gem and a dog? Apartment houses were more than bricks and mortar. There were always people involved, those living in the buildings, the city officials, the superintendent, the managing agent, the owner.

Her office door burst open. Genie looked up, startled. Max had arrived. "Sorry I'm late. How'd it go with Gluck?"

Genie took a long look at her desk clock. It was two-thirty, and she'd missed lunch. She answered sarcastically, "I hope, whoever she was, she was worth it. I'm trying to figure out how it went with Gluck."

Max ignored her sarcasm. "What do you mean? Will the bastard sell anything?"

"He will. Two buildings in fact. Twins. In Philadelphia."

"Price too high?"

"Nope. And that worries me."

"Right. Ralph Gluck does not give away real estate. He's in the business of buying and selling at a profit, and you don't think he'll make a profit on this sale?" Max slid into the chair facing her desk. "Can you find out why he's willing to do that?"

"I intend to try. First I'll have someone examine the tax stamps on the recorded deed to find out what Gluck actually paid for the buildings."

"Very smart. Then what?"

"Then I'll go over the buildings with my handy-dandy magnifying glass and bloodhound's nose for leaky faucets, falling ceilings, buried bones. That done, assuming I don't find anything, you get ready to throw your fastball. We were confident we could sell the apartments in Queens because we knew the buildings and the tenants. I can do the site inspection, but if we buy them without knowing the people, we could be buying a white elephant. You'll have to check out their attitude toward owning their own apartments."

"No way! Forget their attitude. It's too risky. Once they know the buildings are up for sale, any one of them might organize a group of tenants, or even get an outside investor to buy the buildings right out from under us."

"But without knowing how the tenants feel, we're playing blindman's buff."

Max waved aside her doubts. "After we own the buildings is when I really get in and pitch. If some jokers don't want to buy at the start, when I finish explaining the fine points of owning your own master bedroom, they will."

"Go with my blessings." She handed Gluck's presentation to Max. "Have Helen photocopy this and study the offering. See what you come up with. Helen will type up my notes this afternoon, and we'll meet tomorrow. Unless you have another hard night ahead?"

This time Max took notice. "That's a rotten pun."

Genie laughed and then became serious. "Look, Max. As we agreed, your private life is your business and mine is my business. But when either of our private lives gets in the way of work, it becomes the other person's business. Arriving at two-thirty in the afternoon is no way to run this store." Genie saw Max start to react and then settle back. She understood that as a salesman, pure and simple, there were times when he was very busy and other times when he could spend a morning in bed with a woman and be none the worse for the loss of time. But he was no longer that kind of salesman. He was a partner in running a business, and the demands on his time were heavier and would continue to grow.

"Kidlet, you made your point. I'll meet you here tomorrow at eight-thirty."

"No, big brother. Don't overdo it. This is a marathon, not a sprint. Nine-thirty will do."

"Nine-thirty it is. Tell Helen to get me a copy of your notes as soon as she types them. If you need me, I'll be in my office going over Gluck's offering."

"I just wish I could figure out why he wants out so badly."

"You will, kidlet. Believe me, you will."

27

Genie relaxed in a pullman seat on the 7:00 A.M. train to Philadelphia without noticing the countryside race by—not that the run from New York to Philadelphia is famous for its scenic beauty. She was too deeply immersed in the events of the last three days. After going over Gluck's offering and Genie's notes, Max was enthusiastic. "Great buildings! Great locations! Let's go!"

Genie had a second meeting with Gluck to tell him they were interested, and that she wanted to inspect the buildings. Gluck was one step ahead of her again. He'd anticipated her interest and prepared business cards that read Eugenia Szabo, Ralph Gluck & Co., Inc., with his address and telephone number on the bottom of the card. The idea was if she were working for him, the managing agents, Armstrong and Gaites, would supply her with whatever information she wished without suspecting she was a prospective purchaser of the buildings.

Genie's sixth sense was working overtime. The more she considered the situation, the more she realized the managing agents were not the people to speak to first. Didn't Brown, Harris get their reports from her father? And hadn't she, when she managed Husseman's buildings, received her reports from the superintendents? She decided to see the super first. She needed answers only he might have, and since she had to inspect the buildings anyway, he was her starting point.

Genie got off the train in downtown Philadelphia at the 30th Street Station and took a cab for the short ride to the buildings. She stood on the sidewalk studying the twin structures. They looked as good as they had in the photographs, built with white Roman brick and no scrimping. She rang the super's bell. She had to ring three times before a buzzer sounded and she could open the door to the bright, airy inner lobby. She looked around, examining the slate floor, the paint job, and the furniture, and was pleased with the general appearance. The lobby was well decorated and well maintained.

"What can I do for you, Miss?" Genie turned to see a wiry, dark-haired man dressed in khaki pants and a matching shirt. He had a set look on his face, as though prepared for a fight. "I've been busy in the laundry room repairing a washing machine, and I just got a clamp to hold the hose. Look, if you want an apartment, see the managing agents. Armstrong and Gaites on Market Street. But there's a waiting list around the block. Even with the way these buildings are run."

His words and manner registered with Genie. "I'm Eugenia Szabo. I work for Mr. Ralph Gluck." She showed the super her card.

"Gluck!" The man's disgust was obvious. "Yeah. He's in court again today along with Gaites."

"In court? No, he's not. He's in New York."

"Then his lawyers are in court. With another one of those tenants' suits."

"What's this suit all about?"

"Heat and hot water. We didn't get an oil delivery until Monday."

"Why did you allow the buildings to run out of oil?"

"Miss, I didn't let the buildings run out of anything. I tell Gaites when we're running low, and when Gluck gives the green light, he orders it. Then it takes time for a delivery, and we're without heat and hot water for a stretch. So they're suing to withhold a week's rent."

Genie took it all in. "Mr. er?"

"Angelo. Mike Angelo. Pleased to meet you." They shook hands.

"Mr. Angelo, you said another tenant suit. Are there a lot of them?"

"Yeah. Your boss is not the best owner I've ever worked for. So the tenants get mad and keep taking him to court. Gaites spends half his time in court."

"From what you say, I gather you don't order the heating oil. And you said something about just getting a clamp for a washing machine? Don't you keep a supply of clamps on hand?"

"Hell, no! Nothing's in the supply room. Gaites says Gluck

won't allow it. So I don't have washers for leaky faucets, bulbs for hall lights. If an apartment needs a screw to fix a door knob, I have to write a requisition and wait for Gaites to give me permission to buy it. It can take a week before he gets his okay from Gluck and passes it along. And God help us when something happens to a refrigerator or stove that I can't fix. It can take a month before Gaites can get Gluck to agree to buy a new one. Naturally the tenants go nuts and sue to withhold rent. And they blame me for everything. It's not my fault. It's Gluck's. Gaites says he's a cheap bastard.''

"I see."

"You should have heard Harris scream about his refrigerator. He's president of the tenants' committee. I know he had a reason, but he's a real son of a bitch." Angelo sighed. "I thought working in these buildings would be a breeze. But it's shit! Pardon the French. Buildings always need something, and Gluck takes forever to give the go-ahead. So they yell at me. Millie, my wife, says only the cleaning ladies say hello to her anymore. She wants me to find another job."

Genie listened to the outpouring of grievances and filed every detail. Then she said, "Thank you for being so helpful. I would appreciate another hour of your time. I want to inspect the boiler room, the elevators, the roof, the supply room, an apartment, if possible. Everything."

The inspection turned out as Genie had expected. The buildings were in fine shape, well constructed and well maintained, except for the delays in everyday repairs, which were inevitable since the supply room was empty. No bulbs, clamps, wire, fuses, copper pipe, spare refrigerators, or ovens—all standard items found in the supply rooms of well-run buildings. She knew where the trouble lay. Armstrong and Gaites had deliberately interfered with the super's job by taking over and delaying the ordering of supplies necessary for normal building maintenance, and then telling the tenants Gluck was the bottleneck. What a joke! As if light bulbs and fuses interested Ralph Gluck. It amused her to realize the trouble spot would never have occurred to Gluck. In some ways he was a typical operator. He bought and sold buildings, he didn't run them. It was a managing agent's job to run the buildings, and Armstrong and Gaites had convinced him he had a bunch of rotten apples as tenants. The question was, why?

* * *

She entered the reception room of the managing agent's offices on the fifteenth floor of an old building on Market Street. The room was tastefully furnished. She showed the girl at the switchboard her card and said, "I'd like to see Mr. Gaites, please."

"Mr. Gaites isn't in. Will Mr. Armstrong do?" When Genie nodded, the girl rang Armstrong's office.

Andrew Armstrong was an unusually handsome sandy-haired man of about forty, dressed in a beautifully tailored grey flannel suit. His office appeared to be the office of a wealthy, successful man.

"If you'd told me you were coming, we could have lunched at the original Bookbinders on Walnut Street."

"Thank you. I can skip a lunch now and then. Incidentally, do you expect Mr. Gaites shortly?"

"No. He's at a funeral for a maiden aunt."

"Very sad. Then we'll have to talk without him. There's been a number of tenants' suits. Mr. Gluck's lawyers are in and out of court regularly. So he sent me down to find out why."

"I know." Armstrong's voice was sympathetic. "Those tenants! They're an unreasonable group. But at that, you can't really blame them. The building is not very well constructed. Mr. Gluck bought a lemon."

"You think so?"

"We have continual vacancies. Of course the apartments do get rented. They're spacious, and the location is excellent. But we have so much trouble with maintaining the buildings properly, people move out constantly. You know, Mr. Gluck is not an easy man to deal with."

"That's an understatement. I think Mr. Gluck is a cross between Genghis Khan and Attila the Hun!"

Armstrong laughed. "Ah, you do understand." He pursed his lips. "When the buildings came on the market, I must admit I'd hoped one of our friends here in Philadelphia would pick them up. But *c'est la guerre*. Mr. Gluck moved fast."

"He can do that. But this time he may have moved too fast. The buildings are becoming a nuisance."

"I can well understand that. The tenants are difficult."

"As you know, Mr. Gluck is very wealthy. It's possible, if

he becomes irritated enough with the tenants and all the law-suits, he might consider selling the buildings."

"Do you really think so?"

"I don't try to outguess a man who could be president of Exxon. But he might. And then, possibly, one of your friends from Philadelphia might pick up the twins at a good price. Considering the location and the spacious layouts, perhaps with a Philadelphia owner, the maintenance could be improved?"

"Hmmm. Perhaps." Genie could smell the greed pouring out of Armstrong.

Max listened to Genie's report. "Okay, the buildings are choice. Location's excellent. And the managing agents are crooks."

"Let's say it's malfeasance."

"Crooks! We fire them as soon as we take title."

"My thought exactly."

"And we slot in Jack O'Neil. Let's get started." Genie looked uncertain. "It's a sweet ride, kidlet. What's bugging you?"

"Those tenants are organized. I don't like that. They even have a special tenants' committee. I like that less. And the president is a man named James Harris, who I hear is a real bastard. Suppose he takes a dislike to the idea of buying his apartment? He could make a muck."

"That's where I come in. Remember, you buy 'em, and I sell 'em. It's too good a deal for a sane man to pass up. I vote we go ahead. Just give me six months, and I'll have Harris eating out of my hand."

"Or biting it off. But if you will, I will." She repeated their old game.

Genie and Gluck met again. This time he was sitting behind his glass desk with his feet up on the desk, puffing away at his cigar. "Sit down, young lady. Since it's past coffee time, would you like a cigar?"

He deserved to be slapped. "No, thank you." Instead of sitting in the chair indicated and looking up at Gluck, which was what he'd planned, Genie stepped onto the platform and perched on the edge of his desk. Now he was looking up at her. The startled look on his face made her laugh.

After a moment, Gluck began to chuckle. "My compliments. You topped me."

"If you're going to be rude, so am I."

Ralph took the cigar out of his mouth, and the chuckle became a laugh. "Round one to Miss Szabo." He swung his legs off the desk and walked to the chairs where they'd originally sat. "Now, young lady, I assume from your presence here you're interested in my gems?"

"Correct."

"You've inspected the buildings and know all about my ungrateful tenants."

"Yes."

"And you still think you can sell apartments to those lunatics?"

"I do."

"Then you must know something I don't know."

Genie's face was a blank. "Shall we discuss terms?"

They did, and when Genie offered $8.5 million, expecting to settle for an even $9 million, she was surprised to discover Ralph wouldn't budge off his price. "I want the seventy-five thousand dollars to butter my ego for what you know about my gems that I don't."

Finally Genie agreed to the terms. The deal was made, the contract signed, and instead of borrowing the money from the Bank of New York or Bankers' Trust, Genie went back to Raymond Brenner. He'd been their banker when they desperately needed a banker, and she thought he should have first crack at the loan. Prior to meeting with Brenner, Max and she set up a basic business policy. At least half the cash required for any purchase would be borrowed from a bank, thus enabling them to grow faster on their own limited capital. They could get into more deals and hire a sales force. For while Genie could negotiate for more than one building at a time, Max would need help if they were selling apartments in a building in Philadelphia, another in Boston, and a third in Chicago. A million dollars was no money in the league they were entering. Genie borrowed $650,000—a little over fifty percent of the cash payment to Gluck—for six months.

When title passed, Genie and Jack O'Neil visited the managing agents. "Mr. Armstrong," she said. "Mr. Gaites. My brother and I now own the twins."

"You, Miss Szabo? You're a woman!"

"A woman who dislikes managing agents when they deliberatly mismanage."

"Oh!" said Mr. Armstrong and Mr. Gaites.

"Where are the building files?" demanded Jack O'Neil.

Once the management change was made and the proper papers filed in Harrisburg, Max went to work. Although a few tenants signed up quickly, the majority remained indifferent, even hostile. As Genie had feared, Harris was the fly in the ointment. He'd taken early retirement from Wanamaker's, where he'd been a vice-president. At fifty-eight, he was in excellent health, jogging daily to keep in shape for tennis, which he also played daily. He was a snob, high-handed, and had the time and energy to make trouble. His main objection to the Szabos was that the Szabos were New York sharpies out to put something over on the tenants. They were just another version of Ralph Gluck, who had been such an impossible landlord. The fact that the supply room was now properly stocked, leaky faucets promptly fixed, refrigerators and stoves promptly repaired or replaced, and the heat and hot water in plentiful supply made no difference. Harris kept all the old antagonisms alive. If the Szabos wanted them to buy their apartments, something must be wrong with the buildings. As renters, if the buildings fell apart, they could move. As owners, they were stuck.

Every day Genie looked at her calendar, and every day she watched the day when their loan was due come a day closer. Finally, three weeks before it was supposed to be repaid, she went to see Brenner.

"We need a little more time," she said, brightly.

"I know. A little is all I can give." He sounded apologetic. "I'm being pressured."

"Three months will do it."

"Three months is my limit. Pull the rabbit out of the hat, Genie." He sounded more concerned than she thought the situation warranted.

In his frustration, Max shouted, "I'd like to get my hands on that bastard. He'd sign soon enough."

"Oh, Max! That's just what we need. You up on an assault and battery charge. That would make a lot of sales."

Genie wasn't sleeping well. She was too troubled by the situation. She couldn't give up the project, and Max couldn't complete it. She had always believed that, in business, a deal stood on its own merits. Value for value. Clearly, that wasn't always true. Harris had beaten them at every turn. He lived in the buildings. He made neighborly visits. He would block them wherever he could. And he had.

In the dark one particular night, she tried not to think, but sleep was further away than ever. About five in the morning she got up and made herself some coffee. At 6:30 she left her apartment to go to the office. She didn't know what she would do there at that hour, but she felt she should go. She ran into a fellow tenant in the elevator, a young man named Jerry Jerome. Jerome and his wife both worked in the advertising business and usually left the building about nine o'clock, the same time as Genie. Now he was dressed in tennis clothes, carrying a racket and a tennis bag. He gave Genie a silly grin.

"We have a client meeting at five, and Lois has theater tickets for this evening. So the only time I can play is now. I know it's crazy, but I'm a nut on tennis."

"You are? I see. Where do you play so early?"

"East Side Tennis Club. On East 84th Street. You interested in tennis?"

Genie was only half listening. "Very," she answered absently.

She called Max from Penn Station. A groggy voice answered, "Who the fuck is it?"

"It's your sister, Genie. I'm going to Philadelphia. The seven o'clock train."

"For Christ's sake, why?"

"I have an idea. I'm taking the building plans with me."

Max tried to sort out his wits. "You want to tell me about it?"

"Not yet. It's one of my hunches."

When Max arrived at the office at 9:15, he was met by a badly frightened Helen Bradley. "Mr. Szabo, there are two men in your office. They forced their way in, and I was about to call the police."

"If I'm not out in five minutes, call them." Max stormed into his office and glared at the men who had invaded ConVert-Co. One was in a chair facing his desk. Max, who was always alert to physical details, identified him automatically. Scar tissue under his eyes, a swollen nose that had been broken too often, thick lumpy ears, heavy jaw, jowls, and a bulging stomach. He looked like a middle-weight professional boxer who had taken too many punches. The second man was sitting in his chair behind his desk. His feet were resting on Max's desk, and he was playing with the buttons on Max's console. The panel hiding the bar was sliding back and forth and the television set and tape recording machine were being turned on and off. He was a smaller man with a receding chin, sloping forehead, and tobacco-stained buck teeth. His shoes were dirty and needed new soles; his thin black hair glistened with some kind of thick grease. Max decided, brains and muscle, but not much in either department.

Brains spoke first. "Pretty fancy setup you got here, Szabo. Set ya back a good chuck o' dough?"

"You've got exactly five seconds to get your fucking ass out of my chair." Max started counting. "One. Two. Three . . ."

When he reached three, Brains got to his feet and started around the desk. He had a nasty grin on his face. "Carlo, he's tough. A real hard guy." The words were loaded with sarcasm.

The ex-boxer had been hit too often in the throat, and his larynx was damaged. His voice was a soft, hoarse rasp. "Yeah. Tough!"

Max was in no mood to put up with smart behavior. As Brains was about to pass him, he grabbed the man by the lapels of his jacket and slammed him into the other chair facing his desk. He realized they were small-time hoods out to do some sort of job. "Who the hell are you, and who sent you?"

Brains's lips pulled back from his stained teeth. On other occasions one might have considered the result a smile. "Okay, hard guy. When you gonna pay back the loan?"

"Who sent you, punk? Brenner?"

"Brenner! Fuck Brenner! That asshole! None of your fucking business who sent us. I asked you when're you going to pay back the loan?"

Max lifted Brains to his feet. He placed his own face one inch away from the man, ignoring the stench of the rotted teeth, and said, "We'll pay back when we're goddamned ready and not one second before." Then he shoved the man into the chair so hard the chair almost tilted over backwards. As Brains's head snapped back, the cartilage in his neck made a cracking sound. "Drag your asses out of here before I call the police."

"I don't like this shithead. Teach him some manners, Carlo."

"Come on, Rocco. Lay off. We done our job. Let's go."

"I told you to take him. Now take him! And when you finish, we'll wait around. I heard he's got a sister who's supposed to be a great piece of tail. You'd like some fresh cunt, wouldn't ya? Instead of those two-bit whores you been sticking it into lately?"

"Yeah!" Muscles almost drooled.

Anyone who knew Max could have predicted what would happen next. No threat against himself could have caused Max to go after these soldiers running an errand for a Mafia captain. If he'd been rational, he'd have realized fighting with them was worse than pointless. It was dangerous. But at that moment, Max was no longer rational. Not only had they threatened him, they were planning to wait for Genie and attack her. These two pieces of human filth were going to rape his kidlet. All the violence in his nature, which he'd held in check through months of frustration, now had an outlet.

Before the exboxer was halfway out of his chair, Max hit Rocco with the back of his left hand, stunning him. Then he pivoted on his toes and hit Carlo with a left hook, knocking him backwards. He grabbed the man, hauled him to his feet, and hit him with a right cross squarely on his thick nose, squashing it against his face and causing blood to spurt out. A left was buried in his soft belly doubling him over, and Max's knee against his jaw finished that part of the fight.

When Max turned back to Rocco, he saw blood streaming from his cheek where Max's ring had torn the flesh away from the bone. He also saw Rocco fumbling in his pocket for what Max assumed was a gun. Max was on the man before the gun cleared the shoulder holster. "Rape my sister, you bastard!" Max had the gun and tossed it behind his desk. Then he seized the man's arm and twisted it behind him in a hammerlock. As Max applied pressure, Rocco groaned. When Max dislocated his arm and broke it at the shoulder, Rocco screamed. Finally he let Rocco drop to the carpet.

Max stood over both men, panting and trembling. Not because of any effort he'd exerted during the fight but because of the effort he was now exerting on himself not to kill them. When he finally mastered himself, he knelt, lifted both men to a sitting position and said, very slowly and softly, "If I ever see either of you two again or hear any threats against my sister, I will kill both of you. Now get up and get out of here."

Although neither could talk, both were conscious and understood. Carlo got to his feet first and helped his smaller partner stand. At the door, Rocco gathered himself and said, "You won't see us again, hard guy. We got friends. Lots of friends."

Max didn't answer. He followed them into the reception room. "It's all right, Helen. They're leaving." He waited in the entrance to the office until the men entered an elevator and disappeared. He knew he should have handled the situation without hurting the boys as badly as he had. But they'd threatened Genie. That's what did it. He also knew when the errand boys reported back the real trouble would come. Muscle men would be the next callers, and while he might be able to handle one, they came in packs of two or three. Even with the gun he'd taken from Rocco, how was he going to protect Genie then?

Genie left her inspection of the buildings and the garage. She waited until ten o'clock before calling the building architects, Lerner and Lawson, in their New York offices. They had a brief conversation.

"Yes, Miss Szabo. It can take the live load. It's a reinforced concrete slab."

"Thank you, Mr. Lawson," she said and hung up.

When Genie returned to the office late in the afternoon, Max was waiting. So was a message from Raymond Brenner. She asked Max to sit still, because the call from Brenner said urgent. Max nodded, his face ashen and his manner unusually subdued.

"Raymond, this is Genie. What's the emergency?"

For the first time since she'd known him, Brenner sounded frightened. "Have you spoken to Max?"

"No. He wants to talk to me, but I called you first."

"I know you weren't in the office this morning or I'm sure you'd have stopped him. I did the best I could, my dear, but I'm afraid it wasn't good enough."

"What are you talking about?"

"Max had visitors. It was supposed to be a routine call. Two gentlemen were sent to urge that the loan be repaid promptly. Unfortunately, while doing their job, Max beat them up rather severely. The only reason nothing has happened so far is that"—Genie could hear his breathing—"certain people are not completely satisfied as to the stories being told."

"Are you telling me I'm in some sort of danger?"

"You may be. I've been able to place certain actions on hold for the moment. I wish I could promise more. In any case, your loan has been taken out of my hands. It's due in two weeks, and we must be paid. I'm sorry, Eugenia. Max should never have muscled those men."

"I understand, Raymond. I'm sure you did your best."

As soon as she'd said good-bye, Max was in her office. He'd only been waiting until he saw the light go out on the switchboard. "What did Brenner say?"

"He said you beat up two visitors this morning. Sent by our banking friends."

"Some friends! They started it, threatened to rape you, and I blew. How much trouble are we in?"

"Enough. They're calling the loan in two weeks. And just when I thought I had our bottleneck solved. But it'll take longer than two weeks. Now I don't know what will happen. Damn it, Max. I'm scared."

"I've been thinking. I'm going out for a while. Wait for me here."

"Now what?"

"I'm going to collect an old debt, I hope." He was gone before she could ask any further questions.

Ten minutes later a cab drew up in front of the Majestic, and Max jumped out. He was greeted by John, the doorman. "What can I do for you, Max?"

"Call up to Mr. Costello and tell him Max Szabo wants to see him."

John had an answer almost immediately. "He says for you to go up. You remember the apartment—17H."

Max was greeted at the door by a mountain of a man, a man who was almost as tall as Max and outweighed him by well over a hundred pounds. His eyes were cold and suspicious.

"Raise your hands over your head."

"Mr. Costello expects me."

"Yeah, I know." He repeated the order. "No one gets to see the boss without getting frisked." Max raised his arms, and expert hands patted every part of his body where a gun might be concealed. "Okay. You can put 'em down." He called out in a loud voice, "He's clean, Boss."

Max heard the familiar voice of Frank Costello. "Bring him in, Louie."

Max remembered Louie. He was Costello's bodyguard. He also remembered being held in the air by this man when he'd been trying to stop Costello's bleeding. That was fifteen years ago, and fifteen years had turned Louie from a huge, powerful man into a 350-pound hulk.

"Don't I know you, fella?"

"Yeah. I was the kid who helped stop Mr. Costello's bleeding when he was shot."

"Sure!" Louie's eyes changed expression, and his huge face split in a broad grin. "That was a great thing you did for the boss." He noted Max's size and recalled the muscle he'd felt while checking him out. "You lookin' for a job?"

"No. Something else." Max hoped Frank Costello also thought he'd done a great thing.

"Okay. None of my business. Come on in. The boss is waitin'."

He led the way into the living room where a short, stocky man with silvery hair was standing. Costello stood a little stiffly, his feet in worn slippers and both his shirt and pants seeming too large for his aging frame. "Come in, Max. Sorry about Louie, but in my business, you can't be too careful. Long time no see." They shook hands.

Max wrinkled his nose. The apartment reeked of garlic, onion, oregano, and all the other spices he associated with good Italian cooking. Mrs. Costello was probably preparing a huge pot of spaghetti. He glanced around the room. This was the home of a very rich man—once, and hopefully still, one of the most powerful men in the Mafia. He couldn't decide whether he'd changed, or the furnishings had always been the way he now saw them. Old-fashioned, rundown, imitation Chinese furniture, a worn carpet on the floor, an old radio in the corner. The only item that was new was a late model color television set which stood in front of the fireplace with three huge chairs facing it. Apparently Louie and the Costellos watched a lot of television. He noticed several pictures on the walls and recalled picking them up at the framing shop on Columbus Avenue.

"What brings you here, Max?"

Max reached into his pocket and handed Costello a faded piece of paper. Costello glanced at it and put it in his pocket. Although his face didn't register any expression, he said, "Yes, I owe you one. You need my help?"

"If you can't help me, no one can."

"Sit down." He pointed to the chairs in front of the TV set. "And tell me about it."

Max perched on the edge of his chair and started to tell Frank Costello everything that had happened to them since they took their first loan from the Queens-Manhattan Trust, with one exception. He made no mention of the original arrangement between Genie and Raymond Brenner. That would always be Szabo family business. Costello's eyes had the softness Max had come to associate with Italians. He saw them flicker when he mentioned Brenner.

He asked, "Who dealt with Brenner?"

"My sister. You remember her?"

Again that flicker. "Well, we all do stupid things once in a while. Remember, Louie, when I left the twenty G's in the back seat of a taxi?"

"Yeah. In a brown paper bag from the A&P. Boy, was Erickson pissed!"

Costello laughed. "I had to go to the cops to get the dough back."

Louie was laughing so hard he began to cough. "The papers had a hell of a lot of fun with that."

"Go on with your story, Max."

When Max reached the point where he described beating up the two hoods, Costello coldly stared at him and turned to look at Louie. That look frightened Max. The soft eyes had an opaque glitter, and Max knew he was out of his depth. Costello could have, and at one time probably had, ordered the deaths of many men. He was an Italian Mafia chief.

The eyes returned to Max, full of suspicion. "Hold it! What were their names?"

"I only heard their first names. Rocco and Carlo."

"Louie?"

The huge man nodded. "Two punks who work out of Raimondo's family."

"You sure, Max, that was the first time they visited you?"

"Yes. Their kind of visit is hard to forget."

"I don't understand it. They were supposed to give you a warning. That's all."

"Trying to beat me up and threatening to rape my sister? Some warning!"

"You sure they started it?"

"Carlo said something about having done their job, and they should leave, but Rocco wanted Carlo to teach me some manners."

"All right, Max. I'm gonna take your word for it. They started it, and you finished it. But it don't add up."

Max repeated what to him was the most important part of the story. "They threatened to rape my sister."

"Yeah. I heard you. Rape!" He shook his head. "With all the free stuff around? Stupid!" Costello stood and walked to a window overlooking 72nd Street. His hand was in the same pants pocket in which he'd placed the note Max had given him. Minutes passed in which the only thing that could be heard was the faint whistling sound of Louie breathing through a partially clogged nose. Then Costello turned and said in what was almost an apologetic tone, "You know, Max, I'm retired." He touched his chest. "Bum ticker. The doc says I'm not supposed to get excited." Max waited. "No promises, but I'll see what I can do."

"Thank you. How will I find out what's happening?"

"They know where to reach you. You'll know, one way or another."

The two men shook hands. On the way to the door, Louie draped his huge arm over Max's shoulder. "You shouldn't have beat up those boys so bad, kid. It don't look good." He checked the lobby before opening the door. "See you round, kid."

* * *

When Max got back to the office, Genie was waiting. Although it was well after five, Helen had stayed so Genie wouldn't be alone. Both women were very nervous. Max said, "Thank you for keeping my sister company, Helen. You can leave now."

"Should I come in tomorrow?"

"Call in after ten. I'll know then."

Helen hurried out of the office without looking back. After she left, Genie asked, "Where did you go?"

"The Majestic."

"The Majestic? Why?"

"I saw Frank Costello."

"Oh! The real-life Godfather."

"Yeah. Remember the note that came with the three shirts?" Max had memorized the exact words a long time ago. " 'Max, thank you for the use of your shirt. I owe you more than three. Should you ever need more, call me.' This seemed like a good time to call him."

"What did he say?"

"He's an old man, and he said he's retired, but he did say he'd see what he could do."

"Do you think he can help?"

"I don't know. One thing I do know is we should stick together until this is over. My apartment, your apartment, or even a hotel."

"Your apartment is too far east, and a hotel will only delay whatever's going to happen. At least my place is midtown, and a lot of people are always around. There'll be plenty of witnesses."

That night, after eating, Max and Genie watched television so they wouldn't have to talk about what had happened, or how it had come to happen, or what they should do to make certain it would show, and that fear would make sleep impossible. They were going to need all their strength to meet the coming day. So they stared blindly at the television set until midnight. Then Genie made up the couch in the living room for Max and went to bed herself.

She was totally exhausted and hoped she'd fall asleep at once, but she couldn't. Not since childhood, when the family had almost lost their home, had she known such fear. As she lay in bed, she found herself engaged in a confrontation with herself—a struggle in which she had to accept that death was not the worst of what she may have brought down upon them. Max had made a terrible mistake. But his mistake only followed from her own. She was to blame for everything that threatened them. With so many banks ready to finance them, she had gone back to Raymond. Why? Out of loyalty for his original support? And perhaps, even out of some childish notion of gratitude. It was his arrangement that had been pivotal in her final acceptance of herself as a woman, with a woman's right to make independent decisions about matters that concerned only her.

Oh, what a sentimental fool she'd been! To jeopardize their very lives because she liked Brenner. Like him or not, Raymond Brenner was a Mafia banker. If she'd had any sense, she would have faced that fact. Not having grown up within the sphere of organized crime, she had managed to avoid the reality of the Mafia. If, somehow, they came out of this alive and in one piece, she would never make that mistake again. She closed her eyes. What could she do? she heard herself ask God. And when she opened her eyes, it was morning. She got up, used the bathroom, showered, dressed, and went to wake Max.

She stood over the couch staring at him. Max was a marvel. No matter what had happened yesterday or what might happen today, when Max was tired, Max slept. She shook him, and he catapulted off the couch, wearing only his jockey shorts, ready to do battle with the world.

"Relax, big brother. It's only me. The bathroom's all yours. I'll make coffee."

"Whew! Sorry. I'm edgy."

Genie laughed softly. "I wonder why?"

They left the apartment at 8:45. As soon as they reached the sidewalk, Max spotted the black limousine, with what were obviously two bodyguards lounging against the car. "Get behind me, Genie!"

The rear door of the limousine opened and a tall, slim man got out and approached them. "You Max Szabo?"

Max tensed. "Yes."

"I've got a present for you." His hand reached into his coat. The gesture was the same Rocco had made reaching for his gun. Max didn't wait. Instinct made him forget he was carrying Rocco's gun. A gun wasn't his weapon anyway. His fists were. He hit the man, knocking him against the building. "Get inside, Genie," he screamed, turning to face the two bodyguards who were running towards him. Damn it! Instead of using common sense, Genie had grabbed one of them and was trying to stop him. Her arms were wound around his neck and her legs around his waist. Although Max was younger, stronger, and faster than either man, the struggle was short. It ended when Max saw Genie, her arms and legs still flailing wildly, about to be hurled to the sidewalk.

He stepped back. "Okay," he shouted. "Leave my sister alone, and I'll go with you."

A voice behind him said, "Turn around, slowly." He did. The man he'd hit was waiting for him. "Hold him, Tony!" Max allowed his arms to be pinned behind his back. By now they were surrounded by curious passersby on their way to work. They watched, but no one interfered. Then the slim man hit him on the jaw as hard as he could. It was a clean shot, and while it would have knocked most men out cold, Max was only momentarily stunned. He shook his head to clear it, expecting to be hit again. He wasn't. "Christ! This guy's an ox!" Max saw his attacker flex his hand. "I think I broke a knuckle." He stepped closer to Max. "Why did you slug me?"

"What did you expect me to do? Let you shoot me?"

"Shoot you! Me? In broad daylight on Central Park South? With all those helpful New Yorkers watching us? You've seen too many cheap television movies. If we wanted to get you, you wouldn't have made it five feet from the door. I said I had a present for you."

"Yeah. A .38 slug."

"Let him go." Max's arms were released. He looked for Genie. She was standing next to the second man. She was also free. "Here's your .38 slug." He completed the same gesture he'd started when Max hit him. When his hand reappeared, it was not holding a gun but an envelope. "Let's go, boys, before this maniac winds up again." They ran for the car. Taking advantage of a break in the traffic, the limousine glided away from the curb.

"Are you all right, Genie?"

"Yes. You?"

Max nodded.

The crowd, seeing the excitement was over, broke up; each had an interesting story to tell over the water cooler or during a coffee break.

"Open the envelope, Max." He did and handed Genie a piece of paper. It was the note he'd left with Costello. Costello had scrawled cancelled on it and signed it F.C. "What does that mean?"

"I'm not sure." Suddenly Max was bitter. "Cancelled? He's probably telling me he can't help."

"Or he has helped, and he's paid his debt?"

"I don't know. What'll we do?"

"We go to the office. There's no use trying to hide."

"Yeah. They'd find us sooner or later."

When they arrived at the office, everything seemed in order. Genie collected the mail. Nothing important. So they waited in Max's office for whatever would happen. When the phone rang, Max had the receiver to his ear before the first ring ended. "It's for you. It's Brenner."

"Raymond?"

"Genie!" Brenner was excited and pleased. "How did you do it?"

"Do what, Raymond? I've had a rough night. To say nothing of this morning. Give it to me simply."

"The committee gave me back your loan with instructions to renew it." Now he sounded almost hysterical. "They said I could lend you additional money to make up for the trouble they caused you. Also, Rocco and Carlo. They won't bother you any more. As a matter of fact, they won't bother anyone for a while. They're being disciplined for exceeding their authority. But how did you do it?"

"It makes no difference. Thank you for calling, Raymond. Send me the papers as soon as they're ready." Genie hung up. Max had been listening on his own extension. "You heard?"

Max closed his eyes for a moment, allowing the relief to flood through his body. "Who would have thought that old man still had so much power?"

"Just thank the Lord he does." They were silent, each trying to accept what had happened. Then, getting herself in hand,

Genie leaned forward. "Max, it's time to get back to business. I think I have an idea that will get Harris on our side. Listen!"

"Mr. Szabo? What a surprise to meet you here," James Harris remarked.

"Call me Max. I thought I'd take up tennis. I've been spending so much time in Philadelphia, I need some exercise. And tennis seemed a good idea."

"It's great exercise. I play every day. You must know that."

"No, I didn't. Why should I? But that explains why you're in such great shape."

"No. Reach for the racquet and grip it as though you were going to shake hands with it."

"Like this?"

"Like that. If you were such a great pitcher, serving should be a snap. It's exactly the same motion as throwing a fastball."

"These courts are all-weather courts. Personally I prefer a composition like Hardtru. Easier on your feet and knees. But beggars can't be choosers."

"You think Hardtru is a better surface to run on?"

"Absolutely. I've never been envious of rich men. But the one thing I do envy the rich is owning one's own tennis court. Then you can choose the surface you want. You can play when you want, and with whom. And on Sunday, you don't have mobs. Look at this place. It's a zoo."

"You know, Jim, You've given me an idea."

"About how to sell me my apartment?" Harris laughed. "It won't work, Max. I'm against co-oping. But I enjoy teaching you something about tennis. You happen to be a natural."

"That's okay, Jim. I don't mind your being against co-oping. But how do you feel about owning your own tennis court?"

"Me?"

"You. I said you just gave me an idea."

Max was in Philadelphia for two weeks. When he called in, all he ever said was, "Working on it. Optimistic." By the third week, Genie was on pins and needles. She was ready to go to

Philadelphia herself. Then on Wednesday of the third week, Max called in with more information.

"Break out the champagne. I'm on my way to the 30th Street Station with the goods in hand."

"Harris signed?"

"Ten days ago. Your idea of the buildings having their own private tennis club on the roof of the garage was a real winner. And he's been helping me sell the rest of them."

"You bastard! Why didn't you tell me?"

"I wanted to surprise you. I now have signatures and checks from 386 tenants, and the rest will sign within a week or two."

"You did it! We can close!"

"I didn't do it. You did. Without your idea, Harris would never have signed. Where did you get it anyway? You don't play tennis, Genie."

"From Jerry Jerome. He plays at the East Side Tennis Club. On top of the garage. After this, I may take up tennis."

"Stick to your exercise machines. I'm catching the six o'clock train. Wait for me. We'll celebrate tonight."

When Genie totalled up the final results of the venture, she was pleased. It was a lot of money. They'd received an average of $1,700 per room; and after repaying the Queens-Manhattan Trust—that was a great moment—and after all deductions for business expenses, ConVert-Co had netted over $2 million before taxes. And Max and she had learned a lot more about apartment house conversions.

It crossed her mind that over a year had passed since her father's death and six months since her last call to her mother. Maybe it was time to call her mother again. Putting her doubts aside, she dialed Mrs. Sagi.

"Mrs. Sagi, this is Eugenia Szabo. Would it be possible to speak to my mother?"

"I'll find out, Eugenia." Genie waited. "I'm sorry. She still won't speak to you."

"I see. Thank you for trying. Good-bye." Genie hung up, her tears staining the company checkbook. She closed it and continued to cry.

28

And so it began for the Szabos. For Genie it was as relentless a pursuit of a dream as had ever been undertaken by a young woman. For Max, who was equally single-minded, it was not a dream but money that drove him onward. Money! Vast sums of money which would make Genie and him invulnerable to the world. So it was not without reason that in the short time between 1972 and 1982, ten years, they achieved a national reputation in the business community. Although few knew as well as they did what went into the making of that reputation. That it was compounded of grinding, even merciless work, of an instinctive recognition for what made a building a good buy for them, of a genius for selling, and of nerve to take the necessary risks.

Through her travels, Genie became familiar with the current and coming neighborhoods most desired by young marrieds. She recognized which residential districts were hospitable to families with children, dogs, cats, hamsters—and which weren't. She had a knack for knowing where, in which town or suburb, the singles would be swinging. Or wanting to swing. She could point to twelve locations most preferred by middle-income retirees. She never forgot a building in a city, town, or suburb. Beyond the physical condition of the structure, she could tick off the individual advantages of the neighborhood—or its disadvantages.

Along with the locations and neighborhoods, she made it her business to consider the composition of school districts, the crime rate, the cost of heating in the various parts of the nation. To say nothing of the weather, public transportation, and how convenient the shopping malls were. The whole country was her hometown, and she studied it constantly. She knew the building codes and mortgage rates in Duluth, Minnesota, as well as Newport Beach, California, where she learned that mortgages were referred to as trusts.

While her days tended to be unbelievably full and satisfying, her nights at home told another story. Since Paul, she had not thought about love. She had had her share of lovers, which she considered a quaint, romantic word for what they really were. There was no permanence to any of these episodes of the flesh; they were compromised from their inception by the fact that, as the years passed, her life was too pressured by the demands of her career to allow time for romance to flower. Then, too, the truth was she deliberately chose lovers who would accept her self-imposed detachment. For Genie, like Max, was a loner, with large unfilled areas of the heart, like the early maps of the world. Once Paul had filled her heart, but now, had it not been for Max, the lack of commitment would have diluted her personality. With the exception of her brother, she lived surrounded by the superficial, the lustful, and the greedy, who taught her only how to take momentary pleasures without any deepening of human intimacy.

For Paul, as for Genie, the hurried, crowded years moved steadily onward, and by virtue of talent and unceasing hard work, he climbed smoothly and faultlessly up the ladder of theatrical celebrity. In a world so impressed by the gifted, so vulnerable to unexpected good manners, Paul was becoming a national figure. He was interviewed with regularity, and pictures of him stared continuously out of newspapers and magazines. His original Off-Broadway Repertory Company was now a solid production team playing in a theater owned by the company. There was the People's Theater where he and his associates produced plays by unknown playwrights. The tickets were free, on a first come, first served basis. He'd also taken over the Vivian Beaumont Theater in Lincoln Center and produced six smash hits in a row. The latest rumor was that there was about to be a changing of the guard in Washington. It was said that the job as head of the National Endowment for the Arts was his for the asking. And since so many of his plays had taken positions on the major social issues of the day, some speculated he might, one day, wish to test himself in the real world of politics rather than the make-believe world of the theater.

With his hair now turned prematurely white as his father's had, and his strong, mobile face, he had become undeniably distinguished. The success he had hoped to achieve at the start of his career had been far surpassed by his actual accomplishments. But as his life became public, he came to value, even more highly, judgement, coolness, reserve, and privacy. His sexual experiences had given him training in secrecy and deception, and since he was constantly surrounded by beautiful and eligible women, he considered marriage several times. The same question always arose. Suppose he became bored? It was then that he thought of Genie. Of her love, her beauty, her power to absorb his mind, his senses. He'd never grown used to being without her. And the extraordinary happiness of their early years would come back to him with a forgotten melody, a certain scent. The memories of people and of places would melt together, becoming indistinguishable, all feeding his sense of the beauty of that time. When he distilled the fullness of their days and nights into one final essence, the strongest feeling it brought him was of having just that once been joined with life—of not being alone, of loving and being loved.

Then, inevitably, would come the hour when he had to accept again the reason for their continued separation. She could not be trusted. If there had been one banker to whom she had sold herself, who knows how many others had followed? The only difference was the price she now charged. So, if marriage happened at all, it would not be to Genie, and it would have to wait.

Sitting at her desk at home one night, sipping a scotch while reviewing several offerings, Genie took a break to read an article on Paul Husseman which she planned to cut out for her scrapbook. When she finished reading, she felt an anxiety she couldn't repress. It made her question her life. How limitless the possibilities had once seemed! How diminished they now looked. Other than Max, she had no family. Her mother was as lost to her as her dead father. She doubted the breach between them would ever heal. And Paul was gone. In the early years she had postponed thinking about marriage in the secret hope that somehow, one day, Paul and she would be reunited. But as time passed without a word from him, Genie felt they were like people on separate icebergs drifting steadily apart.

She finished her scotch in one big swallow, feeling it burn on the way down. Her dry eyes scanned the room, searching for something to reassure herself. She stared at tear sheets from several magazines. Over her objections, Max had hired a public relations firm. He claimed the publicity would help him sell apartments. Mention of them had appeared in *Time* and *Newsweek*. The latest was a two-page article, complete with pictures, in *People* magazine. The article referred to them as a national phenomenon. Genie turned to a computer printout which detailed a complete history of the activities of ConVert-Co. During the past ten years, they had bought and converted over 650 buildings into condominiums and cooperatives in every major city across the United States. Everything from two-story garden apartments to fifty-story high rises. More people lived in the buildings they had converted than lived in the city of San Francisco. What Max and she had done was important, and she took pride in their accomplishments. Maybe the magazine was right. Maybe they were a national phenomenon.

Genie glanced again at the reports on her desk—among them was a proposal concerning a building in Chicago which deserved further investigation—and seeing them gave her comfort. Her depression eased, and she went back to work. There was always her work. God only knew what she would have done without it.

PART SIX

1983

29

When Genie glanced at the grandfather clock ticking away in the corner of her office, she realized it was almost time to leave for her lunch. Paul's telephone call had badly shaken her, and that shock served as a warning as to what she might expect when they actually met. In a moment of pure panic, she reached for the phone. She'd call "21" and cancel the lunch. She'd say something—it made no difference what—had come up. Then she stopped. What on earth was the matter with her? She must keep the appointment. His wanting to see her after so many years was too strange for the reason not to be important, and in truth, a part of her wanted to see him as well. She didn't understand any of it, including her own response, and she didn't like it. But Paul reminded her that if he could stand their meeting, so could she. He was right. She could and she would.

Genie walked to the window for another look at Park Avenue. Most of the sidewalks in front of the office buildings had narrow paths piled high on each side with freshly shovelled show. There were a surprising number of people struggling to make their way along those narrow paths. Even though it was a short walk from the office to "21", she realized she would have to change back into her ski clothes. This was no weather for pumps and a light dress, even under a parka.

"Ms. Szabo!" George, the maitre d' at "21", greeted her. "What a practical idea. Ski clothes. And so charming!" He scanned his reservation book and looked up, puzzled. "I don't find your reservation. Our mistake, no doubt. There's always room at '21' for you and Mr. Szabo. We see him quite frequently, but we've missed you." Without moving a muscle, he seemed to bow.

"It's not a mistake, George. Paul Husseman made the reservation. Has he arrived?"

"Ah. That explains it. No. He hasn't arrived as yet. The snow must have detained him. Would you like to wait at his table?" Anxious to please, George offered to desert his post. "I'll show you to his table myself."

The ground floor at "21", the only floor that mattered, was divided into two dining sections by a wall which extended more than halfway into the room from the rear of the building. A bar ran almost the full width of the building and faced most of the ground floor restaurant. In theory, this division should have provided an intimate atmosphere. Actually, the bar and the restaurant were noisy and crowded, pulsing with a nervous energy found only in certain very expensive restaurants in New York and Los Angeles. It was tacitly understood by those in the know that the ground floor of the restaurant was reserved for important people. The space was further divided into an A section for celebrities and a B section for those more obscure but steady patrons of "21". Unless business was slow, diners whom management failed to recognize were sent to the second floor—out of sight.

As Genie threaded her way through the mass of drinkers jostling for position at the bar, she recalled how once she had found the atmosphere stimulating. But now, the excitement struck her as feverish. Which was why, despite the restaurant's excellent cuisine, she'd taken to lunching in less frenetic surroundings. It seemed to her the patrons of "21" didn't really come there to eat. They came partially to see and be seen, but mostly to make deals—deals of almost every sort. At each table someone was trying to sell something to someone else. And if there were more than two people at a table, it used to be fun to try to pick out who was the king or queen and who were the sycophants. The game no longer amused her. The servility of one group, matched only by the rudeness and arrogance of the other, came to dismay her.

Paul's table was in the far corner of the A section. Since normally he'd have been placed up front as a showpiece, he must have asked for a table with some privacy. Although the table was hardly secluded, it was the best "21" could offer. After all, placing Paul Husseman on the second floor was unthinkable.

Genie ordered her usual Bombay gin martini and waited. Where the hell was he? She made herself sip the martini with excessive slowness to hide her irritation. She was in great conflict over wanting and not wanting to see him. Added to that, his being late, after all these years, waked old sensitivities, caused old, never completely healed wounds to throb.

She had just finished her drink when she saw him being guided through the closely packed tables toward her. Even under the most adverse conditions, she could not smother her pleasure at the sight of him. The way the light fell on his face, the way he moved and wore his clothes; everything about him was woven into her deepest self, her bones and her blood. He was as tall as she remembered and wore clothes much like those he'd worn years ago. Blue jeans tucked into high boots, an open-throated shirt, and an old tweed jacket. While she'd seen enough pictures of him not to be surprised, nevertheless she was startled by his snow white hair. His high cheekbones, deep-set black eyes, and aquiline nose, which had seemed to be held together only by tightly stretched skin, were now integrated into a single face. The only other difference was that his nose was crooked. It had been broken and badly set, or not set at all. Genie was all too familiar with how his nose had come to be broken. Emotions, which she'd closeted for years, now refused, like respectable ghosts, to stay out of the daylight world.

George pulled the table away allowing Paul to slide into the seat next to her. Noticing her empty glass, Paul said, "George, bring another for Miss Szabo, and I'll settle for a pony of Courvoisier. I'm half frozen."

"The least you could say is hello, how are you? And ask me if I want another drink."

"Hello. How are you? Do you want another drink?"

"I'm all right, thank you. And yes, I want another drink."

"Good. You'll need it."

George left to put in the drink order, and Genie turned to Paul. Keeping her voice low, she said, "Remembrances of things past upset me. Suppose you tell me, as simply as possible, why, after all these years, it is so important for us to lunch?"

"That's why I'm late. I went down to 60 Fifth Avenue to try to get a copy of an article to show you, but because of the snow, the magazine is closed today."

"What article and what magazine?"

Before Paul could answer, the waiter arrived with their drinks and menus. He remained at the table waiting for their order. "I suggest we order, and I'll tell you what it's all about after."

"A bowl of New England clam chowder, a mushroom omelette, a green salad with only a trace of oil and vinegar dressing, and a glass of white chablis with my omelette."

"Steak sandwich. The steak bleu and an endive salad. Bring a bottle of Porter with the steak." He waited for the waiter to leave before saying, "What the hell gave Max and you the brainstorm to hire a public relations firm?"

"That was Max's idea."

"Why did you agree?"

"I had to. Have you ever tried to stop Max from doing something once he decides to do it?"

Unconsciously, Paul's finger ran down the crooked ridge of his nose. "Once," he said quietly. "I wasn't too successful."

Genie ignored his gesture, refusing to acknowledge she understood its special meaning. "Well, neither was I. But what harm can they do?"

"A lot of libel laws might possibly no longer apply to you." Suddenly he gave vent to his exasperation. "Damn it, Genie! As long as you sought no personal publicity, magazines, newspapers, television, all the media, had to be careful about anything they printed or stated about you. No insinuations. No nasty little innuendos. No hints of things they couldn't prove. In short, no smears. Now you may be a public personality. And I know what that means. I live in a fishbowl. So I've learned to be careful."

He paused while the waiter served Genie her clam chowder. She sipped the hot soup before asking, "I'd still like to know exactly what it is you're trying to tell me."

Paul finished the last of his brandy. "Somehow *Forbes* magazine has become interested in ConVert-Co. They've decided to do an article on the company, Max and you." He cleared his throat. "It's rough stuff."

"For instance?"

"Okay. Fasten your seat belt. They have statements from men and women who claim you used prostitutes, physical threats, even blackmail, to force tenants to buy their apartments.''

Genie raised her eyebrows. "It's a lie." It seemed to Paul she was almost amused by the accusations. Her absence of indignation gave him a sense of how far this once naive woman had come, how much sordidness she took for granted.

"The magazine thinks it's true."

"They don't have a story," she said. "Would anyone who was supposed to have been blackmailed tell a magazine there was something in their history which would leave them open to blackmail? Hardly. And prostitutes? Where would they find a woman who not only admitted to being a prostitute but claimed to be working for us? On 42nd Street? It's nonsense. Bribery? I can understand someone accusing another person of taking a bribe. But to have men or women admit they themselves took a bribe? Impossible! What else? Oh, yes. Physical threats. By whom? Max? Were they able to come up with anyone working for us who admitted using threats? Max would take his head off. Accusing is only half a story. Proof is the other half." She shook her head. "None of it is true."

"Then they may drop the story. *Forbes* is a respectable magazine. While they do a number of 'what the kitchen maid saw through the keyhole' items, they're not the *National Enquirer*. As much as they may like juicy stories, they won't invent one."

"If they do, we have lawyers to take care of things like that. And by the way, how did you get into this in the first place?"

"Remember, you got your start co-oping Dad's buildings in Queens. Since Dad is in Europe and refused to talk to them, two reporters from *Forbes* came to see me."

"What did you say?"

"Nothing. To stimulate my memory, they showed me an outline of the planned story. It's a bitch." The arrival of the waiter with their main courses and drinks made him pause. After the waiter left, he continued without looking at her. "There's something in the article about a banker named Raymond Brenner. They interviewed him."

"What did Brenner say?" Genie concentrated on her omelette, holding to her pose of polite interest.

"Not much. You had a good idea, and he backed you."

"That's true." Good for Raymond, Genie thought. There

was nothing to say. It actually had been a straight business deal. Whatever else that had happened between Raymond and her was nobody's business. "He liked the concept. That's the long and the short of it."

"The reporters thought otherwise. One of them made a crack about being willing to bet it was a legs loan. He had to explain to me what he meant." The knuckles of Paul's right hand traced the bridge of his broken nose. "They're going to interview every banker with whom you've ever done business."

Watching him rub his nose, Genie realized that every time Paul did it he passed judgement on her. He knew about Brenner, probably not by name, but he knew. The night that Max had beaten him up Max had been out of his mind. He must have said things about her. Ironic—Max, who cared more for her than anyone, should be the one to have hurt her so deeply. Was it possible Paul's knowledge of Raymond was the reason he had never called her? Even after Joan divorced him? If she read Paul's attitude correctly, he believed she had furthered her business career via the bed. That it wasn't true was irrelevant. That she couldn't have even if she'd wanted to was also irrelevant. What was relevant was he'd judged her and found her guilty. What right had he to judge her? Paul, of all people. All these years later, Paul still lived by a double standard of morality, what a man could do and a woman couldn't.

"Paul, let me ask you something." Her tone was too polite. "Just recently one of the big corporations got a lot of unsavory publicity. Its president was presumed to be having an affair with his female assistant. The board of directors and the media disapproved. So the assistant was forced to resign. But the man remained president of the company. Why? Why are women judged by different sexual standards then men?"

"For the same reason that if a man overdraws his bank account too often, his banker will tell him to take his business elsewhere, while a woman who does the same thing will receive lots of advice from the same banker on how to balance her checkbook. In most cases she will not be asked to close her account."

"Why the difference?"

"It's a matter of honor. A man's honor is still in his wallet. In his ability to earn a living, to support and protect his family. While a woman's honor," and his face was a curious mixture of irritation and acceptance, "is between her legs. In her ability to bear children and know who the father is. Even at the end of the twentieth century, this ancient, stupid code of honor exists."

Listening to his explanation, Genie realized what a tangled mass of contradictions his mind was. Even though he wanted to be free of the old clichés, where they touched his own life—as she had—they still rang true. She sat silent, her mind hardening against him. When they'd been young, he had been the anchor of a small, frightened girl, the beloved of a young woman. Today she felt only blind resentment as his male arrogance. She wished the lunch was over so she could get away.

Paul continued. "And those two reporters who interviewed me prove my point. They weren't interested in Max's sex life, which might make a good outline for a porno novel. Oh, no! They were interested in his business practices. In other words, his wallet. His honor. And they weren't interested in your talent for selecting the right properties and putting together the best financial package. Which would make one hell of a good article. No! They were interested in your sex life. Your honor."

Genie bridled at his words. "They can investigate me till the cows come home. They won't find a damn thing. Not about Max. Or about me."

"Nothing about you?"

The usual harshness with which he'd put the question should have told her how strong his inner conflict was. But she was in no mood to measure his feelings when her own were in revolt. After all these years suddenly to break into her life and assume the right to stand in judgement of her made her furious. It wakened every instinct of pride and self-defense. "Paul, I'm flattered by your concern over my honor. But there's nothing to worry about. My honor is quite safe." She half smiled. "Safer in fact than most of the actresses who audition for parts in your plays."

Paul winced. "That was below the belt. But I guess I deserved it. For your information, my casting couch has been gathering dust in an attic somewhere for a long time. While I'm hardly a saint, that's no longer my form of sin." As he spoke, a gradual change came over his face, its accusing look yielding to an expression of embarrassed relief. "Genie, I realize it's none of my business, and I don't mean to pry. I was concerned. If you say there's nothing, I believe you." The simple words, I believe you, delivered in an almost offhanded fashion, hardly indicated the depth of Paul's feelings. He was well aware that he'd loved Genie since childhood and had fought a battle against that love. What better proof than that now, at thirty-nine, he was still unmarried? Over the years his father had kept him informed as to Genie's extraordinary successes, and like it or not, he'd continued to measure all women against the impossible standard of Eugenia Szabo. Finally he'd reached a point of desperation, and the depth of his involvement frightened him. He'd wanted to call her for a long time, to see her, and somehow get her out of his system once and for all. The *Forbes* article had provided an excuse.

Then, when he'd said I believe you, something unforeseen happened. His relief at believing her and his surprise that he did believe her shook him badly. Such emotions would not help him give her up. If anything, they drew him in more deeply. He tried to understand their source. For years he'd assumed she'd kept cashing in on the market value of her body, and he'd regarded it as a higher form of whoring. But when she said there was nothing for the reporters to find out, his relief was overwhelming. Was it because he wanted to believe her so badly he would believe anything she said? Or was it because he was no longer that proud, self-righteous young man who could neither forgive nor forget the man's voice on Genie's telephone. The man's voice! A startling thought occurred to him. The man's voice was exactly why he did believe her.

Watching the play of emotions of Paul's face, Genie felt the reawakening of their old, close, loving intimacy. The ease with which she'd once attuned herself to his most secret needs now returned like a long unused talent. She as good as read his mind and said, "You've no reason not to believe me, Paul. I never lied to you. That night, when the phone rang at three in the morning, I knew it was you. If I'd wanted to, I could have answered the phone myself." Her words showed how vividly the past was still alive in her. "I didn't. I wanted you to know the truth."

Paul shook his head. He should have known that years ago. "What a fool I've been!"

Genie remained silent while he accepted his new recognition of her. For with it had come a new recognition of him by her.

"I've been a fool as well. Tell me the truth. Did you ask me to lunch to hear me tell you whatever you've been thinking about me all these years isn't true?"

"Possibly," Paul muttered. "I've been thinking about calling you for some time." His discomfort was almost comic. "I . . . Well . . . Er . . . I suppose I needed an excuse. Something to give me the courage. This was it."

Genie had never seen Paul so little the master of a situation. The memories mounted up.

"What are you thinking?" Paul asked quietly.

"Of a hot night in July. Of a boy and a girl, too young and too much in love. I wonder what happened to them?" His question and her perception of why they were having lunch had given her the freedom. The words came to her lips spontaneously.

"I've often thought about them." He faltered. "I think I know where to find them."

Genie remembered when she was sixteen and he was nineteen on the roof of his apartment in the Majestic. Paul in his white tennis shorts and a shirt. She in her too dressy skirt and blouse. His hands caressing her, and their clothes piled in a heap as their naked bodies came together. The redwood lounge with its orange mat. Paul entering her and all the joy she felt. She didn't know, couldn't know then, that twenty years later that would be more real to her than events which had taken place last week.

"Where would we look?"

"Since my apartment is being painted, I'm staying at my family's place while they're in Europe." He gave her a questioning glance. "I think we might find those two teenagers on top of that building on Central Park West."

Her answering smile said she'd been thinking the same thing. "I'd like to volunteer for the search party."

They looked at each other with a kind of surprise, taking unspoken pleasure in the fact that having come together so many years before, having spoiled so much, having wasted so much, something had lasted. Paul started to reach across the table for her hand and pulled back. There was time. "When will the search begin?"

Genie noted the gesture and smiled in appreciation. "As soon as you like."

"Tomorrow evening? If you're free?"

"I'll be in the lobby in front of the C/D elevator line at seven-thirty."

While sliding along the narrow icy paths on her way back to her office, Genie considered everything Paul had told her about Max's business practices. She'd automatically branded the reporters' innuendos as lies. Now she faced the truth. Everything she knew about Max told her they were not lies. There was little Max wouldn't do to complete a sale. She thought of Gertrude Robbins' suicide and wondered how many people Max had hurt. Stacey Moore had repeatedly dropped hints, hints she'd deliberately ignored. She'd also ignored Stacey's girls, whom she'd occasionally seen in the office. They were professionals and not professional caterers. That explained why Max was so adamant she keep out of the selling operation. He'd want to protect her at all costs. Having faced the truth, what could she say to him? Max, I hear you've hired prostitutes and are blackmailing tenants into buying apartments. He would deny everything and insist she tell him where she obtained her information. Worse, his guilt and embarrassment at her having found out would drive a wedge between them. That decided her. She would say nothing. They could not afford to have to worry about their opinions of each other. No matter what, it must remain Szabo and Szabo against the world. So there was nothing to do but wait. If *Forbes* came calling on her, she'd have to tell Max everything. If they didn't, she'd say nothing. There was one thing she could and would do. From now on she'd become more involved in the selling operation. Even though Max wouldn't like it, she'd insist.

When she got back to her office, Genie had trouble concentrating on her work. She kept thinking of Paul. They'd talked but not touched. They hadn't even shaken hands. Yet it was as though he'd taken her in his arms. She felt again the pull of long ago. Curiosity, sadness, and desire mingled as she relived again their shared past. How difficult it was to leave him, even for a day.

30

By the next day the highways leading into the city and most of the main streets in mid-Manhattan had been more or less plowed, and people came to work. Among them was Herbert Gordon, ConVert-Co's lead banker. Gordon was a tall heavy-set man, fifty-five years old, with fleshy features and a fringe of curly grey hair. He was a curious mix of financial sophistication and arithmetic innocence. While his wife had to balance their family checkbook, when it came to lending millions of dollars, he had an almost animal smell for what made a sound loan—and when a loan was going sour—which was why he'd been ConVert-Co's lead banker for almost six years. On the rare times when Herb dragged his feet, Genie learned to look again at her presentation. This time he didn't merely drag his feet. They appeared to be set in concrete.

"As usual, Genie, your presentation looks excellent." But that wasn't the way he sounded. He ran a set of numbers on his calculator, totalled the numbers and asked, "Do you know how much ConVert-Co owes the banks?"

"Your bank? Or the syndicate?"

"Both."

"We owe the syndicate of banks $192.5 million plus current interest. You're in for thirty percent of that"—she did a rapid mental calculation—"or $57.75 million. Our equity in the seven buildings we own at the moment is about $240 million. Your loans are well protected."

"I don't see any profit-and-loss projections."

"I got back from Chicago the day before yesterday and haven't had the time to work them up. As soon as I do, you'll get a copy for your files."

"Now you want an additional $10 million for this new purchase?" The banker closed the file. "I can't recommend it.

369

We'll go $5 million and ConVert-Co or Max and you put up the other $5 million.''

"Why five? Why not three million or eight million?"

"Five seems to me to be the right number."

"It doesn't to me. I'll compromise with you, Herb. Max and I have no objection to putting our own money into a deal. Make it seven-point-five. That will leave us owing you an even two hundred thousand dollars.''

"That's a lot of zeros.''

"It is. With a single two in front.''

Herb considered her proposal. Finally he smiled. "Okay. You twisted my arm. I'll recommend it at prime plus two-and-a-half percent.''

"Two-and-a-half percent? We've never paid more than prime plus one percent.''

"You've never been this extended before. It's the best I can do.'' They both knew she had no choice. "When do you need the money?''

"Ten percent in two weeks. The rest thirty days later.''

"It'll take me a few days to circulate the papers among the syndicate. You know the drill. I'll be back to you on Monday.''

"Isn't that cutting it a bit fine?''

"Tommy's somewhere on vacation. I'll have to find him. And you know Bob and Craig. They always agree, but they have to go through the motions for their own committees. Besides, two weeks is not a lot of time.''

"It's been enough time in the past.''

"That was then, and this is now. Speaking of now, how is Max doing in Boston?''

"He told me he had a handle on it. If you want specific information, call him.''

"No. But it would be nice to see real progress in Boston before we close on this loan.''

"What does that mean, Herb?''

"Nothing. Nothing beyond the fact that the Boston loan has been on the books much longer than either of us figured. I have to keep rewriting my reports. The bank examiners don't like that sort of thing.''

"Neither do we.''

He nodded. "By the way, two reporters from *Forbes* want to

interview me. Did you know they're planning an article on you?''

"I've heard."

"Any reason why they should pick on you?''

"I guess they think we'll make a story."

"Nothing more?''

"Not as far as I know. If you find out anything about the article, I'd appreciate your letting me know.''

"Sure. Last summer they did a number on our European operation. I hope they're kinder to you than they were to us."

"I hope. Are we done for today?''

"I think so."

As she was leaving, Genie turned to ask Herb to try to push the approvals along, but he'd picked up his phone and waved good-bye to her. Later Genie tried to analyze what it was that was troubling her. The meeting had left her feeling curiously unsatisfied. She'd gotten the $7.5 million, which was all she'd expected to get. The interest rate was higher than she'd hoped, but not really out of line. Since she'd owed him the profit-and-loss projections for over three months, that wasn't it. Herb had a right to be concerned about Boston. So was she. Maybe Max had a handle on it, but she wondered which handle? Whores? Blackmail? Bribes? Threats? Whatever it was, she didn't like it. And *Forbes*? How would Herb react to the idea of a legs loan? He'd probably ask them to leave. On the other hand, how would he react if they showed him whatever evidence they'd gathered on Max's sales methods? She wasn't so sure about the answer to that one. None of that explained why she was so uneasy. Then it came to her. For the first time since the start of their banking relationship, Herb was making the loan because he had no choice. The banks were already in too deep. Just as she had to accept the higher interest rate, they had to make the loan. The higher rate wasn't simply a bank's policy of getting the best terms possible. It was Herb's way of telling her he actually didn't want to make the loan at all, and this was the last loan he'd approve until they'd reduced their total bank debt. It wasn't only what he said. It was what he didn't say. For the first time in six years he had not walked her to the door, chatting about his family, his boat, or some other personal gossip. It had been a strictly business meeting, and one that Herbert Gordon, senior vice-president of their lead bank,

wished he could have avoided. She would have to review the
financial stability of ConVert-Co immediately, and in depth.

Genie's memory of her evening with Paul skipped about,
making no pattern. She entered the lobby of the Majestic, the
first time in twelve years, and failed to recognize a single member of the staff. While waiting for the elevator, she glanced
down the empty corridor to where she once lived. To her astonishment, it seemed the door opened, and she saw her mother, a
tall strong woman with black hair pulled straight back and knot-
ted in a bun, greeting her father—a large man with a fierce
black mustache and a gentle look. She had to close her eyes to
rid herself of the vision.

In the Husseman apartment, she watched Paul make her a
Beefeater martini. They were out of Bombay gin. When he
handed it to her, their fingers touched, and for an instant, it was
as though they'd never been apart. Then they were strangers
again, making idiotic conversation.

"One thing I love about this apartment is the dark walnut
parquet floors," he said. "Look at the luster. Did you know
they're dark walnut? They can't make floors like this anymore.
The tree is an endangered species."

"I know. I used to live here." She became flustered. "I
mean downstairs."

"Of course you know. How stupid of me. It's your business
to know."

At some point they climbed the stairs to the rooftop terrace.
Somehow it looked smaller, almost dingy. The redwood stock-
ade fence was broken, the lounges buried under the snow.
There was nothing remaining of that radiant summer when
they'd made love under the stars. It would have been better left
to memory. There would never again be a place like it, because
she would never again be that young girl.

So the evening went in a blur. She had one too many martinis, and he had an extra scotch. She supposed they talked about
the theater and real estate and politics, but she couldn't clearly
remember. Only a snatch here, a fragment there. They had conversations without preludes or endings.

"I've had weeks when I've been in ten cities in three days.
Remember when you thought everything north of 14th Street
was Bridgeport?"

"You mean it isn't" And they both laughed. "Now I know there is Boston, Philadelphia, Washington, Chicago, and occasionally Los Angeles and San Francisco. The theater preview and tour circle. Oh well, there's no provincial as provincial as a New York provincial who works in the theater."

They had dinner, and it was hard for her to swallow the food. The maid served steak. Bleu for Paul. Medium rare for her. Salad. Wine.

"Mouton Rothschild," Genie said. "Full-bodied."

"The fifty-nines are gone. Seventy-three is as close as I could come."

"I'll try to remember to let the wine breathe and take small sips."

"Genie!" Paul's voice broke.

"Don't say it. I know."

They were shy and stumbling in their talk, and when Paul tried to explain about Joan Rosen who had changed their lives and the fact that he wasn't the child's father, he found he couldn't. It had to do with his debt to his father. Genie felt her own awkward pain in a mishmash summary of the years and how they'd passed. She had a bad time explaining about her mother, what had happened to her father, and finally gave up, saying she guessed only a few people got what they really wanted. Because they were willing to sacrifice enough to get it. "But you only know that after you've got it. Or haven't."

Both of them found they didn't want to say anymore than was necessary about the past. They fumbled around talking at each other, over each other, around each other, interrupting each other, until it was almost daybreak. Always making certain to keep at arm's length from each other.

Before Paul took her to the lobby, Genie asked him to dinner at her apartment. He couldn't come for about a month. He had to go to Boston, somewhat further north than Bridgeport, to play doctor to an ailing production. He'd call her just as soon as he got back.

Genie said fine. And as she stepped into her limousine, she felt she was running a high fever. She collapsed against the cushions. When the car pulled away from the curb, she found her eyes were filled with tears. But the tears were not today's tears. They were tears for the boy and the girl of twenty years ago. They had once existed, and they existed no more. Were regrets all that remained? Would Paul call? Would he?

It took three days for the snowplows to clear the 369 miles of Interstate 80 between Pittsburgh and New York. As soon as it had been determined that the highway was completely safe, a large, somewhat old-fashioned, maroon and black Rolls Royce limousine started for New York. The car had an extra high roof, having originally been custom-built so a very tall gentleman wearing a top hat could sit comfortably on his way to the opera at Covent Garden in London. Marcus Cato Telemann—his father had been a professor of Greco-Roman history at the old Mellon Institute of Technology—sat in the rear seat. He'd hung his heavy overcoat on a hanger and adjusted his suit coat and trousers for the eight-hour drive to New York.

Two men sat in the front seat. They wore identical black suits and chauffeur's caps. Marcus Cato was a cautious man. He always travelled with two drivers in case one driver became ill. The travel plan was to make two short stops, one for gasoline, a second for lunch for the drivers and a trip to the rest room. Lunch for Marcus Cato was provided by the family chef, and rested in a compact refrigerator—one of the many amenities the car offered its owner. Marcus Cato had no impulse to open the refrigerator and see what had been packed. Though cautious, he was not an unnecessarily curious man. Whatever curiosity he'd had as a young man had been lost by the time he'd reached his current age of sixty-eight. He'd seen too much, and he had no illusions whatever about the world or people or the possibility of chaos inherent in both.

The years had also made him immune to the teasing he'd received at the hands of the family for his refusal to fly. He'd tried it once and found he disliked everything about flying, from the crowded airports to the hideous meals, even to the first-class seats. And the family-owned jets were not much better. Nor did he like looking down, either at the clouds or at the earth. After that first and only flight, he'd made a rare attempt at humor to explain his position. He said, "When the pilot announces, 'Ladies and gentlemen, I regret to inform you that we are lost in the fog. Unless I can locate our position, there is a good chance we may all starve to death,' then, and only then, will I fly."

As might be expected, his joke made the family assume he had a fear of flying. This was false. Nothing and no one had ever frightened Marcus Cato Telemann. He was cautious because he accepted there were good and sufficient reasons for caution. He disliked flying solely because he disliked flying. And Marcus Cato rarely did anything he disliked. This trip was an exception. When T.E. first suggested he supervise the matter, he'd objected.

"We sold them two buildings, T.E. The Woman carried out her end of the negotiations most professionally. Why do this to them?"

T.E. boomed back. "Family honor, Marcus Cato. Family honor."

"Honor, T.E.? Or pride? Or vengeance?" He was the only member of the family who assumed the privilege of being frank with T.E.

"Words, Marcus Cato. Words. Let's not play word games. The fact is I don't know why, and I expect you to find out. But if you so dislike the project, send one of those bright young men you insist on hiring."

Marcus Cato considered this, then answered, "No. I'll do it. Best to keep it in the family." Marcus Cato had married T.E.'s younger sister and had worked for the family for so many decades his lack of a blood tie was almost forgotten. He was family. "It's been four years since any member of the family has used the Manhattan town house. One must keep an occasional eye even on old family retainers. While I'm in New York, I'll sleep there and run a finger or two over the molding for dust."

"You're right as usual, Marcus Cato. Keep it in the family." T.E.'s voice changed, and for an instant, he sounded vulnerable. "You know this is the first thing my daugher's asked of me in seven years?"

"No one told you to father a child at fifty."

"I was positive it would be a boy. I wanted a male heir."

"I know." Marcus Cato didn't add, so does she. He changed the subject. "I'll look over the documents during the drive."

"When will you be back?"

"I get there Thursday evening. Friday, I'll meet with the bankers. Stay over Friday night and return on Saturday."

"You'll manage to Miss Robert's birthday party Friday night. A family get-together."

"Precisely. That was one factor influencing my decision to go. Emily will represent me."

T.E. laughed. "I'm tempted to go myself."

"No. For you to appear would be like shooting at flies with a cannon."

"I suppose." A light lit up on his telephone. "Ah, my masseuse has arrived. Do we have anything else to discuss?"

"I think not. I'll call you Friday, early evening." Marcus Cato returned to his office and considered T.E.'s daughter. She was worse than a black sheep. She was the dregs of the family, but since she was family, he'd put on his hip boots and wade through the sewers of Stacey Moore's life.

It was 10:05, Friday morning, when Herbert Gordon replaced his phone on its cradle, swivelled his chair so it faced the windows and put his feet up on his credenza. Jack Wainright, the president of the bank and his boss, had just informed him he was sending someone with the incredible name of Marcus Cato Telemann to see him. Jack wanted him to listen closely to everything Telemann said. Which was as clear a signal as Jack ever gave that something had been agreed upon, and Herb's assignment was to execute the agreement. Who the hell was Telemann? What was he supposed to do?

This was turning out to be anything but a typical banker's morning. First those reporters from *Forbes*, a man and a woman. Did they actually think he was so naive as not to understand the implications of the phrase legs loan in connection with Eugenia Szabo? Although furious at the insinuation, he believed he'd handled it well. "I suppose it's possible that a loan officer—when reviewing an application for overdraft privileges or a credit card or even a consumer loan—occasionally might be foolish enough to consider an offer of a personal nature when making a decision. The amount of money involved—several thousand dollars at most—small, the loan officer, young, the woman, pretty." He gave them his best man-of-the-world smile. Then he became stern. "But you're talking about millions of dollars, tens of millions of dollars. With the most accomplished prostitute charging what? You're probably more familiar with the answer to that question than a family man like me, but shall we say five hundred dollars? Your conception of why bankers loan out millions of dollars is, to be polite, right out of bad movies."

Their next question was not so absurd. "Do you know anything about the methods Mr. Szabo uses to sell his apartments?" He didn't, and after listening to the charges—ignoring the lack of solid evidence to support the charges—he was thankful he didn't. The accusations were nasty. If provable, they could trigger several clauses in the bank's loan agreements with ConVert-Co. He'd just finished denying any knowledge of Max Szabo's operation and expressing his strong personal doubts as to the accuracy of the stories when his phone rang. It was Jack. He'd gotten rid of the reporters before returning the call.

On a hunch, he went to his private bathroom to wash his face, comb his hair, and straighten his tie. By the time he'd finished, his phone was ringing.

"There's a Mr. Telemann here who says you expect him. I don't find his name in your appointment book."

"That's all right, Muriel. Take the gentleman's coat and send . . . No. Show him in." When the door opened, Muriel ushered in a short, plump, white-haired man with a round face and bright blue eyes which were magnified by thick wire-rimmed bifocals. Herb glanced at his light grey two-button suit, white shirt, large patterned tie, and made a quick estimate. Midwesterner. Chicago? Cincinnati? Herb felt the superiority of a New York banker for anyone who did not know enough to order his suits at Brooks Brothers or at least Paul Stuart. He greeted his visitor, concealing his scorn as best he was able.

"Mr. Telemann?"

"Good morning, Mr. Gordon." They shook hands. "I appreciate your seeing me without an appointment."

"Sit down, please." Herb indicated a round conference table with a teakwood-grained vinyl surface and six low chairs. When they were settled, he asked, "What can I do for you?"

Marcus Cato opened his attaché case and took out a thick file. "Mr. Wainright tells me you head up the syndicate that backs ConVert-Co."

"We're their lead bank." Could this man be a surprise bank examiner? Something was up. "They're an aggressive, well-run operation. We think highly of the Szabos."

"I'm sure you do," he consulted his file, "Or you wouldn't have loaned them close to two hundred million dollars."

That figure was confidential. Herb doubted even Jack was up to date on the actual dollars. "Without confirming or denying your information, may I ask where you got that number? And whom do you represent?"

"My apologies. Careless of me. My cards."

Herb glanced at the two white business cards Telemann pushed across the table. General Counsel, Director—Moore Industries and President, Director—Moore Investments. Both addresses were the same, the Moore Building, Pittsburgh. Herb's eyebrows shot up. "Moore Industries and Moore Investments are owned by the Moore family?"

"Yes. I would like to see the current financials on Con-Vert-Co."

"Certainly. Excuse me." Herb used the phone on the table. "Muriel, please bring in the file on ConVert-Co." He waited until his secretary left before opening it. "Here." He handed over the papers Genie had given him earlier in the week.

"Hmmm. Are they current on interest payments?"

"Yes." Herb didn't understand the man's interest in Con-Vert-Co. Until he found out what this was all about, he'd reserve any further enthusiasm for Eugenia Szabo. Why the hell hadn't Jack told him who his visitor was? The Moore family owned about nine percent of the bank's stock, more than twice the largest shareholder. If they chose, they could have placed at least two men on the board of directors. Probably this man would have been one of them.

"There appears to be a net worth of some forty million dollars in the corporation. To achieve that number would normally require an orderly liquidation of assets."

Liquidation of assets, Herb repeated to himself. What was Marcus Cato Telemann implying? "Why should they liquidate assets? The company's an ongoing successful operation."

"To repay their loans." The round face opposite him had about as much expression as a puffed-up pillow. "We would like you to call their loans as they come due. All their loans."

Herb swallowed. "That would make an orderly liquidation impossible."

"We don't want an orderly liquidation."

"But a forced sale will only realize a portion of the value of the buildings. I doubt very much if we'd be able to recover our loans.''

"Moore Investments is prepared to guarantee your syndicate complete protection. One hundred cents on the dollar.''

Now Herb partially understood. "I see. You want little, if anything, left over for the Szabos?''

"Not a cent.''

"And the buyers of the properties will be dummy corporations controlled by various Moore entities?''

For the first time he saw a slight change in Telemann's expression. In a face so unusually placid, the change expressed outrage. Herb realized he'd made a mistake. "Mr. Gordon, you misunderstand me. We are not attempting to make money on this transaction.''

"Then why bankrupt the Szabos?''

"That, sir, is a family matter. Well beyond our discussion.''

"I see.''

"No, sir. You don't see, and it makes no difference. My question to you is, as the lead bank in the syndicate, are you prepared to call that portion of the loans your bank has made?''

"I don't believe I have a choice.''

"Not if you wish to remain in the field of banking.''

That said it all. Herbert Gordon had felt the Szabos were in a tight money squeeze and hadn't intended to extend them any additional credit, but he'd expected them to survive. They were smart. They were fast on their feet. They'd ride out the depressed economy. But they couldn't ride out the Moore family. So the Szabos were finished. This made him wonder if possibly some advantage might accrue to him in the demolition process. He had an idea. "Mr. Telemann, I don't quite see the point in calling the loans. They'll file for a Chapter 11 under the bankruptcy code.''

"They won't get it. You will insist on a Chapter 10 bankruptcy.''

"We can insist, but any bankruptcy lawyer will tell you the odds are against us.''

"Possibly, It depends on the judge. We have some influence with judges.''

The openness with which Telemann spoke of controlling judges shook Herb. "I assume there are judges who would be delighted to cooperate with the Moore family. But not all.''

"No. Not all." Herb could hear a note of regret at having to admit the power of the Moore family was not absolute. It offended Telemann's concept of the natural order of things.

"Then, possibly, the Szabos might obtain a Chapter 11 bankruptcy and remain in business. Stop paying interest to us, and should they choose, liquidate at their leisure."

"It is a possibility." The admission was not easily made.

"I have an idea which, if you agree, might eliminate even that small possibility."

"In that event the Moore family would consider itself in your debt."

"Are you familiar with our standard loan agreement?"

"More or less. Is there something special I should note?"

"The morals clause and the clause covering possible criminial activity are unusually strong."

"As well they should be." Marcus Cato Telemann was properly indignant at the idea of anyone involved in immoral or criminal activities. Anyone that is except a member of the family, whose activities, no matter what they were, could never be considered immoral or criminal. It was their right.

"I had a pair of visitors before you. Two reporters, and . . ."

The conversation continued for another twenty minutes. Then Telemann said, "My compliments, Mr. Gordon. That is a most ingenious plan. Proceed exactly as you suggested. It may take somewhat longer, but I believe you will succeed. Then there will be no chance of a Chapter 11 filing. As I said, the family will consider itself in your debt."

Herb was no longer so awed that he forgot a final detail. "There's one more question. Eugenia Szabo is expecting an answer to her request for an additional seven-point-five million dollars on Monday to purchase a new building. What should I do?"

"I noticed the request in the papers you showed me. They're to invest two-point-five million of their own money?" Herb nodded. "Seven-point-five million is such a small amount. Make the loan by all means. We don't want to raise any suspicions." Then he handed Herb back the ConVert-Co file and closed his attaché case. "I think we've reached an agreement as to how to proceed?"

"Yes."

"My next appointment is a few blocks from here. Another of the members of your syndicate. A Mr. Thomas Migliore. If you'll be kind enough to ask your secretary to retrieve my galoshes and overcoat, I'll be on my way. I believe I'll walk. New York is such a stimulating city."

"Tommy's on vacation. I spoke to him yesterday in Antigua."

"He's in his office this morning waiting for me."

Marcus Cato Telemann left as quietly as he'd arrived. Herb's head was so full of the advantages which might come to him through a Moore family obligation, he forgot to walk the man to the elevator. While he was accustomed to dealing with wealth, he had never before witnessed the use of raw financial power—not for profit, which he understood, but solely to crush one man and one woman. And he had no idea why.

31

When Stacey Moore left the offices of ConVert-Co, she felt free at last, free of her disgusting obsession with Max. Free to be who and what she was—the daughter of Thomas Edward Moore and all that that meant. Her liberation was exhilarating. She ignored the snowflakes accumulating on the sidewalks and walked all the way home to her second-floor apartment in a town house on East 63rd Street between Park and Lexington avenues. Striding up Park Avenue, she felt an elation in her newfound freedom such as she had not known in years. Not only was she free of Max, she was free of her need for drugs to get her through the terrors of her days.

Once home, Stacey ran a hot tub, added bath oils and bubble bath soap, and relaxed, soaking the cold out of her joints. While she pampered her body, her mind worked furiously. What did she want to do about Max Szabo? An easy question to answer. Destroy him. There was that article *Forbes* was planning. Her drinking buddies had told her about it. That was what she'd planned to warn Max about. Now the bastard wouldn't know until they'd lowered the boom. Good! She'd talk to the reporters herself. She could give them everything they needed—names, dates—and back it up with testimony from the whores Max made her hire. The reporters would have a field day with all that information. Second thoughts stopped her. What about the stories the whores could tell about her? She was a Moore. T.E.'s only child. How the hell had she been so blinded as to put Max ahead of her family? Max had pictures of her with men—many men. Some with women. Pictures *Forbes* could never print, but knowing Max, the pictures would arrive on T.E.'s desk and in the mail of every member of her family. *Forbes* was not for her. Their story would have to run without her information. This was a family matter. As badly as it frightened her, she'd have to talk to her father. After all, T.E. always took care of his own.

In spite of her exhaustion from her fight with Max, her walk through the snow, and her first solid meal in days, Stacey was unable to fall asleep. Her stomach had shrunk over the past two years when pills, cocaine, and gin had almost replaced food. Now it was heavy, and ached from overeating. Her head whirled with visions of what would happen to Max. Finally she reached for her sleeping pills. They were only thirty milligram Dalmane. Not a real drug. There were three pills left in the bottle. She swallowed two and shook the bottle. That one pill was lonely, and she wanted desperately to sleep. No sense in leaving one lonely little sleeping pill. She took it. Tomorrow would be time enough to order another supply. If her prescription had run out, good old Dr. Wilson would give her another. He always had.

The next day Stacey called the pharmacist and reordered her monthly supply of Dalmane. Then she gathered her courage and called home. Surprisingly, it was easy. Even a hint that she might be home for a visit was enough to start T.E. moving. When she explained what she wanted, he assured her it would take no time. A few days. Weeks at the most. What T.E.'s daughter wanted, she would get, with no questions asked.

A week passed while Stacey waited for her father to call back and tell her it was done. But no call came, and each day she grew more nervous. It had been a long time since she'd gone for a whole week without drugs. Or a man. One morning the phone rang.

"I'll drop off your usual supplies about noon, Miss Moore. Will you be in?"

Stacey started to say no, I don't use those supplies any longer, when she panicked. Max hadn't been home last night. She'd called, intending to hang up once he answered. All she'd gotten was his message machine. She'd called every hour until three in the morning. Max had been with a woman last night, and she'd been alone.

"I have to go to the bank, but I'll be back by noon."

"See you then."

Stacey knew she didn't need the stuff. She'd keep it in a drawer. That was the only reason she'd agreed to accept delivery—to have a supply of cocaine on hand and not use it. It would be proof she didn't need it any longer. She dressed, hurried to the bank to cash a check, and rushed back to her apartment to be there before her source arrived. They met on the street in front of her apartment. It never ceased to surprise her how open and aboveboard everything seemed. The panel truck was white, clean, with neat red letters on each side, Mid-Nassau Supply Company. The driver wore a grey uniform and a heavy coat, and because of the cold and snow still on the ground, high boots and a fur hat. He was a young man with long blond hair extending below his coat collar. Although she didn't know his name, he knew hers.

"Good morning, Miss Moore." The corrugated carton was huge, considering the size of the package they were really selling. Household supplies—soap, toilet paper, floor wax, and facial tissues—were included in the delivery. Stacey gave the man an envelope. "Thank you, Miss Moore. I'll call in two weeks."

"Do that." She tucked the bulky package under her arm and hurried up the stairs to her apartment. The good-looking driver had given her an idea. Now that she was rid of Max, it was time to start seeing new men, men who could provide her with the pleasure of their company as well as their services. There was no shortage of men she could call. After placing the household supplies in the kitchen, she was left with a small white chipboard box. Out of curiosity, she opened the box. Inside were thirty neatly sealed plastic pouches, each containing a white powder. Thirty disposable syringes. Her usual two-week supply. She placed the box in a special compartment in her jewelry box. In a way, cocaine was a jewel. It certainly had given her more pleasure than any diamond bracelet or rope of pearls she owned. But she didn't need the stuff anymore. She really didn't. What she needed was some information on how things were proceeding. She called her father.

"Hello, T.E."

"Stacey!" He sounded surprised.

"How's that little business matter we discussed coming along?"

"Fine, girl. Marcus Cato tells me everything is on schedule."

"When will something happen?"

"Patience, girl. It's happening now. Like fruit ripening."

Damn him! Was he putting her off? He always called her girl when she asked for something. In her father's world, women carried not the slightest weight. Most of the Moore women liked the set-up. They gave lip service to independence and all the new, trendy social causes. That was skin deep. Their jewels, their clothes, their trips abroad were what counted. Only her mother had been different. As was she. She knew she was as smart as any male Moore, and she'd proved it. Running her own business without so much as a by-your-leave from T.E. Sure she'd used money from her mother's trust to get her started. It was her money, and everybody had to get started somehow. "How long will it take for the fruit to ripen, T.E.?"

"I've a report from Marcus Cato. I could read it to you, but it's long and complicated."

"I understand reports, T.E."

"Why bother your head, girl? The bottom line is it will take about six weeks."

"Six weeks!" He was humoring her the way he used to humor her mother. Then he'd forget what he'd promised. "You told me it would take a few days. Two weeks at the most."

"I did say that. But it's turned out to be more complex than I anticipated. Six weeks, girl, is not long to do your dirty work."

Stacey suddenly gave vent to her anger. "If it was your dirty work, or Cousin Jack's, it would have been done yesterday. And don't call me girl!"

The moment the words were out of her mouth, Stacey began to shake. Not even Max could frighten her the way T.E. could. When he answered, his voice was icy. "Stacey, you listen to me. You asked me to do something for you. I agreed, without asking why you wanted this thing done. I agreed because you are my daughter. If I tell you it's being taken care of, it is. In my own way. Any more questions?"

Stacey had none. This was the father she remembered only too well. Any further show of temper or independence and he'd cancel whatever it was he was doing. And he was doing something. She could tell from his words, "because you are my daughter." Though she'd given him no explanation, he was knowing enough to realize it was a matter of personal disgrace. Her disgrace. And where family disgrace was involved, T.E. was a killer. She switched back to her dutiful daughter role. "No, T.E. I trust your good judgement."

"That's better. Now, girl, when did you say you'd visit your old dad?"

Stacey couldn't contain herself. Her tone became an exact imitation of his. "When the fruit is ripe. In six weeks."

"Fine. Good-bye, girl." He hung up before she could answer.

T.E. pressed the intercom and dialed Marcus Cato Telemann's office. "Marcus Cato, would you mind joining me? . . . I understand . . . Fifteen minutes." He hung up the phone and waited. The conversation with Stacey had both angered and amused him. Although, to put a fine point on it, he was far more angry than amused. It was one thing to have fathered a child at fifty. It was quite another thing for the child to have turned out to be a girl. And it was still a third thing for the girl to grow up to be a nuisance. The problem was he'd married the wrong woman—good looks, good bloodlines—but she hadn't been up to the job of being his wife, and she'd passed her weaknesses along to her daughter. Not only was Stacey weak, she was stupid. She actually believed he would consider ruining a company merely because she asked him to. And without his knowing why she wanted it done. He shook his head in silent disgust over what his desire for a male heir had produced.

Fifteen minutes later there was a knock on the door. "Come," he called out in a loud voice.

The door opened and Marcus Cato entered. "No point in shouting, T.E. I have excellent hearing." He sat on the couch. "What is so important I had to drop everything?"

"Did I say it was that important?"

"Yes. Whenever you ask would you mind, you're saying drop everything and do it. What is it?"

"It occurs to me, Marcus Cato, there is something to be said against knowing another person too well."

"It occurs to me that when two people work together as closely as we do, there'a a lot more to be said against not knowing the other person well enough."

T.E. acknowledged the accuracy of Marcus Cato's observation with a humorless laugh. "Possibly. In any case, to answer your question, I have just heard from Stacey."

"And she wanted to know why things were taking so long."

"She did. We had a few words."

"Only a few? My compliments on your unusual restraint."

"I assume everything is proceeding as per your report?"

"Naturally. Would you expect otherwise?"

"Have you received any information as to why we are doing this?"

"Some. I'll have all the confirmation I need in several weeks."

"Care to give me a preliminary report?"

"No."

"That bad?"

"Yes. As a matter of fact, worse."

T.E. showed no reaction. "Humph!" He rubbed his chin. "Do you have a suggestion as to how we might take care of the matter?"

"I do not." Marcus Cato was more emphatic than usual. "She's your daughter. After you read my report, you will have to decide."

"No, Marcus Cato. From what you tell me, this is a family matter. You and I will decide."

Marcus Cato considered briefly the possibility of a joint decision. "You are right about one thing. It is a family matter. However, to repeat, Stacey Moore is your daughter. The best I can offer you is an advise-and-consent position."

"Then that will have to do. Several weeks, did you say, before I receive your report?"

"Possibly sooner. I'll write the report myself. My handwriting is quite legible."

A flicker of surprise passed over T.E.'s face and was gone. Marcus Cato considered the matter so confidential he was not going to allow his private secretary to type it. In addition, he was planning to take two additional weeks to prepare it. T.E.'s long years of having worked first at his father's right hand and then, after his father's death, as the head of the Moore family now served him in good stead. He'd received many confidential reports over the decades and learned, when necessary, how to wait. If he wasn't waiting for word as to the results of an oil drilling venture off the coast of Louisiana, he was waiting for the arrival of a case of priceless artifacts shipped, illegally, out of Egypt, or waiting for a minor coup, financed by the family, to place a government more favorable to the Moore interests in power in a South American country; or waiting for a strike, called by union leaders in the family's pay, to bring a company the family wished to acquire to its knees; or watching the returns on election night to find out how many candidates under obligation to the family had been victorious at the polls; or waiting for a break in a drought needed to save the winter wheat crop so the Moore grain combine could ship millions of tons of wheat to Russia; or . . . No. Waiting several weeks for a complete report would not cause him any undue strain. In fact, he was beginning to become curious as to the contents of the report, and it had been a long time since he'd been genuinely curious about anything. T.E. found his curiosity to be a novel emotion. He actually looked forward to the next few weeks of waiting with some pleasure.

"Should there by any sudden developments, you will inform me?"

"There will be no sudden developments. However, in the event I'm mistaken . . ." Marcus Cato shrugged his shoulders. "Now, if you don't mind, I would like to get back to work. There are several important matters I've left hanging."

Both men were aware Marcus Cato's choice of a phrase similar to T.E.'s was deliberate. He meant to end the meeting. T.E. chuckled and acquiesced with a wave of his hand.

The brief conversation with her father had neither angered nor amused Stacey. It had devastated her, brought back all her childhood years. Watching her mother disintegrate under the pressure of being Mrs. Thomas Edward Moore. Watching her go from being a beautiful vital woman to a helpless alcoholic who refused to stop drinking even after she came down with hepatitis. Later, Stacey understood. It was her mother's way of committing suicide. And by permitting her to drink at times— encouraging her to drink at other times—it was her father's way of getting rid of a woman for whom he had no further use and who had become a nuisance. Since then, Stacey had been running away from T.E. and the family. She knew that if she ever became a nuisance, her father would find a way to get rid of her as he had her mother. For an instant Stacey wavered. She could call the whole thing off and never go home. No! As much as she feared her father, the use of his power, the power of the family, remained the only way to destroy Max Szabo. And no matter what it cost her in the end, Max Szabo must be destroyed. She accepted the fact that, like most things in life, this was a trade-off.

The room felt cold, and Stacey began to shiver. Caught between her hatred of Max and her fear of her father, she felt herself shattering like a dropped glass. She needed help as badly as she'd ever needed it in her entire life. She ran to her dresser and the waiting jewelry box. Just this one time! Just this once! Then she'd be all right. She emptied the contents of the pouch on the back of her hand. Sniff. Sniff. Wait! Nausea. Then whee! The top of her head flew off. And she wasn't afraid of T.E. Or Max. Or anyone. She'd settle with T.E. when she was ready. And Max Szabo? What a joke. Especially on her.

Stacey sat on her bed. Her fingertips ran along her thighs. The touch left a trail of desire that lingered and grew. She wanted Max. She needed Max. Max didn't want her. He wanted his sister. Max didn't need her. He had his sister. She needed a man who wanted her. A new man. Who? If not Max, who? Bruce Welles! Yes! That's who. Bruce Welles wanted her all right, and they'd never been to bed. Because Bruce was afraid of Max. If it could be said that Max had a male friend, Bruce Welles was that friend. She'd eat something, have a drink, and call good old Brucie.

The phone rang. "Welles Ventures."

"Bruce Welles, please?"

"Who may I say is calling?"

The girl on the telephone made it sound like a regular office rather than a room in Bruce's apartment, which it actually was. "Stacey Moore."

"One moment, Miss Moore."

Then Bruce was on the line. "Stacey, baby. Good afternoon. What's gotten you up before three o'clock?"

"Thinking of you, Brucie, I had the wildest dream about you last night. I had to call you."

"Tell me about it."

"Oh, no!" Stacey laughed. "The New York Telephone Company doesn't like its phones used for those kinds of calls. But if you'll take me to dinner, we'll come back here, and I'll tell you all about it. Play your cards right, and I might do more than tell you about it."

She could hear Bruce inhale. "Aaah!" Then there was a pause. Finally, "What about our mutual good friend, Max?"

"Haven't you heard?" She gave her words just the right amount of casual gaiety. "Max and I have gone the way of all lovers. We're ex."

"You're sure?" He'd call Max to make certain.

"I'm sure." Stacey could read his mind. "Call Max. He'll give you permission."

"I don't need his permission. It's a matter of friendship. Male ethics. There are rules about that sort of thing."

"Of course. And you're an honorable man." She kept her scorn to herself. Especially when you're scared Max'll kick the shit out of you. "Tonight, Brucie? Dinner? And I'll tell you all about my dream."

"Sure, baby. You're on. What time?

"Say seven o'clock. We'll catch an early meal and have the whole evening ahead of us."

"Your place at seven. Ciao, baby."

Stacey replaced the phone. She'd been rubbing her crotch the entire time they talked. It felt good. She'd spend what was left of the afternoon at Sassoon's getting the full treatment. If Brucie worked, she'd owe him one. Brucie was a dealmaker. Moore Industries was always looking either to buy or sell something. Brucie would be in heaven. She'd have him around for as long as she wished.

Stacey studied the white powder. She placed a pinch of it on the back of her right hand, closed one nostril, and sniffed. Then she did the same thing with her other nostril. She waited. It always took a little time. Not long. Even the waiting, the expectation was good. Ah! Now! An instant of nausea—going through the coke barrier—and pop! She was on the other side. Riding the wave. Nothing she couldn't do now.

Stacey studied herself in the full-length mirror. She looked great! Skintight black satin pants; no panties to mar the perfect line. A black sequinned, semi-see-through turtleneck sweater. If she turned sideways, one could plainly see the outline of her breasts and their pointed nipples. Stiletto-heeled black thong sandals. A single strand of matching pearls. Her black hair, curled and glistening. It was still early. Time to pour herself a gin over ice. Brucie would get the full treatment tonight. She felt almost virginal. In a way she was. It was like a coming-out party, a debut. After everything that had happened in the last week, Stacey felt she deserved a special evening. She was coming back to life.

He was prompt. Stacey pressed the intercom. "Bruce?"

"No one else."

"Come on up." She opened the door and heard his heavy steps.

"Whew!" This was the first time he'd ever called for Stacey at her apartment. "When are they going to put an elevator in the place?"

"Climbing stairs is healthy." She gave him a gentle push in the stomach. He was soft. "Give me your coat. The bar's in the library."

Bruce looked around the living room with the hard sure eyes of a secondhand furniture dealer, which was what he'd been, buying and selling used hotel furniture. He actually knew more about furniture than he did about deal-making. The eighteenth-century Venetian chest in the corner caught his eye. At least $30,000. The three-legged Queen Anne chairs. Originals. Museum quality. Priceless. The Sheraton highboy. Also priceless. Too much for him to take in all at once. He looked at Stacey. She'd been waiting for him to finish his inspection and had placed herself in front of a lap with a Tiffany glass shade. The light shone through the sequins. She gave him a good chance to inspect the merchandise before leading him into the library.

Bruce was twenty-five pounds overweight. He had shiny black hair and good features beginning to disappear under the flesh. He looked like a sleek seal. But there was no muscle under the flesh. Fifteen pounds more and he wouldn't be sleek. He'd be fat. "What do you drink, Brucie?"

"Scotch and water." Bruce was as impressed by Stacey's library as he had been by the furniture in her living room. Blond oak panelling. One wall covered with books. Mies van der Rohe's Barcelona chairs, leather couch, projection TV, a leather-topped eighteenth-century English desk, built-in file cabinets. The windows were draped in a cut velour, similar in coloring to the wall panelling. "Very handsome room, Stacey." By now Bruce realized he'd missed something important about Stacey Moore. She ran a catering business, and Max had picked her up at some party. But no small-time catering business paid for a full floor on East 63rd Street and the furniture he'd seen. Christ! Those pearls were genuine. Who the hell was Stacey Moore—if that was her real name—and where did the money come from? Even if she was a high-priced hooker on the side, it wouldn't pay for a layout like this.

"Drink up, Brucie. The quicker we eat, the quicker we get back, and I'll tell you about my dream."

"Sure." He drained his glass. "Let's go."

Three hours later they were back in Stacey's library. Although he'd been constrained by their being in a public place, Bruce had spent the time becoming as familiar with the feel of Stacey's body as possible. He told her about the various mergers and acquisitions he was working on. His hands touched her arm, her shoulder, and her knee as though for emphasis. Once, when he placed his hand high on her thigh, squeezing it, Stacey moved it higher between her legs. Dinner ended soon after that.

Bruce was ready. He'd had an erection for an hour. But Stacey wasn't ready. The effects of the cocaine were wearing off, and the fear which always lurked around the edges of her consciousness was starting to return. Tendrils of terror were creeping along her body ready to envelop her. She needed help before they gathered her up. "Fix yourself a drink. I'll be right back."

Bruce was too self-involved to notice any change in Stacey. "Don't take too long. I want to hear about that dream."

Stacey hurried to her bedroom and her jewelry box. It only took a few moments to tear open the plastic and inhale the contents. Now she was all right, and Brucie was waiting for her. Time to change. Shoes under the chair. Pants and sweater tossed into a corner. She placed her finger between her legs. "Ooooh!" She was ready. She slipped on what might be considered an intimate hostess gown. Very intimate for very special occasions. Black lace with patches of black silk covering a few strategic places. All lace in back. She'd give old Brucie an eyeful.

By the time she returned to the library, Bruce had become anxious. He'd finished his drink, taken off his coat, tie, and shoes and was glancing at the door trying to decide if possibly Stacey was waiting for him in the bedroom.

"Wow!" he gasped. "That's quite an outfit. Where did you get it?"

"My little old dressmaker around the corner. Special for Stacey." She turned around. "Look as good from behind?"

"Your behind looks great. Pun intended. Come to Bruce, baby."

They met in the middle of the room. Bruce pulled her tight against his erection. She lifted her mouth to be kissed. Her hands told her he was a soft man. Pneumatic. Everywhere she pressed, she felt his flesh give, only to spring back when released. The only thing hard about Bruce was pressing between her legs. Stacey undressed Bruce, paying no attention to where she tossed his clothes. She dropped her flimsy garment to the floor.

"Come to bed, Brucie." Bruce followed her into the bedroom. She lay back on the bed, and Bruce crouched between her knees. Stacey closed her eyes, giving herself up to the first tremors of pleasure. It was going to be all right. For an instant she exulted in the thought. Then her mind tossed up a picture of Max, and she froze. "Come inside me! Quick!" His penis slipped into her, and although she knew he was there, she couldn't feel him. She could always feel Max. Maybe Brucie was too small? She tried to tighten her vaginal muscles. Nothing! She was dead inside. Max! Max! Stacey couldn't control her imagination. The vision of Max's club buried in Genie and Genie's body throbbing with the ecstasy of her orgasm filled her head. Genie came and came and came. Wouldn't she ever stop? Never! Not with Max inside her. And for Stacey there was nothing. Nothing but this fat sleek thing with something inside her she couldn't feel. Stacey screamed out her frustration. "Aaiiiieeee!"

"What the fuck's the matter with you?"

She didn't answer. Using all her strength, she pushed him off. "Get out, Bruce. Go home."

Bruce had been within moments of his orgasm and had no intention of stopping. "When I'm finished." The bitch wanted him to stop now. She was off her rocker. He'd slap some sense into her. Left. Right. Across her face. With each slap her head snapped sideways. Left. Right. That'll teach her. "Lie there, cunt. I'll go home when I'm done." He was between her legs, his prick searching for the opening.

The slaps brought Stacey's memory of Max hitting her. Bruce wasn't Max. He had no right to hit her. She'd tried to fuck him and couldn't do it. Didn't he understand? She wanted to, but nothing happened. Why didn't he go home? She wasn't a cunt. She was Stacey Moore. Now furious, she decided it was time he found out what that meant. "Look, Brucie." She spread her legs as wide apart as she was able and used her fingers to hold the lips of her vagina open. Rage made her venomous. "Look! There it is. That's what you want. But before you use it, you'd better listen. If your prick touches me, T.E. will cut your balls off."

Bruce reared back. "Tee. Who the fuck is Tee?"

She had him. "Not Tee. T, period. E, period. Moore. Thomas Edward Moore."

Bruce Welles had heard all about T.E. Moore and Moore Industries. He made a horrible connection and hissed through stiff lips, "What's he to you?"

"My father, you asshole!" She urged him on. "Come on, Brucie. Stick it in. How much will you pay for the fuck?" He backed away, his erection wilting. "What's the matter, Brucie? Don't you want to rape T.E.'s daughter? Do it, Brucie, and you'll never make another deal." He scrambled off the bed. "Price too high, lover boy? You don't think one fuck is fair trade for Welles Ventures?"

Bruce had to get away. It all fell into place. The apartment. The furniture. The clothes and jewelry. Everything about Stacey Moore said Moore. Except she was a lunatic. Maybe they all were. He had to get out while he could. "It's okay, Stacey, baby. I understand. You're not in the mood. Happens to everyone. Some other time. We'll try it again."

"That's smart, Brucie. You almost did something real stupid. Get dressed and get out." Stacey was no longer angry at Bruce. Just at herself for thinking she was free. She would never be free. Not as long as Max and Genie were alive. She wrapped her arms around herself, and her body shook as she sobbed out her total despair.

When Stacey opened her eyes, it was day. Her face hurt from Bruce's slaps. Everything she remembered about the night before disgusted her. Mostly herself. What a way to behave! The poor bastard was primed, ready to come, and she'd tossed him out. Why? He'd called her a cunt, and he was right. Thanks to Max that's what she'd become. Her cunt had been used by so many men—she'd put so many things in it that weren't even flesh and blood—what possible difference could one more thing have made? She lay back trying to sort out exactly what had happened. Everything had been going great until Bruce started to fuck her. Then Max and that bitch sister of his were there. That did it. God! Was she going to live the rest of her life in some kind of special hell designed by Max Szabo? Always wanting to come, almost coming, and the same vision always stopping her? Max and Genie! Max and Genie! This very minute she could feel herself becoming aroused. Much as she wanted to touch herself, she was afraid. It was no use. Max would stop her. There was one thing he couldn't stop. The white powder would help her forget.

For the first time, Stacey altered the way she used cocaine. She melted the powder in a silver spoon, mixed it with water, wound a thin rubber hose around her arm, and injected the drug directly into her vein. The effect was instantaneous. She fell backwards onto her bed. Nausea! More nausea! She thought she might vomit. The room began to spin. Slowly at first, then faster.

32

After clearing the table and washing the dinner plates, Nina left. Thursday was her day off, and she often slept at her sister's house on Wednesday nights. Genie gave herself up to restless pacing of the empty rooms in her apartment. She was more than merely at loose ends. She was nervous and tense. There was work she knew she should do, reports piled high on her desk in the study. But she didn't feel like working. Nevertheless, she sat behind her desk as though it was her one place of refuge. She fingered the reports, aimlessly, irritated at her own disquiet. A series of blurred, shifting images ran through her mind. Outwardly, the conditions of her life were reasonably favorable. There had been no call from *Forbes*. Perhaps they'd dropped the article? Herb had agreed to give ConVert-Co the bank loan necessary for them to buy the Chicago building. She'd sensed something cold in his manner and put it down to his being in a bad mood. People do have moods, she reassured herself. There was nothing concrete to which she could point to to account for the intense foreboding she'd been feeling for the last weeks. Was it because it had been over a month since Paul and she had spent the evening at his apartment? Had the passing of time added to her fear he might not call? She didn't know. What she did know was she had a sense of storm clouds gathering just over the horizon—remote, threatening—a darkness starting to fill the sky.

Looking for some distraction, she picked up the scrapbook she kept on Paul. This only increased her depression. When the telephone rang, it took an effort to answer it. It was Paul calling from Boston.

"How are you?"

"Okay. How are you?"

"Okay. I miss you."

"I miss you, too." She said it in spite of herself.

"Are you alone?"

"If you're asking whether there's a man in my bedroom, there isn't. I'm alone, and I have no lover waiting for me."

"There's no lady in mine either. And I have no love who expects me. The ladies come and go. Except you. You go. I should say went."

"I had reason."

"Yes, you did." She heard his hesitation. "Anyway, I'd like to see you. I could fly in from Boston. Catch the eight-thirty shuttle." Again he faltered. "We could have a drink together."

"When would you have to go back?"

"Tomorrow morning. On the seven-thirty shuttle."

"That's time enough for a drink. I'll expect you." Genie stared into space. It was not like Paul to yield to an irrational impulse. He must truly want to see her. What would be the cost? She sat in the glare of forced comprehension. Once she'd wanted to marry him. The truth was she still wanted to. It had taken many years of not seeing him or hearing from him to convince herself of the uselessness of her hopes. Now he wanted to see her again. Probably wanted to make love to her again. What did that mean? Had he changed over the years? He'd not married again after Joan. Was he committed to bachelorhood? If so, considering their history and her own well-being, wouldn't it have been wiser to make an excuse about this evening, to make a date on a more conventional basis? Paul was not a man to mistake such a hint. But her feeling for him colored every other relationship, short-circuiting every other affection. It had become something more than love. It was a part of her body, a growth inside her that could neither be judged nor resisted. She'd been living with it as best she'd been able.

If there ever was a time to resolve the conflict once and for all, wasn't now the time? Otherwise, all she had to look forward to was a future of growing old. Alone.

So she believed, until he arrived. Then her apartment sparkled with welcome. Genie sparkled, too.

"You look wonderful," he said and meant it.

"Thank you." She had changed into a pair of body-molding velour pants and matching top. She had wanted to look her best.

"Better than I remember. If that's possible."

''Thank you again.'' She dismissed the topic. ''Let's have that drink.'' But he continued to stare at her. There are women who reach a certain time of life when the face is as beautiful as it ever will be, the body as graceful and vital. It had happened to Genie. ''Would you like the ten-cent tour first?''

''The works. And I'm prepared to pay.''

She showed him around her apartment, and he was properly impressed with everything—complimenting her on the ingenuity of her exercise room, her heated Jacuzzi, the originality with which she had utilized space, the tasteful, thoughtful design and decor. Then, holding their drinks, they sat, circumspectly, in the living room, both laboriously acquiring the rudiments of a new language. They were as shy and careful as courting children, groping toward each other through a fog of uncertainty. Each beat a devious circle around the outskirts of the desire that lay between them. Every word, every action, took it into account.

''How are the tryouts going?'' she asked, making conversation.

''Rough! We need a new director and a new star. My star, you remember Jackie Bates, is trying . . .''

Genie's instantaneous reacton was blind fury. ''Remember Jackie Bates? Goddamned right I remember Jackie Bates. No wonder it took you a month to call. Between directing her on stage and servicing her offstage, it's a miracle you had either the time or the energy to go to the bathroom. Let alone call me.''

Paul realized his offhand reference to Jackie Bates had been clumsy at best and possibly disastrous. He had to make amends for his blunder at once. ''Hold it, please! You don't understand.''

''I understand well enough. What are you doing here? Is this her night for girls? Or maybe German shepherds?''

''I told you at lunch I no longer fuck where I eat.''

''And I believed you. I must have been out of my mind. Jackie Bates! Shit! Go away, Paul. I have enough to think about without Jackie Bates.''

''Listen to me, Genie. Please?''

Genie calmed down long enough to look at Paul, at his troubled face and body leaning towards her. Either he was a better actor than any member of his cast, or . . . She wasn't sure.

"All right. I must still be out of my mind. I'll listen, but it better be good."

"I don't know how good it is. It happens to be the truth. Do you remember a movie star named Tyrone Power?"

"Vaguely. Why?"

"He was one of Hollywood's biggest stars, and he claimed he wasn't an actor at all. He explained that while he could give a director thirty seconds of any emotion the director called for, he couldn't sustain it. Since thirty seconds was about as long as a single take went, that was all a movie actor needed. But a real actor, a stage actor, has to sustain a role for an entire play. Not just thirty seconds or even thirty minutes."

"So what? I saw Jackie Bates on the stage. She was trained for the theater."

"That was years ago. It's been almost fourteen years since she's faced an audience, and for her to tackle Shaw's *Saint Joan* was a mistake. My mistake in encouraging her to try it, and hers for agreeing."

"What's gone wrong?"

"Almost everything. She's become used to making movies. She doesn't project. She can't sustain a scene. Nothing comes over the footlights. Once the excitement of seeing Jackie Bates in person has worn off—by the middle of the second act—the audience becomes restless. They cough, shuffle around in their seats, some even leave. Now Jackie's scared out of her mind that the Broadway critics will kill her. And it's getting worse, not better."

"What are you going to do?"

"I'm going to find a graceful way for her to bow out. She doesn't like my direction. The production is lousy. They need her for retakes on her last picture. Anything. It makes no difference. Her understudy is good, and she's going to get a big break. Who knows? If we're lucky, after opening night they'll pin a star on her door. If not, we close. That's why I've been in Boston for a month." He waited for Genie's reaction. When none was forthcoming, he risked asking, "Do you understand? I'm having enough trouble with Jackie Bates, female movie star, to consider Jackie Bates, female anything else. Even if I were interested. Which I'm not."

Paul's explanation made Genie feel like a bit of a jealous

fool. She mumbled, "Yes. And I thought real estate has problems."

"Everything and everybody has problems. You. Me. Theater. Real estate. Life is a problem." He half smiled. "And when you think about it, the alternative isn't so good either."

As she had in the past, Genie wanted to go to him. Instead she asked, "So you came here to escape for a night?"

He moved closer to her. "I came here because I couldn't stay away."

"I see. After Jackie Bates, suddenly I'm irresistible." Although she'd meant the words to come out with a touch of amusement, they sounded bitter and accusing. Even to her.

"Things take time. Time has passed. We change."

"Do we?" The color rose to her face. "Now I suppose you want to make love to me?"

"Isn't that why we're here?" Paul put his drink down, and breathing like a man who has run too far for too long, he took her hand and kissed it. Genie felt a shiver run through her body. "Isn't that why?" he repeated.

Genie was full of conflicting emotions—resentment at his having felt free to call her and assume she'd be available, and a yearning to be close to the man she loved. She leaned toward him. Then stopped. She removed her hand from his. "I don't think we should."

"Why shouldn't we? Why did you allow me to come?"

"I don't know. I wanted to see you, and . . ."

"Is that all? What about the way I feel about you? The way I thought you felt about me?"

"I feel everything you feel. That's the least of it."

"It's all that matters."

"That's what you used to say years ago."

Before he'd arrived, Paul had not decided on a set course of action. Except to make love to Genie. Now, as she drew back, his love for her, still so vital a part of him, made him reconsider whether or not she was right. He rose and took a turn around the room. "You don't want to make love?"

"I do. But I'm afraid."

"Of me?"

"Of you."

"How can you be afraid of me? Me, of all men?"

"How could I fail to be afraid of you? You, of all men? I'm

afraid of our past to begin with. And to end with. I don't want that again."

"Nothing is ever the same. Haven't you learned that? What was then is past."

"Is it?" They lapsed into a silence that was a kind of subterranean communication.

"Because it's me. That's why you won't make love," he said at last.

"Because it's you." Her voice wavered. "You mean too much to me."

"Or too little?"

At that she stood up and went to her study. When she returned, she was carrying a heavy, leather-bound, gold-tooled scrapbook. She sat down beside him. "Too little?" She gave a half-hysterical laugh. "I have something to show you."

"What is it?"

She opened the scrapbook on her lap and started leafing through it, showing him the newspaper and magazine clippings. A history of his life in the theater.

"My God!" he murmured, almost speaking to himself. "All those years? You cared enough to collect this?" He took the book from her, closed it, and placed it on the floor. "Then you've no reason to say no. Why are you crying? We didn't do anything that can't be undone."

She struggled against him. "I won't be your girl friend. Or sweetheart. Or whatever. I won't do that again."

"You can't be my 'or whatever.' I couldn't afford you."

He drew her close, pressing her supple body against his lean one. Kissing her throat, her wet cheeks, her ears. "Darling! Oh, my darling!" he whispered. Then his lips were on her lips. She continued to struggle, but her resistance grew feebler, and her every movement enabled him to increase the pressure of his hands, of his mouth. Genie felt the dizziness one experiences when standing before an abyss, powerless to control the desire rising within her.

They stumbled into the bedroom and stood near the bed without speaking. Paul passed his hands over the curves of her body, caressing them, remembering how fine the down on her skin was, how firm her breasts were, how full her buttocks, how slender yet strong her legs. Genie stood before him, dazed, while he undressed, tossed his clothes toward a chair and carried her to the bed. She moved her head in silent protest only to discover she was lying beside him, naked. She couldn't recall his undressing her. The way his caresses made her forget everything frightened her. His mouth was kissing every part of her body, her nipples, her belly, her knees, between her thighs. Her legs parted, and his exploring fingers probed her wetness, fondling, teasing, releasing her from fear. Everywhere he touched her, her skin responded by reaching out for him to make the contact firmer, closer, more intimate. With a moan of pleasure, she began to caress him. Now her lips and tongue worked together around the velvet tip of his penis. Sucking him, Genie became like one possessed. She could not get enough of the taste of his flesh.

Paul could stand it just so long, the exquisite torture of her mouth, but he wanted to come inside her. He raised her head from his sex and placed his hands under her behind. As he did, she arched her body against him to receive his thrust. He slipped into her, easily, smoothly, filling her completely. Touching every part of her. His pulse was racing as wildly as hers. The heat of their desire seemed to fuse them together. Her blood ran through his body. His nerves sent their special message to her brain. When a flash of ecstasy tore through Paul, it was as though Genie almost climaxed. When their orgasms came, they came as one person, each crying out in the joy of the other.

Later, lying side by side, holding only her hand, Paul talked about his life and hers. He struggled against his impulse to tell her what he knew she wanted to hear and his instinct that this was a moment for complete honesty. "I just can't say marry me, Genie. We've only begun again. Who are you now? Who am I? We have to start learning about each other all over again."

Genie knew what he said was true. "Then we'll have to risk it." At that moment nothing was as frightening as the possibility of losing Paul again.

"Risk it? Risk what?"

"Risk hurting each other. The way we did before." Genie's acceptance of her love for Paul forced her to see again the landscape of her life. She was in a new country. What surprised her was the sense of it belonging to her. Things might work out.

They had a chance. "I'm happy you called. Happy you're here tonight."

"Not half as happy as I am." The suddenness of his joy flushed through his skin.

"I feel almost safe with you."

Paul felt a warmth behind his eyes and in his throat. "You mean the way you used to feel with me?"

"Yes. That way." She hesitated. "Maybe I'll fly up to Boston to be with you this weekend."

Paul heard and understood. She did not say, I'll fly up to Boston to be with you this weekend. She asked him a question. Her real question was, do you want to see me this weekend? He was being challenged, and he rose to meet the challenge. He was as committed as she was.

"Could you? It would be like old times. You watching me rehearse my new actress during the day, and after the performance, we'll have the entire night for ourselves."

Genie caught her breath. It was true. He did want her. "It sounds lovely. I'll try to . . ." She broke off, dropping her eyes to revel in the sight of his naked body. "But it's lovely right now." She slid off the bed. "Come. Let's use the Jacuzzi."

Paul's eyes glowed. "You did say it was private?" She nodded. "What a wonderful place to make love."

Once the dam had been broken, the flood waters of desire flowed over Paul and Genie, and they made love to each other the entire night. As often as Paul fulfilled her most erotic fantasies, so often did Genie's passion for him renew itself, rising to an even greater degree of intensity. And no sooner had Paul spent himself satisfying her passion—a passion such as men read and dream of—than his body went on to demand its own special release. Once, when it seemed to Paul he must have drifted off for a moment, he woke to find Genie straddling him, half smiling, as though making love to him without being fully awake. Then there was a time when Genie dozed, only to dream such sensual dreams, she woke to find Paul's mouth between her legs—his eyes were closed—drinking the juices that poured from her body. Finally, exhausted, they slept.

Long before they were ready, it was six o'clock. Barely time for Paul to shower, dress and catch the early shuttle to Boston.

Since neither wished to separate a moment sooner than necessary, without saying a word, they stepped into Genie's large stall shower together. As they soaped and sponged each other, it was as though their night of love had never existed. The need to wash served as an excuse for further caresses, and each caress touched a nerve which somehow had been missed before.

Finally Genie whispered, "We must stop, my darling. Or I'll lock the doors and throw the key into the river. We'll stay here forever."

Paul smiled at the threat. "If we do, what will happen to my plays and your real estate business?"

"Who cares? Theater and real estate have survived for thousands of years without us. They'll continue to survive without us."

Paul roused himself. "Enough. I've got to get going."

While drying each other, they almost lost their way again. Again Paul broke the spell. "I don't even have time to shave. Give me a kiss and send me on my way."

"I suggest you get dressed first. Forgetting about the laws against running around the city of New York naked, it's too cold outside. I'll fix you a cup of coffee." She slipped on a robe and left.

As Paul dressed, he remembered bits and pieces of the night. The intensity with which they had made love frightened him. Genie was thirty-six. At thirty-six, she was at the peak of her sexual drive, a peak that could last for twenty or thirty years. At thirty-nine he was well past his prime and heading downhill. While it was possible for him to be a sexual athlete for a night, a week, or even a month, could he sustain it? Could he satisfy her over a lifetime? He didn't know, and the question bothered him. When they'd been young, her inexperience had given him an excuse to be unfaithful. Now that they were no longer that young, would any serious lessening of his sexuality give her an excuse to be unfaithful?

By the time he was dressed, Genie had a cup of coffee ready for him. "About the weekend, Paul," she asked, "where are you staying?"

"The Ritz-Carlton on Arlington Street. It's an easy walk from there to the Shubert Theater."

"Suppose I take the five-thirty shuttle Friday evening? Logan airport is close by. If you could meet me at the airport, we'd have time for a bite and could be at the theater by eight o'clock.''

"I'll have a seat, fourth row on the aisle, for you. You can tell me what you think of the production." The memory of other similar conversations between them rose, easing Paul's fears about the future. "I've always respected your sense of theater.''

"Only what I learned from you. Reserve a room for me as close to your room as possible.''

Paul was surprised. "Why another room? These days, even in Boston, who cares?''

Genie hesitated. Paul had misunderstood her. Of course she wasn't concerned about anything as foolish as how her spending the weekend with him might look. But making love to Paul last night had produced an explosion of sensuality beyond anything she'd ever experienced. She'd held nothing back, surrendering all of herself to satisfying their needs. Paul worked in the theater, and as Max had pointed out long ago, sex went with the territory. That frightened her. Suppose she couldn't keep up with his needs? What then? Also, it was one thing to spend a night making love. Or a weekend. It was quite another thing to live together without being married. Sharing a hotel room with Paul, without a room of her own to which to retreat, was too similar to living together. She cast about for an excuse which would satisfy him.

"It's not that. I'll be bringing an attaché case full of work with me. With my own room, I'll be able to get some work done Saturday and Sunday mornings without disturbing you.''

"Okay." Paul didn't accept her story about working while he slept for an instant. But separate rooms, even if they never used them, would set a pattern for the future. A pattern with which he agreed. Until he became as comfortable with this Genie Szabo as he had been with the young woman he knew at the Majestic and on 9th Street. Then there'd no longer be a question of separate rooms. His idea of a marriage did not call for separate rooms. "I'll make the reservation and meet you at Logan. Speaking of planes,'' he glanced at his watch. "Wow! Seven o'clock. I've got to get moving.''

Genie walked with him to the door. They were both exhausted by the physical and emotional demands they'd made upon each other, so their good-bye kiss was a hasty, perfunctory peck. Paul hurried down the hall. As he entered the elevator, Genie waved. Then she shut the door. Last night was extraordinary. But it was over, at least until Friday afternoon. Now she must return to the problems of ConVert-Co.

Thursday and Friday morning were like any other days. Time moved at its normal pace. Friday afternoon was another matter. Genie lost count of how many times she glanced at the weekend bag she'd packed that morning. By four o'clock, she gave up the pretense of doing any more work. Using the excuse that she wanted to beat the weekend traffic jam, she called Charlie and asked him to bring a car around to the front of the building. She packed her attaché case just in case she actually found time to do some work, told Max where he could reach her, and left the office. Although they failed to beat the traffic, Charlie weaved his way through the side streets of Queens and avoided the worst of the jams. As a result, they arrived at the special Eastern Airlines shuttle terminal in time for her to catch the last section of the 4:30 flight. She'd be early, but once at Logan, she'd have time to freshen up, relax, and wait for Paul. Sitting at Logan would be far more pleasant than standing in line at La Guardia to board the 5:30 plane.

The first thing Genie did at Logan Airport was dial the weather bureau. If one believed the report, they were in luck. The tape-recorded voice promised fair and unseasonably warm weather through Sunday. Boston was an old city, full of beautiful historic landmarks, restaurants, and special walks Paul and she could take. Odd, she thought, she'd been to Boston twenty or twenty-five times during the past years, occasionally for as long as a week, and all she'd ever seen was the inside of a limousine or a taxi during the ride from her hotel to meet a real estate broker, look at an apartment house, meet with lawyers, and sign contracts. Boston, historic Boston, cultural Boston, the Boston of Harvard and MIT, remained mostly unexplored territory to her. It occurred to Genie that possibly one could be too single-minded in the pursuit of one's goals, and it depressed her to think of how much she might have missed on the way.

"Hello, there." The familiar voice in her ear and the figure standing over her startled her. A breeze of warmth and light seemed to blow through the sterile airport. Paul stood with his hands buried in the pockets of his Burberry. "Have you been waiting long? I planned to be waiting for you."

"I caught an earlier plane. They run almost continuously, you know."

"I know. Still, I wish I'd been here first. Is that your bag?"

"Yes." Although it seemed to Genie that Paul was nervous, it was obvious her coming had made him happy. The two days they were to spend together represented more than just a weekend—it marked a crucial point in their relationship.

His face was comically grave. "I have what I hope will be a pleasant surprise for you." She remained sitting, looking up at him. "When I got to the theater Thursday morning, Jackie and I had a minor disagreement which, by mutual consent, we managed to blow up into a major fight. She screamed. I roared. She ranted. I raged. She laughed. I sulked. In the end, she stormed off the set, and I yelled good riddance. All in the best theatrical tradition."

"But what will you do? Is her understudy ready? Won't you have to spend all your free time working with her?"

"No. That's my surprise. Part of our understanding, Jackie's and mine, is that Jackie's sudden departure has been a terrible blow to me. So terrible I've had to close the show for a week while I work day and night to prepare her understudy, Rhoda Cantrel, for her big break."

Genie's eyes never left his face. He said he had a pleasant surprise. All she could see was a weekend of watching Paul rehearse an unprepared actress.

He sat down beside her and took hold of her hands. "You don't understand? You really don't?"

"No."

"Rhoda Cantrel is up on the part. If necessary, she could go on tonight. So . . ." Paul placed his hands on her face, and for an instant his eyes made love to her. "So I've given the cast the weekend off."

With a leap her heart was in her throat. "And we have the entire weekend to ourselves? No rehearsals? No performances? Just us?"

"Just us."

Genie sat motionless for a moment thinking of the gift of time Paul had found for them. Then she gave up thinking and accepted the gift.

* * *

After they arrived at the hotel and Genie checked in, Paul and she followed the bellhop to the elevators. Her room was in the older section of the hotel. It was delightful. The windows overlooked the Public Gardens and the Boston Common beyond. To her surprise, there was a wood fire burning in the large red-brick fireplace and fresh cut flowers along with a bowl of fruit on a table in the corner. The Ritz-Carlton lived up to its reputation for understated elegance and respect for the grand manner of an older tradition.

Once the bellhop left, Paul and Genie stood face to face, only their fingertips touching. Here, time was not pressing on them. It was one of those perfect moments when they were wide open, and only the slightest touch was needed to make them one.

Paul was the first to move. "You probably want to unpack and wash up. I have to make one short phone call to the theater. I'll be back in ten minutes." Left alone, Genie remained immobile, her body straight, her hands before her, fingertips extended. She had to shake herself before she was able to start unpacking. A knock on the door interrupted her. She opened it. There was no one there. When she looked up and down the wide corridor, she couldn't see anyone. The knock sounded again. Puzzled, she retreated into her room. Another knock. Finally she understood and ran to a connecting door between the fireplace and the window.

"Paul?"

"Unlock your door." She did and she was in his arms, kissing him—kissing his mouth, his nose, his eyes, her tongue tracing the outlines of his lips. Then she discovered he was trembling. Or was she the one who was trembling? Or they both were. He lifted her and carried her over the threshold into his room.

She whispered into his ear, "Adjoining rooms. A suite. How lovely."

"And practical." He was no longer trembling. After that the only sounds which could be heard were the rustle of clothes falling to the floor and moans of pleasure.

Later, much later, they showered and dressed for dinner. Paul had made a reservation in the main dining room of the hotel, one of the great gourmet restaurants in Boston. The restaurant was on the second floor of the hotel and overlooked the trees and dimly lit paths of the Boston Public Gardens. The soft light of the crystal chandeliers and the sound of an equally soft piano being played somewhere in a corner of the huge room gave Genie a sensuous glow, as she smiled the secret smile of a contented woman. Paul ordered what he assured her was the chef's pride, Maine lobster au whiskey. Later they shared an extra special dessert, a soufflé Grand Marnier for two. A brandy was followed by a moment of indecision.

"Your room or mine? Or both?"

It turned out to be Paul's room at night and hers in the morning.

For once the weather bureau hadn't promised more than nature was able to deliver. It was more like a special day in April than early March. Paul bought a tourist's guide to Boston. It turned out that, despite the many times he'd been to Boston and the fact that he'd gone to school at Harvard, like Genie, he'd never taken time from the tryouts and tours of his plays to see the Boston made famous in the history books. Genie selected the Freedom Trail as the one walk they must make. Sticking to tradition, they began the walk in Boston Common.

A wealth of golden sun poured a comforting warmth over them. Soon it was warm enough for Paul to carry his Burberry and Genie her beige cashmere coat. Their first stop was the New State House. It is typical of Boston that the New State House should have been started in 1795 and the cornerstone laid by Samuel Adams. The original dome, now covered with brilliant gold leaf, was copper, purchased from a well-known horseback rider and silversmith named Paul Revere. Paul and Genie held hands during the entire walk. It reminded Genie of how they used to wander through Greenwich Village, stopping to look at small shops and dining in out-of-the-way restaurants. In Boston they stopped to look at American history landmarks and dined in a restaurant on Bunker Hill mall.

When they left Paul Revere's house, with its leaded windows and large fireplace, filled with seventeenth-and eighteenth-century artifacts, they paused to look at the famous Old North Church. The afternoon sun spread its gold on the tall steeple. Paul pressed their palms together. Genie shivered slightly.

"Cold, my darling?"

"No. Not really." She gave him a long look and ran her tongue around her lips. "I can read your mind, you know."

"I was afraid of that. How will I keep any secrets from you?"

"I'll know they're secrets and won't pry."

"Very discreet. Can you read my mind now?"

They were conscious of the same need for each other at the same time. His hand tightened, and while the moment lasted, the suspended happiness in his face seemed waiting to brim over.

"Come. We'll go back to the Ritz."

"Yes! Yes!" She smiled.

It was inconceivable to Genie that they could maintain the passion of that first night, but as the hours of the day slipped away, every time she held Paul in her arms, it was deeper and more satisfying than before. For once, the words making love were appropriate.

On Sunday, Paul rented a car, and they drove across the Charles River and out along Massachusetts Avenue to Harvard Square. Paul showed her the irregular group of buildings which make up Harvard Yard. They walked along the straight narrow paths crisscrossing the yard, over which, every hour, several thousand students flitted from class to class. Their arms were tight around each other's waists. Paul showed her his room at Greys Hall, where he'd spent his freshman year, and the chapel where he'd graduated, and the Harvard Cooperative where he'd bought his clothes, and much more. Genie fell in love with the rectangular structures of old, dark red brick, a few dating back to the eighteenth century, with the sun yellow on their severe faces. To one born and bred in New York, they represented tradition, antiquity, stability—none of which she had ever associated with the Big Apple.

By Sunday afternoon, time, which had been their friend for the weekend, turned against them. They could no longer count on the mornings, afternoons, and nights. All that remained to them was what was left of the afternoon and the early evening. Genie had a ticket on the American Airlines 8:30 flight to New York.

Starting back to the hotel, they became different people. Genie felt a withdrawing in Paul, as though he were preparing for her departure. He drove slowly, pretending to be distracted. Genie watched him closely, and the silence became embarrassing. She could find no casual words to ease the moment.

Once in the hotel room, they quickly undressed. Paul took her with such ferocity that Genie knew he was as shaken by their coming separation as she was. She responded in kind. Somehow the very violence of their lovemaking made it less satisfying. It made her keenly aware that when she left, she would be leaving behind all the new recognitions, all the fresh and quickening hopes she had brought with her.

On the way to the airport, they had a brief conversation typical of lovers who are separating. Each needed reassurance from the other. Genie asked, "Are you glad I came?"

"You know I am."

"Will you miss me?"

Paul's voice was harsh. "As much as you'll miss me. Probably more."

Genie restrained herself from a debate as to who would miss the other more. She asked, "When would you like me to fly up again?"

"We'll be here for another three weeks. When would you like to come?"

Genie had expected a definite answer. Not a question for her question. The ease with which they'd been able to communicate all weekend had shifted into a polite formality. She didn't know how to answer him. She wanted to say, "Friday. Saturday. Next weekend." It made no difference as long as they set a definite date. Instead she asked herself, am I rushing him? What does he want? When does he want me? She had no answers. So she settled for a compromise. "As soon as I know what's going on in the office, I'll call you. Is that all right?"

On his side, Paul was equally disturbed. He'd expected her to say, I'll take the same flight as Friday, and he failed to understand why she didn't. Why should anything that happened in her office affect their weekend? He felt a need to protect himself in what was now a vulnerable position. "It will have to do. Won't it?"

When they reached the airport, their good-bye kiss was closer to a handshake. A quick touch and a separation. Then she hurried to board her plane.

Paul watched her disappear into the boarding platform.

They'd had their weekend, and now that it was over, he felt nothing had been resolved. He knew his fears of being unable to satisfy her were the foolish fancies of an insecure man. But why was he insecure? With Genie of all women? Long ago, there'd been something between them, and now that thing was gone. No matter how much he cared, it would never come back. But they'd found something else. Wasn't he just as pleased with what they had now? Yes, he was. Then why had he allowed her to get on that plane without making certain she'd be back next weekend? He loved her. The new Genie, the Genie he'd made love to all weekend, was the only Genie he could ask for. If she didn't call, he'd have to call her. Tomorrow.

During the flight back to New York, Genie closed her eyes to keep the tears from spilling over. She'd been to Boston, been with the man she loved, made love to the man she loved. And now she was returning to New York without knowing she'd see him again. Why had she been so indecisive? Was it because there had been no mention of marriage? It was too soon for that. One weekend was not enough for a marriage. Why did Paul make her indecisive? Was it because she loved him too much? She hoped he'd call, but if he didn't, she promised herself she would call him. She had to!

33

The morning had been taken up with meetings and phone calls confirming that certain events had taken place. After that there was a long meeting between the two men. Marcus Cato had taken all the time he needed to collect the available information, organize all his reasons, marshal all his arguments. He'd prepared everything necessary to convince T.E. of what must be done. Only when he was ready did he present his handwritten report and accompanying recommendations.

"Nasty business, Marcus Cato. Nasty business. Very much like her mother. What have you done to protect the family?"

Marcus Cato ticked off his answers. "One—the Mid-Nassau Supply Company was closed last week by the appropriate police force. But not before a robbery and fire destroyed all its records. A young man, a delivery boy, died in the fire. Two—several ladies have left for Paris. Bank accounts have been established in Switzerland for them. They understand that in the event they feel a need to return to this country in less than five years, they should resist the temptation. They will. As professionals, they value their good looks. Three—ConVert-Co has been served by the banks with the documents calling their loans and instituting other procedures. Four—Moore Investments has purchased a town house on East 63rd Street. Five—the maid who cleans the apartment on the second floor lost her set of keys when her pocketbook was stolen. Six—the occupant of the second-floor apartment has been placed on round-the-clock surveillance. I think that covers it."

"And Max Szabo?"

"Nothing. You've read my recommendation. The decision is yours."

"You actually believe he represents a threat?"

"He is an intelligent man. Sooner or later he will figure out why the banks are trying to take over his company."

"Assuming he does, what can he do?"

"Legally, very little. However, as my report states, he is a violent man. He will react violently."

"Against Moore Industries or Moore Investments?"

"No. Against you and me."

"And what about his sister, Eugenia Szabo?"

"That's another matter. Remember, I told you she bought several buildings from us, and I was impressed. I believe her brother has gone to great lengths to shield her from any knowledge of the information contained in my report."

"Understandable." T.E.'s face was hardly pleasant. "Though it is quite the reverse of his treatment of my daughter."

Thomas Edward Moore leaned back in his huge chair. He rested his elbows on its padded arms and clasped his hands together. "I accept both your report and your advice as to how we should proceed. And I appreciate and understand your efforts in behalf of—shall we say—my honor?" Marcus Cato's expression did not change. "However, you and I both know that Mr. Szabo does not represent a serious threat to either of us. What you have attempted to do is give me an honorable reason for taking certain actions. I thank you, but I want you to know I consider his misuse of my daughter—a member of the family— sufficient justification for me to act. I do not need any further reasons."

Marcus Cato had not expected T.E. to accept his explanation. The attempt was more important than its success. "Very well. On the assumption that you would agree with my suggestions, my car and drivers have been alerted. We leave for New York after lunch."

"When will you return?"

"Probably tomorrow. The day after at the latest."

"Keep me informed."

Marcus Cato shook his head. "No, T.E. In this case, part of my duty is to keep you uninformed. In fact," he held out his hand, "I would appreciate your returning to me the material you've just read. You know nothing about ConVert-Co, Max Szabo, or anyone else connected with this sordid affair."

T.E. handed Marcus Cato the papers. Before leaving for

New York, Marcus Cato ran everything through his private shredder.

When the maroon and black Rolls Royce started for New York, there were two drivers dressed in similar black uniforms and chauffeur's caps in the front seat. Marcus Cato was as cautious as ever. With one change, a change so startling as to cause anyone familiar with Marcus Cato to develop an intense curiosity as to the purpose of his trip. One of the drivers was a woman, though the sex of the second driver would not be apparent to a casual observer. The woman's dark hair was cut very short. She wore no makeup, and there was nothing of what is usually considered to be feminine in her heavy square jaw, thin lips, suggestion of a mustache, thick eyebrows, and wide forehead. Her coat did little to disguise the breadth and power of her shoulders as well as the strength of her arms. Nevertheless, she was a woman.

The Rolls Royce came to a stop in a vacant space on East 63rd Street. A man approached the car and rapped on the window. The door was opened, and he slid onto the seat beside Marcus Cato. He spoke quickly in low tones.

"The subject left her apartment in the company of a man at seven-thirty. They went to a restaurant. She returned thirty minutes ago, at eleven o'clock. The man did not enter the building."

"Then she's alone?"

"Yes." He handed Marcus Cato a key ring with three keys attached to it. "That large key opens the front door. There are two locks on the apartment door. The key with the white tape is for the upper lock. It's a dead bolt. Use that first. The last key opens the door."

"Thank you. You and your associates may consider this assignment ended. You are expected back at your usual posts Monday morning." The man opened the car door, got out, and walked down the street toward Park Avenue. Marcus Cato used the speaker tube. "Nurse Everitt, do you have everything you need?" The woman in the chauffeur's uniform raised a black bag so it could easily be seen. "Fine. I suggest we get on with our assignment."

Within minutes they were standing in front of a door to the apartment on the second floor of the town house. Marcus Cato listened for sounds. There were none. He had no difficulty selecting the proper keys to open the door. Although the apartment was unlit, there was enough light from the street lamp coming through the windows to make it easy to avoid stumbling over furniture. Another of Marcus Cato's young men had supplied him with a floor plan of the apartment. He knew exactly where to look for her. She was either in the library or the bedroom. He saw a sliver of light coming from under the door leading to the library. Motioning the nurse to follow him, they moved soundlessly across the room. Gently he opened the door to the library.

Stacey had her back to the door. She'd changed from street clothes to a robe, one sleeve of which was rolled up. A syringe had been inserted in her arm, and she was concentrating on injecting the contents of the syringe into a vein. She was so preoccupied, she was unaware of anything else. Marcus Cato seized the nurse's arm to prevent her from interrupting. He waited until Stacey had removed the needle, dropped it into a drawer in her desk, untied the rubber hose from her arm, and placed a small Band-Aid over the puncture. Only after she'd rolled down the sleeve of her robe did he say, "Well done, Stacey. Bravo! An excellent example of how to mainline cocaine."

Stacey spun around. The sight of two people in her apartment would have shocked her had she not immediately recognized Marcus Cato, her father's aide. He could show up anywhere. He must have news from T.E. "You are right, Mr. Telemann. I've become quite adept at the process. I won't ask you how you managed to get in here, because I don't care. But I do hope you've come with a message from my beloved father. For his girl."

"I have several messages."

"Forgive my lack of manners. Won't you and your . . . ? How do you refer to it? Is it a he or a she? Anyway, won't you and your friend sit down? Would you care for a drink?"

"No, thank you."

"And you. You are a woman, aren't you?"

"Yes."

"A woman with a baritone voice. Confusing. I know several clubs where you'd be a sensation. Would you like a drink?"

"No."

"Stacey would. Brandy does wonderful things to cocaine."

She poured herself a generous amount. "Now, messenger boy, tell Stacey your news."

"I assume you will be pleased to learn that the banks have moved in on ConVert-Co. Soon they will be out of business."

Stacey snapped the fingers of her free hand. She downed some of the brandy and did a staggering dance about the room. "Ta-daaa! Good for old T.E. He came through."

"He always does."

"You're sure you won't join me in a drink? This calls for a celebration."

"It strikes me you're celebrating enough for both of us. And I think you should listen to the remainder of my message."

"There's more? Tell! Please tell!"

"You return to Pittsburgh with me. Tonight."

"Pittsburgh! Oh no, I'm not!" Stacey stopped dancing. "I'm not returning to Pittsburgh tonight. Or maybe never!"

"Never starts now."

"No!" A hint of fright crept into her voice. "I won't go."

"Yes, Stacey. You will."

"I will not." Her old terrors were stalking her, dissolving what little courage she had. "You get the hell out of here, you son of a bitch. I'm Stacey Moore."

Marcus Cato was prepared to be reasonable. Up to a point. "The family cannot permit you to indulge yourself any longer."

"You can tell T.E. to take the family and shove it up you know where until it hurts."

"Unpleasant language, Stacey. For the last time, you need help. The family has a place where they will make you well."

The world came crashing down on Stacey. A place where they will make you well. Those were the words she'd heard him say twenty years ago when he had her mother taken away. "The way they made my mother well? So well she killed herself?"

"That was her choice. No one forced her to drink. And no one forced you to take drugs." For an instant he showed his utter contempt. "And no one forced you to become a prostitute for Max Szabo."

"He told you. The bastard told you. Does T.E. know?"

"I have never spoken to Mr. Szabo. I didn't have to. As for T.E., he knows."

Stacey stopped her frantic pacing around the room. "Who told him?" Her voice was a whisper.

"Did you think he wouldn't check on you?"

"He said he wouldn't."

"And you believed him?"

"I'm his daughter." She was speaking more to herself than to Marcus Cato. "He's my father. He promised me, and I believed him."

"He's more than your father. He's the head of the family. You've become what the new slang calls a loose cannonball. You cannot be allowed to roll around wrecking whatever you happen to bang into, endangering the family."

Stacey collapsed on the couch. The brandy glass dropped from her fingers, spilling what was left of its contents over her and onto the floor. She began to cry, wildly, helplessly. Under the choked sounds of her sobbing, Marcus Cato heard her repeat again and again, "I won't go. I'll die. I won't go. I'll die."

"Nurse Everitt. Give her something to tranquilize her. And get her dressed. We've wasted enough time. I want to leave here in twenty minutes."

"Yes, sir."

Fifteen minutes later, three figures emerged from the town house. The one in the middle was being supported by the one on the left. They crossed the street to the parked car. The waiting chauffeur jumped out and opened the rear door. The figure in the middle was lifted up and deposited in the rear seat. As soon as everyone was in their proper places, the car pulled away from the curb and headed west.

Marcus Cato glanced at Stacey slumped against the corner of the seat. Using the speaker tube, he asked, "Nurse Everitt, how long will she remain like this?" Two hands with ten fingers appeared followed by one hand with two fingers. "I assume you mean twelve hours?" The nurse nodded. "Excellent. That gives us more than enough time to return to Pittsburgh and place her in Pine Manor." He yawned. "This has been a full day. I'm going to take a short nap. Wake me in two hours."

Max and Genie were having what amounted to a council of war, and for some minutes Max had been silent.

"What are you thinking?" Genie asked.

"I'm thinking you must be right. I can't come up with any other explanation. Gordon's a scared rabbit. And he's probably scared shitless of the bank examiners. As you say, he's using the *Forbes* article as an out."

"I can't think of any other reason for calling our loans."

"Neither can I, and I've sure tried. Lending us seven-point-five mil one week and calling all the loans six weeks later makes no sense. Doesn't he realize we'll fight?"

"You mean file for a Chapter 11 bankruptcy?"

"Yeah."

Genie shrugged her shoulders. She was relieved Max had accepted her reasoning. Because she herself didn't. Not for a moment. She was convinced something was going on offstage, and she had a nasty hunch as to what it was. It made her thankful Max wasn't much of a magazine reader. He'd missed last week's issue of *Fortune*. They ran an article on Moore Investments. It said they were strengthening their holdings in New York banks. Moore Investments reminded Genie of Stacey Moore. Max had given the girl a rough time. When the notices had arrived from the banks, Genie wasn't all that surprised.

"I've gone over the books and developed a projected cash flow. We're losing money right now at the rate of about a million a month. Mostly interest payments."

"Does that include the Boston building?"

"It does."

"Elliott signed yesterday." Satisfaction momentarily erased Max's concern.

"Off the record, big brother, what convinced him? The truth, please?"

"I grabbed his balls and squeezed."

"What does that mean?"

Max exhaled through pursed lips. The air made a sound like a breathy whistle. "I found the right button to push, and pushed. Hard! Title should pass to the co-op in about two weeks."

"You don't want to tell me what you did?" Max shook his head. "All right, but this is the last time. I know that article was short on facts and long on hints. If I have to, I can do a lot better research job on you than those reporters did."

"Let it go, kidlet. Don't look under rocks."

"I won't. Under one condition. From now on we work on the selling end together."

"Whatever you want."

"So in two weeks we pay off the Boston loan. That drops our cash drain to about seven hundred and fifty thousand a month. Have our original projected sales prices held up?"

"We did better. Over twenty-seven thousand per room."

"That'll give us close to fifteen million more in the war chest. Here's the plan, Max. We drop the lease on the plane and close all the offices except the one here in New York. We'll sell Chicago out of the super's office. How's that going, by the way?"

"Surprisingly well. Chicago likes condos."

"About when do you think you'll wrap it up?"

"Three months at the outside."

"Another hundred thousand a month off the drain. By cutting to the bone—selling this apartment, the cars, everything—we can come close to breaking even. I spent time with Jack O'Neil. He thinks he can raise the rents on the buildings we'll still own by an average of seven-and-a-half percent this year. We'll get through the knothole."

"What's the drill with Herb?"

"Mark Bernstein files for a temporary restraining order. Then a permanent injunction. If he gets it, fine. If not, as you said, we file for Chapter 11. An orderly liquidation of our assets will pay off the banks and leave us in good shape. We'll get it." Genie tried to sound confident. She knew bankruptcies of the size she was considering were tricky things, and there was no telling how much pressure the Moore family could put on a particular judge. "What we have to avoid is a Chapter 10. If Herb and the boys take over, they'll sell everything dirt cheap, pay themselves off, and wipe us out."

"Maybe I can push Chicago?"

"We, Max. Remember. Maybe we can push Chicago."

"Okay, we." Max leaned back, studied the ceiling for a short while and said, "I'm sorry, kidlet. I still feel there's a missing link. The whole thing makes no sense. Even for a dumb, frightened vice-president. It's bananas." His anger rose. "If I could get my hands on him, I'd shake the truth out of him soon enough."

"Stay away from Herb, Max. As soon as we get the restraining order, you go to Chicago or Boston. Wherever you're needed most.''

''I will. Don't worry. I wouldn't touch what's left of a hair on his head. But you can't blame me for wanting to.'' He stretched. ''I am beat. It's home and bed for me tonight. I'll see you in the office tomorrow.''

''Want me to call you a cab?''

''No. It's only a few blocks. Maybe the fresh air will do me some good.''

''Tomorrow, nine-thirty, big brother.'' She kissed him lightly on the cheek.

''Tomorrow, kidlet.''

Max walked slowly up Sutton Place and west on 56th Street. He was completely preoccupied. Why was this happening to them? He kept searching for the missing link his sixth sense told him was there. For a moment his thoughts turned to Genie. There was one thing he did know. No matter what he'd promised her about their working together on sales, it wasn't going to happen. That damned article had done it. Obviously, she suspected something, but there was a gap between suspecting and knowing. He'd spent the last four years—ever since inflation had sent the cost of apartments out of sight—shielding Genie from what went on in sales. Trying as best he was able to make money for them and, at the same time, protect her and her dream. Her dream? Max's laugh of disgust was almost soundless. For all her knowledge of real estate, her numbers sense, she'd been blinded by what she wanted to believe. Her dream was dead. They were no longer selling middle-income apartments to people who wanted to buy the apartments for the security that owning an apartment could bring. They were jamming high-priced apartments down the throats of families who couldn't afford them and didn't want to buy them. It had become a dirty, rough business. What possible help could Genie be? Take Stacey's place? Over his dead body.

Stacey Moore? At first he'd thought she was just another broad. Then, when he found out she was a Moore, of the Moore family, and whoring for him, it had been good for a laugh. Christ! She must be pissed at him. Max stopped dead in his tracks. Stacey Moore! The Moore family! Shit! How the fuck could he have missed it? Stacey was so mad at Genie and him, she must have gone to her family. The Moore family could make the goddamn banks jump through hoops. That was the missing link. He'd have to call Genie as soon as he got home and tell her.

As he neared his apartment, a shadow detached itself from the wall. A voice called out. "Max? Max Szabo?"

Hearing his name, Max turned and looked around. He saw what appeared to be a man dressed in a dark coat. "Yes. Who is it?"

At that moment a car turned east on 56th Street. Its headlights shone briefly on Max and the man. Just enough time for Max to spot the gun in the man's hand. His reflexes took over. As he flung himself backwards and away from the danger, the gun went off. The first bullet hit Max in his left shoulder just below the collar bone. A second bullet glanced off his ribs. Blood spread over his shirt. Max's instantaneous reaction carried him behind a huge concrete tub containing a tree. For the moment the tub protected him. He heard the squeak of rubber-soled shoes coming closer.

Max got to his knees, more aware of his rage than the bullets in his body. Stacey Moore! That drunken, drugged bitch! Ruining their company wasn't enough for her. She hated him so much she wanted him dead. Max began to shake. She hated Genie just as much. That thing coming for him was going to kill Genie next. For the last time in Max Szabo's life, the deep violence in his nature, bequeathed to him by some unknown Magyar ancestor, exploded. All reason, all need to protect himself, evaporated. Instead of crawling away from the shadowy figure, he rose to his feet and moved to meet it. He was focused on only one thing. Stacey Moore had hired a man to kill Genie. Kill his kidlet. He had to save her. As he lurched forward, the man fired again. Max felt the bullet tear into him. Then another. And another. Three bullets hit him before his massive frame reached the killer and dragged him to the sidewalk. A shroud of darkness descended over Max. He could no longer hear nor see, his senses filmed over by hate and death. Even so, his hands closed around the man's neck. What remained of his great strength was concentrated on one last effort of his fingers. Max never heard the sound of the man's neck snapping. Or his gurgle of agony at dying. Moments later Max was dead.

* * *

The ring of her telephone woke Genie. It was 3:30 in the morning. Who knew her unlisted number and was damn fool enough to call at 3:30? "Hello?"

A man with a thick New York accent answered. "Is this . . ." He stumbled over her name. "Eugenia Szabo?"

"Yes. Who is this?"

"Sergeant Brown. New York Police. I'm sorry to call at this hour, but . . ."

"That's all right, Sergeant." Genie sat up. "What is it?"

"Miss Szabo, there's been a death. We need a positive identification."

"My mother? No!"

"No, Miss Szabo. Not your mother."

"Who, Sergeant?"

No matter how often Sergeant Timothy Brown made calls of this type, it remained the side of being a cop he most disliked. There was no way to soften his words, no way to make it easier on the other person. So he did his duty as quickly and simply as possible. "Your brother, Max Szabo."

If Genie had been standing, she would have slipped to the floor. She made noises, audible gasps. "Max dead? N-o-o-o-o!"

Sergeant Brown heard the indescribable sounds. Then silence. "Miss Szabo? Hello?"

"Yes. Yes, Sergeant. I'm here."

"Could you come to Bellevue Hospital and identify him?"

"Yes."

"I'll have a police car waiting for you in front of your building."

"Thank you, Sergeant. I'll be downstairs in ten minutes."

When Genie hung up, she began to shake so violently she had to sit on the bed, her legs locked together, and hold herself. Her head was hunched down into her rounded shoulders, her body rocking back and forth as though praying to an unlistening God.

It took some time for her to regain some control of herself, to be able to stand up and dress.

The car was waiting for her. A black Chevrolet without the usual police markings. Although the driver wore a uniform, the man standing next to the car did not.

"Miss Szabo? I'm Sergeant Brown."

"How did he die, Sergeant?"

The officer had been expecting the question. But it was asked in such a matter-of-fact tone, it took a professional to understand the inherent fear in the question. Sergeant Brown was a professional. He knew that the image of a beloved dying a tortured death was as agonizing as the fact of the death itself.

"Mr. Szabo was shot, and he died quickly. With minimum pain. We don't know why he was shot. At the moment, it looks like a mugging. We'll know more after we check out the assailant's identification."

On the way to Bellevue, Sergeant Brown told her all they knew of what had happened. There had been a witness, the doorman of Max's building. He finished with, "We don't understand why, after he'd been shot, he didn't stay behind the concrete tub. And how, with five bullets in him, he was able to reach the man and kill him."

Genie could not shut out the agonizing picture of Max walking directly into a hail of bullets. She felt herself drowning in waves of horror. Why? Why?

As long as she lived, Genie knew she would never forget the gleaming white tiles, the bare grey concrete steps, and the floor with a dark red line painted down the middle, the brown double doors, and the lit white sign with red letters over the doors. Morgue. The row of slabs, which slid into the wall, looked like large built-in file cabinets. And finally the smell of death.

"Pull out number five, Sam."

"Sure, Sergeant."

The sound of rubber wheels on runners. A body covered with a white sheet.

"Just his face, Sam." The attendant pulled back the sheet. "Is that Max Szabo?"

Genie looked at the face, It was her brother. His face was as handsome, unmarred in death, as it had been in life. She reached out to touch his face. A hand caught her wrist. "Don't, Miss Szabo. Don't touch him."

Genie allowed her arm to be returned to her side.

"Would you mind looking at the other man please? Maybe you can help us?" Genie nodded. "Pull out number seven, Sam." The slab next to Max rolled out. The identical sound of rubber wheels on runners.

"Do you know him?"

Genie could barely look at the man. "No."

"Are you sure?"

"I don't know the man."

The morgue attendant covered the killer's contorted face and pushed both slabs back into the wall.

"Let's go, Miss Szabo. I'm going to need whatever additional information you can give me."

When Genie finished, Sergeant Brown promised Max's body would be released as quickly as possible. Because he'd been murdered and killed his murderer, an autopsy was required. Genie should allow three days. Then the police drove her home.

Genie waited until 8:30 before making the necessary calls. She phoned her mother first, but didn't ask to speak to Anna. "Mrs. Sagi, please tell my mother Max is dead. She'll be notified as to when the services and funeral will take place. A car will be in front of your building to drive her to the church and cemetery, should she wish to come." Then she called St. Elizabeth of Hungary Church and made all the necessary arrangements for the funeral. Max would be buried next to their father. She called her office. "Helen, I won't be in for a while . . . I don't know how long . . . No. Max won't be in either." Genie's stomach trembled. Helen could hear her rapid, shallow breathing, and she waited, suddenly frightened. Finally Genie explained. Her words were choked. "He's dead." She ignored Helen's reaction. She had to or she'd have been unable to continue. "I'll arrange with Mr. O'Neil to take over the running of the office." Her final call was to Jack O'Neil. She told Jack what Max and she had planned to do about the business. Jack agreed to take care of everything. She turned aside his pleas to see her and help her. Then she shut off all the phones. This was the second time she'd known intense grief through the death of someone she loved. And this was far worse than her father. Max wasn't there to share it with her.

The funeral services for Max were short and strictly private. Just before the service began, a figure with her white hair pulled back and tied in a bun slipped into the pew and sat next to Genie. Anna Szabo had agreed to attend the funeral of her only son.

Genie and her mother rode in the same car to the cemetery in northern Westchester. The day was clear, sunny, and windy, with puffs of white fleece dashing across a brilliant blue sky. The two women, mother and daughter, dressed similarly, stood silently as the heavy mahogany coffin containing the body of Max Szabo was lowered into its grave. They neither looked at nor said a word to each other. Genie's eyes were half closed. It was dark under the stark sun and difficult to see. As she stood before the grave, she felt standing beside her, closer than anything she saw, her tall, young, blond brother. His face was full of high spirits, his hand holding hers, the sleeves of his sweater tied around his neck as they had been when Max and she walked home from the baseball field in Central Park on a late summer afternoon.

The grave diggers shovelled the rich dirt over the coffin. Genie wanted to tell them it was a mistake. Max was back in the office. On the telephone. None of this was real. It wasn't! But it was real, and she knew it. Max was gone. It was no longer Szabo and Szabo against the world. There was only Genie.

34

The murder of a prominent businessman and his killing of his assailant was reported in detail by the New York papers as well as local and network radio and television. For forty-eight hours interest ran high. But when the FBI confirmed the identification found on the man's body, and Billy Jack Dupre turned out to be a small-time hoodlum from New Orleans with a long record for committing violent street crimes, interest faded. Max Szabo's death was labeled as one of those things, a fact of big city life. While Sergeant Brown may have asked himself why Max Szabo hadn't remained in a safe place—why he had attacked a man holding a gun—he knew his questions would never be answered. Both men were dead. With nothing more to go on, the case was closed. Unexpectedly closed for Marcus Cato. With an efficiency he liked. As a result he was able to cancel the part of his instructions which had called for Billy Jack to meet with a sudden and fatal accident shortly after his return to New Orleans.

Genie Szabo had ceased to read the newspapers, listen to the radio, or watch television. She wanted to be alone with her pain. Time passed in a kind of hypnotic despair. Genie would lie in bed, motionless, watching the dawn sky grow lighter. Waiting for the beginning of a new, endless, empty day. Thinking was hard. Everything was hard. Some days she was unable to make herself get out of bed and dress. She constantly relived every second of their last evening together. It had seemed no different than a hundred other such evenings. Now she could recall every moment, every detail.

The messages piled up. Paul called again and again. He flew in from Boston several times only to be stopped by the doorman.

"Miss Szabo has left instructions she's seeing no one."

Paul could have forced his way in, but he stopped himself. Genie did not want to see him. That was clear. And he was not her husband. At best he might be considered a once and possibly future lover. As a lover, his rights ended at her closed door. The only thing left for him was to keep on calling, visiting, waiting, hoping.

Her lawyer, Mark Bernstein, called, sent letters, telegrams, documents. Document after document. He'd obtained a temporary restraining order, and he needed her cooperation, her signature, before he could go further. His calls went unanswered. Documents sent for Genie's signature remained unsigned. Herbert Gordon's lawyers were pressing for a dismissal of the restraining order. It was only a matter of time before the judge's patience would be exhausted. "Yes, Counselor, I sympathize with your client's grief. Still, she can sign her name and make one court appearance. Otherwise, I have no choice but to vacate the restraining order."

Jack O'Neil sent many reports covering his success in selling the apartments in Boston and Chicago. Title to both buildings had been transferred to the tenants, and the money to pay back the loans connected with the purchase of the buildings by ConVert-Co set aside. Everything Genie had asked him to do, he'd done. The company was down to a skeleton staff. "Fight the banks, Genie. Fight, and the company might survive."

But Genie would not fight. She would not sign her name. She would not appear in court. She would not see Paul. She continued to do nothing. Her former charged readiness for whatever might happen—the readiness which had been her stance, her way of life—now struck her as pointless. Of what use was it, of what use had it ever been, if it had brought her to this moment, face to face with an empty doorway? Listening for a voice she would never hear again. Looking for a face she would never see again. The past was more real to her than the present, and her deepest fear was she would lose it forever. So she recreated every physical detail of Max, feature by feature, skin, bone, and muscle, until she practically willed him to stand before her. It was a magical rite. It was also futile, wasted. It only intensified the pain which, like some dumb animal, she accepted would be with her for the rest of her life. A light had failed, and there was nothing she could do about it. Genie had come to the end of her romance about her family. All the bold sweeping plans for the rise of the Szabos slept quietly in the grave with her brother.

The weeks passed and became a month. And the month two months. She ate little, slept less, and wandered through the apartment, hopelessly lost. As time passed, she grew thin. Although she was unaware of it, grief added a deeper dimension to her beauty. Her face had a look of resigned calm. Genie had looked beyond the rainbow and found many things there besides the pot of gold. Almost three months to the day after Max's death, Genie's solitude was broken. When Nina answered the ring of the front doorbell, a man handed her an official document. This wasn't unusual, and Nina was ready to sign for it.

"Sorry, I need Miss Szabo's signature."

"Impossible. Madam sees no one."

The man was sympathetic. "Look. I have a court order. A warrant, signed by Judge Carlson, directing me to enter this apartment, if necessary, and serve Miss Szabo personally."

"Madam sees no one."

"I have a warrant. She has to see me." Without meaning to, the man had raised his voice.

Genie heard the noise and appeared at the door, intending to put an end to the intrusion. "What's going on?"

"Miss Szabo, I'm a New York City marshal, and I've been ordered to serve this paper on you."

"Serve it." Genie accepted the paper.

"Sign here, please." Genie signed and turned away. "Miss Szabo!" The marshal was insistent. "I'm going beyond my authority, and I know it. But I want to ask you a favor. Strictly off the record."

"What favor?"

"Read the paper you just signed for."

The situation had become unexpectedly awkward for Genie. Here was a stranger intruding in her life. She had an automatic impulse to insist he leave immediately. Instead, something in the man's face made her ask, "Why?"

"For your own sake. It's my way of paying you back for what you did for me and my family."

"What did I do for you?"

"I'm sure you don't remember us. My name is Hammond.

Years ago, my wife and I, we bought our apartment in Queens from Max Szabo. It was one of the best things we ever did."

"Oh?"

"Now I want to do something for you." Genie was too upset to speak. "Please read the paper. I told Judge Carlson I sort of know you which was why he had me deliver it. If you don't read the paper and talk to your lawyers, there's nothing going to stop your bankers from putting you out of business. I know your brother's dead. But you're not. So maybe you ought to read the paper. Don't you think Mr. Szabo would want you to?"

Genie stiffened. He'd reminded her there were things at stake other than her right to grieve. He was right. Max would have wanted her to read the paper. "I'll do the best I can, and whatever happens, thank you for trying."

She carried the document into her study and dropped it on her desk, unopened. For the first time since Max's death, she realized she had to make a choice. As long as she didn't know what she'd signed for, she could avoid the necessity of doing anything. But if she read the paper, the reading in itself was an acknowledgement that she must reenter the world. Genie sat for several minutes thinking. Seeking guidance. What should she do? She could almost hear Max's words that last evening, "Doesn't he realize we'll fight?" Her hand slid across the desk, picked up the paper and read it. It was a notice of a meeting of the board of directors of ConVert-Co, authorized by Judge Carlson, to be held in seven days. What directors of ConVert-Co? Max and she had been the only active directors of the company. While Helen Bradley was technically a director, it was only because the bylaws of the corporation called for not less than three nor more than seven directors. With Max dead, who besides Helen and herself were board members?

Genie dialed her lawyer. "Mark Bernstein, please."

"Who may I say is calling?"

"Eugenia Szabo."

"One moment, please. I'll get him immediately."

Genie waited. "Immediately" turned out to be several minutes. Then Mark was on the line. "Genie!" There was no mistaking the relief in his voice. He laughed. "Cora got so excited she ran into the men's room to find me. Burns, Matson and Clark will never be quite the same."

"What's this about a board meeting? Who's going to appear?"

Mark Bernstein was usually an excitable man, but this time he made himself talk slowly. "I gather you have not read the many notices I sent you?"

"No. Give it to me simple."

"The morality and criminal action clauses in your loan agreements with the banks give them the right to take control of the board."

"There's been no immoral or criminal action by the company. You got a temporary restraining order to stop them."

"I did. But to make it permanent, you had to testify as to the truth of their claims."

"Which I didn't do."

"Which you didn't do. So the judge dismissed the temporary restraining order."

"The banks now control the board?"

"Not quite. Not if you'll attend the meeting and fight. You are still chief executive officer of ConVert-Co. Remember the way we set up the corporation? Under the bylaws, they cannot fire you until the next official election. That's June thirtieth. They can vote anything they damn please at the meeting. As CEO, you can execute their orders as you see fit. It's a form of veto power."

"Until June thirtieth. Then they can vote me out."

"Only if we let them." Genie could almost see the grin on Mark's face. "Before June thirtieth I get our temporary restraining order reinstated which puts an end to their right to act as directors. Then I make a motion for a permanent restraining order. With you in there swinging, they have to go before the judge and give evidence to support their right to invoke the morality and criminal action clauses."

"They can't prove a thing."

"Agreed. That article in *Forbes* is not proof. What beats me is why Gordon is kicking up such a storm. Why do he and his friendly army ants want to swarm all over ConVert-Co and devour it? Their interest is current. Hell, they're doing a lot better with ConVert-Co than with Brazil and Mexico. Why the ruckus?"

"You're a very fine corporate lawyer, Mark. Don't get out of your depth. There are things in this world you wouldn't understand. Or want to believe. They make a mockery of the law."

Mark Bernstein listened and accepted that here was a situation he couldn't resolve and mustn't pursue. "Consider the matter dropped."

"Done. What shape are we in to fight?"

"Needless to say you haven't read Jack O'Neil's reports either?" Genie didn't answer. "Of course not. There's close to thirty million in the treasury from the Chicago and Boston deals alone. That's right. Jack closed both of them. The army ants want to grab that cash right away."

"You think we can beat them?"

"Now that you're back in the game, we have a fighting chance. Er, you are back, aren't you?"

Genie glanced at the notice. The meeting was set for two o'clock next Wednesday in the offices of ConVert-Co. For the purpose of "determining the best means of disposing of the assets of the corporation to enable it to meet its liabilities, and any other business which may come before the board." Nice! "I'll go over your papers this week. We can meet at your office Wednesday morning at nine, make our plans, have lunch, and go to war."

"Whoopee! Wednesday at nine."

Genie spent the week catching up on her mail and phone messages. She felt like someone who'd been awakened after a long sleep. It seemed years since she'd thought about and dealt with concrete problems. There were messages from Mark. Jack O'Neil. Countless other people. There were also messages and notes from Paul. It was difficult to think about Paul. She wanted to tear up every communication from him as fast as she could. And she wanted to call him immediately. She didn't know what to do about Paul. Until she made up her mind, it was best to do nothing. For the moment, it was first things first. She had a battle with the banks ahead of her, and until she'd settled with them, she didn't dare think about Paul.

Genie arrived at the twentieth floor of 280 Park Avenue, the offices of Burns, Matson and Clark, at 8:45. She knew her lawyer. Mark Bernstein lived on the south shore of Long Island, always caught the 6:15 train and was in his office by 7:20. He was a man in his early forties, average height with small bones, curly hair which he was rapidly losing, the beginnings of a pot belly which mildly concerned him, and a ferocious appetite for work and an equally ferocious drive for success. He was a heavy drinker and smoked at least three packs of cigarettes a day. In spite of all this, his annual checkups showed no warning signs of disintegrating health. Genie concluded long ago that the reason was he seldom kept anything bottled up inside. His emotions were highly contagious. When Mark was angry, everyone ducked. When he was excited, everyone was excited. The fact that, at forty, he was a full partner and on the management committee of such a prestigious firm as Burns, Matson and Clark testified to his success.

Mark hurried out to greet her, and they spent the morning going over their plans. Mark explained, "Our big edge is you're still chairman of the board and chief executive officer. I think their idea is, as board members, to vote in new officers under the other business clause of the notice. I've refused them access to the bylaws of the corporation until after the meeting. It's possible they aren't aware of the unusual election rules of ConVert-Co. If they try that stunt, you simply state they can't vote in new officers until June thirtieth as stated in the corporate bylaws. Elections only happen once a year. I'll have a copy of the bylaws with me, and I'll back you up."

"Max and I never elected each other."

"Yes, you did. All neat and proper. The minutes of the corporation, as prepared through the years by yours truly, show that every June thirtieth you reelected each other."

"Did we now? Thank you." Genie stared out the window across Park Avenue to 299 Park. "So if I hadn't showed up today, our friends would have appointed one of themselves to supervise the sale of our buildings, and it would have been all over." Genie grimaced. "Where have they scheduled the actual meeting to take place?"

Mark hesitated, then blurted out, "Max's office. It's the only office with a large enough table."

A look of apprehension passed over Genie's face. "Okay. Let's grab that early lunch. I want to get there in time to have a look around by myself."

* * *

Mark and Genie arrived at the offices of ConVert-Co at 1:30. The office was not as Genie remembered. Once there had been fresh flowers on the reception desk, and the receptionist's phone rang constantly. Now the place gave off a curious, lifeless aura. It looked like the reception room of a dying company. Old magazines scattered about. A receptionist she didn't recognize. Nobody running from one end of the offices to the other. Phones that didn't ring. They could have been disconnected.

"May I help you?" the receptionist asked.

"Where's Frances Henderson?" Frances had been hired by Genie.

"I don't know. Who are you?"

"Eugenia Szabo. You work for me. Who hired you?"

"I work for Mr. Gordon. I'm here on temporary assignment from the bank."

"Where's Helen Bradley?"

"I don't know."

Genie went behind the receptionist's desk and snapped on the public address system. "Helen Bradley to the reception desk. Helen Bradley to the reception desk."

When Helen arrived and saw it was really Genie's voice she'd heard, her whole face lit up with excitement. "It *is* you. Oh, am I glad to see you!" The women hugged.

"Who's still here?"

"Me. I think I'm here only because I'm a member of the board of directors and assistant secretary of the corporation." She said it with the pride and defiance of a woman who'd been struggling to keep her courage up much too long. Then she spoke in another tone, one that was both awkward and gentle. "I'm so sorry about Max. I wrote you three letters and called many times. You never answered."

"I didn't do a lot of things." Genie's eyebrows drew together, intent on some private vision. Then she said, "Do me a favor. Take care of Mr. Bernstein. I want to wander around the offices alone before the meeting."

"Of course. You can use my office, Mr. Bernstein. If you wish to make any calls, I have a phone that doesn't go through the switchboard."

There were only two rooms Genie was interested in—her office and Max's. She stood in the doorway to her office, paralyzed for an instant. Nothing had changed and everything was different. The office seemed to her to be the office of another person. A stranger upon whom she was intruding. Even when sitting in her own chair behind her own desk, she felt the office no longer belonged to her. Her desk top was clear. No piles of real estate offerings for her to study. Her diary was open to March 18, the last day she'd been in the office. And the notation. "Max. 8:00. My apartment. Discuss banks." Her heart seemed made of lead. A leaden heart which was struggling to beat. Beat, damn you, beat! We have work to do. Without looking at the diary, she flipped the pages. It made no difference which date it was open to, just so long as it wasn't March 18. Her eyes shifted to the far left corner of the desk. There, in a leather-bound double picture frame, were pictures of Max. One side of the frame had a Bachrach portrait Max had sat for several years ago. She'd used it only because Max would have been insulted if she hadn't. It was a profile shot, back lit to bring out Max's screen star looks. For her, the portrait had no life. It wasn't her Max. The other half of the frame had a series of snapshots taken from the time he'd been a teenager until he was in his late twenties. Max in a baseball uniform with a silly grin on his face sticking his tongue out at the camera. She remembered taking that picture. Max with some long forgotten girl. Max against the rail of a Circle Line cruiser with the Statue of Liberty in the background. Max in bathing trunks at Jones Beach. The last show was one of Max standing on the platform of the IRT station at Queensboro Plaza, his head in the sun and his thumb pointing over his shoulder at a large white sign with red letters, Szabo & Szabo—Real Estate. Genie closed the frame as one closes a book and placed it on her desk. She asked herself again the questions she'd asked so often during the past months. "Why?" "What happened?" "Why had it happened?" "What went wrong?" "Had they asked too much from life?" "Was her mother right all along?" She received the same answer as she had during the months alone in her apartment. Nothing.

It was 1:45. Not much time before the board meeting. Genie hurried to Max's office. It affected her the same way her own office had—only the effect was much harder to bear. The office belonged to a stranger. It was cold and empty. Max had taken all the energy and excitement he'd brought to the room with him to his grave. Seated in his chair, she toyed with the buttons on his console. All the gadgets Max loved to play with worked. But without Max to enjoy them, they were lifeless mechanical devices. There was a twin to her picture frame on Max's desk. One half of the frame contained a portrait of her taken at the same time as his. Genie didn't like the picture of herself anymore than she did the one of him. It was a full face shot of an attractive woman, artfully made up to emphasize her full mouth and deep-set eyes, back lit to highlight her black curly hair. But the face was not her face. That cool aloof woman was not the way Genie saw herself. The left side of the double frame contained a montage of snapshots of her. Standing in front of the Majestic. On that Circle Line cruise. In a modest one-piece bathing suit at Jones Beach. Her pointing to the Szabo & Szabo sign. And a photograph it took a moment to place. She was standing on the Husseman roof. Paul had taken the picture using a timer so the picture would be of both of them. Max had cut Paul out of the shot. Genie hadn't the vaguest notion where Max had found the photograph or what it was doing in his collection. She closed the frame, placing it flat on the stainless steel desk.

Paul and Max. Max and Paul. The two names raced around in her brain. Since the beginning of memory there had always been Max. Then, only a little later, Paul. Max loved her, and Max was gone. Paul loved her, but he was never committed to her the way Max was. Nothing had obliged him to love her the way only blood loves. Worse, far worse, suppose she did risk beginning again with Paul? Their brief time together told her how desperately she still cared. And what if something happened to Paul? She couldn't stand it. Not again. Genie had learned a terrible lesson from Max's death—how devastating the loss of one human being can be. She could never go through the same thing again. It was safer not to risk the liability of love. Not give any more than she could afford to lose. Not expect more in return. She'd lived for years on short rations. She could live the rest of her life the same way.

A knock on the door interrupted her vision of the future. "Come in."

The door opened, and Helen's head poked through. "They've arrived." A faint smile played on her lips. "I wish you'd seen their faces when I told them you were waiting in here for them.''

"Where's Mark?''

"With them in the reception room.'' Helen counted the chairs around Max's rectangular conference table. "We're three, including Mr. Bernstein, and they're four. We need another chair.''

"No.'' Genie recalled something she'd learned long ago from Ralph Gluck. "I'll run the meeting from here. We'll move the two chairs with their backs towards me to the other side of the table. Our four bankers will sit facing me, with Mark and you at either end of the table. I need two minutes to shift the furniture before you bring them in. Just knock first.''

"This is going to be fun!'' Genie realized Mark must have told Helen his plan, and Helen was itching for a fight. By the time she knocked again, Genie had rearranged the chairs to suit herself and was ready for the meeting.

The bankers filed in with Herbert Gordon leading the way and Tom Migliore trailing. Herb took one look at the seating arrangement, started to say something and stopped himself. He held out his hand. "My condolences, Genie, and welcome back.''

"Thank you, Herb.'' She shook his hand. "However, since you're in the offices of my company, ConVert-Co, perhaps I should welcome you? In any case, sit down, gentlemen. Mark, you sit there. Helen, there. And you gentlemen, facing me.''

Tommy spoke up. "I must object to this seating arrangement. We're all equal members of the board and should all be seated at the same table.''

"Mark, note for the record Mr. Migliore objects to the seating arrangement. Also note that I object as well. I object to Mr. Gordon, Mr. Migliore, Mr. Engelhardt, and Mr. Winters representing themselves as members of the board of directors of ConVert-Co. They were not elected by the shareholders. They were appointed during, shall we say, my illness.''

Herb cut in. "Genie, our appointments are legal under Articles X and XI of the lending agreements. They were made by Judge Carlson.''

"Articles X and XI refer to immoral and criminal actions which threaten the security of your loans. Herb, you have more of a sense of humor than I realized. However, since in my absence the judge had no choice but to make the appointments, you are board members.'' Her voice flattened out. ''For the moment. Gentlemen, sit down. As chairman of the board and chief executive officer of the corporation, I would like to call the meeting to order.'' The lines were drawn. Genie had established her position. She waited. Unwillingly, the four bankers sat down. ''The first item on the agenda would appear to be a discussion about the disposal of the assets of the corporation for the benefit of the creditors. You gentlemen are the creditors.''

''We must protect our loans.''

''Yes, Herb. But not by gutting the company.''

''Have you read the article in *Forbes*?''

''Months ago. There was nothing to it. No concrete facts. Nothing to concern anyone who didn't want to be concerned.''

''They interviewed me. Interviewed all of us. And we are concerned. Concerned enough to invoke Articles X and XI.''

''And who else was concerned? Do you think I don't know who is behind your sudden interest in the morality of Con-Vert-Co?'' Genie heard the violence in her voice and paused. A loss of temper was a waste of time. ''In any case, as long as I am chairman of the board and chief executive officer of this company, there will be no disposal of assets. Regardless of what this board may vote today. You may tell that to any interested third party. You can call your loans when they come due.''

''And you'll file for a Chapter 11. Which makes that a laugh.''

''That's your problem, Tommy.''

''Genie, are you aware of the methods Max used to sell apartments?''

''Yes. Hard work and offering the best price and terms possible.''

''It's my impression you don't know how Max finally managed to close the deal in Boston,'' Herb continued.

Genie recalled Max's words. ''I grabbed his balls and squeezed.'' She also remembered his refusal to explain what he meant. ''Don't look under rocks.'' She tried to prepare herself for anything that might come. ''Tell me, Herb. How did Max close Boston?''

Herb looked at Mark. ''Off the record, Counselor?'' Mark nodded, nervously. Herbert Gordon seemed too confident.

"He obtained pictures of Richard Elliott's daughter. Elliott was the leader of the opposition. The pictures were compromising. Disgusting. Max used them to blackmail Elliott into buying his apartment. Once Elliott capitulated, the other tenants followed."

"Blackmail, Herb? That sounds melodramatic and far-fetched."

Herb opened his briefcase and took out a large white envelope. He handed the envelope to Mark. "Give that to Genie, please." He spoke with an exaggerated politeness. "These are not pictures I would want my wife or daughters to see. However, Genie, I think of you as a sophisticated, worldly woman. I doubt they will shock you as much as someone more naive."

Genie tore open the envelope. She took out three eight-by-ten-inch glossies. She blinked and caught her breath. Then she recovered. What she saw were two girls, caught by a camera with a telephoto lens, making love to each other. While Genie was hardly an innocent, the pictures were as graphic as she'd ever seen. She could tell from the grainy quality of the prints they'd been enlarged many times. She gathered her strength. "You say Max blackmailed Elliott with these pictures? What proof do you have that Max had anything to do with these pictures? Or that one of these girls is Elliott's daughter?"

"Half of Boston knows." Herb gave Genie an odd little smile. "We only came across the photos because the detective Max hired to take them didn't know Max was dead. Or that Elliott had capitulated. Unable to reach Max, he followed his original instructions and sent the shots to Elliott's wife, his associates at his bank, his relatives, and friends. What Max may or may not have meant only as a threat, the detective took as gospel. Max could be very convincing." Herb waited for this to sink in before continuing. "Then something unforeseen happened. If you look further in the envelope, you'll see a newspaper article from the *Boston Herald*. I suggest you read it. It tells the story better than I can."

Genie pulled out a newspaper clipping she'd overlooked. She scanned the article. Mr. Richard Elliott, vice-president at the New England Trust, and his wife, Emily Elliott, had committed suicide. They were survived by a daughter, Lynn Elliott, whom the police were looking for. When last seen she was working as a topless dancer in South Boston. Against all her will, against all her years of self-taught control, Genie let out a gasp of dismay. She gripped the sides of the desk, and the shock showed in her pale face. Oh, Max! Max! she was silently saying.

"You see, Genie, since we were monitoring the progress of the Boston deal, once that tragedy occurred, we felt it our responsibility to probe further."

"I come from Boston," Tommy added. "I called a few relatives and asked them to look into it. Why? What? How come? Within a week they turned up the photographs you just saw and the name of the detective Max hired to get the pictures. Mr. Barry McCarthy. Mr. McCarthy was more than willing to cooperate. He provided us with all the necessary information in exchange for payment of his bill. A bill that Max's death left unsettled."

"If you want to meet him, we can arrange it."

Genie shook her head. She drew in a sobbing breath, seeing something she'd never seen before. Now, at last, she knew what had gone wrong with their lives. She'd been running away from the truth. In her own way she had helped kill Max. She'd allowed him to run roughshod over people when she alone could have stopped him. And dear God, forgive me, cried her heart. Maybe I wanted the money as badly as Max. What else could explain my looking the other way for so long?

"Are you all right, Genie?" Mark was concerned.

Genie licked her lips and sat up straight and stiff. She'd come to a decision. There was nothing left in ConVert-Co for her. Max and she had seen to that. Its purpose, and hers, had been corrupted. Let them have the company. Do what they wanted with it. Gut it. Dissolve it. It made no difference. "I'm all right. What is it you want, Herb?"

"Your resignation. And a free hand."

"If we agree on a few details, you have it."

"Genie! You know you don't have to go along with any of this."

"I know I don't have to, Mark. I want to."

"I call for this meeting to be adjourned. It's clear to me Genie isn't well."

"I am. Please don't fight me."

Mark Bernstein grew quiet, slumped in his chair. He'd only glimpsed the contents of the envelope, the backs of photographs. A newspaper article. Genie's reaction stopped him from asking to see more. He'd heard talk of a tragedy, of a detective. So what? It was Genie's sudden surrender that made no sense to him. No matter what the photographs showed, or the article said—if they had an affidavit from the devil claiming Max was his henchman on earth—it could all be challenged in court. This detective might prove to be in the pay of the banks. The fact that they admitted paying him his bill was almost enough to discredit him as a witness. The photographs could be faked. The article . . . Mark stopped himself. The answer to everything was not in the so-called evidence which could have been fought. The answer was in Genie. They had struck some chord in her nature. And he had a hunch what it was. She blamed herself for Max's death. There was no use arguing with that kind of guilt. Mark wasn't a brilliant lawyer by accident.

"I'm sure you already have offers for all the buildings?" Genie was saying. "Including my apartment?" Herb agreed. "And, naturally, the total net cash equals all of ConVert-Co's obligations? Not just the banks? Legal? Audit? Everything?"

"We did a little better than that. Even in a buyers' market. There's something left over for you."

"Stop it, Herb." Genie's temper flared for an instant. "I know the market better than you do. I know what I could get for those buildings. Don't waste my time telling me how hard you worked for me. Exactly how much will be left?"

"Close to two hundred thousand dollars."

"I want that money divided up among certain employees of ConVert-Co. Helen Bradley and a few others. I'll give you a list."

"What about you, Genie?" Now that he understood her state of mind, Mark was afraid she couldn't take care of herself.

"I'll be all right. I have a reasonable amount of cash. Some personal holdings in stocks and bonds and my jewelry. Enough to carry me until I decide what to do with my leftover life."

"Want to go to law school?"

"I'll take that into consideration."

35

Genie spent the next months in what seemed to be a whirlwind of activity. She negotiated and signed the final agreements with the banks. She found a two-bedroom apartment in a rent-controlled building on East 57th Street, where she could use one bedroom as an office for some kind of business. She sold the furniture she didn't need in the smaller apartment and disposed of all her jewelry except for one gold pin Max had given her. She was very busy. But beneath all the activity was a cold and profound loneliness. The fear that her mother would again reject her made it impossible for her to call Anna. The decision she'd made on the day she gave up ConVert-Co, that she was not and never would be ready for love, made calling Paul out of the question. The only one who had her unlisted telephone number was Jack O'Neil. He considered it a matter of honor to keep in touch, occasionally to take her out for a quiet dinner. Bereft as she was of all intimate human contact, Genie deeply appreciated his kindness.

Every Sunday she rented a small car, bought flowers, and drove to the cemetery in northern Westchester County. She'd sit on the stone bench next to the graves of her father and brother for hours. Sometimes she'd weep the hard, bitter tears of unrelieved sorrow. And sometimes she'd pray, praying for comfort from those who were gone, yet vividly alive to her. She would beg for a sign, a portent, anything, that told her they heard her, that they understood how much she loved them. She told her father what a wonderful father he'd been. She told Max she forgave him everything, not that it was her right to forgive. She hoped he forgave her. That God forgave her.

On several occasions she noticed flowers lying on both graves. Although she didn't remember asking for the service—her mind was so chaotic after Max's death, she didn't remember much of anything—she assumed she must have. Why else would the church continue to supply flowers?

One Tuesday morning the phone rang. "Good morning, Eugenia."

The voice was familiar, "Andre! Andre Husseman! How wonderful! Good morning."

"Then you don't mind my coercing Jack into giving me your number?"

"I not only don't mind, I should have put your name on my privileged list of callers. People who are welcome to ring up at any time. It's a very select group."

"If I were a modest man, I'd say far too select for me to be included. But, then again, I'm not that modest. It's both a blessing and a shortcoming," he said dryly. "Which brings me to the reason for my call. Do you think you could find time from your other pressing duties to meet me at my office this afternoon?"

"I can always find time to meet you. Although you must know I have nothing but time these days."

"Jack did fill me in. My deepest condolences about Max."

"Thank you."

"Sara and I have been in Europe for the past six months which is why you haven't heard from me sooner. We saw a great deal of Rebecca. She's now living in Paris as a wife and mother. She sends her regards."

"How nice. Give Rebecca my best."

"Would three o'clock be convenient?"

Genie laughed. "It seems to me three o'clock was always your favorite time for meeting."

"Three is my lucky number. See you then, Eugenia."

During the hours between Andre's call and the meeting, Genie considered the possible reasons for the call. To offer condolences? He'd done that on the phone. He couldn't have a building he wanted to sell her? Since he'd talked to Jack, he must know she'd lost—or given up—control of ConVert-Co, and had neither the cash nor the banking connections to purchase an apartment house. The call confused her. Andre usually called on business matters, and she was no longer in business. Still, the idea of seeing him carried with it a familiar glow, a feeling which had been in short supply for her for a long time. Andre's call cleared the air. The sunlight streaming through the window seemed brighter. She took a deep breath, pushing her desolation back into the corner of her mind where she could forget about it for a while. This was a trick she'd been teaching herself. Suddenly she frowned. Had Andre asked to see her because he wanted to talk about Paul? Oh, no! That couldn't be Andre's reason. It wasn't in Paul's nature to consult with his father about her. Andre had intruded himself between them once, and that one time he'd had his own personal reasons. Now there could be none. She would have to wait until three o'clock to find out what he had in mind.

When Genie arrived at Andre's office, Harriet Greenspan was waiting for her. Harriet was ageless, and she greeted Genie cordially, as she always had in the past.

"Mr. H. is waiting for you." Harriet picked up the phone. "She's here!" Genie heard a note of pleasure in her voice. "Go right in."

Andre met Genie in the middle of the office and shook hands. "Good afternoon, Eugenia," He stepped back to look at her. "You look very well, my dear. Very well indeed."

"Do I?" She sounded half surprised. "I feel as old as the hills. And no wiser." In reality, she had changed. Her mouth turned down slightly. It had known deep pain and was more vulnerable. Her eyes, so beautiful in shape and color, were different from the eyes he remembered. One could almost see the veiled suffering.

"You've had a difficult time."

"I've had trouble. Most people do, at one time or another." She gazed at him appreciatively. "But you look wonderful." And it was true. A glow, something which had been missing from Andre's face ever since he'd lost his condominium project to Jake Rosen, was back. He appeared years younger than the last time she'd seen him. Younger than she estimated his actual age to be.

"Shall we sit?" He guided her to the table by the window where they'd always sat. Genie glanced around the office. It remained a credit to Andre's taste and his ability to afford his taste. "Do you mind if I smoke?"

The automatic question, and her equally automatic answer.

''Of course not.'' She watched him light a cigarette. Gauloise? She wondered what tobacconist still carried the brand.

Andre inhaled deeply, allowing the smoke to fill his lungs before exhaling it towards the ceiling. He needed time to consider exactly how to present his idea to Genie—the reason why they were having a meeting. From the beginning, he had not thought it would be easy. Jack O'Neil had filled him in on how stricken Genie had been at Max's death. That was to be expected. Max was at the core of her life, and his death crushed her. It was Jack's opinion that her grief had so overwhelmed her she'd even given up ConVert-Co without a fight. That was not to be expected. As he understood it, Genie had gone to a meeting with her bankers. It was Andre's opinion a woman of Genie's temperament did not attend a meeting to surrender her company. She went prepared to do battle, and something had stopped her. Andre assumed it must have been something to do with Max. Which raised the next question. Had whatever happened immobilized her forever? Seeing her now in his office verified his instinct that he must proceed with extreme caution. Not only for her sake. Equally for his own.

Genie waited patiently for Andre to speak. They were like two old equally matched chess players, each familiar with the other's game. Andre had something on his mind. For one reason or another, he was having difficulty expressing it. But he would get around to it. He always had.

And Andre did. He would try a gambit. He pushed forward a question lazily, but under the mask of politeness, his eyes were very keen. ''I understand from Jack you have been in retirement, shall we say, for the last months?''

''A retreat would be more accurate. Or, to be euphemistic, a vacation.''

''I find I only enjoy vacations when I'm working. And as for retirement, it's a total bore. Though I will support a museum exhibit and do enjoy concerts, I'm not one for sitting on museum boards. Or the board of the Philharmonic.''

''I guess we're old war-horses, Andre. We only enjoy working our tails off.''

''But you haven't been doing that. You've been vacationing.''

''Consider it a forced vacation.''

''As I understand it, you gave up ConVert-Co voluntarily.''

Genie grew wary. "My lawyer, Mark Bernstein, and Jack O'Neil believed it was voluntary. And in a way it was. Perhaps I could have kept control."

"But you didn't want to?"

"I really had no choice. You see, I'd fallen out of love with my company."

"As a result of Max's death?"

Genie's shoulders hunched forward ever so slightly. "Max's death made me see more than I'd seen before. I thought I could change the world. Play God. And I was punished." Genie drew a carefully casual breath. "I think I was far too committed to my dream, to its success."

"Nothing is accomplished without commitment. And you accomplished a great deal."

Genie met his words head on. "Possibly. But our accomplishments caused more harm than good."

So there it was. Out in the open. Something so unsavory had happened it had turned Genie against herself, and against her life's work. "I think you did more good than harm."

"If that were true, Max might be alive today." Her words popped out of her mouth before she could stop them.

Andre was far more adept at understanding other people than most men. He knew how Genie's mind worked, and that the load she was carrying was very heavy. Speaking in a measured tone, he tried to make it clear that he did not judge her. "We are human beings, Eugenia. With the weaknesses and failings of human beings. Something even beyond Max's death is troubling you, and I want to make clear to you that whatever it is, there is nothing you could possibly tell me which would change the impression I formed of you years ago. Nothing you could say could make me think less of you or like you less."

The weariness Genie had felt for so long seemed to be lifting a little. Her guilt at having failed herself and Max eased slightly. "Thank you for saying that, Andre. It does help."

"Don't thank me for anything. Or if you want to thank me, remember who you are."

"What do you mean?"

"You have a talent, Eugenia. A great talent for real estate. You would thank me sufficiently by using that talent."

"That talent, as you put it, did a lot of people damage."

"It also provided a lot of people with something they lacked. The security of owning their own homes."

"There were too many people who didn't want that security." Genie wasn't sure if Andre was being sympathetic or for some reason bent on tormenting her with reminders of her past.

"I know you benefited far more people than were ever harmed." Andre had prepared for her resistance and laid his plan accordingly. "As I told you, when I learned of Max's death and what happened to ConVert-Co, I was in Europe. So I called Jack O'Neil from Paris and took the liberty of asking him to do me a favor." Andre opened the drawer in the table and removed a pile of papers. "Letters, Eugenia. This is just a sampling of the hundreds of letters collected at my request. Would you mind if I read one to you?" He didn't wait for an answer.

Dear Mr. O'Neil:
In response to your inquiry concerning the purchase of our apartment at 64 Wyndam Terrace in Denver, Colorado, from ConVert-Co and Max Szabo, I would like you to know that my wife and I regard our purchase of the apartments as the single most important financial investment we ever made. Exceeded in importance only by my choice of a career. Not only has it given us the security necessary for peace of mind, but when we needed money to send my daughter to a college of her choice and later law school, and student loans were hard to come by, the fact that we owned our apartment—we were not renters—was a major factor in convincing our banker to lend us the needed funds. Need I say more?
Sincerely
Edward Collins

Andre handed the letters to Genie. "Read them, Eugenia. Every one of them says something along the same lines."

Genie clutched the letters, searching for the proper words, tears in her eyes. Finally she managed to ask, "Then what went wrong? Why were we punished?" The agonized look on her face made Andre turn away to do battle with his own thoughts.

When he looked at her again, his features were composed, permitting no glimpse of what went on behind them. "Eugenia, each of us has something in us which will not be denied. Max had what he had. You have what you have. We are what we are. We may know what we are doing is wrong, even before we do it, but that does not stop us. And what happened to you is what happens to people like you. And Max. And me." He was speaking quietly but with the full weight of personal experience. "In the scramble for success, to win the game, we move too fast. Distinctions between what is right and what is wrong become blurred."

Genie nodded. Max and she had wanted success desperately. In their own minds, they'd never stopped thinking of themselves as the super's kids. She tried to wipe away the tears. She had no right to embarrass Andre with them. He'd seen too much, won and lost too much, lived too long with the knowledge of his own mistakes, and never burdened anyone with them. What right did she have to tears? "Did you gather those letters to help rebuild my ego? Or did you have something else in mind?"

"I have a number of things in mind." Though Andre was now at his most tense, he sounded most matter-of-fact. "A strong, healthy ego in a partner is always easier to live with than a weak flabby one."

"A partner? Were you thinking of me?"

"A partner. I was thinking of you. I see no point in standing on my dignity. I need you as a partner. Badly."

"For what?"

"To help me retire from retirement. Before it kills me."

"Andre, you're pure steel. Nothing could kill you."

"Not true. Doing nothing will kill me. Once I understood that, I realized I had to get back to work. But I need the right partner."

"To do what?"

Andre opened the drawer in the table again. Genie leaned forward. Over the years that little drawer had contained many documents which had made huge changes in her life. What now? He placed a second pile of papers on the table. "At the moment, I own fifty-four apartment houses. All are within fifty miles of New York City, and all could be called middle-income houses. In fact I've always believed in your idea to turn middle-income rental apartments into cooperatives and condominiums owned by the families who live in them." For the first time in all the years she'd known him, Andre began to speak rapidly. His words tumbled out in a burst of enthusiasm. "I would like to go into business with you. I own the properties, and you know more than anyone in the country about converting them into co-ops and condos." He handed her the pile of papers. "Here are the details on all the buildings. Jack O'Neil prepared the numbers."

"Jack knows about this?" she asked, placing the papers next to the letters on the table.

"He does, and he's urged me to go forward. He's already established what he considers a fair price for each building. That is, the price I might expect to obtain if I sold the buildings to an ordinary investor, not the tenants. I suggest an operating company be formed in which we have equal ownership. The company would function as follows. Say Jack has set a sale price of a million dollars on a building, and we co-op the building for one million two hundred fifty thousand dollars. I receive the first million and pay you a commission based on the standard real estate board rates. The two hundred fifty thousand dollars remaining goes into our operating company to cover overhead and provide capital to purchase buildings from other owners. Incidentally, I've sounded out Ralph Gluck on the idea. Don't smile. He and I may have had our differences in the past, but that was the past. He still thinks your idea is too good for the damn fools." Genie had a vision of Ralph Gluck, his feet on his desk, a thick layer of cigar smoke swirling above his head, growling about the stupidity of mankind, and at the same time selling his buildings for resale to those idiot tenants. It occurred to her, if he were approached properly, he might be willing to join them. "Anyway," Andre continued, "Ralph always has something to sell. It's his business." There was a quiet during which the loudest sound which could be heard was the sound of Andre tapping the long ash of his cigarette into an ashtray. Then, "Does my plan interest you, Eugenia?"

As he had so many years ago, Andre Husseman had come to her aid again. "Yes. It interests me very much. It's a little like coming back to life."

Genie walked around the table, leaned over, and kissed Andre on the cheek. She was very happy. She wanted to say, "Thank you, Andre," but despite her best efforts, the tears spilled over and ran down her cheeks. And, seeing the delight in his face, she realized it wasn't necessary to say a thing.

Andre waited quietly for Genie to regain her poise. When he thought she was ready, he said, "There's one more bit of unfinished business." He went to the door that led to the small office Genie had never seen but from which she remembered Joan Rosen appearing. He said to someone in the room, "I'm sorry to have kept you waiting so long. Come in, please."

Genie struggled to speak. Only one clear word emerged. "Momma!"

Anna Szabo crossed the room to her daughter. The look on her face shocked Genie. There was not a trace of the bitterness Genie had seen all through the years. Anna put her arms around her daughter, and the women hugged, their eyes filling with mutual tears of joy. When they looked for Andre, he was studiously staring out the window at Park Avenue.

"Why, Momma? Why now? After so long?"

"Because now I know I was wrong. I didn't understand. Listen to me, Genie. Paul and I . . ."

"Paul and you?"

"Paul and I. We have had many talks. Whenever he drove me to the cemetery, we talked and talked."

"You were the one who left the flowers?"

"Yes. Paul and I. He explained to me how he felt about you. He explained many things to me. Things about this country I didn't understand. You see, Genie, something happened in Hungary a long time ago. Before I met your father. I will have to tell you about it." She said, softly, "It made me believe things which I now know are not true, and I let it spoil all our lives."

"Eugenia, my car is waiting," Andre interrupted with studied casualness. "In the hope that you would accept my proposal, Sara has arranged for all of us to have dinner tonight at our apartment."

"All of us?" Genie asked.

"All of us. You. Your mother. Sara. Me. And . . ."

"Paul?" Genie's eyes roamed the room without seeing it.

"Paul. The Hussemans would appreciate the company of the Szabos at dinner tonight. Paul is doing the cooking. I believe he's planned for us to eat on the rooftop. I hope being a bachelor has taught him something about cooking."

"Momma," Genie had only half listened to Andre, "will you tell me about Hungary? What made you afraid?"

"It made me afraid for all of us. For you and Max. For the family. Especially for you." She was pleading with her daughter. "Maybe, when I tell you why, you will understand and forgive me?" Her voice broke. "Maybe Papa will? And Max?"

Genie turned away from the ravaged face of her mother. She needed time to calm herself, time to understand what was happening. "Did Paul arrange all this?" she asked Andre.

"Not the business part, Eugenia. That was my idea. Although he approves of everything."

"I'm not sure I'm up to more than the business part. Dinner may be too much."

Suddenly, Andre felt like a fool. With Genie's best interests in mind, he hadn't told her the exact truth. The truth was he'd been searching for something to do for years, and it had been Paul who had made the original suggestion he work with Genie to convert his buildings. He'd eagerly seized upon the idea and presented it as his own—assuming correctly that that change made it more likely Genie would agree to the plan. As in the past, in his eagerness to settle his own personal problems, he'd been utterly blind and utterly self-centered. It had taken him to this moment to grasp fully what Paul had been doing. Paul's business suggestion to him. The time Paul had spent with Anna Szabo. Paul's wanting Genie to meet her mother at his office. Paul's eagerness that Genie and her mother come to dinner. All of it had been part of Paul's plan to reestablish his relationship with Genie. And now Genie was backing away.

Andre became concerned lest he fail his son again. "Eugenia, this is a celebration dinner. You can't refuse to celebrate with old friends."

"I'm not up to it, Andre."

"Genie." Anna had been observing her daughter. "Now you are afraid. It is wrong to be afraid."

"It's not the same as it was with you."

"It is the same. Fear is always the same. You want to be safe, Genie. So did I, and look what happened. Nowhere is safe. You should know that now." Anna pronounced each word with the reverence of one viewing a precious new truth.

Listening to her mother, Genie felt a welcoming and an understanding such as she had not known in years. Or thought she was ever to know again. She felt the entire history of her past rising within her; memories of her family and of their life together came back to pierce her with their beauty.

"Momma, you want me to have dinner with Paul?" she asked, almost as a child.

"Yes. He is the right man for you."

It was true. He was the right man, the only man, for her. But dare she risk loving him again?

Genie looked around the room. Suddenly, it seemed different—lighter, more spacious. She had a strong impulse to move, to act. It was all right. This was the way life was lived. You win. You lose. There were no guarantees. She took a very real comfort in the knowledge that she was not alone. Paul wanted her. He was ready to risk loving her, and would be with her as he had been all her life. She asked herself the question again. Dare she risk loving Paul? And the answer came to her in another question—dare she not risk it?

So Genie's life began again when she smiled and said, "Very well, Andre. The Szabos will be delighted to accept the Husseman invitation to dine this evening."

Her heart had decided for her. She had no choice but to give love, and Paul, another chance.

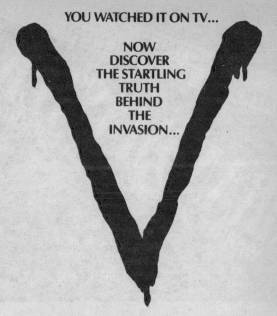